DUC

DUCKLING

Eve Ainsworth

PENGUIN BOOKS

PENGUIN BOOKS

UK | USA | Canada | Ireland | Australia
India | New Zealand | South Africa

Penguin Books is part of the Penguin Random House group
of companies whose addresses can be found at
global.penguinrandomhouse.com

Published in Penguin Books 2022
001

Typeset in 10/15.2 pt Palatino LT Std
by Integra Software Services Pvt. Ltd, Pondicherry

Printed and bound in Great Britain by Clays Ltd, Elcograf S.p.A.

The authorised representative in the EEA is Penguin Random
House Ireland, Morrison Chambers, 32 Nassau Street,
Dublin D02 YH68

A CIP catalogue record for this book is available from
the British Library

ISBN: 978-1-52915-724-6

www.greenpenguin.co.uk

To Simon.

I'm so grateful for your continued support and encouragement.

You have faced so much and yet barely complained.

You are my hero. Love you so much.

Chapter One

I thought I was alone when I buried the creature, but someone was silently watching my every move. The sun had only just begun to rise, stretching its weak fingers of light across the poky, stripped-back garden. The air was still sharp with the scent of morning dew and the grass felt squidgy and damp beneath me as I moved barefooted across the lawn, clutching the bloodied ruins close to my chest.

I chose a small patch of soil at the rear of the communal lawn, sheltered from public gaze by the overgrown conifer that towered over the space in a jumbled knot of branches and leaves.

It was an ideal place to conceal the body. No one would come this far down the garden. Most of the residents chose to lie further up on the yellowed, patchy grass, spreading out their towels and blankets and letting their kids run loose, belting footballs against the low brick walls or climbing the spindly trees that were clinging to life nearest the road. This was the no-man's-land, unloved and unkempt. The scraggy arse end of the garden that even the stray cats avoided.

There were a couple of old beer cans and greyed scraps of paper discarded on the ground that I pushed to one side. I dug quickly with an old fork that I had snatched from the kitchen on my way out. The weak metal was bending uselessly against the solid clay. I held up the wonky tines against the watery light and cursed, then in frustration I threw the tool to one side and used my fingers to rake at the ground instead.

The result was a scrappy, gaping mouth in the earth, ready and waiting for its offering. I hesitated for a moment, a tremble forming.

I wouldn't want to be buried like this, I thought, staring blankly at the dark hole.

I laid him carefully in the newly dug earth, my fingers working further to make the space a little bigger. He looked quite peaceful if that was possible. Snug. Certainly, a lot more presentable than when I first found him, splayed out on my kitchen floor, his sorry little eyes blinking up at me in bewilderment.

There was a sharp intake of breath behind me. It made me jump back a little. I don't know what I was expecting to find there, but it certainly wasn't the little girl. She stood there quite squarely, her hands planted on her hips, her teeth chewing on her bottom lip.

'What are you doing?' she asked me accusingly.

I was suddenly conscious of how I must look crouching down there in the mud, wearing an oversized greying Madonna T-shirt and a pair of bright pink holey tracksuit bottoms. I pushed my hand through my straggly hair, managing to drag dirt into the roots, and pulled uselessly at the T-shirt. Quickly, I put my glasses squarely back in place and tried to make myself appear remotely normal.

The little girl was dressed in her pyjamas and her long dark hair was loose and messy, sticking up like candyfloss around her face. Her cheeks were pink with the cold, round and bright like ripe apples. She was wearing shiny green wellies that seemed to be on the large side. It made her feet look strangely fat and not at all fitting with the rest of her skinny frame.

I blinked, realising who she must be.

I had met the girl only briefly outside our flats as they were moving their belongings inside, and I was leaving for my normal shift at the bookshop. The young woman, who I assumed was her mum, had blurted out a quick greeting, certainly nothing memorable. If only it had been, because right now I couldn't for the life of me remember either of their names.

I really needed to get better at this.

'You've just moved in next door, haven't you?'

'Rubi.' The girl frowned a little. 'I'm Rubi.'

I nodded. 'Rubi. That's right, of course it is. And your mum is ...?'

'Cassie.'

'Yes. Cassie,' I said. 'I knew that.' But of course I didn't. I could only just recall her face. A young woman. Skinny with blonde hair, long, delicate eyelashes and glossy lips that were plump and rich with sparkle.

'So, what are you doing outside in the gardens so early? Why are you digging around in the mud?' Rubi's eyes widened suddenly. 'Are you burying treasure?'

I stared back down at the ground, at the discarded bent fork and rusting beer can.

'How long have you been watching me?' I asked instead.

3

'Only for a bit. I woke up and I couldn't go back to sleep. Then I saw you out here, creeping around.' She stepped forward so that she was next to me. She smelt faintly of lavender. 'What are you doing, then? Are you looking for something special?'

I sighed and then shifted to one side so that the half-covered grave was exposed. What was the point in trying to conceal it? It wasn't as if I was doing anything wrong. I poked at the hole, trying not to dislodge my offering. I was suddenly envious of the bird, tucked away securely in the mud, more or less hidden from view. He'd never have to explain himself to a small child in wellington boots.

'Well ...' I said, 'I'm just burying this poor thing.'

She moved closer; I could feel her breath hot on the back of my neck. 'Oh! What is it?'

'A bird ... a baby one, I think.'

'Ugh. It's all gross. Where did you find it?'

'In my kitchen.' I paused, feeling unsure. I glanced over my shoulder, checking behind me. I'd thought I was alone out here, but perhaps I was mistaken. Could anyone else see me? What if someone was peering through their poky windows, sneaking a quick fag and staring down at the view below? Would they see me here? The crazy neighbour, out in the early hours digging around in the mud ... Should I even be out here talking to this girl – a stranger, really? Was this the appropriate thing to be doing?

'Maybe you should go back inside, hey?' I said. 'I'm not sure you'd want to see this. It's not nice at all. And it's cold out here ... Won't your mum be worried about you?'

Rubi didn't seem to hear me and peered further forward. I thought I saw the slightest flinch as she neared the broken body, but she didn't pull back. Instead, her forehead crumpled into a small frown.

'Is it a pigeon?' she asked finally.

'Yes, it is. Or rather it was.' I scooped some more earth and scattered it over the grey, bloody body. 'My Boris has always had a thing for birds. He really doesn't like them much. I think they must annoy him.'

'Is Boris your cat? That's a funny name.' She paused. 'Is he named after that man on the TV? The Prime Minister?'

'Oh no. I don't think so.' My fingers toiled with the loose crumbs of mud. 'The rescue home named him, not me.'

'My mum says that man has funny hair,' Rubi confided. 'She calls him bad words when she thinks I'm not listening.'

I thought of my pampered cat, now probably lazing on the chair, his own fur coat a mass of uncombed fluff. I couldn't deny that there were certain similarities between the two Borises, although I was pretty sure our Prime Minister didn't hunt for birds in the early hours.

I peered up at the little girl who was staring back so intently at me, I think waiting for me to say something. Oh God, I was no good at this. What was I even meant to say to a child? I had no experience of this at all.

'So, erm … do you like cats, then?'

It seemed a daft thing to say, but really, what else could I talk to her about? Cats seemed a safe topic of conversation.

'Oh yeah, I love cats. I'd love to have four. I'd keep them all in my room, on my bed.'

'Well ... cats are the best,' I agreed. I could've said more, of course. I could've bored her silly, telling her the million and one reasons why I thought that cats were a superior species, but I didn't. In truth, I was hoping that this conversation would quickly end, and I could return to my happy isolation.

'I think they are cute and clever, and they don't let anyone mess around with them!' Rubi said, prodding at the mound of earth with one of her tiny pink fingers.

I nodded. 'Erm ... Well, yes. They are cute. Especially Boris, even when he brings me dead pigeons at six in the morning.'

'Do you wake up early too?' she asked.

'Er ... no. Not normally. Boris woke me up with his loud meowing. I knew he was up to something.'

In truth, I would've given anything to still be in bed. My mornings were usually as lazy as possible. My shifts were always in the afternoons, so I visited Dad on my way to the shop in the late morning. It meant that early morning and evening were my perfect times to relax. Rubi crouched further down, her hair swinging forward, thick and tangled. She sighed loudly.

'Poor little bird, though. Do you think he was hurting a lot – you know, before ...?'

'Well ... I don't know. I don't like to think that he was in any pain.'

I continued to cover the bird up, moving quickly now. I expected Rubi to move away, I kind of hoped she would, but instead she lingered beside me, breathing heavily through her mouth. Simply watching me.

'Are you sending him to heaven?' she asked. 'Is that what'll happen now?'

I smoothed over the rough earth. There was nothing there now, not even a lump in the ground. Before long, this bird would be swallowed by the earth and forgotten. Not a trace left behind.

'She's in heaven now, Duckling – looking at you from the clouds ...'

'He'll be OK,' I said, slowly standing up, ignoring the sudden spark of pins and needles in my legs, the dull ache in my calf.

I needed a shot of caffeine and some more sleep, preferably another eight hours curled up beside Boris. What I wouldn't give to live the life of a cat. It must be so much simpler not to have a worry in the world. I began to move back towards the flat, my body heavy. Rubi remained behind, her head dipped towards the grave, her body turned away from mine.

'You should go back to your flat now, your mum really will worry,' I called back. 'You should talk to her about this sort of stuff, heaven and that.'

I reached the gate that led out of the shared garden, directing the path towards our monolithic block. I was ready to go inside, but something instinctively pulled me back. The thought of Rubi standing on her own by the grave made me shudder. It didn't seem right somehow. I turned around.

'I'm sure you shouldn't be out here on your own,' I called, louder this time. 'It's too early. Wouldn't your mum wonder where you are?'

This was an assumption. Maybe it was fine for kids to be out and about at all hours. For all I knew she was quite happy for her daughter to be outside in the early morning, with ill-fitting boots and unbrushed hair?

There was no reply. I waited at the gate, my fingers pinching the wood. For goodness' sake, this girl wasn't my responsibility, yet I felt awful walking away and leaving her there by herself. Shaking my head in frustration, I found myself turning back towards the small child.

'Come on,' I said. 'Why don't you come inside with me? I don't want your mum to worry.'

Rubi shrugged, still turned away from me. 'It's OK. I think she's still asleep.'

'She won't be for much longer, will she? She'll wake up and find you gone and then what will she think?'

Rubi shook her head, a tiny smile etched on her face. 'It's OK. Really it is.'

'Still . . .' I said. 'I'd prefer it if you came.'

'All right then!'

She turned and we both walked down the narrow path towards the main building. 'My mum knows I have trouble sleeping. Sometimes I go to bed late, sometimes I get up early. That's just me.' She grinned. 'But it's safe here. Mum knows that. She says that it's all good now.'

She waved and continued to skip along the path. I hung back a little, unsure if I should follow too closely behind her. The cool air whipped behind me as I watched her slip back inside the warmth of the building.

She was safe. A sense of relief washed over me.

Now I could return to my own cosy routines.

I had been living in the Cherry Blossom Estate for just over ten years that spring. The towers were named optimistically after the luscious tree that was torn down during its development. I certainly saw nothing in common with the beautiful blooming tree and the grim, grey concrete blocks that contained us. The sixties development was tired and dirty, battered around the edges and stained with pollution and graffiti. The local council named each block after other trees, thinking it would provide a 'warm' and 'homely' environment, but there was nothing homely about the dark lift lobby and heavy wooden doors that led through to our poorly lit corridors. I lived in Sycamore. Or as it was known to us locals – simply 'sick'. The smell of acrid piss or sweet-smelling weed that hovered around the lift and in the walkways did little to make me feel comforted and safe. But at the same time, I knew it could be so much worse, so it really wasn't right to complain. I heard of other people who lived in unsafe housing, in flats with dangerous cladding. I knew in many ways I was lucky to be somewhere safe and secure. Number eighteen was my little flat on the end of the row. A stunted, dark arrangement of rooms on the second floor with a view overlooking the car park, and if I craned my neck sideways to the left, the small, tatty allotments and busy railway line into London. This flat was squat, and it was quiet, and it was all mine. I loved this private space, my little nest. For me, it was perfect. I could ask for nothing more.

And next door, just on my right, were my new neighbours – Cassie and Rubi.

Of course, they weren't my first neighbours.

I'd only known one before. But I never quite appreciated how special she was.

Joy Adeyemi was an elderly Nigerian lady with a wobbly chin and a predilection for playing the country singer Jim Reeves far too loud at night. The first time I met her was the day I moved into my flat. I was nineteen years old, alone and feeling completely out of my depth. The flat itself was pretty much empty and all I had was a few pitiful boxes and a couple of bags of clothes. My dad had helpfully managed to secure me some second-hand bits from one of his 'mates' down the pub and I was waiting hopefully for them to arrive, peering out of my door like I expected him to pop up at any moment. But he was already an hour late and I was sure I knew why. The pub was a nice little detour, and I knew his 'mate' was a regular drinking buddy. It was becoming pretty clear that I wouldn't be seeing my mattress any time soon.

It was at the moment when I was about to retreat back inside my new, bare home when Joy stepped out of the neighbouring doorway and slowly looked me up and down.

'Jeez, you're tall,' she breathed, puffing out her lips. 'Were you grown in compost or something?'

I blushed, my knees buckling a little as they always did when I became aware of my height. 'I suppose I am … My mum was the same.'

I blanched a little at the mention of her name, but Joy didn't seem to notice.

'Some would say it's a gift to be so tall,' she said, her smile stretching across her face. She could've only been just over five foot herself. As she moved slowly towards me, I felt like a giant. 'Are you living there by yourself, then?' She gestured at the door.

'Yes.'

She nodded, her dark eyes analysing me. 'You look so young!' She took a few steps closer. I noticed how her hip was slightly twisted forward and her hand nestled against it, as if holding it in place. I wondered how much pain she was in. She peered behind me, through my open door.

'Pretty empty in there.'

It was a statement, not a question. I shrugged in reply. 'My dad is bringing some bits. A mattress and that.' I floundered. 'I think he's been held up.'

'Oh.' Her eyes were studying me again and her tongue darted out of her mouth, licking her lips. 'Well, if he doesn't turn up you'll be stuck, won't you? It's no fun sleeping on the floor.'

'I'll be fine.' I attempted to smile back, to look relaxed and chilled about it all, even though I was fuming inside. I was so angry at Dad for putting me in this position, for letting me down once again.

Although I couldn't expect anything more. It wasn't his fault, after all. This was back when I still felt angry at Dad, before I understood that it was pointless to feel anger at something I couldn't control.

'I have large sofa cushions,' she offered. 'You could use them, perhaps, if you need to? I'm guessing they would make a good enough bed.' She paused. 'Until your dad gets here, of course.'

'Oh, there really isn't any need,' I said quickly.

'Don't be silly.' She shook a dismissive hand at me. 'And I have food here. Plenty of it. Perhaps you can eat something?'

'Really. I'm absolutely fine.'

Her eyes widened. 'Well – you know where I am. Just knock, tall girl.'

'Lucy,' I corrected her. 'My name is Lucy.'

She smiled again. 'Such a pretty name,' she said, before carefully walking back into her flat.

I stood for a while staring at the closed door. Behind it I could hear the mournful tones of a country singer. I imagined this woman inside, cosy with all her belongings and life around her. How kind she had been to offer her help, but I knew I couldn't accept it. To do so would only serve to complicate things further. It was better to manage things on my own like I always had. It was far simpler that way.

I trudged back into my own flat to wait for my dad. I knew he'd show up eventually, even if I had to wait until the next day. I remember being painfully aware of the stark, exposed walls that night. I pressed my hand against the party wall and felt the soft rumble of music under my skin. It was soothing.

Two hours later there was a gentle rapping on the door. I opened it cautiously, knowing full well Dad would never knock like that.

Joy stood before me, holding up a plate of biscuits. 'At least you can eat something while you wait,' she said. 'And I'll sort out those blessed cushions for you.'

After that, Joy sort of became part of my life, although I don't think I ever actively encouraged it. She became like a friend to me, I suppose, or the closest thing I'd ever had to one in adulthood. I tried to politely explain to her that I wasn't the type to socialise or mingle with other people. I just liked to keep myself to myself. Joy would simply tut loudly and fix me with her beady stare.

'You keep telling me these things,' she'd say, her hand clutching another freshly made cake, or a parcel she had taken in for me. 'But why is it I don't believe you?'

I did start to pop in on Joy too, especially towards the end when her legs got too bad, and she couldn't move far from her chair. It wasn't any real problem, until that one final time, a few months ago.

That time, she placed her small, crumpled hand over mine. I remember peering down at the bulbous veins that pressed out of her drying flesh. It made me think of the fat worms at the bottom of the garden.

'Look at you,' she said in her husky, deep voice. You could still hear the beautiful melodic tones, a richness that seemed out of place in our shabby commuter town. 'You're all sharp corners and rough edges. I feel like if I were to rub up against you too close, I'd hurt myself.'

I pulled away from her. It wasn't the first time she'd said something like this to me.

'All these years and I still feel like I barely know you.' She sniffed. 'Yes, yes, I know you pop by now and again, but I know nothing about you. Even now. You've never let me in.'

'There's nothing to know,' I told her firmly, picking up my bag.

'I never see a soul enter that flat of yours. Ten-odd years now and apart from your dad coming over in the early days not one person visits you.'

'My dad is too sick to visit now.'

'But there's no one else. No one at all.' She swiped her hand over her mouth. 'You go to work. You come home. You go and see your dad. That's it. You're only thirty. Where is your life? Why aren't you living it?'

I stiffened; my bones felt rigid, my skin damp with sweat. I felt so big in this room, taller than ever and completely exposed by Joy's cool and calm analysis. I didn't want her probing me like this. I didn't want my life to be questioned in this way. How could she ever understand me? She didn't know what I'd been through, or what I'd done.

'I'm all right, Joy. I've told you before, I just like my own company. Now are you sure you'll be OK? Do you need me to get you anything?'

'No friends at your age?' Her beady eyes followed me as I went to leave the room. 'I find that rather strange, Lucy. I wonder what secrets you're hiding. I wonder why *you* are hiding?'

I smiled. I could feel it stretching out over my teeth, like a mask. It felt heavy and unnatural. Suddenly all I wanted to do was go to bed, pull the covers over my head and sleep for a very long time.

'I'm going now, Joy,' I told her. 'We can talk another day.'

'Secrets are bad for your soul,' she said as I walked away. 'You should tell them to someone one day. It might help you. You need to let people in, girl.'

I ended up slamming the door. I suppose I wanted her to stop talking. Or maybe I simply wanted to stop listening.

I was sad when she went into hospital two days later, her tiny, thin frame swallowed up on the huge white stretcher. I remember her eyes as she looked up at me – hollow and dark, like shrunken conkers. She smiled nervously and offered me a little wave, like she was the bloody Queen on her way to Ascot.

'I'm off for a bit, Lucy,' she said weakly. 'I'll be back before long. Could you turn my big light off for me?'

When the ambulance left, I crept into her flat with the spare key that she hid under the broken Buddha on her front step and quickly flicked off the main light in the living room. The great oversized lampshade had a pattern that was so faded, I couldn't work out what colour it once was. The room seemed different in the gloom, sadder somehow, like it was slipping away also. Days later the council were in her flat, dressed in heavy white overalls like they were clearing out a cesspit. They looked like bright white maggots, sifting through all of her belongings. Joy's bits and pieces were bagged up and boxed away – stacked in the gallery like a misplaced jumble sale. I felt sad then. Joy was probably the only person in the flats who knew I even existed. It seemed wrong that her worldly possessions could be handled so carelessly.

I took her Jim Reeves CD. I felt like I had to. Even though I couldn't bear to play the thing, I didn't want to think of it all smashed up in a bin bag. I took the lampshade too, God knows why. It had been sat outside my toilet ever since, upside down and still covered in dust.

She was right, of course. I didn't have any friends. Apart from my work at the bookshop and seeing my dad, I was pretty much alone, and to be honest, I liked it that way. It was much easier to live an uncomplicated life in the shadows without having others bothering me. But now every time I walked past Joy's stupid lampshade an ache throbbed deep inside my heart. I couldn't quite bring myself to throw it away. There was so much I could have told her.

Three weeks was all it took for Joy's flat to be cleared out and her memories packed up. And then, so quickly, it all changed again.

I saw the new neighbours arrive just a few days later, or to be more precise I *heard* them. The door of the stairwell had crashed shut, like the wind had taken it in a sudden gust. Then there was a sound of roaring laughter and a bright voice sweeping across the deck. It was a sound quite unfamiliar on this floor. It seemed wrong somehow and out of place.

'Are you all right with that box, babes? It's pretty big.'

'I'm fine! It's not heavy at all. I'm strong, Mum. See!'

At that point, I stepped outside. I was on my way to work anyway, but curiosity made me tug my coat on a little bit quicker. I stood and watched at my door, taking time to lock it, as these two figures approached me. One was tall and skinny, the other much smaller and wobbly and very clearly a child. They were both clutching oversized and overstuffed boxes, so I couldn't see their faces properly, but they were giggling like this was the most fun they'd ever had.

The woman stopped outside Joy's door. She planted her box on Joy's old, faded doormat and caught her breath. The bright bracelets on her thin arms rattled as she reached up to her blonde hair and tightened her ponytail.

'This is it. This is our home,' she announced.

The child placed her box down with a groan. As she straightened, I could see her dark hair was styled in the same high ponytail. Her face glistened and a smile lit up her face. She reached towards Joy's door and touched it, like it was magic.

'I like it, Mum.'

The woman laughed. 'How do you know? You haven't even been inside yet!'

The girl simply shrugged. 'I like the door.'

There was a look that passed between them, I couldn't quite work out what it meant – but they were looking at each other so intently, it made me shiver. I suddenly felt out of place here, like I was watching a private moment between them.

I tried to pass them casually, without fuss, offering a shy smile in their direction.

The woman lifted her hand in a half-wave. 'Hi! I'm Cassie. We're moving in today.'

'How lovely,' I replied. 'Do let me know if you need anything.'

But I was already marching past them, towards the stairs, aware that her name would soon be lost in my jumbled, confused thoughts. My head throbbed as I walked and an empty feeling opened up within me, like an aching wound.

I knew it was daft and I knew full well I was being unreasonable, but Cassie moving in made me realise that things were moving on. Joy had only been dead a short time. Her memory was already being erased.

Everything was changing so quickly.

Chapter Two

Cassie first knocked on my door a few days after the incident with the bird. It was late morning, and I was getting ready for work. They'd only been living next to me for a week or so and I was still getting used to the new sounds through the thin wall that divided us.

Rubi was standing beside Cassie, her hair once again tied into a high ponytail. It swung from side to side like a dark whip, her bright eyes still fixed on mine. On her cheek was a swipe of what looked like biro. I stepped back a little, surprised to see them both there.

'I'm so sorry to bother you,' Cassie said, leaning in a little through my doorway. She was wearing her hair down this time and it fell smooth against her shoulders like a golden sheet. Her eyes were wide and beautifully made up. She seemed to actually sparkle in the poor light of the outside deck. 'I'm Cassie, your new neighbour. We met briefly before.'

She pointed loosely in the direction of her flat. 'I know we waved at each other, but I thought I should say a proper – well, hello.'

'Hi,' I said, shyness creeping back like a familiar friend. 'Well, I'm ... I'm Lucy.'

Cassie brushed the top of Rubi's head. 'I hear you met my daughter the other morning. She was telling me all about the incident with the dead mouse.'

'Bird!' Rubi corrected her sharply. 'It was a bird, I told you that!'

'Oh, bird, mouse – same difference ...' Cassie flapped her hand dismissively, the bangles on her arm jangling. I noticed she had dark gold eyeshadow dusted on her lids and as she leant towards me, I caught the scent of fresh, slightly sweet perfume. 'I hope she wasn't any bother. She's always been an inquisitive one, my girl. She likes to know what's going on, especially if it involves animals.'

'No, not at all.' I smiled, still staring at her sparkly eyes which glistened in the light. They reminded me of the sherbet sweets I used to love when I was small. 'It ... well, it was nice to meet her properly.'

Rubi lifted her chin and seemed to study me more closely. I noticed how her bright eyes twinkled as they made contact with mine. She reached up and pushed her long fringe out of her eyes. 'I liked it,' she said carefully. 'It was a nice thing to do for the poor little bird.'

Cassie half laughed. 'Well – I could think of more exciting things to be doing first thing in the morning, but hey!' She caught my gaze, but I quickly looked away again. I certainly wasn't the type to be doing anything particularly exciting. Not unless you counted breakfast TV and a cuddle with a dribbly old cat as an interesting morning activity.

'Well, it's lovely meeting you ...' I started, before Cassie jumped in.

'Actually, I wondered if I could nick some washing-up liquid. I thought I had enough but obviously not – and I'm out of cash till Friday.' She smiled widely and I saw the small gaps between her white teeth and the bright flash of a tongue piercing dancing between her lips.

'Sure,' I replied, shrugging. 'Luckily, I always stock up.'

She waited while I retrieved my spare bottle. On the way back through the hall, I caught sight of myself in the mirror. My glasses were smeared. I hadn't brushed my hair yet and there were toast crumbs on my lips. My short dark hair was standing up in wavy tufts, like frizzy balls of hay. I quickly brushed my lips with my fingers and attempted to flatten my curls before returning to her, feeling my cheeks burn red.

'Thank you!' She took the bottle eagerly, inspecting the label as if it were wine. 'My flat is such a dump still, I really just want to get going on stuff, you know? I'll just pour a little into a mug if you want. I don't want to leave you short.'

'It's fine,' I said, flapping my hand. 'Just take the whole thing. I have another.'

'I haven't disturbed you, have I?'

'Er ... no. No ...' I glanced down at my work clothes, basic black trousers and plain white shirt. 'Actually, I was just getting ready for work.'

'Oh. Where's that, then?' she asked, seeming genuinely interested.

'It's a bookshop across town. Words End.' I scratched at my neck. 'It has all sorts ... if you like to read?'

'Oh, books!' she scoffed, as if I had tried to sell her insurance. 'I don't have time for that.'

I smiled politely, but I noticed Rubi was frowning slightly. I wondered if she agreed with her mum.

'So, who lived there before?' Cassie asked, gesturing back towards her own flat with a jerk of her head. 'It's pretty grim in there, you know. A bit old, and I dunno – tired, dusty ...'

Her nose wrinkled a little.

I frowned, not able to stop myself. I thought of Joy and how proud she had been of her home. 'She was an elderly lady, a lovely one. I think the cleaning got on top of her a bit, but she was very nice. She used to like playing music and baked the most amazing biscuits. That's until her legs got too bad.' The words came out in a rush. My cheeks felt hot. Had I said too much?

'Oh ...' Cassie paused and her eyes seemed to suddenly sparkle. 'My God – she didn't ...' Her hand fluttered to her mouth.

'What? Oh God ... No! No ... she died in hospital,' I replied quickly. 'Sadly. That really was the last place she wanted to be. I think she would've preferred to slip away in that old chair of hers.'

Cassie shuddered. 'Well, personally I'm relieved. I'm no good with ghosts and that. I don't trust them.'

'Ghosts aren't real, Mum,' Rubi said sharply, shaking her head. Her ponytail bobbed up and down, looking even more like it had a life of its own.

Cassie laughed brightly. 'I don't rule out anything,' she said. 'I've watched programmes on it. People can communicate with the dead and all sorts. Bugger that.'

'Well ... I don't think there's any ghosts around here. I'd like to believe the easiest option anyway,' I said, moving back a little, trying to indicate that I needed the conversation to end now. My head was hurting a bit.

'I guess you're right. Sometimes the easiest option is the best one,' Cassie agreed. 'But I always thought ghost hunting looked fun – just a bit, well, risky …' She widened her eyes in mock horror and Rubi nudged her.

'Mum! Ghost hunting is silly.'

'Well – maybe not silly,' I said, catching Cassie's eye. I thought she looked a bit sheepish. 'I suppose I can understand why people do it, looking for answers in the unexplained—'

Cassie jumped in eagerly. 'Exactly! See, Rubes! I'm not so daft. Even Lucy, who seems a very sensible woman, agrees that there could be more to it all.'

I smiled hesitantly, but inside my internal cogs were whirling. Why was this woman wanting to chat to me for so long? I really had nothing interesting to say. I couldn't believe for one second that someone as confident and, quite frankly, as stunning as Cassie would enjoy my company. Was she after something else from me, perhaps? Not that I had much to offer …

Rubi was frowning in my direction, obviously a little disappointed at my earlier response. I could've said more, of course. I could've told them both that I'd long given up on ghosts or anything remotely otherworldly, but I didn't like to make Cassie feel silly in front of her daughter. Nor did I want to dampen her obvious excitement on the subject. The truth was I didn't really know what to do. I just wanted to go back into the safety of my flat. I wasn't used to any of this. I wasn't a natural when it came to flowing, easy conversation.

'Well, that flat is fine, I promise,' I said instead, trying to bring an end to matters. 'If Joy was to be haunting anyone it would be Jim Reeves, not that old place.'

'Jim who?' Cassie looked at me blankly.

'A country singer. She was a huge fan.' I thought of his CD still sitting on my bookshelf and suddenly felt sad. I really should play it one last time. I was pretty sure Dad would let me borrow his CD player. But somehow, I couldn't quite bring myself to do it yet. I wasn't ready to hear that voice again.

'You're really tall, aren't you?' Rubi said, looking back at me as if she'd only just noticed my size.

'Er – well, yes – I suppose I am.' I peered down at myself. It wasn't like I could forget, but suddenly my limbs seemed longer and more gangly than before. I could feel my shoulders start to slump in response.

'How tall are you then?'

'Er … I'm not sure.' I paused. 'Six foot two, I think. Maybe a little more in my boots.'

'You're lucky,' Cassie said. 'And those cheekbones too. You could grate cheese on them. A lot of women would die to look like that.'

My fingers touched my cheek, feeling the sharpness of the bones under my skin. No one had ever said anything nice about them before. Dad always said I looked gaunt. *'My duckling,'* he used to laugh when I was young. Always so tall and clumsy. Always falling over her own feet. My gaze flicked back briefly to Cassie. Was she being cruel and mocking me? I searched her face, looking for clues, the sneering lips or narrowed eyes that girls I knew before used to flash at me. Girls like Cassie who were pretty and confident. Cassie, however, was still looking relaxed and open. She smiled back at me and her eyes lit up with warmth. There was no threat there, nothing that I could detect anyway.

Cassie continued talking. She told me that she had moved over from North London, 'in a bit of a rush'. She smiled then and winked at me as if I knew what she meant. She told me she had recently lost her job, cleaning in a local office. So, if I heard of anything? School hours? I nodded politely, even though I was probably the last person to get wind of a new job around here. She said she was glad to be making a fresh start for her and her little girl. At this, she acquired a softer expression and reached out to touch her daughter's head. 'Rubi,' she said. 'It's such a pretty name, isn't it? Unusual. It's Rubi with an "i" not a "y" – it drives me nuts when people get it wrong.'

'There's a song, isn't there?' I offered lightly. '"Ruby Tuesday".'

Cassie blinked at me. 'Never heard of it. Is it old?'

I blushed again. 'Yes, I guess it is …'

'What's it about?'

'I'm not sure.' I paused. 'I could ask my dad, he might know.'

'I hate Tuesdays,' Rubi stated flatly. 'It's the worst day.'

I was about to answer when I heard my phone ringing inside my flat. I turned instinctively towards it. Finally, I was saved by the bell.

I knew it could be one of two things. My dad. Or that call centre that seemed convinced I'd been in a recent accident. I was reluctant to speak to either, in all honesty, but it was an excuse to break up this long and quite exhausting chat.

'I should—'

I gestured behind me.

'Oh, yes, you must go. It could be important. Me and Rubi have to get back anyway. We have lots to do in the flat.'

'Well ... I'll be seeing you around ...'

Cassie grinned, holding up the bottle of washing-up liquid with one hand and lightly touching Rubi's shoulder with the other. 'Oh, I'm sure you will, Lucy. It's so nice to finally meet you.'

I smiled back weakly, wondering what they must really think of me. Would they be like Joy and end up judging me for having no visitors and seemingly no friends? Would they also suspect that I was hiding myself away?

But Cassie was simply smiling. A fresh, honest smile that seemed to light up her entire face.

'Thank you,' she said, still clutching the bottle like it was some kind of prized jewel. 'Thanks so much for helping.'

Back inside my flat, I closed the door with a satisfying click. As I rushed towards the phone, I could smell the scents of my home again. The cinnamon sticks that I left in the hall, the coffee in the kitchen, the faint, musty stink of Boris. It made me feel so safe. *Settled*.

I picked up the phone hurriedly, my fingers clumsy. I didn't think to check the number.

'Hello?'

There was a long silence on the other end. My jaw clenched. This was becoming so familiar now.

'Hello?' I demanded again, just to be sure. I couldn't risk that Dad had fallen, that he was lying on the ground crying out for help. Finally, there was a digitalised sound of buttons being pressed, a brief burst of static and then a loud, northern voice greeted me.

'Hello! We have reason to believe you've been in an accident recently ...'

I slammed the phone down in disgust. Who had time for this nonsense? Certainly not me.

Cassie's visit had made me late, and now this would make me later still. I really wasn't the best person at dealing with added pressures on my carefully structured routines. It left me feeling unbalanced.

Over the next few months, I saw less and less of Cassie and Rubi. We did still exchange smiles if we passed each other outside, but that was about the limit of it. Rubi would be glued to her mum's side, a quiet shadow, occasionally shooting me a curious look as if she couldn't quite figure me out. And I would nod back hesitantly, never sure what to say and believing, as always, that it was usually better to remain quiet.

So apart from the odd thud and intermittent sound of music, I couldn't really complain about Cassie and her little girl next door. They were quite different from Joy, but maybe that was a good thing. They really did leave me alone.

Until September, when it all suddenly changed.

*

'I've got a bad feeling about today.'

It was a Friday afternoon. I was at the bookshop and after an unusually busy few hours, I was sitting at the main counter with Jimmy, my manager, while we waited for the last hour of the shift to pass. It was always the longest hour of the day and both of us were willing it to end.

'Really? Why do you say that?' he asked, a little distracted, as he leafed through a catalogue.

I often heard Jimmy talk at work about his own family – his sisters, who he obviously loved, and their young children that he saw regularly. His life was very different to mine. Sometimes I wondered if he had any notion what I was really like.

'They're so noisy,' he'd laugh. 'But I love being with them. We always have fun.'

I had just nodded along, half listening to what he was saying. It was always hard for me to join in these sorts of conversations because my own experiences were so very different. I didn't want to make Jimmy feel sorry for me or bring down the mood by talking too much about my childhood. Jimmy told me how close he and his sisters were, and that idea alone seemed so alien to me. Would it have been so different if I'd had a brother or sister? Would my life have turned out another way?

Jimmy's life seemed to be lively chaotic and full of love. He was open and honest about his life and as a result I knew more about him than he did about me. For example, I was aware that he was one of three children and the only boy, that his parents had moved to England from Jamaica in the early fifties and that his uncle had found success and riches as an independent music producer before dying young from a heart attack. His family often threw parties and gatherings that Jimmy grumbled about but I think he actually cherished. I also knew that Jimmy had recently broken up from a long-term, eight-year relationship, after he found out his girlfriend Ria had been cheating on him with one of his best friends. I hadn't liked that period one bit. I didn't like seeing him upset and angry and I never knew the right thing to say to make him feel better.

I didn't tell Jimmy much about my life because there really wasn't much to say.

By comparison, my own family was very small. It was just me, Dad and an uncle somewhere up north who I barely knew. I was dimly aware that Mum had had more relatives – second cousins, a great-auntie somewhere, perhaps. But Dad had cut ties with them soon after her death. Both Mum and Dad had been only children with older parents, a sad connection that linked them together. Dad said that they found each other because they were both so similar. Two lost souls. I suppose I quite liked this romantic image, but I couldn't help wondering what a bigger family would've felt like. We always seemed so fragile, like we could snap apart at any time, even before we did, when Mum died.

'Well …' I said finally, tracing my finger around the mug of tea Jimmy had made me. Drinks were not allowed on the shop floor, but Jimmy was in one of those 'oh, who cares about rules' moods today. 'First of all, Boris brought in another dead creature this morning. This time it was a frog. I swear he's doing it to wind me up now.'

'Don't cats do that as a sign of affection? Him bringing you gifts?'

'I don't think so. Not when it hasn't got a head, anyway.' I shuddered.

'Wasn't it a mouse last week?'

'Yeah, and a bird before that. I'm getting quite an animal graveyard going on outside mine.'

Jimmy sipped his own black coffee, his smile barely hidden behind his huge yellow mug. 'You always were a soft touch,' he said. His voice had an almost melodic tone to it, which made him sound chilled no matter what else was going on around him.

'Well, with animals, I suppose I am. They need looking after, don't they?'

'I suppose they do. So, what else has put you in this negative frame of mind?'

'Well, I was late today, wasn't I?' I said. 'And I crashed into that stupid new bestseller display of yours and hurt my hip.' I rubbed it, as if to make the point. I was bound to get another bruise to add to my collection. 'I still don't think it needs to be so close to the door.'

'Hey! It's not stupid! You're just complaining because you don't like change.'

'That's not true,' I grumbled. Even though I was pretty sure it had looked better before.

'By the door more people will see it and will be enticed to spend their money,' Jimmy said in his matter-of-fact way. 'I can't help it if you come running into the shop like a demented fawn.'

'I was late! And I swear when I run my limbs are even less co-ordinated than usual.' I frowned at him. 'It's not fair. You're over six foot too. How come you aren't clumsy like me?'

Jimmy was a stocky, muscular man who seemed to take over the entire counter with his presence, but for a man of size, he always seemed to move with grace. He also had a stillness about him that I'd not seen in many others, an ability to be perfectly at ease simply sitting and watching the world go by.

'It's just a gift, I guess.' He nudged my arm gently. 'So what? You found a headless frog and you managed to wake up some sleepy customers with your grand entrance. What else is worrying you?'

I pushed aside some invoices that I was meant to be processing. 'Oh, I don't know. It's my dad, I suppose ...'

'Your dad?' Jimmy put his mug down, his eyebrows raised. 'What's happened now? Is he all right?'

'I don't know. He didn't answer the phone this morning. He usually does when I call him – we have an agreement.'

Jimmy nodded. He knew a little bit about my situation with my dad. It wasn't that I particularly wanted him to know the details of my life, but there had been times in the past when I had called in late for work, or even not come in at all. That had been when Dad's drinking was really bad, when he fell or was very sick after a binge. At first, I used to make up excuses and lies to cover my absences. But then, at the beginning of the year, Dad had a bad seizure and ended up coughing up blood. He was in a terrible state and so was I. After that, I had to tell Jimmy that my dad had a drinking problem and he had been this way for a long time. I admitted that I was more or less his carer now and Jimmy, being Jimmy, supported me. He even let me have a paid week off to look after him.

Since that seizure, Dad hadn't touched a drop of alcohol. He'd promised me that would be the very last scare. But it was so hard to believe a man who'd always failed to keep those kinds of promises in the past. We'd been here so many times before. The feeling of dread always lingered. I was simply waiting for everything to go wrong again.

'You can't panic,' Jimmy said kindly. 'He might've just forgotten or been distracted by something.'

'My dad is never distracted,' I scoffed. 'He has nothing much to be distracted by now.' I sighed, stretching my hands out on the counter. 'It's fine, you're right. I probably am worrying for nothing, but it still is, isn't it? A worry.'

'You need to give yourself a break, Lucy. You do so much for him. All the calls, visiting him nearly every day. You're wearing yourself out.'

'I'm all he has,' I said. 'I have to be there for him.'

I had no choice.

There were things Jimmy could never know. He could never know the true reason why my dad turned to drink in the beginning. Nor could he ever know about the guilt that raged deep within me.

Because deep down, I knew that I was the one to blame for all of this. It was only right that I look after Dad now, given that I was the one who had ruined both our lives.

*

At last the shift came to an end. I busied myself tidying up the few disturbed bookshelves whilst Jimmy cashed up, humming tunelessly under his breath.

'Are you planning anything fun this weekend?' he asked finally as he shut down the till.

'Only the usual. *Columbo* tonight and a relaxing bath. Dad's tomorrow morning and then back here. Sunday – I dunno – my usual walk, lunch at the café.'

'You always have it all figured out.' He leant on the counter, resting his chin on his large hands. 'Do you ever fancy doing something different?'

I shoved the last book in place, ran my finger across the lovely neat row I had formed. Books always looked so beautiful lined up, like colourful straight-backed soldiers. Everything in its right place.

'I like my life the way it is,' I said. 'Anything different would throw me out of sorts. I wouldn't know how to cope.'

'I'm sure you'd do better than you think.'

I glanced away from Jimmy's stare and continued to walk towards the back office, pushing up my glasses as I passed him. 'Well – anyway, I better go. Lots to do, as you know ...'

'Yes, yes, of course.' Jimmy hesitated. 'But first I want to show you something. I've been meaning to give it to you.'

He lifted a bag off the chair and handed it to me. It was a small, white, insignificant-looking bag that had been sitting there all day. I'd barely acknowledged it before.

Jimmy squirmed a little. 'I just ... well, saw this when I was out getting stock. I ... well, I thought of you. Just a silly thing really. To say thank you – for your hard work and ... and for being such good company when we work together. You've helped take my mind off things.'

Good company? I had to fight back a laugh.

'Really? Me? I didn't think I'd done that much.'

'Of course you have. You listened when I moaned about Ria. I practically poured out my broken heart to you when we split up.'

'It was nothing,' I said honestly. After all, I really had done nothing. I wasn't able to offer him any helpful advice or love tips. How could I? I was a work colleague with barely any life experience and no love life to speak of. I'd just let him talk and hoped he wouldn't ask me for an opinion.

'You listened and that really helped, trust me,' he said. 'Now go on, open the present.'

Jimmy was still staring intently at me and I felt flustered, not used to being centre stage. Instead, I concentrated on the bag, reaching in carefully and pulling out a flat cellophane package. My fingers stroked the cool wrapping.

'I hope you like it,' he said.

Gently I peeled back the tape and drew out what was held inside. In my hands was a folded white T-shirt. I could just about make out the face of Columbo staring back at me, his thoughtful, kind eyes, his wry smile. Underneath were the scrawled words: *Just one more thing ...*

'Do you like it?' Jimmy asked. 'I really hope it's OK. I know how much you like *Columbo* ...'

It was as if someone had turned on the central heating in my heart. I wanted to whip him up in a hug and squeeze him. I wanted to thank him so much for being so kind and for thinking of me. I wanted to tell him that I couldn't remember the last time I'd actually received a present. I wanted to say all these things, but as usual my tongue remained glued in my mouth, the words rattling inside me, unsaid. I knew once I released them, I would be revealing too much. I would be opening myself up to him.

And also, I knew that I didn't really deserve any of this from him.

So, instead, I tilted up my chin, bit the inside of my lip and nodded. 'Thank you, Jimmy.'

'It's a small thing, Lucy, I know, but ...' He shuffled on the spot. 'I like seeing you smile.'

My cheeks reddened. I stuffed the T-shirt back into the bag, my fingers feeling like they were made of rubber.

'Make sure you look after yourself tonight,' he said as I walked towards the back door. 'Try not to worry too much about your dad.'

'You don't have to worry about me,' I said.

'Maybe,' I heard him reply. 'But somebody has to.'

Back inside my flat my body seemed to instantly unwind as soon as I unlocked the door. I kicked off my shoes, dug my feet into my cheap but still soft carpet and breathed in the heavenly scent of home. This always happened when I came back. This was where I felt safest, where I could truly relax. I stepped over the snoozing body of Boris in the living room and wrapped my perfectly worn and ever-so-slightly tatty cardigan around my shoulders.

Peace.

I got this flat from the council after some help from social services when I was nineteen. Before that I'd been living with Dad, which had been very difficult, especially as he'd been a much heavier drinker back then, and things could get quite nasty. It was considered safer for me to be moved into a place of my own.

It had taken time to make this flat feel like mine. Fresh paint in the kitchen, a nice bright yellow to remind me of sunshine, charity shop knick-knacks to make the place feel cosy. I was especially proud of my Columbo print, which hung on the living-room wall. It had been an expensive buy from America, but well worth it in my view. Every day I stared up at Columbo's kind, twinkling eyes and felt comforted that he was looking after me. I knew it was a bit daft, but it made me feel good. My other prize possession was the battered African figurine that Joy had given me a few months before she died. She swore to me that it would bring me luck and new opportunities. I hadn't seen much sign of that yet.

I padded out into the kitchen and made myself a quick cup of tea. Then, after some thought, I drizzled some Dettol on the floor where the headless frog had been deposited hours before. Boris really did impress me at times. I wasn't even aware that we had any water sources nearby, but my clever cat had obviously sought them out. My mop had seen better days, so I used an old tea towel and skimmed the cracked tiles with my foot.

From the living room I heard Boris move himself on to his favourite chair. He lived life at a very slow pace; even stretching seemed to take a lot of effort. He was an old man now. If he was human, he would've been consigned to a retirement home by now – rocking and farting gently in the tatty winged chair in the corner.

'Poor old boy,' I sighed. 'I remember when you used to dangle from my curtains upside-down. Like a bat. Do you remember? So full of life.'

Boris ignored me – he often did nowadays. His tail flicked slightly in protest at being disturbed.

'It's OK, mate. I won't bother you any more,' I muttered, pulling out my mobile. I leant against the counter and pressed the button. I had Dad on speed dial, of course. It was one of the few numbers I had stored in there, apart from Jimmy's, the dentist and a few other standard emergency numbers. Dad answered first time this time.

'Duckling. You OK?'

'Dad!' I breathed out in relief. 'Are you OK? You didn't pick up earlier.'

'Oh, I'm fine.' He coughed; the deep rattle vibrated down the phone so I pulled my ear away briefly. 'I'm sorry, Lucy. I had a bad night last night.'

An invisible thread twisted around my stomach and pulled it tight. 'Dad – were you ...'

He coughed again, shorter this time. 'No, I wasn't drinking. I just felt a bit unwell, that's all. Nothing major.'

'Are you sure?'

'Of course I'm bloody sure!' He sighed. I imagined him sat on his ratty old armchair, rubbing at his face, frowning at my words. 'Duck, I'm dry, OK? You have to trust me. You're talking to me all right, aren't you? I'm not slurring and struggling?'

'Yes. I guess.'

'And you'll see tomorrow. When you come you can check the place. There are no bottles here.'

'I won't need to do that, Dad,' I said, even though we both knew I would.

'But you'll still come tomorrow, won't you?' he said, sounding more earnest.

'Of course. You know I will. Ten o'clock.'

'Good.' His breath was heavy. 'I've been busy today. I've got stuff to show you, I think you'll be pleased.'

I smiled weakly. This was typical of Dad, to start projects and never finish them. I thought of the half-built kitchen cabinet in the garden shed, the beginnings of a police detective novel typed up on his battered computer. Dad tended to start things and then quickly lose focus or confidence in it.

'Oh, that sounds good,' I replied as I absently stroked the kitchen worktop. My finger found a rough bit and began to fiddle with it, picking at the edges. 'But are you sure there's nothing wrong?'

'Of course there isn't! Why do you keep worrying?'

My eyes scanned the floor where the dead frog had lain. 'I dunno, just a bad feeling, I guess.'

'You and your bad feelings,' he scoffed. 'There's nowt wrong. I just want you over here tomorrow, like normal.'

'I'll be there,' I promised.

'Thanks, Duckling.'

I ended the call, trying not to feel angry at him for still using the nickname I hated so much. It didn't matter how I begged; he couldn't get in the habit of calling me Lucy. Not when I was a teenager – not now. To him, I was always his Duckling, or Duck. To him it was a term of endearment, something he had called me since I was small. I was his 'cute and awkward little Duckling', the child who never quite fitted in. He didn't seem to understand that the term only reminded me how different I was from everyone else. It also reminded me of the times he had slurred the name at me in a drunken, cruel state, the word striking me with his own sharp spittle. I plugged my dying phone in to charge by the kettle and briefly closed my eyes.

I'd had that bad feeling before, so many times. With Dad, of course, knowing when I was likely to find him drunk again, but far worse was the feeling I'd had long ago, the first time I knew something really bad was going to happen.

The night my mum died.

My eyes opened again as I shook away the memory.

No. Not now.

I eased open the balcony door, letting the cool evening breeze sweep into the flat. I needed the air, needed to take my mind off these horrible, corrosive thoughts. I couldn't let them take over again. My gaze flicked over to next door. They had an identical balcony to mine – small, squat and north-facing. I saw that Cassie had stacked some pots in the far corner and whatever was in them was failing to grow in the weak light. Rubi's pink bike stood pressed up against the railings; it had been there since they'd moved in. I wondered when she had last taken it out. It seemed such a shame to leave it there, neglected and unloved. I hadn't seen them for a few days now and I wondered how they both were. I thought of Rubi and her sharp, intense gaze. What would she have thought if she'd seen me again this morning burying another dead animal? I was thankful that she hadn't. It would have only created more awkward questions. I just hoped that she didn't think she'd moved next door to a secret animal killer.

The cool air was beginning to nip at me. I went back for my tea and took it into the living room, sinking down heavily in the ancient, falling-apart sofa, the one my dad had picked up for me all those years ago. I ran my fingers over the soft, faded fabric, my body instantly relaxing. My feet kicked up on to the battered coffee table and, gently, I eased my hand down the crack between the cushions. It was there again, where it always escaped – my crusty, held-together-with-Sellotape remote control.

I smiled. 'Good to see you again.'

I nestled back, finding my snug spot. As Columbo's face lit up the screen, my entire body began to warm and unwind. I breathed in the smell of my room. My space. The scent of warm toast, biscuit crumbs and the hint of dust.

This was just how I liked it.

Lovely, sweet solitude.

Maybe I'd been wrong. Maybe the bad feeling was nothing, and this weekend would be OK after all.

Maybe everything would be absolutely fine ...

But then there was a knock at the door.

Chapter Three

My ears pricked up. It was just after six on a Friday night – who would be calling now? Perhaps I should just ignore it and the person on the other side would go away.

Whoever it was kept on knocking. Could I pretend to be out? But a nagging insistence told me that I shouldn't ignore it, just in case. What if it was something important? I heaved myself up, my feet scuffing at the floor in a hurry to find my torn rabbit slippers.

'All right! Hang on … I'm coming!'

I hurried down the hall, hoping it was simply a salesman, or someone I could politely shoo away. All I wanted to do was return to my snug, scruffy sofa and shut out the world.

They knocked again, harder this time. Whoever it was clearly suspected I was in the house.

I opened the door cautiously, preparing to send my visitor away. But then I saw who it was. Immediately I noticed again how pretty Cassie looked. Her hair was brushed loose around her shoulders, her eye make-up was dark, but perfectly applied with a cat-like flick at the end, and her lips were shiny pink pillows.

'Lucy!' she said, her voice firm but her smile spreading. 'Thank God you're there!'

I blinked at her. Where else would I be?

'I need to ask you a favour. Please. It won't take long. Can I come in?'

So, what else could I do? I slowly stepped aside and let her drift past me. I caught her scent again as her body brushed past mine, so rich and floral. It made me think of summer.

'I'm so sorry, Lucy. Did I disturb you?'

Cassie's eyes had already trailed across my sparse living room. She noted *Columbo* on freeze frame on the TV. I saw a small smile curl on her lips as she nodded towards me.

'Oh – you were watching something?'

'Oh no ... not really. It's OK,' I said, pulling my baggy cardigan across my body.

'Can we go outside?' she asked. 'Just so I can hear Rubi from the balcony. I like to know she's all right. She's by herself next door.'

'OK.'

I watched as Cassie tugged open the stiff door that led outside. A cool breeze immediately swept into the room and I hugged my arms tighter around my body as I followed her.

Cassie was already leaning against the railings on my tiny balcony as I stepped out, looking down at the bleak concrete view. From here I could catch the drone of Rubi's cartoons from their open balcony door and the occasional childish giggle. I pictured her inside, curled up on a sofa, perhaps completely unaware that her mum was here.

Cassie's body rocked in the breeze; she gripped the railings tighter, and I watched as her knuckles turned bright white. Her tiny frame, which had seemed so upright and strong before, now seemed to be more vulnerable somehow.

She reminded me of one of the sapling trees that the council had planted outside the flats to replace the bigger ones they had originally torn down – they usually get blown about in all directions but hold their roots firm. Except this time, a storm had pulled Cassie completely out of shape. She looked younger and more fragile now, and there was something else too – a kind of desperation in the way she was looking at me. Her legs, tanned brown and shoved into high ankle boots, looked so thin that they reminded me of Twiglets. I was sure they would snap right in front of me.

'Lucy – are you OK?' Cassie turned and was peering over at me with her darkly rimmed eyes. 'You look a bit weird.'

'I'm fine,' I said, pausing for a moment. 'Erm ... Is there anything I can get you? A tea, maybe?'

Cassie snorted. 'Got anything stronger?'

'No ... No, I don't think so. I don't really drink, I'm sorry—'

I felt her hand on my shoulder. Her sharp nails grazed my skin. 'I was just messing. I don't want a drink.'

She wiped her nose with the back of her hand and turned her attention back to the view from my balcony. I followed her gaze. The car park was pretty quiet at this time of evening, but I could see the soft glow of fire at the allotments. Another bonfire probably, there had been so many recently. I liked the smell it produced. Acrid and rich, flavouring the sky like an autumnal spice.

Cassie leant further against the railings, as if she was looking for something. It made me nervous as one of the posts was a little loose.

'Maybe you should move away from there? Come inside?' I said hesitantly. 'It's getting a little cold.'

Cassie blinked back at me. 'I'm fine here. I need the air.' As if to prove the point, she sucked in a breath and tipped her head back a little as she exhaled. 'Oh God – that's much better.'

'OK ...'

'Can you see someone down there?' she asked, her finger drifting back towards the car park. 'I thought I saw someone.'

I squinted in the direction she was pointing. Apart from a couple of beat-up cars and a discarded fridge, I couldn't make much out. But it was getting dark, and my eyes were well overdue a test, so I probably wasn't the best person to ask.

'I don't think so. Perhaps it's one of the kids?'

She shrugged, and there was a pause. I cleared my throat, feeling impossibly out of place.

'Cassie, what's going on?'

She didn't speak for a moment; her attention still seemed fixed on the empty car park. Her jaw was working, like she was grinding her teeth. I stood there awkwardly beside her, not sure what else I could say. What was Cassie doing here? Had she just come over for a chat? Did that mean she thought we were friends? I almost chuckled at the idea. No, of course, Lucy! Why on earth would she think that? I was getting it all wrong again. Other people were good at this stuff. Jimmy, for example. He always knew how to talk to customers and put them at ease. But I wasn't so good at things like that. That was why I mainly worked out in the back where I couldn't get in the way or say the wrong thing. I guess that's why I always felt safer with my routine life. Going to see Dad, going to work with Jimmy, coming back to the flat. That was pretty much it. Even I couldn't mess that up too badly.

Life didn't seem so scary when you knew what to expect.

I sighed. Cassie still seemed to be in a world of her own and I was growing impatient now. It was cold out here and I really wanted to go back to my TV.

'Cassie—'

'I'm sorry,' she said finally, her voice flat and drifting.

'Do you need money, Cassie?' I stammered. 'Because I'm not sure I can help with that ... you know how it is ... I've had a few heavy bills this month and my dad has needed stuff. The bookshop hardly pays that well and I'm not sure my manager could fix me an advance ...'

That wasn't exactly true. We had worked together for five years and Jimmy had been my manager the entire time. He lived and breathed that bookshop and did all he could to try and make it succeed. But he was a good boss and a kind person, and I knew he'd help me out if I needed it. I just didn't like to ask him.

Cassie was chewing her lip. 'I don't want your money,' she muttered. 'I just need a favour. That's all. I'd never ask you for money. I'm not like that.' I could hear anger in her voice, and I instantly flinched, once again not knowing what to say. Why was I getting this all wrong?

My fingers traced the roughness of the wall beside me. 'OK, so what is it? What *do* you want?'

She hesitated a little, a tiny sigh shuddering through her body, then slowly she turned to face me. 'I just need you to watch Rubi for a bit, that's all. I have no one else to ask.' Her eyes went wide, I could see how blue they were. Pure blue like the sky on a really clear day. 'Lucy, I wouldn't ask unless it was a real emergency. I really have no other choice. I have to pop out tonight. There's something I need to do.'

'Where are you going?'

'I just—' She shook her head. 'I just need to see someone. Away from the house. It honestly shouldn't take long.' She was talking in a rush, her eyes fixed on me. I dropped my gaze and noticed that her fists were clenched. I could see her sharp fingernails pinching into her skin.

'Cassie – I'm not sure I'm the best option. I've got no experience with kids and I'd just mess it up, so I don't think I can.'

Cassie reached forward suddenly and gripped my hand. The gesture surprised me so much that I didn't immediately pull away.

'I'm not good with children, I'm really not,' I continued, my voice trembling a little. Inside my heart was hammering. How could I look after Rubi? I didn't have the first clue about kids. And I didn't want to upset the safe routine that I'd taken so long to create for myself.

'But she's so easy to look after, Lucy, I promise. Dead easy. She's such a good girl and really mature for her age, all her teachers say so!' Cassie's tone was insistent now, drilling through me. 'I wouldn't ask anyone else, honestly. I know you'll be responsible with her. I can tell you're the type.' She smiled wanly and then her voice dropped a little, almost to a whisper. 'All you have to do is sit with her for an hour or two, that's all. She'll be as good as gold and I'll be back as quick as I can.'

She released my hand. I flexed it, feeling a little sick with worry. I looked past her, towards the greying sky and wispy clouds. It would be night soon. How did it get late so quickly?

'Please, Lucy.' She paused. 'There's no one else I can ask, and I think I can trust you. I can tell you're a good, honest person. You won't mess me around. Do you trust *me*?'

I looked at her, unsure. Did I? That was a good question. To be fair, I barely knew her, but I had no reason *not* to trust her.

I flapped my hands uselessly. 'But I could be anyone. I could be ... I don't know ... an animal serial killer,' I blurted out clumsily.

Cassie stared back at me for a second or two, her expression confused, and then she giggled. 'Oh, that's funny. Animal serial killer. Love it.' Her eyes twinkled. 'Lucy, I get vibes about people, I've had to learn that over the years, and I get vibes about you. Good ones. I can tell you're nice, sensible, kind. It's something you give off.'

'I do?' I blinked at her, surprised.

She nodded. 'You really do.'

'I didn't know that.'

'Well, just trust me on it,' she said gently. 'And let me trust you. I promise, it's just this once. I'll never ask again.'

'Well – I – I guess.'

'Well then,' she beamed. 'It's sorted. You really will be helping me out, Lucy. I'll be so grateful.'

I sagged a little, feeling beaten. 'OK ... What would I need to do?'

'Nothing. Not really.' Cassie looked much brighter now. 'It's getting late, I know, but Rubi doesn't sleep well so she won't be going to bed for a few hours yet. Maybe she could just sit up with you and watch some TV until I get back? She'll need feeding – just a quick tea, nothing special – and then it's really just a case of keeping her company in the flat until I get home.'

'But how long will you be gone?' I said, frowning.

'Not long,' Cassie replied firmly. 'But it might drag on a bit, a couple of hours or so. It's nothing dodgy, I swear, just family stuff. You know how families can be, right?'

I hesitated, my teeth chewing on the rough part of skin in my inner cheek. Finally, I nodded.

'So, you can understand why this is important, then.'

'And it's just for a couple of hours?' I said. 'Not late?'

Cassie nodded. 'I promise. If I'm honest, I doubt it'll even take that long.'

'OK,' I found myself replying again. I tried to ignore the unsettled feeling in my stomach and instead focused on the soft whooping sound that Cassie made before she rushed over to hug me. My body immediately stiffened, my arms falling like poker rods at my sides. I wasn't used to this. In fact, I couldn't remember the last time someone had hugged me like that.

Cassie released me and I could see her face was glowing.

I was helping someone here. They needed me. They wanted my help.

I could do this.

After all, how hard could a few hours with a little girl really be?

Cassie left, saying that she didn't like to leave Rubi for too long on her own. I told her that I would follow on shortly, I just wanted to smarten myself a bit. I didn't think any child should be exposed to my unbrushed hair and bare, knobbly feet. I took a few minutes to run a brush through my unruly locks, wondering jealously what it must be like to have thick, glossy hair like Cassie. I brushed my teeth, pulled on some socks and grabbed my handbag. I was about to throw my phone into it when I realised it was still on low charge. The thing was so old, it took ages to build up its power again after use. I suppose it was a bit like me. I shook my head, raging at my bad organisation skills. If Dad were to call while I was at Cassie's, he would only worry. But would he call this late? It was unlikely. I was more likely to get another bloody call from that stupid call centre. Taking my charger to Cassie's seemed a bit extreme. After all, Cassie had assured me that she would only be quick. I plugged it back into the socket in the kitchen, deciding I was fretting over nothing.

I had a quick glance in the hall mirror as I was leaving. My big, moon-like face stared back at me. My glasses were smudged, my nose had a spot on it, my lips were dry and chapped. I looked tired. Really, really tired.

'What are you doing?' I whispered to myself. 'You could have said no. It's not like you need the bother.'

But despite the nagging doubt, I found myself leaving the warmth and security of my cosy little flat and crossing the outside deck towards Cassie's.

The chill of the evening breeze whipped around my body as I hesitantly knocked on her door.

Being inside Cassie's flat was strange, because I hadn't been in there since Joy died. I almost imagined I'd still see her, bent over in her chair, the news blaring out full blast on the TV. That big, dusty light swinging above her head like a floral UFO.

Everything was different now.

Cassie's flat was identical to mine in layout, but her belongings obviously marked it out as a completely different habitat to my own. Whereas my flat was simple and minimal, Cassie's place was more chaotic despite the fact she had only recently moved in. A small dining table and chairs were shoved to one side, a cracked leather sofa ran the length of the room and the largest TV I'd ever seen sat glowing on the wall. There was a desk in the corner, stacked with paper, pens and magazines. Across the floor lay the discarded debris of their lives – a hairbrush, an odd shoe, some well-loved toys, a pile of towels, a hairdryer – and sitting cross-legged in the middle of all of this, quietly reading a comic now, was Rubi.

This flat was so much 'fuller' than mine and far more homely. I could see traces of Cassie's and Rubi's life every-where, from the lip balm on the table to the discarded colourful drawings on the floor. I stood awkwardly gazing around, my arms clamped to my side. I was scared I might knock something over or step on one of Rubi's drawings with my clumsy big feet.

My mind wandered back to my own flat, my own space. My episode of *Columbo*, now put back, unwatched. I still felt unprepared, like I had just been planted in an unfamiliar country. I wasn't aware of the rules and was barely sure if I could speak the language. I was totally out of my depth.

Cassie was already belting up her coat. She turned to look at herself in the mirror and ran her fingers through her long, wavy hair, shaking it into place. It fell perfectly smooth against her shoulders, like a golden sheet.

'Shit, I look a mess. I do, don't I? I actually look bloody awful.'

I wasn't sure if she was asking me as she wasn't looking at me – her eyes were glued to her own reflection, her lips curling in horror. I wondered whether I should tell her she looked fine – but the words seemed silly, clumsy, and why would she care what I thought? So I remained silent, my eyes fixed on Rubi instead, who seemed totally indifferent to my presence.

Cassie spun round again, walked over to the desk and began rifling through the papers. 'My purse is here some-where ...' Her long fingers pulled out sheets, letting them flutter to the floor. 'Rubes, have you seen my purse anywhere? Have you moved it again?'

Rubi looked up calmly. She didn't seem like the other children in the flats that played outside, shouting excitedly at the tops of their lungs. Her hair was hanging dark and heavy, falling on to her shoulders in a glossy curtain. Her fringe was a bit too long now and I could only just make out her eyes peeking through. She looked quite different to Cassie, a darker beauty to Cassie's golden one. But they shared the same large blue eyes. Eyes that seemed to pierce right through you.

'Did you look on your bed?' Rubi asked her mum matter-of-factly.

'Yes ... No ... Hang on!' Cassie flew out of the room. I heard crashing and thumping before she returned clasping both her phone and her purse in her hand.

'Colin was sitting on them!'

I turned to her in alarm. 'Colin?'

Cassie laughed. 'Colin. He's our pug. How have you not seen him? He's been here about a week now. They're bloody expensive things, you know. But one of my old neighbours was getting rid of him. She said she couldn't stand his snoring.'

'His snoring is so cute,' Rubi said. 'He sounds like a little pig.'

I shook my head. 'I had no idea you had a pug.' My mind cleared a little. 'Cassie, I should warn you, I'm not really a dog person. I'm more used to cats.'

Cassie was now busy texting on her phone; she didn't bother to look up. 'He's just a tiny thing. He doesn't bother anyone, does he, Rubes?'

Rubi was staring at me with her half-shielded eyes. 'Pugs are very good pets,' she said firmly. 'And Colin is the best.'

'OK,' I said, feeling more out of my depth by the second. 'But I don't really know what to do with dogs. I've never had one before.'

Rubi's eyes widened a little. 'He's easy.'

'If you say so,' I mumbled.

Cassie walked over to Rubi and lightly ruffled her hair. 'Rubi? Will you be good for Lucy while I'm gone?' She was almost pleading. 'Please. I promise I won't be too long.'

Rubi muttered something under her breath, her feet scuffed at the floor.

'What was that?'

'What if she kills Colin by mistake?' She glared at me.

'She won't kill Colin,' Cassie said firmly. 'Will you, Lucy?'

'I won't kill Colin,' I said. I looked carefully at Rubi's face. She looked wide-eyed with concern and I wondered if she was thinking of my animal graveyard. I hoped she really didn't think I was a serial killer. 'I'm just not very good with dogs, that's all, Rubi. I'd never hurt one. I promise ...'

But Cassie had already lost interest. 'Of course you won't! Why would you? Colin is a breeze. I really shouldn't be long. I think there's some tea for Rubi in the freezer – just fish fingers and chips – that'll do, and squash in the cupboard. If I'm late back, which I shouldn't be, can you just put her into bed and wait till I get home?'

I nodded. That sounded easy enough, even for me.

Cassie was looking at her phone again. 'What's your number? I'll punch it in now, so I'll call if I need to.'

I recited the number and watched as she tapped it in with speed.

'Shall I give you my number?' she offered. 'Just in case you need it?'

'Oh.' I patted my pockets, remembering. 'I left my phone charging in the kitchen. Shall I nip back and get it?'

Cassie held up her hand. 'No. Don't worry. I really need to go. I'll write it down for you.'

She moved back to the desk and picked up a small blue envelope. Her expression changed briefly as she glanced at it and I noticed the sweep of a frown cross her face. As she turned it over, I could see neat handwriting printed across it, clearly stating her address. She tore the back of the envelope away, then leant across the desk and began to write on the smaller piece.

'If you need me, call me. I'll pick up, OK?'

Her smile returned, her eyes softening as she handed me the paper. I nodded mutely.

'And Lucy, please – I know I don't really know you that well, but like I said before, I trust you. I really do. Please don't let Rubi go anywhere with anyone else. Just keep her with you, OK? Keep her safe, until I get home.'

I nodded again, then gazed across at Rubi, who was still reading quietly. But what was I to her if not a stranger? She barely knew me, after all. I wondered how she must be feeling about the whole thing and quietly hoped she wouldn't get upset once Cassie was gone. I didn't have the first idea how to deal with a tantrum.

'Just remember I trust only you,' Cassie said firmly.

I blinked back at her. My entire body was so tense, I felt like I could snap myself in two. My mind was bubbling over with conflicting emotions. She trusted me. Trust was good, of course it was, it was nice to have it. But was she right to trust me? I knew it was just a couple of hours, but what if something happened on my watch?

'It'll be fine,' I forced out, my lips curling against the words.

She folded up the letter in her hand and shoved it into her bag without another glance. Her fingers zipped the bag shut. The noise made Rubi look up. Her expression suddenly paled.

'I don't want you to go, Mum,' she wailed.

Cassie ran over to Rubi and wrapped her into a tight hug; her lips brushed the top of her shiny hair.

'I won't be gone long, baby girl. I promise. You're safe here with Lucy and I'll be home before you know it.'

'Promise?' she whispered.

'Promise.'

I looked away briefly and busied myself with cleaning my glasses on my cardigan. I felt suddenly uncomfortable, like I was intruding on a precious moment between them.

Then slowly, as if she was being dragged away, Cassie moved towards the front door. She blew a kiss to Rubi, then turned to me and flashed a thin smile. Her gaze shifted again, back to Rubi, and I saw something sparkle behind her eyes.

'We'll be fine,' I said, feeling the need to reassure her, but also to reassure myself.

'Thank you,' she said softly, her smile returning. 'Really. Thank you. I'll be back soon. In no time at all.'

And then she was gone.

Chapter Four

The first thoughts that darted through my head as I stood in this strange new space were: *How am I going to get through this? Can I really look after a little girl, when the only little girl I've ever known before is me?* I wondered who my mum would've asked to look after me when I was small. There had only really been my nan on my dad's side. I saw her a few times when I was younger. She had a small council house on the south coast. I don't remember much about the place, or her, in fact. I know she smoked a lot of cigarettes and collected brass ornaments that I used to play with on a large, faded carpet. They were funny little things that she picked up in charity shops – a bell, a girl in a flowing skirt, a mouse nibbling cheese – but I used to make up the most wonderful adventures with them. Nan also decorated the hall walls with commemorative sailing items – a bronze picture of an old ship was hung by the front door, and several decorative anchors ran alongside it. She had fluffy white hair, like cotton wool. I imagined if I touched it, my fingers would disappear through it, like stroking a cloud. Being at her house was like drifting back in time, the slow-ticking clock in the background, the dark hues of the faded curtains, the hiss from the electric heater in the living room. It was all so comforting.

I sat kneeling on her rough carpet, laying out the cards she kept by for me. They were from tea packets and they still had a slightly bitter, dusty scent. I loved the decorated pictures, of flowers and plants – each one so different and beautifully drawn.

I listened as Mum and Nan chatted in the kitchen. Nan might not have been her mum, but they got on well and enjoyed each other's company. Dad on the other hand sat quietly in the corner of the living room with me, nursing his cup. I glanced over at him and saw that he was rubbing his face and frowning.

'I wish we came here more,' I told Dad, as I carefully laid out my cards in a circular pattern, each one placed at a perfect equal distance from the others.

Dad laid down his cup. 'We can't, Duckling. It takes too long.'

'But doesn't Nan get lonely, here on her own?' I asked, my fingers stroking the rough fibres of the carpet.

'Your nan copes perfectly well.'

'And Mum likes coming here.'

As if on cue, Mum's laughter pealed through the room.

Dad sighed. 'Aye, that's true.'

'So why don't you like it here?'

Dad didn't answer me at first. He leant forward in his chair, his fingers gripping the arms as if he were about to get up. Then – 'I don't know, Duckling. Sometimes I just think I'm the type of person who's not very good with other people ...'

He glanced over at me and smiled hesitantly. 'Maybe one day you'll understand?'

I suppose that was one of the few things that Dad ever got right about me.

*

I moved across Cassie's living room, feeling like I needed to do something, but not sure what. I rubbed my hands absently against my cardigan as I stared out of her window. The streetlights had just flickered on, their amber glow spreading across the narrow paths that led out of the estate. Another Friday night was beginning. I remembered Cassie telling me that Rubi hadn't eaten yet. It seemed quite late for her not to have had dinner, but maybe this was normal for a girl her age nowadays. I wouldn't have a clue.

'So, I expect you'll want something to eat, then?' I said to Rubi as brightly as I could manage.

She remained huddled up against the sofa, her nose still buried in her comic. She barely spoke, or moved for that matter, but every so often her eyes would flick up and she would catch my gaze. She had an intense, unsettling stare and I found myself having to quickly break away. It was as if she could see right through me somehow.

As it was, I was hardly feeling at ease standing in this once familiar, now unfamiliar flat with a child that I didn't know. The place even smelt different from before. I sniffed at the air, trying to remember what it had been like when Joy was here – dusty and a little bit sweet. It smelt of Cassie now – of her perfume, the rich floral scent that made me think of the countryside. The walls were painted white and decorated with large, colourful prints of tropical islands and exotic-looking animals. By the TV there was a framed ceramic handprint that looked very small. I was guessing it was Rubi's cast when she was a baby.

I walked over to the bookshelf in the corner beside a small cabinet, which was black and stacked with more magazines, a vase of fake flowers and a framed photo of Cassie and Rubi that looked as though it had been taken quite recently. In it, both of them were smiling broadly at the camera, sunshine sparkling against their faces. I realised that it must look like I was snooping and glanced over at Rubi, who was still staring intently at her page. I didn't want her reporting to Cassie, saying that I had been looking around the place as soon as her back was turned.

But even so, it was interesting to know these things. To learn a little about the woman I was helping. I thought once again of Joy, how she'd had a similar bookcase in the same place – except hers had been crammed full of ornaments and interesting, unusual reads.

After about a minute spent standing at the bookcase, wondering what to do with my hands, Colin made an appearance. He was a fat, squat creature with a sad-looking face and an obvious problem with his sinuses. He trotted into the room, paying no attention to me at all, and instead curled up beside Rubi. She immediately threw her thin arms around him and drew him into a tight hug. He snuffled back at her, definitely sounding more like a pig than a dog. I hoped his habits were cleaner.

'Colin!' she cooed. 'Who's the best dog ever?'

Only five minutes had passed since Cassie had fled out of the door, and already my brain was working overtime. I stretched out my arms and flexed my hands.

'Rubi,' I tried again. 'Would you like some tea?'

'Mum was going to do me something earlier.' Rubi's fingers were working into Colin's fur, rolling the soft flesh under her fingertips. 'I think she forgot.'

'Oh – OK.' I shifted on the spot. 'Well, she's obviously got a lot on her mind.' I frowned, hoping that didn't make me sound judgemental. 'What does she usually make you? I think she said something about fish fingers?'

I studied her face, praying she would agree to this. Cooking was not my strongest point. Cooking for children, even less so.

'Yeah. I like those with ketchup.'

Rubi looked up at me expectantly. Colin huffed beside her and she lifted her hand to pat his head. He snorted in contentment. I noticed that each of her fingernails was painted a different colour; they looked like tiny sweets glinting in the light.

'Well, I'm sure I could manage that,' I said. 'Is there anything else you'd like?'

Rubi shrugged. Her nose wrinkled a little.

'I'm sorry – is that a yes or a no?'

'No.' She looked up, her eyes assessing me again. 'Thank you.'

'OK then ... Good ... fish fingers and ketchup.' I straightened up and nodded to myself. 'Good.' And that was one of her five a day, wasn't it? Ketchup must count, surely? It had tomatoes in it, after all. Maybe I wasn't so bad at this.

I walked over to Cassie's tiny kitchen which, like mine, was attached to the living room but separated only by an archway. Unlike mine, Cassie had made a feature of her arch by decorating it with an array of Rubi's paintings and drawings. I paused and peered at them for a moment. They were pretty good. Most of them were family portraits, depicting a small girl with a ponytail, a woman with a wide smile, a triangle for a body and spaghetti-looking hair, and a dog-like creature with a bone in his mouth. I smiled as my fingers touched the thin paper.

The one thing that had remained the same as in Joy's occupancy was the kitchen – the same shape and size as mine, but with much older units and painted a strange yellowy-brown colour. In fact, looking again at the single cupboard without a door, which had been a source of many of Joy's grumbles over the years about the council's cutting of corners, I wondered how they had passed any kind of inspection. They were supposed to carry out checks in between residents, but you did wonder who was responsible for holding them to account. The surfaces were all clean, but the oven was so old and sad-looking … I could see areas where food stains had baked in, probably too ancient to clean properly now. I imagined Joy standing here in this small room, long before her legs got bad. She used to love cooking, but towards the end she became reliant on the Meals on Wheels service. She was always grumbling about the bland taste and lack of flavour.

I gripped the worktop and felt a rush of sadness. Oh, poor Joy. Should I have done more for her? Maybe I should've visited more. I was always in such a rush, and now it was too late. I sucked in a deep breath and attempted to steady myself.

I couldn't start to think these things now. I had to focus on the task at hand.

'Are you very hungry?' I called out to Rubi.

'A bit ...' came her uncertain reply. What did 'a bit' even mean? How was I supposed to fill her up 'a bit'?

I opened up the freezer, surprised to find it almost empty. Folded inside a drawer was half a bag of chips and two rogue fish fingers, unboxed and totally encased in the ice.

As if on cue, my stomach growled. I thought of my own kitchen, of my microwave meals that were waiting for me. I was pretty sure my chicken madras for one wouldn't appeal to a little girl. It stung my own mouth badly enough.

'Rubi? When does your mum get the shopping in?' I called out, curious. My head was in the main fridge now, regarding the half-pint of milk, a stumpy lump of hard cheese and a cheap packet of bright pink ham that looked suspiciously crispy around the edges. Seriously, what were these two living on?

'I don't know,' Rubi called back, sounding confused.

'When does your mum go shopping, to get food?'

'Oh ... We wait till Mum's money comes in and then we go.'

'And when did her money last come in?'

'I don't know.' Her comic rustled. 'She says she needs a new job, because the old place didn't want her any more. But I don't like her going to work. It makes her tired and grumpy ...'

I walked back into the living room, wrestling with my options. At the present time, they seemed limited. Colin lifted his head and looked up at me, trying to work me out. He eventually let out a long sigh, as if disappointed.

I made my mind up.

'Rubi, come on. Get up. Put your shoes on. I think we should go out and get something.'

Rubi stood up slowly and stood blinking at me, her hand still gripping her comic. 'Where are we going? I thought we were supposed to stay here and wait for Mum?'

'Erm ... Well, I think we should get something nice to eat.' I paused. 'I guess you could call it a treat!'

She frowned at me. 'A treat? Why? What have I done?'

I hesitated. 'Well, have you done anything bad?'

'No!' She seemed horrified that I should suggest such a thing.

'Well then – I'm guessing a surprise treat today is deserved.'

'Will Mum mind?'

'I'm sure she won't,' I said, pushing back any uneasy thoughts. 'She has my number, so if she gets back earlier than she thought she can call me. I won't text her yet. I don't want to disturb her in case she's busy, but we can always leave her a note, so she'll know where we are.'

Rubi nodded, seeming to like this suggestion.

'Maybe we can get a milkshake?' she said hopefully.

'OK. That sounds like a plan,' I said, reaching for my handbag. 'So, where do you want to go?'

'McDonald's?' she asked shyly.

'Do you go there with your mum?' I asked. Personally, I was quite happy with McDonald's, but I was vaguely aware that some people felt differently, especially some parents. Jimmy was often complaining about his sister's latest health-food obsessions and reluctance to let her children eat 'fast food' or sugary treats. '*I don't know what they think will happen,*' he had grumbled once. '*The kids' heads won't fall off after one visit.*'

'We go sometimes.' Rubi's voice was quieter now. 'We go when Mum thinks we need a cheer-up.'

I stared down at her small, pale face. Did Rubi need cheering up so soon? Was I that bad that twenty minutes of my company had made her feel sad already?

Something inside me cracked open. How must Rubi be feeling – stuck here with me, someone she barely knew? I really was unknown to her and this wasn't easy for either of us. Surely we both needed cheering up, now more than ever.

'OK,' I said as brightly as I could muster. 'McDonald's it is.'

Rubi stuffed her feet into the scruffy-looking trainers that had been left outside the front door. It took her a long time to get them on. I did offer to help but she resisted, telling me she was fine. I stood back nervously, watching. She didn't seem fine, as she banged her foot impatiently on the floor in a desperate attempt to ease it in. She had already shown me where Cassie kept her spare keys, hanging on a hook by the front door, so I took these and placed them carefully in my pocket.

'Are they too small?' I asked, pointing at her shoes.

Rubi shook her head. She was scowling furiously. Finally, she let out a grunt and managed to force her foot in. I stared down at the battered, scratched-up leather and the gunked-up Velcro fastenings. She was certainly no Cinderella.

'I think you need new shoes.' I paused. 'Perhaps you should tell your mum?'

Rubi's frown deepened. 'It's fine,' she muttered, but her eyes quickly shifted away from me and her sad expression suggested this really was far from fine.

'I hope they don't hurt you,' I said. 'I had shoes once that were too small. I struggle to find any in my size, if I'm honest. I found those ones in a charity shop. I loved them, but they pinched every piece of my skin. I ended up hobbling to work covered in blood and blisters. I was lucky not to lose a toe.'

Her expression suddenly seemed to brighten. 'You nearly lost a toe? Really? Which one?'

'No, no, I didn't really,' I replied, feeling flustered. I wasn't used to this, talking to a child. I forgot that they could take things literally. 'I just thought I might because I was in so much pain. Tight shoes are no joke – you can do a lot of damage and we need to look after our feet. They're pretty important.'

Rubi peered down at her trainers. 'I suppose so. Although there's a man on TV who can walk on his hands.'

'He must be very clever.' I buttoned up my cardigan. 'But he probably has very sore hands that he needs to take care of, so either way you need to look after yourself.'

Glancing down at my own bitten and scabby nails, I realised I wasn't the best person to talk. I quickly rammed my hands in my pockets before Rubi noticed.

'Jessie Simpson at school lost her finger last year,' Rubi said earnestly. 'No one knows how, but some people say she stuck it in a piranha tank, and they shredded it down to the bone.'

'And do you believe them?'

She giggled softly. 'Of course not, that's daft. Anyway, there's no piranhas around here. But it sounds funny.' She prodded my side, making me jump back a little. 'Did you know that piranhas are like one of the oldest animals on earth?'

'Really, are they?'

'Uh-huh. I learnt that in my comic.'

'You read a lot of comics, then?'

'When Mum can get them. I like animal comics best, or animal books.' She puffed out her lips. 'Or anything with animals in.'

'Well ... that's good ...'

My eyes rested on the discarded scooter that stood by the front door.

'Rubi, maybe you're better bringing that thing inside? It really shouldn't be left out here, you know. There's bad people around who might take it.'

Rubi shrugged, not seeming that bothered. 'Mum doesn't like the mud getting into the hall.'

'Erm ... I guess we could just bring it on to the hall mat. That way we won't be trailing any muck into the carpet.'

'OK.' She smiled, and then proceeded to yank the awkward contraption through the door. I did wonder if I should help her, but she seemed pretty confident on her own. I watched her in fascination. I was pretty sure I'd never had her confidence at the same age. I wondered if Rubi had had this spirit her whole life.

She lifted the scooter with one hand and heaved it over the front step, but the scooter swung suddenly and clattered against the door frame.

'Be careful!' I said a bit too sharply, terrified that she might mark the wall, or injure herself. What would Cassie say then?

Rubi scowled, dragging the scooter in behind her. 'Mum says I'm too clumsy. I always crash into things.'

I smiled. 'Oh, me too, all the time. My dad used to say I was always too big for my body – all arms and legs. I guess I suited his name for me, Duckling.'

She leant the scooter up against the hall wall. 'Duckling? But ducklings are small and fluffy, aren't they?'

'I suppose.' I shrugged. 'But it was a song he used to sing to me – "*There once was an ugly duckling*—"'

I stopped. The words tasted bitter in my mouth.

'Why does he call you ugly?'

'He doesn't call me ugly, just Duckling. He still calls me it now,' I muttered.

'You should tell him to stop.'

'It's too late now, it's been going on forever,' I said. 'He's an old man, set in his ways. I don't think he realises how much the name annoys me.'

'Because of the ugly duckling song?' she asked.

'Well – that doesn't help.'

Rubi was still staring at me; her hands on her hips.

'You're not ugly, though. You're pretty.'

'Pretty!' I snorted, pushing my glasses up my nose. 'God, I'm far from that!'

'You're a bit like Velma from *Scooby-Doo*. But more stretched out.' She considered this for a bit, her head tipped to one side, assessing me. 'Yeah – a very thin Velma. With fluffy hair.'

I paused, touched my glasses briefly. 'Is that a good thing?'

'Well – she's cool, she solves mysteries.'

'Like Columbo!'

Rubi looked at me blankly.

'He's a detective I like to watch,' I explained. 'He's really good.'

'Detectives are cool,' she replied. 'They get to solve crimes and catch the bad guys. I'd love to be a detective, but Peter Ramsey in my class says you have to be a policeman first and I really don't want to be a policeman.' She shook her head. 'I don't like hats.'

I hesitated for a moment, my hand on Cassie's front door, ready to close it. 'Do you know what, Rubi, I'd love to be a detective too. I'd love to be just like Columbo. Wouldn't that be a great job?'

She smiled up at me and nodded.

'I don't think Duckling is a very nice name either,' she said suddenly, as if she'd only just made up her mind on the matter. 'And you made a funny face when you said it.'

'Did I?' I said, surprised. 'I didn't realise.'

'Yes, like this.' Rubi screwed her face up a little. She looked like she had just swallowed something sour.

'I did not look like that!' I said, shocked, touching my face. I wasn't even aware I could twist it into that shape.

'You did!' She giggled. She pulled the face again, just to confirm.

'Well – that's something I never knew I could do,' I said. 'Anyway. Enough of this. We need to get on.'

I eyed up the dog, who was snoring loudly by the door.

'Will he be all right left here by himself?'

'Of course,' said Rubi. 'He's our guard dog. He keeps us safe.' She paused. 'As long as we don't leave him too long or he might piss all over the floor.'

Her hand flew up to her mouth. 'Oops. I'm sorry, I said a bad word. Mum'll kill me.'

'Well ...' I said, unsure what I was meant to do. 'Just ... well, just don't say it again. OK?'

'OK.'

I stared down at the tiny, smelly creature sprawled out on the mat and wondered how he'd keep anyone safe. Perhaps as a trip hazard? He certainly didn't seem capable of bringing a potential burglar to his knees. He did, however, look like the sort of creature who would be quite happy to cover the floor in urine. In fact, his expression was almost smug, like he was already planning it.

'Don't even think about it,' I hissed as I eased the door closed.

We walked outside on to the shared gallery. The evening air was already much sharper now. For a moment neither of us moved. I could hear the shouts and thuds above our heads, children playing. In the distance, the familiar sound of Friday-night sirens pierced the sky. I sucked in a deep, smoky breath. I wasn't usually out at this time. I looked back longingly at my own front door – to its glass and chipped wooden panels. To my taped-up sign which was looking rather tatty and lopsided now.

'Wait there,' I said to Rubi. 'I just need to get something.'

Inside, I unplugged my phone and looked longingly at Boris who'd taken my place on the sofa. He meowed in his usual lazy style, his eyes blinking slowly back at me. What I wouldn't have given to flop down beside him and lose myself once again in an episode of *Columbo*.

'Not long, Boris ...' I whispered as I left. 'Not long ...'

Back outside, Rubi was picking at my sign, her face screwed up in concentration.

'What does this say?' she asked. Then carefully she began to read my angrily stamped-out words. 'No charity. No can – canva – canvassers. No religious groups.'

'Well read,' I told her. 'Now come along.'

I was keen to get her away, even though my own eyes were still fixed on the door, thinking how easy it would be just to slip back inside ...

'Why were you telling those people to go away?' Rubi asked.

I turned around, put my hand on Rubi's shoulder and quickly eased her in the right direction.

'Why, though?' she pressed as we walked. 'It doesn't seem very nice.'

'It's not very nice to annoy people in their own homes,' I said quietly. 'I just like to be left alone.'

'Are you very busy, then?'

I knew my cheeks were turning red. 'Yes – yes. Always. I have lots to do. I have my work, my dad to look after – I have so much going on.'

'Do you live with your dad?'

'Oh ... no! Not any more. I'm all by myself.'

'Like the lady who lived in our flat before?'

I cast my eyes back towards Cassie's door, a tiny shudder fluttering down my spine. 'Yes … yes, just like her.'

'Oh …' At least she was walking now, albeit in a slow, dragging-feet fashion. 'Mum said you weren't busy. Mum said—'

'What?' My voice was sharp. We were at the lifts now. I pressed the call button several times, my finger stabbing the cold metal. 'What did your mum say?'

Rubi was twisting her T-shirt, her eyes fixed on the cool grey doors. 'I … I'm not sure now … She just said you seemed to be on your own lots. That you were probably lonely. That we should be nice to you.'

'Really?' A cold, empty feeling opened up inside me. I'd felt it before – it was like I could be seen, that people could see right through me. They knew what I was. My cheeks were hot. I pressed the call button again, desperate to get away. To get this whole evening over with.

The lift bleeped. The doors slowly drew open and a waft of stale metallic air swept over us both. There was no one else inside, thankfully, so we stepped in. If it had been full, I would've made us take the stairs. I pressed the ground-floor button, trying to ignore the graffiti on the walls. I stood in the centre, well away from the wall, trying to ignore the dank stench. Rubi stood a little way apart from me, her fingers still twisting her T-shirt, her focus very much on the doors.

'I'm not lonely,' I said finally. 'I'm really not. I like being the way I am.'

Rubi turned to me, nodded. Her small apple cheeks were bright pink. 'OK.'

'You can tell your mum that. You can tell her she got me all wrong. Tell her I'm not lonely.'

She nodded again, bit the corner of her lip.

I tutted to myself. This was no good. I was just making Rubi look sad again.

'Look,' I said, waving my phone. 'I'll ring your mum now. I'll tell her where we're going. She should be pleased to hear that we're doing something together.' I hesitated, hating saying the next words. 'You can stop me being lonely.'

A tiny smile snaked across her face. 'But you said you didn't want to bother her?'

'Well, a quick call can't hurt, can it?'

I pulled out the scrap of paper Cassie had given me and punched in the number. With the phone pressed to my ear, I made myself smile back at Rubi. See! Everything was going to be OK ...

The phone rang. It continued to ring. I frowned. That was odd. Surely Cassie would've picked up straight away. She had told me to call her if I needed to. Wouldn't she have her phone available just in case?

The voicemail snapped on the same time as the lift doors eased open, revealing the foyer and another strobing light above us. I ended the call, keen to shepherd Rubi safely out of the stale, stinky box. I hated leaving messages at the best of times, never quite sure what to say.

'Is she not there?' Rubi asked, her voice a little high.

'Oh, she must be busy. Maybe she's talking,' I replied. 'I'll try again later.'

'She'll be back soon, won't she?' Rubi suddenly said, her hand gripping the edge of the steel door. 'We can't be out long. She might get cross.'

'We won't be long, I'm sure,' I said.

At least, I seriously hoped not.

It really wasn't far to go. McDonald's was further up the main road opposite the flats. The luminous bright yellow 'M' seemed to call out to us from across the street, daring us to walk faster. My stomach was already rumbling.

'I've been trying to avoid this place,' I told Rubi matter-of-factly. 'I've spent so much money in here in the past, my stomach basically turned into a McMuffin.'

Rubi giggled at this, her gaze drifting over my tummy.

'Don't you cook?' she asked.

'Not really,' I replied. 'I never really learnt how to, if I'm honest. I had to cook for me and my dad when I was growing up, and it was always just me heating up ready-meal stuff. Now I've just kept that going. I should be healthier, though. Jimmy is always telling me to try. He says my cholesterol will end up through the roof.'

'What's cholesterol?'

I screwed up my face. 'I'm not even sure. Something to do with lots of bad fat in your body, I think.'

'But you're skinny!'

'I think this is the type of fat that hides away inside you.' I shrugged. 'I don't know, really. You'd have to ask Jimmy. He has books on it.'

'Who's Jimmy? Is he your friend?'

'Oh no,' I chuckled. 'He's just my boss at the bookshop. He loves his food, that's all. He's always talking about it; he likes to cook properly and he's always bringing fresh fruit to work. He tells me off for being lazy and then I tell him off for being a nag.'

'He's a nice boss, then?'

'Well ... er ... yes, I suppose he is.'

But he was nothing more. As much as I enjoyed Jimmy's company, I knew that it was better to keep it purely professional. Despite what other people thought, despite the questions asked of me before by the likes of Dad and Joy, I knew I didn't need friends around me. I always had to say the same thing in reply – *'I'm fine as I am'* – and then silently remind myself that *'I don't need anyone else.'* Friends only complicated matters and I really didn't need that extra worry in my life.

'My mum used to like cooking but now she says she's too tired,' Rubi said. 'I don't mind. I like fish fingers.'

'And McDonald's?'

'Of course! I like the milkshakes best. Chocolate especially.' Her eyes seemed to brighten as she spoke. 'Sometimes we come here, and Mum gets me one with a burger. But only if I've been really good, like at school or something. But we can't if Mum doesn't have enough money.'

'She was a cleaner before, wasn't she?'

'Yeah ... She liked cleaning things. But they told her they didn't need her any more.'

'It must be hard now she's not got her job.'

Rubi chewed her lip again. 'Mum hates it. She gets mad and shouts a lot. Sometimes she kicks things, or she shouts down the phone at people. She hates not having money.'

I considered this. 'I can understand that your mum is probably fed up.'

Rubi shrugged. 'Yeah, I guess, but Mum says lots of people are in the same boat.'

'I think she means a lot of people are the same as you,' I said. 'I know on the news they were talking about more people being out of work.'

'Mum says that the lousy bloody government doesn't care about us and that makes her cross. She says that everyone in charge is an ar—'

She paused; her eyes flicked away from me. 'I'm not going to say the word because it's a bad one.'

'That's OK, I think I get the idea.'

Rubi peered up at me, her eyes wide. 'They wind her up. She always says she wants things to be different, but I don't really know what she means.'

We crossed the road carefully. It was a busy junction, and I wasn't sure whether I should take Rubi's hand or not. Again, I felt silly and inexperienced. I made myself walk right up close to her. Guiding her along without actually holding her hand.

'It'll be OK,' I muttered as we eased through the traffic. 'That's it. It's OK.'

Once again, I wasn't quite sure whether I was saying these things to Rubi or myself, but it seemed to help. We reached the other side unscathed. I rubbed my arms and smiled in relief.

'There. We made it.'

Rubi pulled a quizzical face. 'Duh. Of course we did. I can cross a road, you know! I do it all the time. I always look both ways.'

'I'm sure you do,' I muttered, even though I wasn't sure of anything any more.

McDonald's stood before us, the holy grail. Rubi hovered outside by the overflowing bin, almost as if she was unsure whether to step inside or not.

'Go on,' I said in my gentlest voice.

She grinned and strolled in, with me following behind nervously.

'So, what do you fancy?' I asked her as we approached the menu. 'A Happy Meal? That's what kids have, right?'

I felt Rubi stiffen next to me. 'I'm not a baby. I don't get those any more.' She tipped her head up and squinted at the choices. 'I want a Big Mac. And fries. Large fries, please.'

'Really? You can manage all of that?'

'Yeah – of course I can.' She puffed out her stomach, as if to prove it. 'I have a big appetite.'

I nodded, impressed. 'Fair enough. Sounds like a good choice. I'm getting the same myself.'

The queue moved slowly; in front of me a mother with a young toddler in her arms stood glaring at her mobile phone, ignoring the child who was reaching over to a nearby table.

Within seconds the child's pudgy fingers gripped a straw and tugged it hard. The drink in question lifted momentarily, before rocking mid-air and then tipping and falling back down, spilling cola all over the table and on the young man who was sitting beside it. He leapt up in disgust and shouted, 'What the hell!', his hands trying desperately to push away the liquid that was already soaking through his skinny jeans.

'He looks like he's wet himself,' Rubi said, sniggering. 'He needs a nappy!'

'Oh, Rubi – I'm not sure …'

She was still laughing, her hand clamped over her mouth to try and smother it. The infectious sound made my mouth twitch. Despite myself, I snorted.

The child had moved back up into her mum's arms. She was still clutching the straw, which she was now busy trying to ram into her mouth sideways. Her mum had barely noticed what had just happened, and simply shifted the child slightly on her hip, shushing her under her breath as her dull eyes still scanned her screen.

'I want a phone. Mum won't let me,' Rubi complained. 'All my friends have one. I'm the only one in my class who hasn't.'

'How old are you? Seven? Surely you don't need a phone?' If I barely needed my phone, I couldn't imagine why Rubi would.

'I'm nearly eight, and yes I do.' Rubi glared at me. 'I could message my friends. I could play games. I could call Mum whenever I wanted to …' Her voice broke; she immediately looked at the floor. 'I could call her right now and tell her to hurry up because I miss her.'

'Yes, I suppose you could,' I admitted, realising Rubi had a million more reasons than I did.

We shuffled to the front of the queue and I finally gave our order to an older-looking woman behind the till. She had greying hair tied back in a bun and a worn, thin face. Her light grey eyes surveyed us carefully.

Rubi gave her order excitedly, her fingers gripping the counter. I stood just behind her, amazed by the speed with which she spoke.

The lady smiled at her. 'My, that's a lot of food for a little girl.' She glanced towards me and winked. 'And what does Mummy say about that?'

'Oh …' I stepped forward. 'Oh … Oh, no! I'm not her mummy. I'm just looking after her, that's all.'

'OK!' The woman snorted. 'No need to get your knickers in a twist, I was only saying.'

Rubi giggled next to me. I glanced over at her and it only seemed to make her giggle again. 'She said "knickers" …'

'That'll be ten pounds eighty,' the woman said, more stiffly now. 'Just wait over there.' She flapped her hand to one side.

'This should be delicious,' I said, trying to sound enthusiastic as we moved to the left of the counter. 'I wonder if she's always worked here. She looks like she should be somewhere completely different, like in a school,' I said out loud, not meaning to.

'What do you mean?' Rubi asked.

'Well, that she doesn't seem to belong here. She looks out of place.'

'Like you,' Rubi said, looking up at me and then away again.

'What do you mean?'

'You just seem different to us. Clever and a bit ... I don't know. Mum said you looked ...' Her face scrunched up. 'Loof?'

'Aloof?'

'That's it!' She nodded. 'Mum was being nice when she said it, but she didn't think you looked right in the flats. She said she could imagine you in a big house somewhere. Painting or something. Being married to a rich man.' She giggled. 'Having a house with a huge library inside it.'

'I can't paint. Not like you. I saw your lovely paintings in the flat.'

Rubi nodded. 'I like painting.'

'Do you want to be an artist when you leave school?'

'No, silly. I told you, I want to be something exciting, like a detective. And I want a big house and lots of cats.'

'I've never had a big house. I've never even been inside one! But I wouldn't mind a big library.' I paused. 'Can I tell you something, Rubi?'

'What?'

'I'm not even very clever. I left school at seventeen, I didn't take my A levels.' I smiled sadly. 'Maybe I seem different to you because I'm quiet and keep to myself, but I'm really not so different.'

Not in the way she thought, anyway.

'You're like the woman,' Rubi said, her eyes moving towards the grey-haired worker again. 'You seem a bit sad.'

'Yes … maybe I do.' I frowned slightly, not enjoying this turn in the conversation. 'So anyway, what does your mum order when she comes in here with you?'

'She doesn't. She just has a coffee and watches me eat,' Rubi replied. 'She says she likes doing that.'

The woman placed the tray in front of me. 'Have a nice day,' she said flatly, her dull eyes locking on mine. She then turned to Rubi and her tone brightened. 'And don't get a tummy ache too fast, will you?'

'I won't.' Rubi beamed.

We sat at the back, at the only free table in the corner, right by the loos. Every so often, someone would fling open the door and radiate the scent of sharp disinfectant over us. I huddled up against the wall and tried not to breathe in through my nose.

'Aren't you going to eat any more of those?' I asked.

Rubi stuffed a floppy fry back into the cardboard container and sighed heavily. 'I'm not hungry any more. My tummy hurts.' On her tray a half-eaten burger sat neglected, looking like a soggy, burnt half-moon.

'You should eat. It'll make you grow.' I was chewing on my own burger and wondering why it was particularly tasteless today. 'My dad used to say that to me all the time, and the funny thing was I didn't bloody stop growing, so I think he soon regretted saying that. I overshadowed him by the time I was twelve.'

'Don't you have a mum too?' Rubi asked.

'I did.' My finger circled the straw of the milkshake. If I squinted, I could still see her face, just. But it was fading now, like a photograph that had been left out in the sun too long.

'Do you miss her? Your mum?' Her voice was as soft as a breath now, gently stroking my cheek. It took me a moment to answer. I quickly sipped my drink and busied myself with my handbag, opening and closing it – checking that everything was still there.

'No,' I said finally. 'I don't really. It was too long ago now.' That was the first lie I told her.

Chapter Five

I checked the time on my phone as we walked back home. It was nearly eight o'clock. Internally the timer in my brain was ticking down – Cassie should be back anytime soon. I checked my call log, wondering whether I might have missed a call from her, but there was nothing there. Maybe I should have left a message for her, asked her to call me back, but something in my brain niggled. Wouldn't she check a missed call? Wasn't she concerned?

Beside me, Rubi was walking quickly to keep in step, her spindly arms swinging freely by her side. I was glad to see that intense little look of hers had melted away and her expression was far softer.

'It's not been so bad, has it?' I said, as we crossed the road and headed back towards the estate. The crowds were thinning now. Somewhere up ahead, probably in the allotments, someone was still burning a bonfire. The smell was much crisper and thicker.

Rubi twisted her head a little to look at me. 'You didn't want to do this, did you?'

'Do what?'

'Look after me.' She reached up to her hair and tugged on her ponytail, pulling it tighter in place. 'I heard you talking to Mum on the balcony before. I heard you saying you didn't want to do it.'

I froze for a moment. God, how bad was it that Rubi thought this of me? I really needed to learn to lower my voice.

'Well ...' I paused, considering how best to answer this. The breeze was really chilly now, so I found myself wrapping my arms across my thin coat and drawing it against my body. 'Well – to be honest, Rubi, I didn't really want to do this. That's not because of you, or anything like that. I'm – well ... I'm just not used to being around children.'

'I'm not a child. I'm seven,' she huffed.

'Oh ... I'm sure you're very grown up for your age,' I offered. 'I didn't really mean that. It's just me. I don't really know how to be around ... well, young people.'

'Because you haven't got any? Because you're all alone?'

I had to take a short breath and lower my gaze away from Rubi.

'Well, that's true,' I said. 'I'm used to being by myself a lot.'

Rubi nodded, seemingly satisfied with my answer.

'You must have good ears to have heard me talking,' I said.

Rubi grinned, her ponytail bouncing high once again. 'I do. My mum says they are like a bat's, just not as pointy. Or hairy.' She pulled a face. 'Did you know that bats live for over twenty years?'

I shivered. 'No ... I didn't know that. You certainly are full of facts.'

She nodded proudly. 'And also ... some bats don't live in groups. They live on their own, in caves, like you.'

'Really ...' I paused. 'Although I don't exactly live in a cave.'

'I wouldn't like to have their hairy ears, though. That's just gross.'

'You should see mine first thing in the morning ...' I saw Rubi's look of horror and shook my head quickly. 'No, no, I'm not being serious. My dad, on the other hand – urgh ...'

'He has hairy ears?' Rubi creased up her nose. 'Can he hear well, too?'

I snorted. 'Barely.'

'Do you see him a lot?' she asked.

'Usually every other day.' I clenched my arms tighter to my chest. 'He isn't very well so I go round to help with things.'

'Why don't you live with him? Like I live with my mum?'

'Well ... I'm much older than you are, Rubi, and I lived with him for a long time before.' I paused. 'I think we get on better living apart.'

'Don't you like seeing him?' Her voice was sharp, chipping away at me like a tiny hammer. I tried not to flinch, but instead I turned my face away from her.

'He's my dad, Rubi, but it's complicated; these things often are,' I replied. 'He needs my help. He likes to know I'm there.'

I didn't mention the numerous phone calls I received from him each day. The constant checks to make sure I was still around and would be visiting soon. They'd increased significantly since he'd stopped drinking.

We continued walking in silence, slipping through the main entrance of the Cherry Blossom Estate. I had to watch my pace; my long strides meant I was leaving Rubi slightly behind. I found I had to walk at an almost half-step to keep her beside me. Across the way, in the car park, someone was revving up a clapped-out Mini. From one of the flats came the blast of loud dance music and high-pitched laughter. Friday night was by now in full swing.

'I don't have a dad,' Rubi said finally.

I stopped walking and glanced at her, wondering if she wanted to say more, but her attention had already switched to the patchy playing fields. I wondered what she meant by that comment. I'd assumed before that her dad was no longer around, but had he ever been involved in her life? Did he know her at all?

'Look! A cat!'

We both watched as the black creature slunk across the grass, its movements careful and considered. I wondered briefly whether it might have been the same one bothering Boris, a few weeks earlier – yowling and creating outside the window. It seemed the brave type, like it would be the sort to pester others.

'Cats kill other animals, like yours did,' Rubi said flatly. 'I wish they didn't do that. I wish they could be nice.'

I chuckled softly. 'It's survival instinct, nothing more. Remember, cats are related to tigers and panthers, to great big strong animals. They do what is instinctive to their breed; very often they only act like they do because they have no choice.'

'I know that, but I still think it's horrible.'

'That's just the way the world sometimes is, Rubi.'

She shivered; I saw the tiny goosebumps pop up on her arms almost instantly.

'Let's go inside,' I said quickly. 'It's getting cold, and your mum will be back before long.'

'But what if she ...' Rubi's voice trailed off. She rubbed at her arms and turned away from me. Slowly, almost sullenly, she began to walk back to the flats.

'What if what, Rubi? What are you worried about?' I called after her.

But her back was straight against me and her head held high; she might as well have put an invisible barrier between us. Whatever she'd been going to say, she wasn't about to continue it now.

Back in Cassie's unfamiliar but thankfully warm flat, I tried to make myself relax a little. A glance at her clock on the wall told me that an hour and a half had now passed, and Cassie still wasn't home. My phone still sat silent on my lap. Perhaps I would leave it a tiny bit longer and then try her again? That would be OK, wouldn't it? I only wanted to know when to expect her back.

It was difficult making myself comfortable here, but I think that was mainly due to my own insecurities rather than the comfort of the flat itself. Cassie's sofa was large and soft but buried under stuff – mainly clothes, a heap of Rubi's drawings and comics and what looked like a chewed-up dog's toy. I didn't like to move anything that wasn't mine and, as usual, felt like a big, lumbering idiot trying to squeeze my bottom in the small space available. Rubi was parked in front of the TV, too close perhaps. Didn't people worry about things like that? Vaguely I remembered someone talking about 'square eyes' but I couldn't recall where from. I decided now wasn't the best time to make a fuss about it. The dog, Colin, was curled up beside her, snoring quite loudly and making odd spluttering noises in his mouth. A couple of times I was convinced he was choking, but Rubi assured me that he made these old-man noises all the time and it was cute.

My eyes scanned the front door, thinking of my own flat lying just beyond. I started to think about my usual routine and what I should be doing right now. I thought of poor Boris, all alone and probably quite hungry and searching for food. I quickly sat up.

'Rubi,' I said. 'Can we just nip next door, to mine? I really need to feed Boris. I don't like leaving him on his own for too long. He gets lonely.'

I was expecting protests, but instead Rubi heaved herself on to her knees.

'OK,' she said brightly. 'But can I have a biscuit first?'

Rubi was walking inquisitively around my living room, nibbling the one bashed-up custard cream I had found her at the bottom of Cassie's biscuit tin. I quickly fed an impatient Boris and dumped the empty can in the bin. Being back in my own space was reassuring, like having my first cup of tea of the day. I leant up against my own bare arch that linked the kitchen and living room and took a few deep breaths.

'You have so much space,' Rubi said, spreading her arms out wide.

'Not really. My flat is the same as yours,' I replied. The only difference was mine barely looked lived in, compared to Cassie's place. The only suggestion of clutter was my discarded cup of tea, left on the coffee table from earlier, and Boris's bed and scratching post in the corner of the room.

'Your TV is so tiny,' she said, standing directly in front of my perfectly adequate twenty-inch flat-screen. 'I like our TV. Mum took it from Gav before we left.'

'Oh.' I wasn't quite sure what to say to this. 'I guess that's ... good?'

'I dunno. Mum called him lots of bad names and hit him with one of her boots. She told him the TV was payment for mugging her off.'

'Well ... Then he probably deserved it,' I decided.

Rubi sighed dramatically, stretching her arms out in front of her and peering at her nails. I was about to say something, to ask her if she was all right, when my phone started to buzz in my hand. I blinked at it for a moment. It was an unknown number.

Cassie?

I instinctively walked into the kitchen for the quiet, before swiping the green phone logo.

There was silence on the other end; echoey, horrible silence.

'Cassie?' I hissed. 'Cassie, is that you?'

A pause. And then –

'Hello! We are calling because we have reason to believe that you were involved in an accident in the last—'

'Oh, why don't you lot just bugger off!' I snapped, slamming the phone back down on the kitchen worktop.

Disappointment overwhelmed me. I'd so hoped that it would be Cassie. I thought she might be telling me she was on her way home and not to worry.

Instead, it was the same bloody call centre that rang every time. They were calling me more than my dad at the moment, and that was saying something.

'I'm not falling for it again,' I muttered. 'I'm not answering any more unknown numbers.'

It was too much. They were giving me a headache. If it was anyone important, well, they could just leave a message, couldn't they?

Rubi was sitting on the chair when I walked back in. She seemed to be a little stiff and uncomfortable, her hands placed neatly on her lap.

'Where's my mum?' she asked quietly. 'She's taking ages. What's she doing?'

'She's ... er ... well, she's running some kind of errand.'

'What errand? What is it?'

I stared at Rubi blankly. 'Well ... I don't know for sure. I guess it must be important.' I realised I was twisting my hands in front of her and made myself stop, but it was hard to keep still. Thoughts were bothering me like hungry bees. I didn't actually know what Cassie was doing. Or where she was. In fact, I didn't know much at all.

I drifted across the room, picking up the cup that I'd left out earlier and straightening the table so that it was in line with the chair.

'You don't have many things,' Rubi said, almost accusingly. 'And your walls are pretty empty,' she continued, her gaze trailing the room. 'You have no photos, nothing ...'

Her arms spread out wide as if emphasising the point. She was right, of course. Apart from my cherished print of Columbo, my walls were bare. I'd never really thought much about it before.

'I like it like this. It's soothing.'

'I can paint you a picture if you like? Mum loves putting my pictures on the wall – she says it brightens the place up.'

I hesitated. I wasn't sure I wanted scraps of paper tacked up on my wall, but I didn't want to hurt her feelings. 'Yes, OK. Maybe.'

She grinned. 'I'm going to do that. I'm going to paint you the best picture ever.'

I forced a smile, but it felt heavy on my face. Just the thought of Rubi wanting to decorate my walls or invade my space any longer was making my head spin a little. I was tired. I desperately wanted my quiet space back. I slowly moved towards the door, trying to steer the conversation towards her.

'Maybe I should take you home now,' I said.

'I don't want to go back. Not without Mum.' Ruby's voice was a whine now. She was rubbing at her eyes. 'I want you to get my mum.'

'Well – I'm sure she can't be much longer,' I replied hopefully.

'It's not fair.' Rubi flopped back on the seat, her ponytail bouncing. I noticed how red-rimmed her eyes were. How there were shadows under them, like lightly sketched half-moons.

'Rubi, I think you must be tired.'

'I'm not.'

'Well ... you look tired ... I know I am.' I paused. 'Let's go back to your flat, get you ready for bed. Hopefully by the time we've done all that, your mum will be home.'

'OK ...' She stood up. 'I suppose ...'

Boris was now sitting on the kitchen counter, looking at me suspiciously. He knew better than to sit up there, but I felt guilty telling him off when I was about to abandon him again.

'I won't be long,' I whispered. 'I'll be home again soon.'

I went into the kitchen to grab my phone. It was still on silent. I never particularly liked to have the sound on, much preferring the vibrate. I noticed the light was flashing, telling me I'd missed another call. Not the call centre again, surely? Quickly, I swiped through the menu, calling out to Rubi at the same time.

'Hey, do you want to grab your shoes from the hall? I'll just listen to this and then we'll make our move.'

I heard Rubi clatter back into my hallway, while my answerphone kindly told me that I had two new messages. Two, seriously? I'd only been out the room for a few minutes. Who ever thought I could be so popular? Surely the call centre hadn't bothered leaving me a message?

I walked back into the living room, nestling the phone under my chin.

When Dad's voice flooded my ear, my breath caught in my throat as it always did now. Even though he called frequently, the same worries hit me every time. Was he OK? Would this be the call telling me that he'd broken his resolve? But thankfully, I could immediately tell by his steady voice that he was still sober. I let out a long breath.

'Duckling – are you there? It's your dad again.' He coughed before continuing, 'Look, I know we only just spoke earlier, but I wanted to check you're still coming tomorrow. I forgot to say before, but I really need to talk to you. Is that OK, Duck? You'll come tomorrow? I'll have the kettle on ready.'

Then the beep sounded, and he was gone. His voice was still echoing around my head. He had sounded so lost and apologetic, which made my heart hurt. He was OK, though, I reminded myself. This wasn't one of his drunken, rambling messages like the ones I'd endured in the past. This was quite different. I stroked the phone absently, my mind wandering. Maybe I could let myself believe ...

I was just about to press the button to call him back, to reassure him that I would be coming tomorrow, when the voicemail beeped again. The second message. Was it him again? Surely not? But this voice was younger, the tone higher and faster; I had to pull the phone away slightly so that the words didn't burn at my ear.

It was Cassie.

I barely recognised her voice.

'Lucy – I'm so sorry ... Look, something has come up. I'm, I'm being held ... OK, OK. I'm being held up, yeah? Yeah, do you understand? Please – please just look after Rubi for a bit longer. I'll be home soon, Lucy, I promise – just keep her with you ... I'm sorry to do this ... Just keep her safe, OK? And I'll be home soon. I owe you, Lucy, I really do. I won't forget this ... Tell my baby I love her ... Tell her to wait for me, OK? Tell her I'm so sorry.'

The voicemail beeped again, one final time. There were no further messages. I closed my eyes briefly. How long was I now going to be stuck at Cassie's flat, waiting for her? This was not how I had planned my evening to go. What on earth was Cassie up to, and how long exactly was *soon*?

I glanced at my phone, almost willing it to start ringing again, for Cassie's voice to flood my ear in real time. For her to tell me that it was actually OK and that she was coming straight home. But of course it didn't. I did, however, notice that the small envelope was flashing in the corner. Hope surging, I opened the text. It was Cassie again. But her message was just one word.

Sorry xx

I re-read the word, almost unable to take it in. Was she sorry? Or was she busy having fun somewhere, while I babysat her kid for free?

Somehow this word felt flat and meaningless, and a trickle of rage coiled down my body. What about poor Rubi? Was Cassie even thinking about her own child? She needed to go to bed. Whatever I thought of Cassie right now, I still needed to make sure her little girl was settled.

I turned and walked through into the hall. 'Rubi. Rubi. We need to go now, back to yours.'

But as soon as I stepped inside it was clear that she was no longer there, and the front door stood wide open.

Chapter Six

I couldn't see Rubi anywhere. Where on earth was she?

'Rubi!' I called out hopelessly.

I ran to the front door. It was like an open mouth, yawning, taunting me.

I stepped back outside on to the cool walkway. Quickly I scanned both ways, but there was no one out there.

Making sure I had the keys in my pocket, I closed the door behind me and rushed over to Cassie's flat. We had closed it up earlier, but I had to check – maybe I'd made a mistake. But the door was firmly shut and locked, and Rubi didn't have a key. I still did. I leant my head against the door and swore quietly under my breath. Rubi must have heard the message, got upset and run off. After all, who could blame her? Being stuck with me for even longer! It was bound to make her panic.

This was just typical of me, getting it all wrong. I only had one job to do, and I was messing it up already. I'd let a small child run out of the flat. She could be anywhere. This was why I should never have been trusted to look after a child. How did I let myself get talked into this? Why on earth did Cassie think I could be trusted?

I took another deep breath and straightened up. She had only been gone a few seconds, hadn't she? With those little legs she couldn't go far. I strode across the deck, trying desperately not to worry too much.

Above me I could still hear the thud, thud, thud of children playing outside on the gallery. A man's voice shouted at his child, caught up in the breeze. 'Oy!'

I peered over the balcony. On the snaking paths below I saw no one, but the view was limited. There were shrubs and a collection of small trees that a child could hide behind. I looked around me, trying to work out where she had gone. The estate itself was made up of three large, looming blocks, surrounding a concrete forecourt and playgrounds. Could she have run into another block? Perhaps she was hiding in a stairwell? My eyes followed the path leading out of the estate, the one that we had walked along into town, not so long before. Could she be heading that way? Would I even be able to find her if so? The other paths twisting behind my tower led towards the communal gardens and the stubby field and railway beyond. I gripped the bars tighter. Could she have made her way there again? After all, that was where I'd met her that first evening. But the path wasn't well lit, and I really wasn't sure if she would go there in the semi-darkness. Was it even safe for her?

I decided that was the most logical direction Rubi would have taken. After all, it was a place she had gone to before. It was as good a starting point as any. If I was lucky, she might still be waiting by the lift. The bloody thing was always temperamental and often slow. Maybe she would be standing in the main lobby, safe and sound and waiting for me there.

I walked as fast as I could down the gallery, my lungs feeling tight and the muscles in my thighs already pinching. My eyes scanned the doorways, the shadowy little areas by the bins and drains. She might be hiding, of course. This could be just a silly little game of hers. I shook my head at the thought – surely not? She had seemed tired and a bit stroppy before. It was more likely that hearing Cassie's message had made her run.

How would she be feeling if she'd heard it? Upset? Angry? Or maybe she was frightened? If that was the reason then it was my fault. Come to think of it, whatever the reason, it would be my fault. I had caused this. I should have been aware of her standing in my tiny flat, listening out for any reassuring words. She'd already told me about her bat hearing. I should have considered her feelings as I casually held her mum's message away from my ear, allowing her words to flood the small room. Why hadn't I thought of Rubi at the time?

At the end of the outside gallery, the lift stood like a solid silver shadow, waiting for me. No sign of Rubi. I pressed the call button, half hoping she would pop out like a playful jack-in-the-box. But instead, the doors opened to reveal empty space. The weight inside me grew heavier.

'Oh Rubi,' I whispered as I stepped inside. 'Please be OK.'

I couldn't lose her. I couldn't mess this up. Not this time. Not again.

I tried to stop the memories which grew within me, but even shutting my eyes couldn't stop them. This feeling was familiar – the panic that comes when you suddenly realise that something is slipping away or has already been lost. Immediately I saw my mother's face as she turned towards me on that last day. Her eyes dull and unloving. Her hand flapping at me, telling me to go. I felt powerless and useless to stop things from escalating then and I felt the same way now. It was an awful, overwhelming feeling of hopelessness.

I saw myself back then, turning on my heel and leaving her. Shutting the door behind me.

Hiding away.

My eyes snapped open again; my heart thundered in my chest.

I couldn't be trusted with anything. The lift seemed to be taking forever to move and it was sucking all the air in from around me. I swear it stank more than it ever had before. There was a heady stench of booze in the air that made my skin crawl. On the metal someone had sprayed the word 'Sick' in lurid yellow.

The lift shuddered as if it was giving up and was shrugging its shoulders back at me. Slowly it began its rickety descent before finally creaking to a stop. The doors inched open. There was an older man waiting, wrapped tightly in a tired-looking raincoat. He nodded at me briefly as I stepped out and went to move past me.

'Excuse me ...' My voice was a little too shrill.

He looked up. He had a gentle-looking face, round and podgy. His large eyes twinkled in the poor light. 'Are you OK?' he asked. His hand reached out to the opening, holding the lift doors open.

'Have you – have you seen a little girl?' I stuttered. 'She's about seven years old, has dark hair. I think she may have come this way.'

The man frowned for a second and then nodded. 'There's a little girl just outside. She has dark hair. Is she yours?'

'Yes, well yes, sort of ...'

What else could I say?

'She's just out there,' he pointed to the main doors. 'She was with a lad.'

'A lad?' My heart was beating that little bit harder.

'Yeah, one from that group of boys – you know. The ones that are always hanging around here.' He shrugged. 'She seemed to know him. I assumed it was one of their sisters or something.' He hesitated, his frown deepening. 'Why? Is there a problem?'

'No,' I said. 'No, not at all. You've been so helpful. Thank you.'

I hurried to the main doors, feeling a rush of energy surging through my body.

'Please still be there, Rubi,' I whispered. 'Please be OK.'

Outside the smoky air struck me, cooler now and threading around me. The trees that lined the forecourt were now darker blurs, moving slowly in the breeze, scraping at the sky with spiky claws. Perhaps it was just the worry about Rubi, but all of my senses felt heightened. The lights from the windows of the flats were like glaring eyes staring down at me and the pavements themselves seemed harder, more unforgiving. As I moved, I could hear the screech of brakes, a dog barking, the dull beat of music coming from an open window and the distant sound of laughter and shouts.

Evening sounds were harsher out here. I found myself moving even faster, my feet scuffing the ground, making me almost trip. I just wanted to find Rubi and get back inside and safe.

Where was she?

I turned the corner of the path and then stopped in my tracks. I saw her first, sitting on one of the low walls that lined the patchy stretch of grass between the blocks. This was meant to be a pretty area full of flowers and blooms, but the bulbs had been kicked out long ago and now all that was left was muddy, rucked-up earth and dried-out weeds. Someone was with her – the boy, I assumed, his back to me.

'Rubi!' I called. 'Rubi!'

She turned, squinting in my direction. She didn't exactly seem delighted to see me, but she didn't run away either, so I took that as a good sign. I rushed towards her, relief overtaking me.

'Rubi,' I said again, firmer this time. 'There you are! You had me so worried.'

Rubi didn't move, but the boy turned to face me. I vaguely recognised him from around the estate, one of the older teens in the gang that hung around. I always avoided them, afraid of what they might think of me and scared that they might shout something out or confront me. They always seemed so loud and confident. This boy's short dark hair stood up in spiky tufts and his eyes glinted in my direction. His heavy, black clothes seemed to swamp his thin, wiry body. My gaze swept behind him, but to my relief he seemed to be alone.

'What do you want?' he grunted. 'Who even are you?'

'This is Lucy,' Rubi said brightly before I could reply, standing up. 'She's the one I told you about. She's looking after me.'

He scanned me up and down, then his mouth curled into a sneer. '*She* is?'

He turned back to Rubi and rested his hand on her shoulder. His fingernails were chewed to the quick; I could see blood and swelling around his cuticles. A fat gold sovereign ring was shoved on to his bony middle finger, looking strangely out of place, too large and gaudy on his pale, delicate hand.

'Rubi – do you even know this lady? What's going on?'

I flinched, not liking the direction of the conversation. All I wanted to do was get Rubi safely back inside. Cassie had specifically told me not to let Rubi go with anyone else and I'd already messed that one up. I'd been so fixated on the phone calls, I hadn't even heard Rubi sneak out. How bad a childminder did that make me?

Rubi shrugged. 'She's our neighbour. Mum said it would be OK to stay with her for a bit.'

He looked me up and down again like I was an item of furniture on a market stall. I slumped a little, aware of how tall and spindly I must look beside him. He made a strange sucking noise in his teeth. 'Rubi, this is no good ...' he hissed. 'Seriously? You don't know her. I don't know her. How long has she even lived on the estate?'

'Ten years, actually,' I replied coolly.

The boy stepped back; his eyes widened. 'You're joking me! Why have I never seen you round here before, then?'

'I keep myself to myself,' I said, trying to keep my voice polite, but I didn't really know why I was having to explain myself to this kid. 'I don't get myself involved in other people's business,' I added to make my point.

He held his hands up defensively. 'Hey! I'm just checking, OK? For all I know, you're some weirdo that Rubi barely knows. You could hurt her or something.'

I flinched again. His words were hitting old scars. 'Cassie didn't think so,' I said finally. 'And for that matter, I don't even know who *you* are. Do *you* know Rubi?'

The boy nodded slowly. 'Yeah, I do, and I found her out here on her own! Looks like you're not doing a very good job of looking after her.' His eyes drilled into mine. It made me feel exposed and vulnerable and I had to quickly look away.

'Do you know him?' I checked with Rubi, shifting my body to one side so that I didn't have to face the boy.

Rubi's head was dipped; her eyes met mine through her long fringe. 'He's Liam. He knows Mum,' she said.

'Yeah, we go *way* back,' Liam said.

I sighed. None of this mattered now, really. 'Rubi, you shouldn't have run off like that. I was worried. Why did you do that?'

Her head dropped even further. 'I wanted to go to the gardens. I wanted to see the bird grave again.'

'And then I found her,' Liam added. 'Sobbing and making a right noise. I thought someone had hurt her. I needed to check she was all right.'

'When I heard what Mum said on the phone, I wanted to get out. I just wanted to be on my own ...' Rubi whispered.

OK, this was something at least I could relate to.

'I get that, Rubi, believe me I do, but you can't do things like that. You need to come—'

'I don't want to go with you!' she snapped. 'I want my mum.'

She began to cry, huge, ugly sobs that took over her tiny body, snot bubbling in her nose. I went to move forward, reaching out to her, but she immediately recoiled from me as if I'd struck her. I stepped back, pulling my hand away clumsily. How was I getting this so wrong?

'Rubi—'

'She was OK before you came,' the boy hissed. 'I was with her, I'd calmed her down. She was fine with me.'

'Well,' I reasoned, 'I didn't know that, did I?'

He sniffed. 'You don't know much. You made it worse.'

I glared at him, the words lodged in my throat.

He was right, of course; I had made it all worse.

I squeezed my hands into a fist. I didn't want to think about that now, it wasn't helpful. I took a sharp breath. Rubi was talking again, her voice sounding fractured and small.

'I go outside sometimes when I'm angry. I just sit in the gardens until I feel better. I'm sorry, Lucy. I didn't mean to scare you. Liam was here so I thought it was OK.'

'Your mum lets you out at this time?' I asked.

Rubi's cheeks reddened. 'Yes,' she said, though she didn't make eye contact.

'So she won't be angry if I tell her what you did?'

Rubi looked up quickly. 'No, no – don't tell her.'

Liam sidled next to me. He pulled a slow, snake-like smile that didn't reach his eyes. 'You're not going to tell her mum, though, are you?'

I hesitated. 'Well – I wasn't …'

Liam continued smiling, but his eyes remained cold and hard. 'Because if you tell Cassie, maybe someone else will tell her how you weren't looking after her properly. How you let her run off because you weren't paying proper attention.'

'But that's not what happened! I was on the phone. I was—'

He held up his hand. 'I don't want any more trouble for Rubi, that's all. Don't you think the kid's been through enough tonight?'

I glanced back at Rubi. She looked sheepish now; her wide eyes still peering up at me, smudged with dark shadows. She looked exhausted. 'Well, I guess there's no point stressing your mum out unnecessarily.'

'And she said she'd be back soon,' Liam said, his voice softer now. 'She's probably just enjoying herself, eh?' He winked at me. 'Doesn't she deserve some fun?'

I hesitated before speaking again. 'Well, that's just it. Like Rubi told you, I was listening to a message from Cassie when Rubi ran outside. I think that's what got her upset.'

Rubi simply sniffed in response.

Liam frowned. 'And what did she say exactly?'

'That she was going to be longer. That she was held up.'

Liam shrugged. 'So – I guess her thing took longer than she thought …'

I paused, wondering whether I should convey my doubts. But Liam had said he knew Cassie from way back. Maybe he could be useful here.

I lowered my voice a little. 'I don't know. Maybe ... I just got a feeling. Cassie sounded different ...'

'Different in what way?'

'I'm not sure ... I can't put my finger on it. Rushed, I guess. And she seemed insistent that I should understood what she was saying.'

Liam rubbed at his chin. 'And you're getting a bad vibe, yeah?' He looked concerned.

Vibe. That was something Cassie had said to me before. That she had got good vibes about me. Was I feeling a similar thing here?

'Yes ... I think I am ...'

Liam nodded slowly. 'It's probably all right, you know. Cassie is clued up, she must be doing something important. Just sit tight, yeah? I'm sure she'll call again soon.'

'Do you think I should call someone?'

'Like who?'

'I'm not sure.' I hesitated. 'I mean, I wasn't meant to be looking after Rubi for long and this feels a bit wrong—'

'So what? You're thinking of the police?' He sucked in his breath. 'Nah. Not just yet. Wait, like I said. She's told you she's a bit delayed, that's all. You don't want to be making trouble for Cassie. She doesn't need that.'

'But—'

He held his hand out. 'Chill. Just wait and see if she calls again.'

His tone was light and confident, but there was something in his expression, a haunted look in his eyes that made me think he was more worried than he was giving away. I went to say something more, but Rubi shuffled up beside me.

'Is my mum OK?' she asked, her voice suddenly wobbly. 'What are you saying about her?'

Liam ruffled her hair playfully. 'Your mum won't be long, babes, promise. Try not to worry, OK? And any problems, come and find me, yeah? This lady here, well, I don't know her, but your mum obviously trusts her. I'm sure she'll look after you well, yeah?'

The 'yeahs' were soft, gentle as a stroke. His face was quite different when he spoke to Rubi, losing all the hard edges, making him look younger.

Liam turned back to me. 'If there was a better choice ...' He let the sentence hang. I knew what he was saying. It was like he could see inside my head.

'I'll do my best with her,' I muttered. That was all I could say.

Liam nodded at us both, then smiled sweetly at Rubi. It was the first sincere smile I'd seen. Then, just as quick, he snapped it off and the dark, cool look returned. Slowly, he moved away, his body as controlled as a cat.

Rubi took my hand without me asking and we quietly walked back towards the flats.

I was glad to get back indoors. Once inside, I ignored the over-excited Colin as he greeted us at the door and instead poured us both a glass of water.

'It's late,' I told Rubi, watching as she took a reluctant sip. 'Maybe you should go to bed and get some sleep. You look very tired.'

Rubi rolled her eyes. 'It's not even nine o'clock. I always stay up later on Fridays. Mum lets me.'

'Really?' I said, trying to keep the desperation out of my voice. 'But surely the sooner you go to bed, the sooner your mum will be home,' I reasoned. 'It'll make the time go faster.'

'Really?' Her eyes were hopeful.

'You'll wake up and she'll be here!' I said. Because she had to be, didn't she? I was clinging on to the hope that she would soon be home like she'd promised, and we could all go back to normal.

Thankfully Rubi went to bed with little complaint, suddenly seeming quite tired and subdued. I watched as she climbed into her tiny bed, drawing the covers high over her head.

'I want Mum,' she muttered into the pillow. 'She always puts me to bed. She's been gone too long now.'

'It's only been a few hours,' I said, turning off her pink bedside light. 'But I understand. I want her home too.'

Rubi peered up at me in the gloom. 'I'm sorry,' she whispered. 'I shouldn't have run away from you.'

'That's OK.' I paused. 'But how about you don't do that again.'

She wiggled in the bed. 'I won't, Lucy. I promise.'

'Sleep tight,' I whispered, padding over to the door and closing it gently behind me.

I trudged back into the unfamiliar living room, sat on the sofa and tried desperately to relax. I put the TV on low, liking its reassuring glare. I wished I could play a *Columbo* episode. Perhaps 'Try and Catch Me' – my personal favourite where a wonderfully charming mystery writer imprisoned her nephew in a safe. That would have been a perfect antidote to a stressful day.

Instead, I had to make do with just sitting back and trying to concentrate on a mind-numbing gameshow, the snoring but thankfully quite docile Colin lying on the floor by my feet. He tried to jump up beside me, but I quickly dissuaded him. Tiredness swept over me and slowly, cautiously my body began to unwind.

I had to sit and wait a little bit longer. It was all I could do. I had to try and relax.

But all I kept seeing was the haunted look that had filled Liam's eyes earlier.

What was he keeping from me?

Chapter Seven

Oh God . . .

I woke up suddenly. My neck was aching badly. I had fallen asleep in an upright position, my head angled towards the headrest. Now it was stiff and throbbing. I sat forward and massaged the sore point with my fingers, feeling a hard knot bobbling just under the skin. It took a few moments for me to remember where I was. Then my heart sank a little. The large window was casting early-morning light on my out-of-place body. Time had passed.

I was still here . . .

What was going on?

I looked down on to my lap. Colin was now sprawled across the sofa and his back legs and tail were slung upon me in abandon. I eased them off carefully. He snorted in protest and curled himself into a new position, his nose firmly wedged into his bottom.

'Sorry, mate,' I whispered. 'I don't think Boris would approve if I went home stinking of dog.'

Home . . .

My eyes drifted towards the door. It was still dark in the room, but I could make out the shadows of my exit route; beyond it I could picture the cold deck of the gallery and my own scruffy but safe front door. I reached towards my phone which was resting on the arm of the sofa. Swiping at the screen I discovered it was five o'clock in the morning. I shouldn't still be here. The phone remained blank. No more messages.

Thoughts tumbled inside my mind like fluttering birds.

Where on earth was Cassie? Why wasn't she back yet?

I rubbed my neck again, groaning slightly at the pain. My entire body was so tense and stiff, I swear I could've snapped myself in two. How long was I expected to just sit and wait here? I couldn't leave Rubi, but at the same time I couldn't sit around much longer doing nothing. Why wasn't Cassie home? Surely she would be doing everything in her power to get back here quickly.

Unless . . .

Another thought trickled in.

I didn't know Cassie that well, did I? Not really. She was just a neighbour that I'd said hello to a few times, nothing more. Why had I been so quick to believe her when she'd said she'd only be a few hours? Why had I been so accepting of her frantic phone message, apologising for being held up? What if this was a simple ruse? Maybe Cassie had planned this all along. Perhaps she had seen it as a way of getting a free babysitter so she could have a proper night out without Rubi. After all, she only needed some poor mug to fall for her lies and it looked as though she had succeeded with me.

I pictured her, all made up and dressed up for town, her hair beautifully straightened, her face perfect. She probably had more make-up stored in that huge bag of hers to touch up when she left here. She would be happy out there somewhere, having fun and laughing at the stupid old cow who she'd tricked into staying behind and waiting for her. My skin glowed. Where was she now? Was she still out at a club, dancing and drinking? Or was she with a dodgy bloke she'd picked up, enjoying a rare night away from the responsibilities of being a mum?

My head pulsed; my cheeks were on fire. Anger throbbed inside me like a second heartbeat.

She was out having fun while I sat here next to her smelly, farting dog who was still showing too much interest in his own backside. I was fed up, tired and uncomfortable. Despite everything, despite all the worries, I'd done this thing for her – because I thought she was a young, struggling woman who I had recognised. A woman I'd seen before, long ago in my past. My mum.

I thought this time I could get it right, but it looked like I had been tricked all along.

Cassie was obviously nothing like the young girl I thought I knew.

I pulled myself up from the sofa, my head spinning with tiredness. There was nothing I could do about this now. I was so exhausted I felt sick. I could consider my next move in the morning after some proper rest.

'Well, Cassie,' I muttered. 'If you get to go out all night, I get to lie on your bloody bed. Fair's fair.'

I stumbled into her room, trying to ignore the piles of clothes on the chair by the bed and the large, damp towel that spread across the floor like a dark puddle. The air was still thick with the smell of sweet, cloying perfume, but it was better than dog. I let myself sink on top of her surprisingly comfortable double bed. My eyes closed immediately, a tiny smile resting on my face.

I soon drifted back into heavy, dreamless sleep.

'Lucy?'

My eyes shot open. For a few seconds I couldn't recall where I was, especially as my first sight was a bedside table crowded with nail polish bottles and empty mugs. I scanned the room, taking in the bright floral wallpaper, the soft fabric curtains that I'm sure were once Joy's. Above me dangled an extremely ornate crystal chandelier. Well, I assumed it was a plastic replica – and it was certainly far too big for this room. Cobwebs dangled between the beads. I stared up at it for a moment, admiring the delicate silver strands. Spiders really were such clever creatures.

I groaned, wiping away the tiny pool of dribble that had formed between my lips. My eyes were caked with gunk and my entire body ached from sleeping on the sofa. I groaned again, feeling about eighty years old. My long limbs moved stiffly against the bed.

'Lucy?' I felt someone tug on my foot. 'Lucy? What are you doing there? Why are you sleeping in Mum's bed?'

I turned my head slowly. Rubi. Yes, of course. She was standing frowning at me. One hand was gripping a teddy. Her cheeks were bright pink, and her eyes were squinting at me as if she couldn't quite make me out.

'I – I was tired ...' I swiped at my damp mouth.

'But where's Mum?'

'I ...' Easing myself up, I glanced around the room. 'I don't know. What time is it?'

I answered my own question by looking once again at my phone, which was sat next to me. It took me a moment or two to focus on the screen. Half past seven. Still early. The screen remained blank. Still no messages from Cassie. No missed calls.

'Rubi? Is your mum back?' I asked her, confused.

'She's not in the living room,' Rubi whispered. 'And she's not in the toilet. I even checked the shoe cupboard. She's not in there either.'

'Oh – well, that's good, I guess,' I said, imagining Cassie crumpled up in that cramped space.

'Why isn't she home?' Rubi demanded. 'She should be home now. When will she be here?'

I paused. How best to answer this? With honesty? Or with a brush-off until I had a better answer? Being the coward I was, I picked the latter option.

'She's on her way, Rubi, I'm sure. Perhaps it's taking longer to get back than she thought. We just have to wait a bit longer.'

'Do you really think so?'

'Yes, of course. Where else would she be?'

'But—'

Rubi's bottom lip jutted out; she looked to be on the verge of tears.

'Rubi, it's OK. Liam told us, didn't he? He said your mum will call and he's right.' I made myself smile at her. 'I'm sure she's just having trouble with her signal. Or maybe her phone broke.'

'She does drop it sometimes. She has a cracked screen already …'

'See. That'll be it, then. She probably dropped it down the toilet. I did that once.'

'Yuck.' Rubi wrinkled her nose. 'Did you wee on it too?'

'Luckily not, but it took forever to dry out.' I paused. 'Do you feel a bit better now?'

'A bit.' Rubi looked at me and frowned. 'You look funny. Your hair is all sticky-up.'

I reached up, attempting to flatten it down – it never behaved itself first thing. I still felt fuzzy and un-programmed, like I hadn't been turned on properly; I was still rebooting. I wasn't sure what to do next. I had to sit for a moment just to breathe and give my thoughts time to settle. I wasn't used to waking up in a bed that wasn't mine in a room that I didn't know, and I certainly wasn't used to waking up and finding another person there with me, albeit a very small, confused one.

Rubi walked towards me and rested her free hand on the mattress. Her eyes were puffy and still sleep-ridden; I saw sleep dust matted in her long eyelashes. She rubbed her face and yawned.

'Lucy – I'm hungry … My tummy keeps making noises.'

'Really? Does it?' I made myself force out a hollow smile. 'OK. Shall we try and do something about that?'

'Can you help me, Rubi? I don't know where anything is.'

I thumped through the cupboards, looking for something. *Anything* that might be suitable for a tiny, grumpy person to eat. But aside from a handful of tins and some dog food, there really was very little. At last, in the furthest cupboard I discovered a packet of sugared cornflakes. I pulled it out reluctantly, jiggling the contents. It looked old and in truth the contents were more dusty than sugary.

'Will these do?' I said finally, holding the packet aloft for Rubi. She was sitting slumped at the table, making little circle shapes with her finger. Every so often she would sigh loudly and look at the door. She didn't seem keen to engage this morning.

'Rubi?' I shook the packet. 'I've found these, but they don't look very appetising. Will they do?'

She shrugged. 'It's OK. I'll have them.'

'I think I have some bread left next door. I could always make you some toast there?' I offered, my stomach rumbling at the thought. I peered inside the packet. I certainly didn't fancy this sugared-sawdust option.

'I don't like toast.' She pulled a face, like I'd offered her one of the dog tins. 'I want my cereal.'

I rummaged in the cupboard to find a bowl, then opened the fridge and took out the half pint of milk that was sitting there. Sadly, one gut-wrenching sniff told me it was on the turn.

'Are you OK having your breakfast dry?' I said. 'The milk's off, unfortunately.'

Rubi shrugged again, which I took as a reluctant yes. I handed her the bowl and watched as she began to eat. I couldn't believe that this was the best breakfast to be giving her, but what other choice did I have? I guessed it was better for her to be eating something. She seemed to rush each spoonful, like she was worried it was going to suddenly disappear or be taken away from her.

'You'll get indigestion eating that fast,' I told her. 'Aren't you meant to chew each mouthful carefully?'

She scowled back at me. 'I'm hungry.'

I glanced around the room again. My own stomach felt hollow. I cleaned my glasses on my top as I digested the situation. Saturday was such a busy day usually, I had so much to do. I needed to check in on my dad this morning; then I had to tidy my own flat and get myself ready for my afternoon shift at work. I glanced bleakly over at Colin who was now busy gnawing at his own paw. I guessed I would have to walk this dog at some point too. He couldn't stay shut in the flat all day, could he? That was hardly fair on him.

My thoughts drifted again to Cassie and my stomach was no longer hollow; it was heavy with dread. What was she doing right now? Where on earth was she? Surely I'd have to call for some help soon. I didn't want to, but I would be left with no choice.

'What does your mum usually eat for breakfast?' I asked Rubi, trying to force my troubling thoughts away.

'She doesn't, normally. Sometimes she'll have a biscuit if we have any.'

A biscuit? I raised my eyebrows and then sighed.

My mouth was dry. I ran the tap for a bit and then helped myself to two glasses of cool water, glugging one after the other. The lack of tea in here was distressing. I had to have a morning cup – it kept me going throughout the day. I swear it was the only thing that kept me going sometimes.

'Do you drink tea?' I asked Rubi.

She looked back at me in disgust. 'Urgh. No. I like Ribena but I finished the last bit yesterday. Mum was going to get some more today ...' Her voice drifted off and she looked at the door again. Her body slumped and she returned to her bowl, this time making circular patterns with her spoon, grinding the remaining flakes into the bottom.

'Maybe she's getting it now,' I said hopefully. 'She might be stopping at the shop on the way back. It could be why she's late.'

Rubi didn't reply. I turned back to the sink and rinsed out my glass. Then I poured out some more water.

'Will you have some of this?' I asked, offering it to her. 'You really should drink something. You might get a headache – I know I do if I don't drink lots.'

She took a sip and then screwed up her nose. 'It tastes weird.'

'It really doesn't. In fact, it really doesn't taste of much at all.'

'It's horrible.' She glared at me like I was trying to poison her. 'I hate water. It tastes of yuck. I want Ribena, or orange juice. Or Coke.'

My eyes scanned the kitchen; I really couldn't see anything like that here. I also wondered how Rubi knew what 'yuck' tasted of.

She soon finished her small bowl. Then, without another word to me, she walked back into the living room and began to fuss over Colin who was rolling around on the carpet making more strange grunting noises. I busied myself clearing away her bowl and washing it up in the sink. The routine movements were strangely soothing.

'Lucy!' Rubi suddenly shouted. 'Colin has done a poo by the door.'

'Great!' I hissed under my breath. This really was the last thing I needed. I raced into the living room and, sure enough, there was a pile by the front door. I stared at it bleakly for a moment or two. It was surprisingly large for such a small creature. I wondered how he'd managed it.

'Oh God,' I muttered. Colin sat up and looked over at me, his head slightly bowed. His eyes were large and dark as if begging for my forgiveness.

'It's not Colin's fault. We should've walked him last night,' Rubi said firmly, her hands planted firmly on her hips. 'Colin's toilet is outside. What else could he do? He can't hold all his poop inside. He'd explode.'

'No, I suppose he can't ...' I replied. The thought of an exploding Colin certainly wasn't a nice one.

'Poor Colin,' Rubi cooed, rubbing the dog's head. 'He thinks you're cross now. Look at his sad face.'

'Well, I'm not cross at Colin,' I said.

But I was cross with Cassie. This was all her fault. Because of her irresponsibility, I not only had a small child to look after, but also a dog, neither of which I had any experience with.

Stomping back into the bare kitchen, I gathered what little equipment I had. A tired-looking dishcloth, the washing-up liquid and thankfully some battered old scrubbing brush that I found buried right at the back of the under-sink cupboard. Judging by the age of it, I suspected it was one of Joy's. I held it for a second, a calm feeling washing over me as I remembered my old neighbour. What would Joy make of all this – me stuck in her old flat, looking after a little girl I barely knew? Would she be surprised? Would she look me up and down with her beady eyes and point out that I was clearly out of my depth?

Oh Joy. If only she were still here. She would know what to do. She would help.

I continued rooting around in the drawers and finally came across some washing-up gloves. I nearly wept with relief. They looked unused.

I cleaned up as quickly and efficiently as I could, all the time trying not to gag at the smell. Then I double-wrapped all the bits in plastic bags and threw everything away. I wasn't sure Cassie would approve of my methods, but I couldn't worry about that, I was doing my best.

'We need to go back to mine for a bit,' I said finally, my mind made up.

Rubi stared up at me. 'Why?'

'I just need to go home,' I said flatly, thinking of my own lovely space, my familiar smells. 'I need to check on Boris again, I need to eat something, and I need to wash and change. I stink.'

Rubi wrinkled her nose. 'You're right. You do.'

I smiled, not able to help myself. 'And most importantly, I need a cup of tea!'

Rubi came back to my flat reluctantly, but only on the proviso that: a) we walked Colin afterwards and b) we left a note for her mum telling her exactly where we were. I agreed to both, and a tatty, hand-written note by Rubi was Blu-tacked above Cassie's letterbox.

'I wrote in big letters so she can't miss it,' Rubi said. 'Even from very far away.'

'Good idea,' I agreed, smiling at the huge 'MUM' she had scrawled, along with about ten exclamation marks. 'WE ARE AT LUCY'S. COME NOW. XXXXXX'

'Are you sure you're allowed to wear that?' I said, as Rubi walked across the gallery with me to my own front door. She paused for a second, bent over and inspected her choice of outfit. She had insisted on getting herself dressed, assuring me that she did it all the time.

'This is my favourite,' she said, tugging on the red sequin dress that only just skimmed her bare legs. On her feet she was wearing strappy silver sandals and over the top of her dress, she had pulled on a bright pink cardigan that hung loosely on her arms, only allowing the tips of her fingers to peek through. It was a very colourful and chaotic ensemble.

'Are you sure it's not a special one?' I said, squinting at the dress. 'It looks *very* special.'

She pulled a face. 'It's only a little bit special. But I want to look nice for when Mum comes back.'

'OK, I just hope your mum doesn't mind,' I said, still uncertain.

'She won't.'

Once back inside my flat, I rushed into the kitchen to put the kettle on. Boris raced to greet me, winding his warm body between my legs and complaining loudly about my absence.

'I know, I know,' I soothed, stroking his soft fur, desperately hoping I didn't stink too much of Colin. I didn't want to offend him. 'I missed you too. I won't be gone for much longer.'

'Do you hate it that much at my house?' Rubi asked quietly. She was standing at the doorway, peering in, her expression sullen.

I stepped back. 'Oh no ... Rubi, it's not that. I just like being home, that's all.' I waved my arms around the small space. 'I'm so used to being here all the time and it just being me and Boris ...' I faltered, unable to think of the right words. 'I find it hard ... I don't know ... being somewhere different, that's all.'

'I don't like that either.' Rubi settled herself on the floor and began to pet Boris, tickling him lightly under the chin just where he liked. 'I went to a sleepover. It was Rosie Edwards in my class, she's like the most popular girl.' She looked up to see if I understood and I quickly nodded to show that I did. 'I was so excited, but after a couple of hours there I got really sad and scared. Then I felt really sick and Rosie's mum had to bring me home. I didn't want to be there any more, I didn't know why. I wanted to come back to Mum.'

'I'm sorry,' I said. 'That sounds horrible.'

She looked up, her eyes wide. 'Mum said it was OK. She said it was normal to miss your own home. She said you get used to things being a certain way and that those things make you feel safe and good.'

I nodded. 'Yes ... yes, they do.'

We locked eyes and then Rubi smiled shyly. I smiled back. It was nice to have someone understand me for once, albeit a small person. I felt a strange urge to sit down on the floor next to her but I held back, unsure. Boris was less inhibited. He rolled on his back, his mouth dribbling. He really was turning into the soppiest thing ever. Rubi ran her fingers through the thick hair on his tummy.

Hunger was now taking over, so I raided the bread bin. Thankfully it was reasonably full.

'Ah, toast,' I said thankfully. 'Are you sure you don't want any, Rubi?'

Rubi's pretty smile disappeared as she turned up her nose again. 'I told you. Toast is yuck,' she declared, like I should know this already.

I ate quickly, once again churning over the things I had to do today. I badly needed a shower, I still had to visit Dad and then there was my afternoon shift at the bookshop. My eyes drifted towards the front door, praying that Cassie would knock on it at any moment and I could stop worrying.

'Are you OK to wait while I freshen up?' I asked Rubi. 'I'll just have a quick shower; I won't be a minute.'

She nodded and then slowly walked into the living room. I watched as she circled the room and then sat herself carefully on my sofa.

'I won't be long. Maybe you could put the TV on?' I hovered in the doorway. 'But Rubi, no running away this time, eh?'

She frowned. 'I won't,' she said. 'I told you that.'

I watched for a moment as she inspected my battered remote control; then, happy that she was able to work it out (which she did straight away), I slipped into my small bathroom.

I think I had the quickest shower ever, but it was still blissful. The hot water pummelled and drilled at my skin, easing my stiff neck and soothing my tired muscles. I sighed as it poured over my face, waking me up. This was just what I needed. I stepped out on to the cool floor and dried my body as fast as I could, moving awkwardly in the tight space. As always, my elbows struck the shower cubicle and the side of the sink. This room was certainly not designed for tall people. Luckily, I had a clean top hanging up on the back of the door. After a spray of deodorant and a brush of my teeth, I felt halfway human again. I inspected myself in the mirror. I still looked a sight and my hair needed a decent wash, but at least I felt a bit better.

Coming back into the living room, I found Boris now purring contentedly on Rubi's lap.

'Well, look at that. I really have never seen Boris so soppy,' I said. 'He's not normally a lap cat at all. He usually prefers floors and boxes.'

I bent down to fuss over him, loving the feeling of his soft, clean fur under my fingers again. Rubi shifted on the seat under him.

'I know you don't like Colin as much,' she said suddenly. 'But you should try and be nice to him. Mum says dogs know when you don't like them. They get sad.'

I stood up, feeling weary. 'I don't not like him, Rubi. I'm just not a dog person, that's all. It takes some getting used to.'

'But you like cats more?'

'Well – probably ...' I chuckled nervously. 'I like cats better than most things, if I'm honest. Even people.'

Rubi's eyes were glinting. 'But I'm a person.'

I moved towards her. 'And I like you. Of course I do. I guess I'm just ...'

What? What was I? Oh yes, different to everyone else. As Dad used to say, *'You're the same as me ... A bit of an outsider.'* Dad and I had always been a bit that way but became so much worse after Mum's death.

It would never change, even though Dad was trying with the drinking. I didn't think it ever could. We were too set in our ways.

Rubi was looking beyond me. 'Your phone is flashing,' she said quietly. 'Do you have another message?'

Her eyes looked hopeful. I knew who she was wishing it would be. I hurried over to where I'd left my phone resting on the table and scanned the screen, then grinned.

'It's your mum, Rubi! Hang on! Let me see it.'

But then I read the message.

And my smile slipped away.

Chapter Eight

I read the text again and again, my eyes blurring. Rubi stood quietly next to me, her intense stare burning into me once again.

'What does it say, Lucy? Is it my mum?'

'Yes – hang on. Let me read it again.'

Lucy I'm so sorry. Things are taking longer here. Please can you keep hold of Rubi for a tiny bit longer. I'll be back soon, I promise. I'll explain everything when I'm home. I really owe you one.

The tone seemed quite flippant and upbeat but in effect she was still telling me nothing. I read back the words.

'I really owe you one ...'

Well, she was right there! I put the phone down and rubbed my arms. How was I going to manage this? I had things to do. This was going to cause so many problems for me. It was going to upset my entire routine. I closed my eyes and tried to settle myself, but it was so difficult. I was used to my Saturdays panning out a certain way, and this wasn't how I imagined the day going.

I wanted my normal back.

And yet, alongside my irritation, another feeling buzzed in the background. It wouldn't leave me alone. Something wasn't right here. Maybe I had watched too many episodes of *Columbo*, maybe I was looking for something that wasn't there, but my instinct was telling me something was off.

I stared bleakly at my phone wondering what I could do next. Maybe find Liam, ask him what to do? I chewed at my lip, instantly dismissing this. Liam was a young lad – how could he help? I didn't even know his connection to Rubi. And he hadn't exactly been that friendly towards me.

Should I contact the police now? I churned the thought over in my head. Really? And tell them what? That I was looking after a little girl for my neighbour, and she was delayed. Surely they would laugh in my face if I said I had a bad feeling. They didn't have time for that sort of thing. I really didn't want to waste anyone's time.

I picked up the phone again and re-read the message. Was Cassie simply taking advantage here, or could there be something else going on? She'd been a bit upset yesterday, but she'd also seemed rational – there was no suggestion that she was going to take off, simply leave Rubi behind like a sack of rubbish. She had been calm and caring towards Rubi. She'd also seemed insistent that I look after her properly.

Oh Rubi …

I recalled her face when I'd told her that her mum was going to be late and the idea that she was stalling even longer filled me with dread.

I felt worry build up inside me like I was a Coke bottle that had been shaken up, all the bubbles and fizz fighting for space inside my stomach. How could I carry on doing this? I wasn't used to caring for a young child. It was only luck that had got us through so far. What if I were to mess it up or get something badly wrong? The more time went on, the more likely that became, and the idea of it filled me with horror.

'What is it? Your face has gone all weird. Is Mum OK?' Rubi was now pulling my arm, trying to see the message.

Not sure what else I could do, I held the phone down towards her so that she could read Cassie's text.

She read it carefully, slowly, stuttering a bit over some of the words. Her brow was furrowed, and her teeth grazed her lips. Finally, she shook her head. 'You told me Mum was coming home soon.' She paused and pushed the phone back towards me. 'You lied.'

'I didn't lie, Rubi. I didn't know.' I paused. 'I really thought she would be home by now.'

'Why isn't she coming back?' Rubi's eyes were welling up.

'Rubi – I don't know, but there must be a reason for this. Maybe she's seen an old friend? Or lost track of time. Or ...'

I glanced at the message again. 'She did tell me before that this was all to do with family. That it was complicated.' I sighed softly. 'If there's one thing I understand, that's how families can cause bigger headaches than you imagine.' I rubbed at my own head. 'I think we just have to trust what Cassie says and wait for her.'

Rubi scowled, but her voice was small. 'That still doesn't make sense, Mum doesn't talk to her family. It's just us. Only us.'

'I just think ...' I hesitated, realising what I meant was, *I hope*. There was no point filling in Rubi with my worries. 'That there is some valid reason for all of this. Your mum will come home and explain everything to us and suddenly it'll all make sense.'

Rubi shook her head. 'She always says ... She always says that she would never ever leave me. That was our deal ...' She sniffed loudly. 'She said that when we left our house before. And when we left Gav. She kept saying it to me. She kept telling me she'd never leave me on my own.'

'Oh.' I stood awkwardly. Finally, not really knowing what else to do, I laid a hand softly on Rubi's head. Her hair was soft and silky. To my surprise she didn't flinch away, and I didn't pull my hand away either. We remained like that for a moment. Still.

I stared at the blank screen, uncertainty tugging at me. 'I suppose I could try calling her. At least that way she can explain for herself. We might know one way or another.'

Rubi nodded and then ducked away from my hand. She stood to the side of me, her arms pulled tightly across her body, her eyes lowered.

I hated making phone calls usually – they were always a bit too direct for me – but this really did seem the best thing to do now. At least I might get a proper answer. I told Rubi to settle herself back in front of the TV to try and take her mind off things and then I scuttled into the hall to make the call. I needed quiet. I needed to focus.

My phone instantly connected with Cassie's. I waited for it to start ringing, but instead it flipped straight through to her voicemail. She must have turned her phone off, or maybe it had died. If it was anything like my useless mobile, it would need charging every few hours even when it wasn't being used.

The voicemail message burst into life. Cassie's bright, friendly voice was actually welcome relief.

'*Hey, this is Cas! Thanks for calling. Sorry I'm not around. Leave a message or call back soon, yeah?*'

The beep sounded. I coughed, feeling uncomfortable. What should I even say?

'Cassie, it's Lucy. Listen, I received your last message and I'm sorry but we're getting a bit concerned now. Are you OK? Where exactly are you?' I coughed again, trying to clear the lump that was forming in my throat. 'I mean, I'm not even sure I'm the best person to be looking after Rubi now and I'm not available for much longer. So, if you get this message, Cassie, call me. I need to know what's happening.'

I hung up the phone and placed it back down on the table. I was shaking with frustration by now and sick with worry. 'I can't wait forever, Cassie,' I muttered out loud, running my hand across my face. 'It's not fair. If you want to be a bad mum, that's your business, not mine, and I'm sure social services or someone would love to know ...'

I swear I forgot about Rubi, but she was suddenly there, standing behind me, and as soon as my stupid words left my lips, I felt my cheeks flame with shame. *She would have heard everything!* I turned to face her. To apologise for getting frustrated and to tell her that I didn't mean any of those words at all.

But Rubi was already slumped on the floor, sobbing her heart out.

*

Social services – I knew immediately once the words had left my mouth that it had been the wrong thing to say. 'Social services' used to be hissed at me in spite by Dad when he had drunk too much when I was little, his threat that would have me sent away. He would stagger back from the pub, his eyes glinting, his body primed for a row – one I was never prepared to have. I learnt over time that 'social services' was a bad word around our estate. You didn't threaten it and you certainly didn't call them unless it was a true emergency. As Dad used to say, 'We look after our own. We don't need nosy buggers poking around in our business.'

It had started with a few drinks after work, but soon escalated into drinking at home, after Mum's funeral. I was the same age as Rubi, and suddenly facing life as a cook, cleaner and carer. I struggled. But it was my life. I accepted it. We made the best of things.

So social services were bad words for me to say. They brought back awful, scary memories. When they finally became involved in our lives, I was sixteen. It was already a little too late by then. School had finally become concerned about my attendance, about my unkempt appearance. I hated the long, drawn-out meetings, the probing questions, and Dad hated it even more. It seemed to drive another wedge between us. The only good they ever did was helping me get this flat.

At least with some distance between us, Dad and I were able to be close again – especially when he eventually stopped drinking.

But despite all this, I knew these words should never have been uttered by me, of all people. They made me feel shaky inside. I clenched and unclenched my fists, trying to move the fear away from the centre of my body.

I shouldn't have said that. Not in front of Rubi.

Rubi and Cassie were not like me and my dad. I knew that.

Once again I'd badly messed up.

'Rubi. Please stop crying.'

She didn't. She carried on, louder than before. More like a howl, high-pitched and piercing. I thought that being firm and calm might be the best solution, but it obviously wasn't working.

Rubi turned to me, her eyes red and her mouth swollen. 'I just want my mum,' she gasped, between sobs.

'I know. I know you do.'

'I don't want you.'

'Rubi ... Please ... I know. I know this is horrible. I'm really sorry, but at the moment you're stuck with me.' I tried to force a smile. 'I know that's a bit scary, isn't it?' I crouched down so that I was at her level. 'Look at me! I'm terrified. I'm making this up as I go along. I haven't got a clue what I'm doing.'

Rubi sniffed hard, then wiped her hand across her dripping nose. 'I just want Mum. Where is she? Why is she taking so long?'

'I don't know, Rubi.'

'It's not fair.' She sighed, a shuddery sigh that seemed to shake her whole body.

I hesitated for a moment, trying to process everything. I needed to keep Rubi calm and happy, and I wasn't sure how.

My eyes fell on my picture of Columbo hanging on the wall. I always ended up looking to him when I felt stressed or anxious. Sometimes, although it was daft, I would talk to him. Ask him what he would do. I squinted at his face, at his wise, kind eyes. An idea struck me.

'Rubi … Do you remember you said you wanted to be a detective?'

Rubi nodded, still sniffing.

'Well, over there on the wall is the greatest detective ever. Columbo.'

'The one you like?'

'Yes.'

'He's old … and funny-looking.'

I stiffened a little. 'He's the best, Rubi, not funny-looking at all, and do you know what Columbo would say right now if he was in the room with us?'

Rubi's eyes widened. 'No … what?'

'I think he'd tell us to get off our bums and try and investigate this. We can put our clever heads together and work out exactly where your mum is.'

'Like a proper detective!' Rubi said, brightening.

'Exactly.'

Rubi swiped at her nose, leaving a snotty trail on her cheek. 'I want to do that! I'd be a good detective.'

'I'm sure you will,' I said, looking around the room. 'Now, first we need paper and pen – like all good investigators would use. Can you find that for me? Maybe in my kitch—'

She jumped up and across the room. I heard some banging and crashing, before she returned clutching one of my old spotty notebooks and a giant pencil that Jimmy had given me once as a joke.

'This is all I could find ...' she said hopefully.

'That's fine. That's good. Now, to start with, I want you to write down some names. Do you have any other family? Someone who might be able to help us, who might know where she is?'

'Liam?' she said finally. 'Mum likes him.'

I hesitated. 'OK. Well, write down his name. How exactly does your mum know him? Can you remember?'

'Mum knows his mum, Jo, on the first floor. Mum said she was a – a ...' Rubi's face screwed up, trying to think of the word, and then she stopped herself. 'Mum likes Liam. He makes us laugh.'

I frowned. The thought of having to track down and possibly meet more people I didn't know was very over-whelming and, in all honesty, a bit terrifying, but at least we were getting somewhere. Friends might have answers or sug-gestions that could help us.

'How does Mum know Jo?' I asked. 'You'd only just moved here. Where were you before? Wasn't it the other side of London?'

Rubi nodded. 'But Mum used to live around here before, years ago. She knows Jo from school, she said they were naughty together. That's why she came back here. She said it was the best place to be.'

I nodded. 'Well, write down Jo too.'

I watched as Rubi struggled with the oversized pencil, her tongue poking out of her mouth in concentration.

'So, your mum must have other relatives around here? Uncles or aunts, maybe? I'm trying to figure out who she might be meeting.'

Rubi scowled. 'I don't know. She never said.'

'What about your nan? You must know if you have one?'

She glared at me, her watery eyes looking colder now. 'Nanny doesn't live in London any more. I think she lives by the sea. Mum says she's horrible now. They argued a lot.' She paused. 'We used to see her, though, when we lived there.'

'That's funny, my nan lived by the sea too. I used to love visiting her there,' I said, a tiny smile settling on my face at the memory. 'So, you lived there too? Near your nan?'

Rubi nodded.

'Was this before you moved here?'

'No. There was another place before here ...'

'It's a shame that you don't see your nan any more.'

I thought of my own nan, long dead but not forgotten. Of her soft voice and gentle hands. I still missed her, although it had been so long ago now.

'I don't care. I don't want to see her again. She made Mum sad.'

I hesitated. 'I think we still need to put her name down. Just in case.'

Rubi frowned, but she did as she was told.

'So, what about your dad? Can you tell me a bit more about him?' I pressed, feeling a little uncomfortable. I knew I was risking upsetting her, but I wanted to know if he was a part of Rubi's life in any way.

Rubi's body stiffened and she threw down her pencil. 'I told you before, I don't have a dad!'

'OK ...' I said carefully. 'Let's leave that one, then. I really didn't want to upset you.'

She picked her pencil up again and nodded.

'How about where you lived before, after you lived by the sea? Is there anyone there your mum might have gone to visit?'

Rubi now muttered through her fingers, so I had to lean in closer to hear her. 'I don't know. I don't think so. Mum hated it there. She said we'd never go back.'

I felt restless, like I needed to pace the room or something. There had to be someone else who could help us. Someone who might know where Cassie was.

'Rubi, is there anywhere else? Anyone that you can think of that knows you or your mum? Someone that can help?'

She looked up at me. 'No,' she said. 'It's just us. It's always just us. Me and Mum. I told you that. She said it had to be that way.'

I could see the tears were starting again. There was nothing I could think to say to make her feel better. I turned away from her. I wished I could just lay my head down and get some rest. But I knew I couldn't give up. I owed it to Rubi to try and work this puzzle out. After all, it was what Columbo would do.

'Rubi,' I said, suddenly feeling decisive. 'We are going back to yours. There must be something we are missing.'

*

I stood in the middle of Cassie's flat clutching the list that Rubi had written out at mine. It felt wrong to even be considering this, to want to pry and peek around the hidden spaces of her life, but I was convinced that there had to be clues. Watching endless episodes of *Columbo* had taught me one thing – people usually leave something behind. There must be something in the flat that could help me figure out where Cassie was. Despite feeling uneasy, I had to snoop.

'Rubi, do you know where your mum keeps special things – letters? Photographs?'

Rubi scowled. 'Mum has photographs on her phone ...'

'But does she have anything else that she keeps in a special place? Can you think?' I tried to keep my tone light, upbeat. 'Remember we are being detectives now. We have to try and find some clues.'

Rubi's face lit up. She tapped her mouth with her finger thoughtfully. 'We could try that cupboard,' she said, pointing to the white cabinet in the corner by the bookcase. 'I think Mum puts her letters in there. Or there's a cupboard in her bedroom where she says her private things are ...'

'Do you want to look in the bedroom?' I asked. I wasn't sure I felt comfortable searching in there. 'See if you can find notebooks, or diaries ... or photos?'

Rubi nodded, already moving towards the room, and cast a cheeky look over her shoulder at me. 'I'm going to be so good at this.'

I smiled encouragingly. 'I'm sure you will, Rubi.'

The cabinet in the corner was quite small, with three snug drawers. On top there was a green vase, a stained coaster and a pair of pretty hoop earrings. Reluctantly, I tugged open the first drawer, whispering under my breath.

'Please forgive me, Cassie. I'm doing this for you, I promise.'

The drawer was rammed full of envelopes, takeaway flyers and several newsletters from Ruby's school. I dug through it carefully, moving the items around. There were a lot of unopened letters and, as I looked more closely, I could see that there was one that seemed particularly urgent, with black official writing stamped on top of it – Phillpotts and Braithwaite Management. My stomach churned; I recognised that name. It was one Dad had ranted about in the past; he'd told me how his mates down at the pub had taken loans out with this company and ended up crippled by the interest they ended up adding on. Dad had always warned me against them; they were notorious in the area. The letter itself was unopened like the rest in here, but my intuition told me it wasn't good. Was Cassie in trouble? Did she have debt that she was struggling to manage? I already knew she had lost her job – maybe it was cash that she was trying to sort out.

I placed the letter carefully back and then checked the second drawer. This one wasn't as full, and mainly contained Rubi's drawings and scribbled stories. However, as I leafed through the sheets of paper, I discovered a small passport photo. I pulled it out.

It was Cassie, a much younger Cassie, a teenager probably. Her face was fresh, her hair was worn in a high ponytail and her eyes were sparkling with joy. Next to her sat a man, his face pressed up against hers. His expression was serious, gruff-looking. His features were dark. He was much older than Cassie, I was guessing in his late twenties at least. I flipped the photo over. On this side were the words:

Best day with Babe x

Rubi came running back into the living room, disturbing my train of thought, and without thinking I stuffed the photo into my pocket. Rubi stood in front of me, looking a bit disgruntled.

'I went through all her drawers – her knickers and everything . . .' she said. 'I couldn't find anything.'

I nodded. 'That's OK, Rubi, at least you tried.'

'I'm not a very good detective, though.'

'Of course you are! Being a good detective is looking and thinking hard. You don't find all the clues straight away.'

I thought of the photograph and the letters stuffed in Cassie's drawer. 'Don't worry, Rubi. We are getting closer. I can feel it.'

I took a breath. Right, what would any other person do in this situation? My mind shifted and then suddenly cleared, a chink of light showing me the way. That was it. I had to think like an expert, like someone skilled in these sorts of situations. What would Columbo do? Columbo would never panic, for one thing. He'd look at all the facts and weigh them up one by one. He'd be analytical and logical. Perhaps he'd make a list of his options.

I scuttled over to Cassie's table and picked up a discarded magazine and a chewed-up biro.

Quickly, I re-read the list that Rubi had made, adding notes of my own.

Mum/Cassie – keep trying

Jo – a friend of Cassie's? Maybe?

Nan – try and find out address/contact details. Cassie doesn't like her – why?

Dad – who is he? Where is he? Is he 'babe' in the photo?

Other friends/relatives – keep searching for more clues

Loan company – is Cassie in debt? Has she run away? Or has she got a boyfriend, someone helping her?

The police – really? As this would lead to social services. Do we want that? Too extreme? Would Cassie ever forgive me?

I looked back at the list with pride. Columbo would be chuffed. This was a far more rational and sensible way of dealing with the situation.

I decided the final point would be my last resort. I had other options to explore first. The most logical one was to speak to Jo. At least she might know where Cassie had gone, and she might (you never know) offer to take over the care of Rubi. Idly I wondered why Cassie hadn't asked her in the first place – as another mum, surely this would've been the better option.

Why on earth had Cassie resorted to me, a neighbour she hardly knew? Someone she considered a bit of a loner.

I glanced at my phone. There was another text message.

But this time it was from Dad.

Duckling. Remember I need to see you this morning. It's important. 10am x

Uncertainty began to gnaw once again at my stomach. Surely I shouldn't leave it too long before trying Jo. I needed to speak to her, but on the other hand Dad needed me too. I still had my own responsibilities, and it didn't take long to pop over there.

And then I thought of all the years Dad had spent in the police force before he got too ill.

He might be able to help me figure this all out.

Perhaps it really was the best place to be.

Chapter Nine

I sat down with Rubi and carefully explained my plan.

'I'd really like to check in on my dad first,' I said. 'He's not been very well, and I worry that if I don't see him, something bad might happen ...'

I guessed it wasn't appropriate to tell her about his drinking and how I was worried sick that any change to our carefully orchestrated routine might upset things. He obviously badly wanted to talk to me, and I was worried that if I didn't do so, something could go wrong. Or he'd use it as an excuse to break his sobriety.

'Shouldn't we see Jo now?' Rubi asked.

'Well, we could,' I said, considering the options. 'But I'd like to give your mum a little more time before we start worrying her friends. This way I can still see my dad as planned and you can get a little fresh air.'

Rubi shrugged. 'OK.'

'Also, my dad used to be a policeman, so he might be able to help us in our detective work.'

'Oh ...' Rubi's eyes widened. 'Does he still have the funny hat?'

'Not any more, but I'm sure he'd love to tell you all about it. And then, once we're back, if your mum still hasn't come home – well, then we'll go and visit Jo. See if she can help us.'

I was hoping that Jo would be able to confirm that Cassie was probably with a new boyfriend or something and had lost track of time. It was certainly better than the other options that were flooding my aching brain. Either way, the detective game seemed to be keeping Rubi occupied at the moment and I saw no reason to spoil it by telling her my theories.

'With any luck your mum will be home by the time we get back from my dad's and we won't even need to disturb her,' I added. 'The mystery will solve itself.'

Rubi finally agreed to come with me as long as we left another note for her mum, sent her a text and took Colin as I'd previously promised. I glanced over at the dog and I swear the mutt was grinning smugly at me.

'I'm not sure what Dad will think,' I muttered. 'He's not a great lover of dogs either.'

'I'm not coming, then ...' Rubi huffed, folding her arms tightly.

I drew a deep breath. 'OK, OK. He can come, I suppose ... Get his lead and his bits. But he'll have to stay in the garden when we get there.'

Rubi ran off and then quickly returned holding a yellow lead, some equally bright bodily contraption and a handful of dog poo bags. I took the contraption thing from her and stared at it bleakly.

'What is this?'

'His harness. You have to fit it over his head and between his legs. It stops him pulling on the lead.'

I looked first at the twisted knot of material and then at Colin who was staring at me with hooded eyes. Sighing, I bent down and attempted to hook the largest hole over the dog's squashed-up face. Colin began to snort and squirm. Frustrated, I tried to pull his legs through the bottom part. Stepping back, I quickly realised something was wrong. Half of Colin's face was now obscured by yellow mesh and his right paw was being yanked up by one of the attachments. He looked like he'd got himself trapped in a fishing net. He snorted at me in protest – I think he could tell how utterly hopeless I felt.

'You've done it all wrong,' Rubi told me.

'I gathered that,' I replied dryly. 'But it's far too complicated. I don't know why they can't make these things easier ...'

Rubi stepped forward and unhooked the dog. Within seconds, she had whipped the harness round the right way and secured it tightly. I stood watching her like she was a superhero.

It was the first smile I'd seen from her in ages. Her entire face brightened again. 'Shall we go, then?'

I nodded, trying to ignore the roiling feelings that were growing inside me. This was how I always felt going to Dad's. It wasn't really fair, because he hadn't drunk anything for months. He'd done so well. But the sense of dread never really left me. What if this was the day when it all went wrong again? I never quite knew what I'd face behind that front door. To complicate matters, I was now bringing Rubi with me. I'd never taken anyone back there before, least of all a small child. What on earth would Rubi make of my father? And what would he make of the situation I'd got myself into? It was all such a confusing mess.

And then there was the other worry – why did he want to see me so badly? Dad never wanted to talk unless it was to tell me about another job that he needed me to do for him. I certainly wasn't prepared for it today. I had enough on my plate already.

'Come on then, let's go,' I said, opening up Cassie's front door. I was careful closing it behind me, for attached to the letterbox was a new note for Cassie, this time written in my quick scrawl.

Just popped out. Back by 12

I'd sent her a text message saying much the same thing.
I was hoping that she would be back before us.
Surely she had to be?

It wasn't a long walk to my dad's. Sometimes if I was feeling lazy or in a rush I'd take the bus. But today, I had Rubi and Colin, so walking felt a better option. It felt strange, though, taking a little girl and dog with me. I was like an actor playing a part in a role I hadn't even rehearsed for. I was sure that other people must be looking at me and seeing what I saw – an awkward woman, out of place with these two new, smaller, additions tagging along.

We turned right out of the blocks, walking down the narrow criss-cross paths that led to the back of the estate, towards the gardens and playing fields.

I liked this time of day best, especially in the sunshine. The estate didn't look so cold and imposing, and at times the greenery around the flats made the place look softer and quite appealing. Obviously, you had to ignore the litter buried in the grass, the graffiti scrawled on the walls and the burnt-out car rammed up against the far wall. But, if you could turn a blind eye to those things, you could almost pretend that this wasn't such a bad place to live. It was vibrant at times and full of colour. It was forever evolving.

I could feel my mood lift a little. The sunshine on the back of my neck was helpful and almost healing. We continued walking out to the footpath that wound its way up through the fields and the rail track beyond. As usual, the bushes and verges were covered in rubbish. My fists clenched at the sight of a newly discarded mattress, filthy and wedged awkwardly between the walls and spiny trees.

'I hate seeing this,' I said. 'Some people are so selfish.'

Rubi jutted out her chin a little and nodded. 'Mum says some people are dragged up.' She frowned. 'I'm not really sure what she means.'

I laughed. Cassie had a point there. 'Well, it's true, some people don't realise the damage they are doing.' I pointed at the discarded object. 'Not only does it look awful, but it could harm other creatures. Look at the sharp springs coming out of it. That could snag on a fox or a cat ...'

'Or Colin ...' Rubi agreed, trying to pull the dog back. It didn't work. He lifted his hind leg up and let out a stream of dark urine, soaking the corner of the mattress.

'He obviously agrees with you,' I commented.

We carried on walking, over the steel bridge that led us across the tracks. I had to remember to slow my pace so that

Rubi could keep up. She was talking gently to Colin the whole time, encouraging him to walk quickly and not pull on the lead. He didn't appear to be listening and instead chose to sniff everything we passed, which made the journey take much longer than usual. Colin really was the complete opposite of me: whereas my legs were gangly and took long strides, his were stunted and short and could only shuffle along. We really were a mismatched pair.

'Oh Rubi, we didn't brush your hair,' I said, suddenly noticing how matted it looked at the back. 'And your teeth! My God, how did I forget that? How stupid of me not to think!'

'It's OK, I did it myself,' Rubi said proudly. 'Mum forgets sometimes too. Don't worry, I did them extra good. Front and backs.'

'That's good.'

I smiled weakly, but once again felt out of my depth. This should have been something I had checked before. God knows what else I might have missed. I needed Cassie's advice. But Cassie wasn't here, was she? She wasn't even available to ask. I pulled my phone out of my pocket and glanced at it again. I had now switched the volume on high so as not to miss any calls, but even so I liked to check. I kept telling myself she would be in contact soon.

The screen remained blank, almost taunting me.

'What is your dad like?' Rubi asked. 'Is he nice?'

We were clearing the field now. It was open here, more exposed. Across from us, some boys in brightly coloured bibs were playing a football game. Their parents stood off to the side in a tight cluster, coffee flasks clasped in their hands.

'My dad?' I paused. 'He's …'

I struggled to find the words. How could I describe him accurately to a young girl? Everything that came to mind seemed to be inappropriate somehow. Grumpy. Sullen. Most days, especially when he was off the booze, he was tolerable – but others … Well, those days weren't so good.

'He's quite tall, but not as tall as me. And he's got grey hair and very blue eyes. He is strong,' I said finally. 'Well, he used to be anyway. Like I told you, he used to be in the police. Not much scares him.'

'Was he really brave? Did he get shot at?'

'No – nothing like that. He was a constable. He was never shot, but he hurt his back quite badly, so he had to leave. I suppose that made him quite sad.'

I didn't mention the drinking that got worse after Mum. That the drinking was what injured his back in the first place. That the drinking ensured he could never return to the job he'd loved so much.

'What happened to your mum?' Rubi asked quietly.

The sharp sting was there again, right there in my chest. Funny how it never went away, even after all these years. I rubbed at my eyes. I didn't want to see her face. Not now. It was too much.

'She died,' I said flatly. 'When I was six years old.'

'Oh …' Rubi's feet were scuffing the ground; she looped Colin's lead tighter around her hand and pulled him towards her. 'That's really sad.'

'I guess it is.'

We passed the football team. One of the boys had just blasted a ball through the makeshift goal of cones and some of the gathered parents roared.

'How did she die?'

Broken images filtered in my mind. Mum staring up at me, her face tear-soaked, her lips dry. Her hand reaching up – telling me to go.

'She was sick,' I said.

Rubi coughed, a delicate noise. Then carefully she asked, 'What's it like? Not having a mum?'

I could picture her now, my mum, walking beside me. We'd both liked walking, Mum and me. But she could go out for hours on end. Her legs were strong and muscular, almost like a man's. Her towering presence had been calming somehow, a reassurance that she was in control. That everything would be all right as long as she was there with me.

Except one day, she wasn't any more. People later told me she had suffered for years, had a blackness inside her that took over her mind and made her do things that she shouldn't.

But even so, she meant what she said. I was the one who ultimately let her down.

Our pace had slowed and I realised that Rubi was looking up at me, waiting for an answer. Swallowing hard, I tried to think of the right thing to say.

'I don't really like talking about this, Rubi,' I said finally. 'Is that OK?'

She fixed her gaze on me for a moment or two. I saw something there – was it pity? Then she smiled and tugged gently on Colin's lead, encouraging him to walk faster.

'It's OK,' she said.

We continued the rest of the walk in comfortable silence. Dad's house was a tidy little terrace on a small back street that was now overshadowed by a towering warehouse. Years ago, fields had been there; it was where I used to run and play. But now the giant, corrugated metal-clad building backed on to his garden, blocking the light, the sky and anything that used to be any good. At night you could see the glow of soft green lights in the back rooms. It wasn't the same. It was like living in an industrial estate.

Number eleven, Daventry Row. I used to think it sounded posh, but in reality, this was just a dusty finger of a street, now rammed into a tight little space, with clapped-out cars and neglected wheelie bins lining both sides. Each front garden had long since been concreted over, with only occasional dashes of patchy green. It looked worn out and neglected now. A road that no one cared about any longer and probably no one would choose to live in.

I usually hated coming back here; every time I would hang back a little, hesitating at the mouth of the road, my legs turning to brick, crumbling with every move.

You can never fully hide from your past.

'Why are you stopping?' Rubi asked, pulling my arm.

'I'm not,' I said, forcing my legs forward. It was like wading through sludge.

'Are we here?' Rubi whined, her pace slowing. 'My foot really hurts.'

I glanced down at her feet. The strappy silver sandals that she had insisted on wearing did look a little big on her, and as I peered forward, I saw what looked like the start of a blister on her right heel.

'Oh, Rubi. That looks sore!'

'It is!' she cried out. 'I'll have to hop!'

'At least we're nearly there now. I'm sure Dad will have a plaster; we can fix it up once we're inside.'

Rubi nodded and then proceeded to hop down the rest of the street, her tongue planted in her cheek as she focused on her balance. It did mean I was left walking Colin, who shuffled along beside me like a furry pig.

Dad's house was in the middle of the row. It wasn't one of the neater examples; I guess you could say he had let the place go a little after I left home. Even his cherished old Ford Sierra sat rusting on the front drive.

'You have to be good,' I told Rubi as we drew near. 'Be polite and quiet. And we'll need to leave Colin outside, there's a post there that we can tie him to.'

'That's cruel. Colin likes to run,' she said softly, looking back at the dog. 'He'll get upset if we tie him up.'

'It'll only be for a little while,' I insisted. 'I just want to make sure my dad is all right.'

She nodded reluctantly. 'But not for long. He'll get scared if we take ages.'

I rang Dad's doorbell and stood back a little, taking a deep breath. I imagined what he was doing in there. Reading, perhaps. Or watching the news on cable TV. He wouldn't go out in the garden until the afternoon and his daily stroll was always at three o'clock, rain or shine. Some things never changed.

The door opened and he pressed his face into the gap. All I could see was thin, greying flesh and large blue eyes, yellow now staining the white. He stared intently at me for a second, as if he was worried I might be someone else.

'Dad,' I said. 'It's only me.'

He nodded gently. 'You came, then … good. I'm glad.'

The door swung open fully. He was wearing simple grey trousers and a loose blue sweater, despite the warm weather. I could see the folds of his swollen belly spilling over the tight waistband.

'Good. You're OK, then.' I said, breathing out. 'You're not—'

'What? Pissed?' He snorted. 'I should be so lucky. I keep telling you, I'm off the stuff for good this time, Duck. You need to start believing me.' His tired eyes skated over towards Rubi who was jiggling on the spot beside me. 'What's going on here? Who's this little one? Is she with you?'

'This is Rubi. She's just keeping me company this morning,' I said, trying to avoid his burning gaze. I knew he must be curious, wondering what on earth I was doing with her, and that made me feel uncomfortable. I felt like Dad's eyes could see right through me. He knew too much.

'And I'm not that little,' Rubi huffed. 'I'm one of the tallest in my class.'

Dad considered this for a moment. 'Well, it's good to meet you, Rubi. How unexpected.'

'It's been that kind of weekend,' I muttered.

Rubi was still hanging back a little, unsure. She was testing this situation out. Colin was safely tied up on the post behind her. He'd already rolled on to his back and started to lick himself, seemingly unbothered by the whole situation.

Dad rubbed his chin and said something incomprehensible under his breath. I noticed he badly needed a shave. I noticed too how the blue shadows under his eyes were larger than before and wondered how much sleep he was getting. He coughed and I heard the soft rattle in his chest.

'I'm OK really,' he said. 'You didn't need to rush round.'

'But you messaged me. You reminded me to come.'

I glared at him, confused. Was he really OK? He'd seemed so insistent on the phone earlier – why was he acting so casual now? Was it because Rubi was with me?

'Well, that's true. I suppose I'm used to you coming at a certain time.' His gaze drifted to the ground. 'I'm a daft creature of habit.'

I shifted on the spot, feeling immediately uneasy. Dad seemed different today – sadder, I suppose, and more sluggish.

'It's OK if you're busy. I can see you have your hands full.' His eyes lingered on Rubi for a moment and he frowned. 'Is everything all right here, Duck?'

I nodded. 'It's fine, Dad. I'm just helping out a neighbour.' I gestured towards Rubi. 'Rubi is her daughter. Her mum had to pop out and she asked me to keep an eye on her.'

He half laughed. 'My God, your neighbour must've been desperate.'

I knew he was trying to tease, but it still struck an old bruise. I found I had to take a sharp breath and steel myself. 'I'm just joking, Duck,' he said weakly, obviously noticing my reaction.

'I know,' I muttered.

'Look, why don't you both come in?' he said finally, his voice softer now. 'There was another reason why I wanted you here. I was going to show you what I've been up to the last day or so.'

I glanced quickly over at Rubi. She simply grinned back at me, her eyes wide. She seemed keen to explore my dad's dark house.

'OK,' I said. 'We were going to pop in anyway.'

We followed him in slowly, keeping behind Dad and his ridiculously slow pace. It was only when we got fully inside that I saw what he'd been up to.

'Bloody hell, Dad, what's going on?'

Chapter Ten

Dad's house, which was never in the best-kept state, now looked like a bomb had exploded. There were bags stacked in the hall and large bin bags piled up on the stairs. It seemed like Dad had spent the past few days packing up his entire life. I stepped into the living room and saw there were more boxes and bags thrown about inside. He'd even started removing books from the shelves in there and put away most of his DVD collection.

'I was only here on Wednesday,' I said, shaking my head in confusion. 'When did you start this? Where did you get all the boxes?'

'Fred next door gave me a load; he works at the warehouse round the back,' Dad replied casually, following me in. 'I made a start after you left the other day. I've not done a bad job, have I?'

'Have I missed something? Are you moving out?' I asked, squeezing myself through. 'How on earth did you manage to do all this with your back?'

He shrugged. 'Fred helped me out for a tenner, he got a load of stuff down from the loft for me. I can do quite a lot by myself if I take it slow.'

'But why?'

'It's what I wanted to show you,' Dad replied, running his hand across the top of one of the boxes. 'I thought you'd be pleased. You don't want the burden of sorting out my junk when I've gone, so I thought I'd make a start. It's actually quite therapeutic. I wish I'd done it years ago.'

I looked around me, still feeling a little unsettled. 'But Dad, these are your things! Surely you need all of this.' I stared at him blankly. 'You don't need to be worrying about this sort of thing yet.'

Dad smiled at me sadly. 'Well – the thing is, Duck, I wanted to—'

'I think it's cool!' Rubi interrupted.

We both turned round. Rubi had now strolled into the room and was moving around the boxes, her eyes lit up in glee. I had completely forgotten she was there and I stepped towards her, feeling instantly guilty.

'Do you?' Dad asked her, clearly pleased.

'Yeah,' Rubi replied. 'My mum always says that it's good to tidy up. She makes me clean my room out all the time. She says it's fungy pee.'

Dad frowned. 'That sounds like some kind of nasty disease.'

'I think she means feng shui,' I told Dad softly. 'The art of having good energy and organisation in your spaces. I read a book on it.'

Dad's face screwed up even further. 'Well, I'm not sure about that either. My spaces have never been full of good energy.' He snorted. 'I suppose it's never too late to change, though. Maybe we should have that tea, eh? All this talk is making me thirsty.'

We eased our way into the kitchen. The situation was no better there. Boxes and bags were stacked all over the table – it looked like someone was trying to pack Dad away.

'Wow – your dad is really messy …' Rubi breathed behind me.

'I needed to do it,' he said, already breathless. He leant against the kitchen counter and ran a hand through his straggly hair. 'I have far too much stuff. It's getting silly.'

'You're telling me.' I looked around. I never knew he had so much to throw away. Where had he kept it? 'What are you going to do with it all?'

'Who knows. I'll probably dump most of it. It's mainly crap. But I have to sort through it – you know … just in case. I'm guessing you might want some of it. In fact, I've got a box for you upstairs somewhere. Some of your old bits.' He flapped his hand towards the kettle. 'Do you want a cuppa, then? Are you staying?'

'For a bit.' I watched as he filled it up, his back turned to me. I tried not to stare at the curve of his spine and the gentle slope of his shoulders. He moved carefully across the kitchen, as if he was walking on ice.

'What does the little one want?'

Rubi stiffened behind me. 'I keep telling you, I'm not little. I'm seven.'

'Well, you're little compared to me. I'm seventy-six.' He snorted again. 'Although I feel about a hundred and six and I'm shrinking by the day.'

'Are you OK, Dad?' I asked, studying him. Was I imagining it, or was he moving more slowly than usual?

'Of course.' He flicked the switch on and stood back with a sigh. 'It's doing me good, having this sort-out. I had all this crap up in the loft, filling up the spare rooms. And what good was it doing me? I can't take it with me, can I? I need to get my affairs in order.'

I gripped the table, feeling unsteady. 'OK,' I said. 'But I still don't understand why you're doing it now. Why the sudden rush?'

'At my age, there's no point messing around.' He glanced at Rubi. 'But we can talk about this later, yeah?'

While Dad busied himself with the drinks, I checked through his cupboards to see if I needed to pick him up anything in the week. Although Dad bought things from the local shop, they didn't tend to be the healthiest or the most appetising. Of course, I was also doing my other check, the silent inspection. Dad said nothing at first as I peered behind his jars and tins, but then he slammed one of the cups on the counter.

'You'll find nothing there, Duck. I keep telling you, I've stopped for good this time.'

'So you keep saying.' I sniffed and ran my eyes across his meagre food stash. Typically, he was running low on biscuits and crisps. I swear McVitie's were keeping him alive. The fruit bowl, as usual, stood untouched. I scanned the bin and fridge, checking for evidence of drink, but there was none. It had been weeks now. This had to be a good sign.

Perhaps vomiting blood had been all the warning he needed – who knew? Nothing else had made him stop for so long. Not me begging him. Not him being arrested. Every dry period in the past had ended in bitter disappointment, for both of us.

'You still should eat these,' I said, gesturing to the apples, which were now a little soft and bruised around the tops. 'You know you should be healthier. You *need* to be healthier.'

He shrugged. 'I try, but they always get stuck in my teeth.' He opened his mouth and prodded at his few remaining molars. 'I can't afford to lose any more, Duckling.'

Rubi squeaked behind me, making me jump. 'Why do you have no teeth?' she asked.

I blushed, feeling bad for Dad, but also for her. What seven-year-old child wants to see a rotten old mouth? It was the stuff of nightmares.

'It's what happens if you don't brush your teeth and eat too many wine gums.' Dad winked at her and then laughed to himself.

Or smoke forty a day. Or fall over, drunk as a skunk, and smash a few out on the fireplace, or drink sickly-sweet alcopops by the gallon because they were on offer for months at the Co-op.

'I brush my teeth twice a day,' Rubi told Dad, before glancing at me shyly. 'Well – usually I do. Perhaps you should too.'

Dad nodded slowly. 'Aye – maybe I should ...' He paused, stirring the tea. 'Or maybe it's just too late for me now.' He flinched suddenly, teaspoon still clamped in his hand. 'Eh, little one, why are you looking at me so strangely? Have I got something on my face?'

I glanced over at Rubi, who had her head tipped to one side and was studying Dad as if he were some kind of exotic animal in the zoo.

'I'm trying to see if you really do have hairy ears. Like Lucy said.'

'Rubi!' I gasped. I turned back to Dad. 'I'm so sorry, I just meant—'

He flapped the teaspoon at me. 'Oh, don't worry yourself, Duck. You're right, I do have hairy ears.' His eyes gleamed. 'And hairy toes and nostrils. I think it's to make up for my receding hairline.'

Dad gave me a tea, stewed just as he liked it. Just like him and Mum both liked it. It was no use asking him to add more milk, he'd only argue. I grunted a thank you and sipped it, trying not to flinch. I could never like it dark like this, it tasted too bitter. I felt like I was drinking wood.

'So – how long are you babysitting for?' he asked, his mouth curling into a grin. 'I mean – I'm not being funny, Duckling, but I'm surprised that she asked you. A cat, maybe. But a child?' He shook his head. 'It's not really your thing, is it?'

'It's not for long. She was only meant to be gone for an hour or so, but she got held up.' I checked my phone again. It was still blank. 'She really should be back soon ...'

Dad raised an eyebrow. 'Did she say where she was going?'

I glanced over at Rubi, who had walked back towards the hallway and was looking out at the front door. I guessed she was worrying about Colin.

'Well, that's the thing, she didn't tell me exactly. She just said she needed to do something important.'

'And what was that exactly? When did she leave?'

I shook my head, feeling foolish. 'She left last night. I didn't ask where she was going, it didn't seem that big a deal. She was so casual about it, just mentioned something about family ...' I faltered, realising how naive I was sounding. 'I honestly believed her when she said she was just nipping out.'

'Since last night?' His voice was clipped. 'My God, I thought you were just talking a few hours.'

'She's called me, though, and left a message and a text to say she's just been held up.' I sipped my tea again, flinched. 'She told me she won't be much longer.'

His voice lowered. 'And do you believe her? Or do you think she could be up to something else?'

'I ...'

I glanced towards Rubi again, worried she might be listening in, but she was out in the hallway, her thoughts probably still absorbed with Colin. Her fingers were picking at the loose paint on the door frame. I didn't bother to tell her off. From the state of the place, I didn't think Dad would mind, let alone notice.

I stared back at Dad, trying to take in what he'd just said.

'I don't know, Dad,' I said finally. 'I guess it's possible that she's messing me about, but I have this bad feeling that I can't shake off. I'm worried she might be in some kind of trouble ...'

Dad's cool eyes stared at me. I could almost hear the police brain inside him ticking over. Even after all these years he couldn't let it go. He reminded me of Columbo in that respect.

A man who needed answers. A man who didn't like messy problems or things that didn't make sense.

'You've got a feeling? Nothing else?'

'Well ... it's nothing I can put a finger on.' I paused, feeling a bit ashamed of my snooping. 'I did look around Cassie's flat. I found a letter from that bailiff company – Phillpotts and Braithwaite. I wondered—'

'If she has money worries,' he finished for me.

'Well, yes.'

'To be fair, most folk around here have money problems. I think those chancers are shoring up half the estate.' He sighed. 'But it could be a reason why she's held up, I suppose. She might be trying to get some funds together.'

'That's what I thought,' I said. 'Either that or she has some new boyfriend. Someone else she is enjoying spending time with alone.'

He rocked back on his heels. 'Well, yeah ... She's a young single mum, isn't she? I suppose she doesn't get an opportunity to go out much. Maybe she just saw her chance and grabbed it.' He paused. 'You hear these stories – mums leaving their children while they go off gallivanting on holiday.'

I glanced at Rubi again, remembering her sharp hearing. 'Dad – be careful,' I warned.

He shrugged apologetically. 'OK, but you need to get hold of this woman, Lucy. You need to ask her what she's doing. If not—'

He didn't say the word. We both knew what the 'if not' meant, but we weren't prepared to say it in front of Rubi. I didn't want to upset her. Not again.

'I'm hoping she'll be there when we get back,' I said softly. 'I'll wait till lunch and then see.'

'And then you'll do something? You know my feelings on this. The police should be involved.'

'I know, it's just we know the police will lead to other things …' I hesitated. 'You know what will happen, Dad …'

His eyes locked with mine. An understanding passed between us. He nodded briefly.

'I know. I know. But you have a responsibility, Duck. You have to do what's right for the little girl. You're not her mum.'

I nodded. Of course. My gaze drifted back to Rubi again; she was running her fingers down the rough edges of the door frame between the hall and the kitchen, her expression lost and far away. I wondered what she was thinking.

'Hopefully it'll be a simple thing,' Dad said finally. 'These things often are. Perhaps she got carried away. Lost track of time. We've all done it.'

'My mum isn't like that,' Rubi said sharply. She was now standing in the doorway. Her hand slapped against the woodwork. 'You both talk about her like you know her and you don't. Mum wouldn't leave me. She wouldn't.' Her cheeks were red and her eyes blazing fire. She stepped back into the room. 'I heard you saying bad things. You think I'm silly and I can't hear. My mum wouldn't leave me to go on holiday, or to galli-vant.'

Dad bowed his head. 'I'm sorry, love. You weren't meant to hear that.'

'My name's Rubi,' she replied stiffly. 'Not "love".'

'I'm sorry too, Rubi,' I said. 'We shouldn't have said those things. It was silly of us.'

'And wrong!' Rubi spat, still angry.

Dad nodded. 'Aye, I'm sure you're right. There probably is a simple reason behind all of this. Don't worry, little lady.'

'I'm not worried,' she said and then, even louder, 'and I'm not little.'

'No – you said before.' He chuckled. 'I must say, you look like you can handle yourself, probably a lot more than my girl here can.'

'Yes, I can!' she replied flatly.

'We'll say no more about it,' Dad said, but his weary gaze hovered on me.

I glared back at him. 'On that note, is there anything you need me to do? While I'm here?' I asked coolly, putting the tea back down. 'I can't stay too long – obviously I need to get Rubi back.'

Dad sighed gently. 'I don't need anything, and you don't need to stay. I'm OK. I'm watching my programme anyway and then I've got all these boxes to go through.'

'I can come back tomorrow like usual.'

He coughed loudly and his entire body shook. It was getting worse – I swear I could hear his lungs crying out in pain. It took him much longer to regain his breath, and as he did it came out in short, wheezy bursts.

I leant towards him. 'Dad? Are you sure you're OK? Do you need me to make a doctor's appointment for you? Do you need more antibiotics?'

He held out his hand, palm up. 'No ... no ... I'm fine ...'

'Has he got a cold?' Rubi asked, peering at him. 'Is it a bug?'

'He smokes too much,' I told her. 'His lungs don't like it.'

Her eyes widened. 'You shouldn't smoke,' she told Dad stoutly. 'It's really bad for you. Mum showed me a cigarette packet once, with a picture of dirty lungs on it. It was so gross.' She breathed out. 'Mum said if I ever smoke, she's going to boot me up the bum.'

Dad smiled weakly. 'Your mum sounds like a wise woman.'

'So why do you do it?'

He shrugged. 'I guess it would be harder to boot an old man around the room.'

'Don't tempt me,' I hissed. I turned to Rubi. 'Dad has been smoking for so long now. It's a habit he can't stop, even if it's bad for him.'

'Well, I think he's stupid,' Rubi said bluntly. She sank down on one of Dad's rickety kitchen chairs and tugged at her sandal. 'Lucy, my foot is really hurting and – and it's bleeding now.'

Her foot! A fresh wave of guilt washed over me. With everything going on, I had forgotten all about it. I studied her heel carefully. The skin was really raised and red. It did look pretty grim.

'OK, I'll just pop upstairs. You'll have a plaster up there, won't you, Dad? Rubi has a nasty blister on her foot.'

'Probably, somewhere in that cupboard in the bathroom,' Dad muttered. 'Excuse the mess up there, though – it's just as bad, to be honest ...'

'Well, like I said, I can come back tomorrow, and I'll help you tidy it up a bit.' I eyed the sink that was piled high with plates.

'You really don't have to, Duckling,' Dad said, lifting his head towards me. 'It's not necessary.' He sank back a little on his chair. 'But maybe we could watch a *Columbo* together. There's one on the cable TV, one of the early ones. It'll be nice to spend some time with you.'

I felt an uneasy spark settle at the base of my spine.

'Seriously, Dad. Are you OK?' I asked. 'I mean, really OK. Don't fob me off now.'

'Of course I'm all right. I just fancied watching some *Columbo* with you, that's all; maybe have a little chat. Nothing sinister.'

'Do you like him too?' Rubi asked, sounding surprised. 'He has a really funny name and a squashed-up face. But Lucy says she really loves him.'

Dad nodded. 'He's the best, you know. He reminds me a little of me when I used to fight crime.' He lifted his arm and flexed his muscle. 'I was tough then, Rubi. And quick. Nobody got the better of me.'

Rubi smiled. 'Lucy told me he has a wooden eye.'

'A glass eye,' I corrected her gently.

She shrugged. 'Same difference.'

'Well, not really ...'

'So tomorrow, then – me and you and Peter Falk. Is that a date?' Dad looked up at me. His face was so thin, his eyes shiny and damp.

'Dad ...'

'I'm fine, Duckling. Stop going on.' He held up his hand. His stare was harder now, more familiar. 'The plasters will be in the bathroom. Stop faffing and go and get them. This poor girl doesn't want to wait around forever with her foot in the air. She'll get a cramp.'

'But …' I floundered, uncertain.

'Just go! Hurry up,' he said in a forced light tone and turned away from me.

Upstairs was much worse than I had expected. The landing, which was usually pretty clear, was piled high with more boxes and bin bags. How had he even had the motivation for such a major clear-out? He usually complained if he had to move to pick up the remote control.

'What are you up to?' I whispered. 'And how did I not know that you owned so many things?'

Curious, I stuck my nose in the nearest bag. It was full of paperwork, most of it ripped or scrunched up into tight little balls. I pulled out a sheet and straightened it out. It was a utility bill from years ago. Ten years ago, in fact. I pulled out more sheets, but they were all old bills and reminders. There were even crumpled-up leaflets and circulars that should have been binned on arrival. I had no idea that he had been keeping it all.

But to be fair, when had I ever seen him throw anything out? This was just like Dad – to stuff things into drawers and cupboards to sort out another day.

I pushed the bag back with my foot and peered into one of the boxes. This one was rammed with books. Old paperbacks, with faded spines. I ran my finger across the covers of the top few – they were old, yes, but they were still in good shape. Vintage Penguins. These were decent. Jimmy would love books like these. Had they even been read?

The other boxes and bags were crammed full of random objects. Headphones. An old portable stereo. A bunch of tangled coat hangers. One lone brown leather shoe. For some reason I found myself plucking this out and nursing it against my chest as if it were a small creature. The leather was cracked and the sole well worn, but I didn't recognise it. I couldn't even recall the last time Dad had dressed smartly. Nowadays he just seemed to live in his socks or battered trainers. Tears pricked at my eyes. When I was much younger, he'd been such a strong man, so in control and full of authority. Yet bit by bit, parts of him had broken down. The grief after Mum's death and the drinking that followed had chipped away at the last bits of him. I realised how bitterly sorry I was. He had never been able to cope. When had he last been truly happy?

It wasn't his fault, all of this.

I picked my way over the clutter and peered into his bedroom. The dark duvet had been pulled roughly over his unmade bed. Piled up on the end of the mattress were more, smaller boxes. His wardrobe stood open, the doors hanging as if preparing for an embrace. I stepped into the room. It smelt dusty and stale in here, like the windows hadn't been opened in a very long time. I faced the wardrobe and stared into the vast, empty space, tasting mothballs on my tongue. He'd cleared it. Apart from a few shirts and two pairs of trousers, hanging neglected on the rail, it was empty. Where were his nice chinos that he wore for best? Where was his wedding suit? The back of the wardrobe stared back at me.

I walked over to Dad's bedside cabinet and pulled open the bottom drawer. I braced myself, but there were still rolls and rolls of socks inside. He'd left this part alone. Right at the bottom were the still-unopened packs. I took one of these and bunched it into my pocket.

And then, slowly, reluctantly, I walked around the bed. I didn't like doing this. Even now. I hated being here. I hated being on this side. My eyes grazed her pillow. I could still see her. Her face turned towards me. The duvet pushed back, her bare arms exposed.

Her mouth open.

I blinked and looked away again, turning my attention instead to Mum's drawers. I tugged gently on the top drawer but I knew already; it slipped out far too easily. Empty, of course, as they had been for years.

Mum's things had gone a long time ago. He'd never kept her stuff. That was one thing he'd never clung on to. I don't think he could bear it.

My gaze fell on the bed again, but further down this time, to those boxes. I reached into the nearest one and dug inside with my fingers. Carefully I drew out a handful of photos. They were old ones, I could tell immediately. Some were irrelevant, of people I didn't know. But then I found one of Dad when he was younger, dressed in tight blue jeans and trainers – his hair longer, a mop of sandy yellow. He was standing laughing in a crowd, a beer can in his hand. And then Mum. This was Mum standing next to him, her dark hair falling into her eyes, bright blue eyeshadow lighting up her face. White top. Pink skirt. White tights. They looked so young. My thumb traced the image. I'd never seen it before.

The only photo I'd ever seen of Mum was the one Dad kept downstairs of their wedding day. Tears stung my eyes. This was a different Mum – so young. So innocent. This was a Mum I never knew.

In the next picture she was alone; it must've been taken on the same day as she was in the same clothes. She was leaning up against a car – an old Datsun. Her chin was tipped back, her face unsmiling, but those piercing eyes were firmly fixed on the camera. She looked so strong. In total control. This was before me, of course. This was when she was really happy.

I slipped the photo into my pocket. It would nestle alongside Cassie's one. He wouldn't miss one, surely? There were loads in there, by the look of it. I wanted to take time to go through them all, but I couldn't. How could I when Rubi was waiting downstairs? And what would Dad say if he saw me going through them? He'd kept them hidden from me for so long.

I walked out of his room. The bathroom stood across from me, so I slipped swiftly in. The suite was old and tired, and the grime seemed to cling against the bright pink ceramic. I glanced at the sink, looking sadly at Dad's single toothbrush sitting in the mug. It seemed so lonely just waiting there. There was nothing in this room, just an old bottle of shampoo and a well-used scrap of soap.

I reached up to the cabinet over the sink and opened it. There was barely anything there. Some forgotten eardrops, headache tablets, shaving gel. A tub of talc that looked like it was caked in dust and the plasters, tucked away in the corner, the packet frayed and ripped. I pulled a couple out, hoping that they weren't so old that they wouldn't stick.

It was only as I stepped outside that I finally forced myself to look at my old bedroom. The door was closed, of course. It always was nowadays. I could still see where I had stained the paint with marker pen. So long ago, but I could still make out the faint lines – Lucy. Mum had shouted at me for that, for spoiling the new door. She shouted and then she had cried. She hated it when I was naughty, or when I caused her bother. But then again, Mum seemed to hate most things towards the end. Even the smallest thing would make her cry or lock herself away. Later, Dad would tell me not to worry. He said I was his silly duckling and he didn't mind when I did something wrong.

This room had been my first sanctuary, my safe place. I'd close the door behind me and try to shut away all the pain and worries that lingered outside. In my room it was quiet and small. I could think. I could pretend that everything was OK. I could forget, or at least pretend to.

I became so good at hiding away. Dad was the same. We were similar in that respect.

But I was good at hiding the truth, too.

I continued to stare at the door, and I thought of that last, awful night. How I had run here, thrown open the door and slammed it behind me, tears coursing down my cheeks, breath hot in my throat and the image of my mum's face burnt forever in my mind.

Dad might forgive my silly mistakes, but I wasn't sure that he'd forgive the terrible thing I'd done that night. He would never understand. And because of that, I knew I would never tell him, and the secret would continue to rot inside me.

Chapter Eleven

Leaning against the landing wall, I attempted to gather my thoughts. I took a huge lungful of air and closed my eyes.

I clenched my fists, squeezing so tight that my nails almost pierced my skin.

Here I was, stuck in this house with a girl I barely knew. Why on earth had Cassie trusted me? I just screwed everything up.

Downstairs I could hear the murmur of Dad's TV and the gentle rise and fall of conversation. They were OK down there; they were getting on. I had to get back to them, back to the flat, get Rubi back to safety. I didn't have time to start thinking about the past again.

As I walked back down the stairs, I heard Dad talking. I froze for a second, keen to hear what he was saying.

'... ah, so the name Duckling came about because she was an awkward little thing as a child. All arms and legs. Do you know the story, Rubi? Of the ugly duckling?'

'Yes, of course I do, it grew up to be a swan,' I heard her reply.

Dad coughed again, loud and drawn out. 'Yes. Yes, exactly. I mean, Lucy's hardly going to turn out to be a swan, that's why she kept the name, Duckling. Suited her much better, I think. Did you know that she was really named after an old song? By the Beatles? You must've heard of them?'

'No – who are they? Why are they named after insects? That's silly.'

'The Beatles were one of the greatest bands ever. And they were not named after insects! It's BEAT-les. Like the music beat.'

'My mum says that Madonna is the greatest singer ever. But I'm glad I wasn't called Madonna. I want to be called Esme like my best friend.'

'Well, to be fair, Lucy doesn't really suit her name. That's why Duckling is far more appropriate.'

I couldn't stand to hear any more. I made myself hurry back into the room. Dad barely moved, just slurped his tea and stared up at me, a curious expression on his face.

'I was just telling Rubi a bit about you,' he said matter-of-factly.

'Really. That's nice,' I said as casually as I could. I smiled loosely at Rubi to try and show her that I wasn't bothered, but she was looking at me strangely, like I was wearing horns or something. I immediately felt uncomfortable and shifted myself to the side of the room, wishing I could blend in against Dad's white chipboard units.

'Why is your face all red?' she asked.

I touched my cheek. 'Is it?'

'Yeah. You look all sweaty.' She squinted at me. 'Did you run down the stairs or something?'

I screwed up my face, feeling myself grow hot. 'Of course not.'

'You look like you do when you're all wound up about something,' Dad said. 'I hope it wasn't my mess up there. I told you not to worry, I'll sort it out soon.'

I avoided his gaze. 'No, why would I be? But there does seem to be an awful lot of boxes up there.'

'I'm just tidying up, Duck, I told you. I have too much. An old man like me doesn't need to be surrounded by loads of things.' He paused, his eyes softening a little. 'Did you go in your room? I found some old bits of yours in the loft from when you were young and put them in there. Books and things, that huge doll I got you when you were little. I thought maybe we could go through it—'

I stiffened. 'No,' I said quickly. 'I didn't go in there.'

'Oh.' He nodded. 'Well, maybe we can another time?'

'Maybe,' I said. 'But I'm not sure there's anything I'll want to see. I thought all that stuff was thrown away.'

Silence filled the air. Words were lodged in my throat, but I forced them back. It had to wait.

'Can we go soon?' Rubi asked finally. 'I'm sure my mum will be back by now.'

'Yes, yes. We should go now.' I walked towards her and my hand scraped inside my pocket again, catching the edge of that photo. A shiver curled down my spine. 'But first of all, put this plaster on. We don't want you hobbling again on the way home.'

As I passed Dad he reached forward and took my hand. I looked down, surprised. It was so unlike him. In fact, I couldn't remember him ever grabbing me like that. I noticed how saggy and grey his skin looked in mine, like dough that had been left outside too long. I thought of Joy. How she had taken my hand that time, all those months ago. Of the words she'd said.

'Secrets are bad for your soul ...'

'You will do as I say, won't you?' Dad asked gently. 'If she doesn't come back. You'll do the right thing?'

'I told you I would.'

'I remember a case I worked on, not long before I stopped. Such a sad one. Little boy was left all on his own in a flat for three days.' He shivered. 'The mum had gone off with her new fella ...'

'Dad ...' I warned, sneaking a look at Rubi who was concentrating on her plaster. 'I will do the right thing, OK?'

He nodded. 'I know you will. Thank you for coming to see me, Duckling.'

'It's OK. I'll be back soon. You know that.'

'Can you remember to come back tomorrow, though?' His voice dropped a little. 'I still need to talk to you.'

I let go of his hand. 'Look – are you sure everything's all right?'

'It is, but I do need to see you again alone, that's all. Just come over.'

I hesitated. He rocked back in the chair, his body looking so tired and frail, like a worn-out shell. How had I only just noticed how old he was looking? Or was it the stress of the past day bringing it to light? I swallowed hard. Why did I have such a horrible, sinking feeling that I didn't want to hear what he wanted to say to me? Did he have something bad to say? Or had he finally worked out the secret I'd been keeping from him for so long?

'I only want to talk, Lucy,' he said, as if reading my mind.

I ducked my head, nodded slowly. 'Tomorrow, then.'

He smiled weakly. I could see his eyes were watering a little. Then he turned away from me, sniffing, and took another shaky gulp of tea. 'Call me later, Duck. Let me know what's happening. I want to know that the little one's OK.'

'I will.' My eyes lingered on him warily, I wanted to say more, but he spoke again.

'I'll be fine, you know. Everything will be just fine in the end.'

But I didn't know who he was talking to.

Me or himself.

'Your dad is really sad. Why is he?'

We were walking back, all of us much slower; even Colin – who Rubi complained was annoyed at being tied up for so long – was dragging behind. We were going back a different way via the housing estate, cutting across in front of the supermarket.

'We should be home in ten minutes,' I muttered, distracted. 'Hopefully your mum will be back and then I can go into work as planned.'

I couldn't let Jimmy down at such short notice. I'd never forgive myself. He'd struggle on his own.

'What if she's not back?' Rubi asked quickly.

I kept walking, picking up the pace a little. I didn't have an answer for that; not yet, anyway.

I rifled through my bag as we walked, checked my phone for about the twentieth time that morning. It didn't matter how many times I looked, there were no more messages. I glanced over at Rubi, but she was distracted by Colin, cooing down at him. Without thinking too much more about it, my finger swiped the screen and I pressed Cassie's number again. A bubble of anxiety danced in my belly. I needed an update.

To my surprise, the phone was answered almost immediately. I heard what sounded like slow breathing on the other end.

'Cassie, it's me, Lucy.' I tried to keep my voice as light as possible. 'Are you on your way back? We just wanted to know ...'

Silence. I pressed the phone closer to my ear.

'Cassie? Are you there?'

In the background I could hear another voice. A male voice. He seemed to be talking loudly, but the sound was distorted. I couldn't quite make out the words.

'Cassie? Cassie, are you there?'

Another sound. So subtle I could barely make it out – but it seemed like a sigh. A long, drawn-out sigh.

And then, just like that, the phone went dead.

I stared at it blankly. What on earth was going on?

Numbly my finger pressed redial. The phone buzzed once and then the depressing automated voice greeted me:

'The number you are calling is not available at the moment. Please try again.'

'Is Mum there?' Rubi asked.

'No. Not at the moment,' I replied as calmly as I could. 'I'll try again in a bit.'

I placed the phone inside my bag, making sure it was resting on top. I wanted to hear it if it went off. I was hoping

Cassie would call me back straight away. Did she pick it up in error? Was she drunk, perhaps, not aware of what she was doing? My fingers shook as I slung my bag back over my shoulder. I just couldn't shake the feeling that something was wrong here. People always say you should follow your gut instinct, and right now mine was a vibrating knot of jelly.

We waited to cross the main road. Rubi made Colin sit beside her and then took my hand. I was startled for a second, not expecting the sensation of warm, damp skin against mine. But I didn't pull away. Instead, I let her hand sit loosely in mine.

It's OK. We can do this.

I kept this mantra in my head. After all, if I believed it enough, surely it would make me feel more confident and in control. If I could be those things, then everything would work out just fine. Like Columbo. He was always in control. He always believed in himself. Dad had told me to do the right thing and that was what I was trying to do. I wanted to see if I could work out where Cassie was, before I had to involve anyone else. Surely that was better for Rubi?

'Why is your dad so sad?' Rubi asked again, as we traced the main street back to the estate.

I shook my head. How could I even begin to answer that?

'He's been like that for a long time now,' I said. 'I think he's sad that he never got to do a lot of what he wanted to do. So many things went wrong, and when my mum died ...'

My voice drifted. I let go of her hand and rubbed at my face. I could feel the tension rising under the skin, knots building in my temples and pressure burning beneath my eyes.

So many things have gone wrong for both of us.

Rubi didn't reply, but I knew she was still looking at me. I could almost hear the mechanics in her head churning everything over and working it all out. I wished I could stop her. I didn't want her to do that. If she knew too much it could ruin everything.

'He's old, too,' I added finally. 'And ill. I think every day is hard now.'

She nodded. 'He told me that his bones hurt all the time and that I should never want to get old.' She frowned. 'I thought getting old was a good thing.'

'It is,' I said. 'Except when you are actually old, then sometimes I think you feel grumpy about it.'

'That's sad. I want to get old. Really, really old. Over a hundred.'

'I'm sure you will, Rubi.'

We passed a small playground and Rubi begged to go inside. It seemed a bit mean to say no when she had been so good for me this morning, but I was still conscious of the time ticking away.

'Just five minutes,' I insisted. 'No longer, we really need to get back.'

I stood by the gate with Colin tied up safely beside me and watched as she moved around the equipment, her face calm with concentration.

Another woman came up to the gate, pushing a bright red buggy, and smiled shyly at me. I turned my face away, instantly uncomfortable. The woman didn't seem to notice.

'Is she yours?' she asked.

Mine? I blinked, stumped for a moment, and then realising what she meant I felt my cheeks colour. 'Oh no. I'm just looking after her.'

'She's a pretty little thing.'

'Yes. Yes, she is,' I said, feeling strangely proud and accepted. I was seen as another mother. Someone like her. Perhaps I didn't look as out of place as I felt?

The woman smiled again, and I watched as she manoeuvred her buggy into the park, all the time talking and cooing to the small child who was obviously hiding under its pink blankets.

How did some women find all this so easy? It seemed so completely natural to them. I guessed that the baby in her pram had been loved and wanted. She had probably nurtured her in her belly for nine months, excited for her arrival. A cool feeling washed over me.

What must that feel like? To really want something? To love another person so unconditionally?

Rubi ran over to the fence, her cheeks bright pink, her breath rapid.

'We have to go now,' I told her.

'Aw.' She made a whiny sound that I hadn't heard from her before. 'I love that slide. It's so big and fast.'

'It does look good.'

Rubi beamed. 'Do you like slides?'

'Well, I've never actually been on one.' I hesitated. 'Well – only once. A long time ago.'

I don't remember Mum ever taking me, because of course towards the end she was at home a lot, in bed or curled up in front of the TV. I'd like to think that she did when I was a baby.

But I do have a clear memory of one sunny afternoon with Dad. He'd been in a particularly jubilant mood; I think he'd won some money the night before. I recall him going on and on about his luck turning, then he made a snap decision to take me out.

I must've been younger than Rubi, perhaps five, but I remember that hopeful feeling. Excitement trickling through me. I had also been a tiny bit scared, because this behaviour was different to normal and it unsettled me.

I screwed up my face trying to recall the day, the few hours that we had spent together. We had gone to the duck pond. He had pointed out the mallards and called them lazy buggers. He had tried to scare the geese and ended up being chased by one. We had escaped to the playground, and he had taken my hand and guided me to the swing. Lifting me in it, he told me he was going to push me to the stars.

As the swing moved higher and higher, it almost felt like I was. My stomach had swooped and swirled, and I had laughed out loud. Behind me Dad had cackled, 'Lucy is in the sky!'

It had been a wonderful afternoon. Too short. Too long ago now. But for a brief time, we had been completely joyful and without any worries.

Rubi's voice interrupted my thoughts. 'You've only been to the park once! That's awful!'

I pulled open the gate, about to tell her again that it was time to go, but before I could, I realised Rubi was tugging on my arm.

'C'mon,' she urged. 'It's not fair that you've only been to the park once. You need to go again.'

I gently shook her off. 'Rubi. I can't, we need to go. I—'

'Lucy!' Her voice was firmer now. 'Just have one quick go.' She stared up at me, making her eyes go all wide and soppy-looking. 'For me?'

Somehow, I couldn't resist that look. What harm could it do?

Cautiously, I walked over to the next swing, ignoring the looks from the other mother, and nestled myself into it. It was quite a squeeze. My bum spilled over the sides and my long legs dragged hopelessly on the ground.

Ruby was laughing. She ran over to me.

'Can I push you?'

'Can you manage? I'm probably quite heavy.'

'I can try. I'm really strong.'

She stood behind me and I felt her small hands reach under my bottom and clutch on to the soft rubber. With a defiant grunting sound, she managed to give me a gentle shove.

'Nah. You're too heavy!' she moaned after a moment. 'I can't move you.'

She clambered on to the swing next to me. 'Let's have a race. Let's see who can go higher.'

I pushed up hard with my feet on the patchy rubber surface. My head tipped back; my eyes automatically closed. I could feel my tummy begin to twist and turn, but in a good way. Next to me Ruby was exploding with excitement.

'Lucy, you're going so high! Open your eyes. Look!'

I opened my eyes. The swing was moving at speed now, creaking gracefully with every arc. My feet were so high, almost touching the clouds. I leant back, gulping mouthfuls of clean, crisp air.

I was in the sky again.

As we reached Cassie's flat, something inside me knew she wouldn't be back. There was some kind of instinct – a nagging voice inside my head that was telling me the flat was still empty. On the door, our note flapped uselessly. Unread. Unseen. Rubi tore it down in frustration.

'She's not here, is she?' she said. But it wasn't a question, it was a statement. Her tiny face was full of fury.

I couldn't blame her.

I opened the door and walked in. There seemed to be more space now, a gaping hole where Cassie should've been. I imagined her sitting, watching TV, jumping up when we arrived. Sweeping Rubi up into a hug. Telling us she was so sorry for going for so long and thanking me for being a good person and helping them both out.

But of course, there was nothing.

Resentment clawed at me. I shouldn't even be here. I should be next door. Hidden away, minding my own business. What would I normally be doing right now? Probably having a cup of tea in front of that Saturday-morning cookery show. Then I would think about getting ready for work. These would probably seem like boring, uninteresting things to someone like Cassie, but they mattered to me. They were part of my lovely, safe normality.

Rubi let Colin off the lead. She walked slowly around the flat, peeking into each room, then she stood in front of me. She looked small and tired and suddenly a lot younger. She tucked a long strand of hair behind her ear and looked at me mournfully.

'Where is she?'

'I don't know,' I said quietly. 'I'm sorry, Rubi, but I just don't know.'

Anger was creeping in now. I thought of Dad's words earlier. Was Cassie really messing me around here? Maybe she had fled to some exotic place, leaving me behind with her child, like she was some plant to be watered.

And yet, that argument still didn't sit right with me. I just couldn't see Cassie doing that. I might not know her well at all, but what I did know did not match a neglectful or uncaring mum. Not at all.

There was more to this. There had to be.

'She'll be OK,' Rubi said, as if she was reading my mind. 'Mum always is.'

'I don't know, Rubi, maybe we should ...'

But what? If I called the police, I knew that could cause more problems for Cassie, and was I ready to do that to her? What would they do with Rubi? What would Cassie say if she suddenly came back and discovered I'd broken her trust? After all, she had left me messages. She had asked me to wait with Rubi until she called again. There could be a reasonable explanation for all of this. I could end up looking like a complete idiot.

Anyway, there was another reason I couldn't ring the police. I couldn't risk it for poor Rubi; just looking at her sad, scared face confirmed that for me. Not yet anyway. Not until I had more information. Despite what Dad had said, I needed to wait just a little bit longer. It had to be the last resort.

'What do we do now?' she asked, her eyes wide, her face pale.

'Now we go and visit your mum's friend Jo,' I said. 'We see if she can help us.'

Rubi insisted we leave another note on the door. She wrote again, this time taking more care with it. I have to say, I was quite impressed by her neat, cursive handwriting. Rubi noticed me looking and smiled.

'Miss Gibson says I have the best writing in my class,' she said proudly.

The note was pretty much to the point:

Mum. We have gone downstairs to see Jo.
Please wait here. Do not go Anywhere!

'She can't leave again,' Rubi said, Blu-tacking the paper to the door. 'I'm not going to let her. Ever.'

'Has she ever left you like this before?' I asked, though from what I'd seen she was a good, conscientious parent and Rubi had always seemed to be rooted to her side.

'Never,' Rubi replied firmly. 'She even hates me going to school, she says she misses me too much. She's always with me.'

I could see her bottom lip jutting out, wobbling a little. She wiped her eyes, but I could see no tears there. Not yet, anyway.

'Maybe you can stay with Jo for a bit?' I said lightly. 'I'm sure it won't be for much longer. Do you like her?'

Rubi shrugged. 'She's all right.'

'But of course your mum didn't ask her to help in the first place,' I mused.

There had to be a reason for that. Maybe Jo was unavailable? Or unwell? Or could it be something more concerning? Rubi's silent, sullen face wasn't telling me anything.

We walked over to the lift. It was colder now, so I drew my coat tightly across my chest. Looking over at Rubi, I realised she really was dressed inappropriately in her thin pink cardigan. I cursed myself for not picking up something for her to wear over it.

'Aren't you cold?' I asked.

'No.'

'We can go back and get your coat?'

She shook her head, her fringe dancing above her eyes. 'It's too small for me now. Mum needs to buy me a new one. She said I had to wait till she gets more money.'

'Oh, I see.'

The lift came quickly and we stepped inside. I let Rubi press for the first floor, wincing at the sight of newly applied chewing gum against the buttons. She didn't seem to mind. Then I stood in the centre, well away from the stained walls and especially away from the suspicious-looking puddle that had formed in the corner.

'What's this Jo like?' I asked, suddenly feeling nervous.

Rubi blinked back at me, taking a moment to think about this. 'She shouts a lot. And she keeps pet snakes,' she said finally. 'Loads of them.'

The doors slowly creaked open and we stepped out on to the first floor. Rubi led the way, drawing me down the deck. This was a far more cluttered floor. The first flat had bikes piled up outside it and the next had a collection of overflowing (and fairly dead-looking) plants. We eased ourselves past, trying not to stumble over the mess.

Finally, Rubi stopped outside the penultimate door. I guess it had been blue once, but most of the paint had chipped away. The letterbox was hanging off at a strange angle and the glass above had a long crack running from corner to corner. By the neighbour's door there was a plaque with a very plain-looking dog with the number eight painted on it, below a very tatty 'Beware of the Dog' sign. I quickly returned my attention to the first flat.

'There's no bell,' I said.

'It's OK.'

Rubi rapped hard on the glass. I automatically sprang back, convinced that the glass would splinter and shatter upon us.

There was no reply. Weirdly, I was quite relieved. *OK, we've tried this option and it hasn't worked out. Fine.* I was happy to trudge back upstairs and not come back. There was something about this place that unnerved me.

'Shall we go back?' I suggested. 'Maybe we can give your mum another half-hour? I don't start work until one—'

Rubi frowned and then banged on the door again. Inside I imagined snakes awakening, uncurling their bodies and focusing their attention on the door.

'Let's go,' I said, turning to leave.

But it was too late. The front door flew open, and a woman dressed in bright yellow pyjamas stood there. Her short hair was the colour of fire and her eyes were heavily lined with dark pencil. She looked cold and angry. She didn't seem to see Rubi as her focus was purely on me, her thin, red lips curled into a sneer.

'What the fuck do you want?' she slurred.

It seemed I was right to think this was a bad idea.

Chapter Twelve

Jo's bleary eyes rested on Rubi. She wobbled slightly on the spot and grabbed the side of the door frame for support. I noticed two of her long red nails had snapped off, which gave her fingers an odd, stumpy look.

'Rubes!' she said in a breathy voice. 'What are you doing here?' She turned to me, took a long, hard look up and down and then sucked her teeth. 'Who is this woman? Should I know her?'

I glanced over at Rubi, not able to hide my shame that she already knew more people on my estate than I did. I remembered she had told me that Jo knew Cassie from before, but it was still a stark reminder that I hadn't got to know any of my neighbours in my time here. Apart from Joy, of course. She was the exception.

'This is Lucy. She's looking after me,' Rubi said calmly.

'Who?' Jo stared at me, still looking me up and down. Her hand wiped her mouth. 'Who is she?' She flapped her hand towards me. I flinched instinctively. 'Cassie shouldn't be leaving you with strangers. What was she thinking?'

I moved closer to Rubi, feeling suddenly protective. 'Cassie is my neighbour. I must admit we're not best mates, but I'm hardly a stranger.' I paused. 'She obviously trusted me.'

'She probably wasn't thinking straight,' Jo hissed. 'I'm not being funny, love – but what are you even wearing?'

188

That stung. I glanced down at my comfy trousers, at my favourite charity-shop boots. I knew I wasn't exactly dressed in the latest designer gear, but the criticism was coming from someone still in her nightwear!

I pushed my glasses back up my nose. 'I'm sorry. I wasn't aware my clothes had anything to do with this.'

Rubi stepped forward. 'Lucy is just helping us, me and Mum. Don't have a go at her.'

Jo shrugged, looking bored. 'OK, fair enough. So why are you here? What can I do?'

'We thought you might be able to help,' I said, trying to keep my voice level. 'I thought you might know what Cassie might be doing.'

A tiny frown dented her forehead. 'What about her? Why do you need to know?'

'We don't know where she is!' Rubi said, louder this time.

Jo seemed to consider this for a moment. 'What do you mean, you don't know where she is?'

'Just that,' I replied as calmly as I could. 'Cassie left Rubi with me, but she said she'd only be a little while. A few hours maybe. Then she left a message saying she'd been held up. Then a text saying I had to keep hold of Rubi and that things were taking longer than she had planned.'

Jo seemed to relax; she pulled a face. 'So? What's the problem?'

'So I'm getting a little concerned,' my voice wobbled. 'Cassie has been gone since last night. I don't know if this is usual for her, but it's getting me worried. I tried calling her and she answered, but ...'

'But what?'

I shook my head. 'Well, nothing. There was silence. I'm not even sure she picked it up properly.'

'Me and Lucy are being detectives,' Rubi interjected. 'We're trying to find out where Mum is.'

Jo's eyes widened but she said nothing. Her gaze was still fixed on me, but it had softened slightly.

'So, can you help us?' I persisted. 'Is there anywhere you think Cassie might have gone? Anyone she might be with? It could help.'

Jo sighed and ran a hand through her dry, wild hair. She was quite small and far too skinny. She and Cassie could have been matchstick sisters, except Cassie would be the far more glamorous one. Her skin had a weird sticky sheen to it, like she had been sweating out in the sunshine.

'I dunno,' she said finally. 'Me and Cassie don't talk so much now. But I suppose Liam might have an idea.'

'Liam?' I frowned. I wondered whether he'd want to help; he'd seemed a bit defensive before.

'Yeah, my boy Liam. He knows lots of people. He hears lots of things.' She glared at me, her sour mouth curling. Then, seeming to change her mind, she sighed again and told us to come in. 'We can talk better inside. But I'm warning you, I don't want any grief ...'

'That's the last thing I want, believe me,' I muttered.

And the last thing I'd asked for when all of this started yesterday.

*

This flat was dark, more tired than Cassie's and mine, and seemed so much smaller inside. Jo stood in the main hall and called out Liam's name a few times. Her voice was strained. His name seemed to echo through the walls, bouncing around us. Jo didn't seem particularly bothered when there was no reply.

'I never know if the fucker's in or not,' she said finally. 'Looks like he's out after all. No bloody change there. So you'll just have to see if I can help.' She gestured that we follow her and we moved into her living room.

It was difficult to breathe in there. The stench of stale smoke seemed to hang heavy in the air. I imagined it soaked into everything – the drab grey sofa, the worn carpet, the clothes that littered the floor. The entire place was a nicotine sponge. Even the ceilings were stained a dirty yellow colour, darker in areas where I assumed Jo lingered with her cigarettes, mapping her movements.

'I need to hoover,' she said, then she laughed, kicking aside a discarded jumper. 'You can report me for this if you want. For making a fucking mess in my own bloody flat. I bet you'd love that, wouldn't you? You look the type.'

I kept quiet. I thought it was best. My eyes were fixed instead on a glass tank in the corner of the room. It seemed so out of place there, propped on top of an old table that looked desperately unstable. I squinted a little, taking in the shapes. This was not your usual fish tank. This glass cage contained three large snakes. I imagined the lid propped open, the snakes uncurling themselves slowly like they do in the Indian baskets in films. Their jaws would open wide, a forked tongue exposed, and they would aim their fangs and strike straight towards me.

Jo frowned and then suddenly burst out laughing. It was an explosive, raw sound, breaking the silence and making me wince.

'Why the fuck are you gawping at my snakes?' She snorted. 'What? Are you scared? Oh my God, you are, aren't you? Do you want me to drape one of them over your neck? Big buggers, aren't they? They're my babies.'

Rubi didn't seem fazed at all. She walked towards them and pressed her nose up against the glass. 'I like the yellow one,' she said gently. 'He has really pretty patterns on his skin. Did you know that snakes smell with their tongues?'

Jo's face seemed to soften, although she was still shaking her head at me like she couldn't believe my reaction. I wished I could've hidden my fears better; it was just making me look even more out of place here.

'That one is Ambrose,' Jo was telling Rubi. 'He's pretty chilled. His brother Clyde is a bit of a handful, though.'

'I like them,' Rubi decided.

'How long have you had them?' I asked quietly, trying to show interest.

'Two years,' Jo said, her lips so firmly pressed together that the words were forced out. 'And don't think you can have me on that, either. I've checked the rules. I can keep them as long as they stay inside that thing.' She pointed back at the cage and smiled smugly.

'And do they?' I asked, worry prickling me. 'Do they stay in there all the time?'

'Of course.' Jo touched her chest in mock offence. 'Would I break the rules of the tenancy?'

Again, I didn't bother to reply. I didn't know why Jo was so convinced I would report her. I glanced down at my plain, drab clothing. Jimmy always joked that I looked like an old-fashioned librarian. I guess that meant I looked a bit uptight too. I had to fight back a wry grin. If Jo had seen the home that I had grown up in she might think differently – the beer cans littering the kitchen floor or the vomit staining the living room. She might see that I was in no position to judge.

This all felt so familiar.

'Is this the first time you've met the snakes?' I asked Rubi.

She nodded. 'Liam told me about them before. I've been wanting to come inside for ages.'

Wasn't that strange, considering Cassie and Jo were old friends? Surely Cassie would've been in and out of here loads of times. Rubi said she went with her mum everywhere ...

Except for now.

'Does Cassie not visit, then?' I asked Jo.

She sighed and flopped herself down on the sofa. Her top rolled up, exposing her tight pink belly and the silver threads of stretch marks. 'Not really, as it goes. I mean, we were good mates – still are, I suppose, in some ways. But we had a little fall-out after she moved back to the estate.'

'You fell out? Why?'

'Yeah, we fell out. So what? People fall out all the time. I can't even remember what it was over now. Cas has always had a gob on her. She probably wound me up over something.'

My mind searched for further questions. I struggled to think of the right thing to say. I was sure there were correct things I should be asking, obvious things. My mind floundered. I thought of Columbo, how he could calmly bring down a suspect with a choice line or two. Even my dad, trained in such matters, was good at it. Why couldn't I be more like them? My mind buzzed for a moment or two and then finally settled. I knew what to do. I had to keep things simple, like Columbo would. Ask general questions. Find out more about the woman I was worried about.

'Jo ... What is Cassie like? I mean, you know her pretty well by the sounds of it. Would she normally go off like this?'

Jo shook her head. 'Nah. No way. She never takes her eye off Rubi normally.' She wriggled on the sofa, her face creasing into a frown as she considered her next words. 'Cassie is the good one, yeah? She always tries to do the right thing. She's had a rubbish taste in men before, but haven't we all? But she's honest and she bloody loves the bones of Rubi.'

'I thought so ...' I said, feeling my unease grow. 'This is why this doesn't make any sense.'

'There will be an explanation. She'll have a good reason for doing this,' Jo insisted. 'And she's been texting you, hasn't she? She obviously thinks Rubi is safe with you ...'

I looked over at Jo and saw she was staring at me, her mouth curled into a smile. She shook her head sadly and muttered something before reaching forward for a can of beer that was resting on the table in front of her. She took a long slug, wiping her mouth with the back of her hand.

'Are you really worried, then? About Cas? Do you think something has happened to her?' she asked finally.

'I don't know. It's just nothing makes sense.'

'She wouldn't leave Rubi normally,' Jo repeated softly. 'That's true enough. That's not like her at all.'

I wobbled slightly on the spot, the familiar uneasy feeling swimming inside me. It was like my bones were turning to rubber. I hated this.

'Liam told me that you were angry with Mum about Gav,' Rubi said suddenly, her back turned to us, still staring at the snakes. 'Liam said you were angry that Mum hurt his feelings.'

Jo sniffed. 'Well, he is family. She shouldn't have done that.'

I felt lost. 'Who's Gav again?' I asked, remembering the name. 'Is that Cassie's ex-boyfriend?'

Jo glared at me again, like she had forgotten I was there. 'Gav's my cousin, yeah? He's like my brother really. He means the world to me. He's a good guy and she broke his fucking heart.'

My brain was still whirring, trying to process this new information.

'Is that who she left when she came here? Is that why she moved?' I asked. Jo nodded reluctantly. 'OK,' I continued. 'Could she have gone back to him, then? Is that where she could be now?'

Jo half laughed. 'Unlikely. He never wanted to see her again. She treated him like shit – sorry, Rubes, but she did. The poor guy was broken after she left.'

'So if she's not there, where can she be? A new boyfriend?'

Jo snorted. 'Unlikely. She's only just broken up with Gav. Even Cassie doesn't move that fast.'

'What about other exes?' I reached into my pocket and carefully drew out the photo from Cassie's flat. 'Do you recognise this man?'

Jo's face paled a little. She took a sip of her beer and swiped her lips. 'I don't know … It's a long time now …'

'But he looks familiar?'

She shrugged. 'Maybe. It's not a great photograph.' She squinted at it again. 'But it could be one of her old boyfriends from way back.'

'Do you remember his name?'

Jo sniggered. 'Love, I can barely remember what day of the week it is … It was something twatty, I think. It might come to me later …'

I stared at her dazed expression. I didn't think her memory would be improving anytime soon.

'OK … but could she be with him?'

'What?' Jo almost fell off the sofa. 'No way! He buggered off years ago. Last I heard he was out of the country. Cassie would no sooner meet up with him than she would hack her own nose off. I'd lay money on that!'

'OK …' I paused. 'So, you have no other ideas where she might be?'

Jo rubbed at her head. 'No … I mean my head is a bit muzzy at the moment, you know? All the late nights …' She caught my eye. We both knew what had been causing her sleepless nights, but I didn't comment. 'I can't help you, love.'

I leant in a little more, kept my voice low. 'To be honest, if this carries on much longer, I'm thinking of calling someone.'

Her watery eyes suddenly widened. 'Who? Who the fuck would you call?'

'I don't know.' I was wobbling a bit now. 'The police? Maybe they could—'

'No!' Jo's hand flew out in a 'stop' motion. I stepped back automatically as if she had actually struck me. Jo kept her hand in place as she talked, her voice now strangely calm. 'You do not call the police, you hear? We don't do that round here. Once they get involved and start sniffing around, fuck knows what will happen. They always think the worst about the likes of us.' She glanced over at Rubi who was back chatting to the snakes. Jo dropped her voice. 'Do you know what trouble that could cause? They'll think Cassie left her on purpose or something – they'll involve the social. They would take Rubi away.'

I shook my head, even though these were the same thoughts that were troubling me.

'I dunno … maybe they could just help find her?' I whispered, my voice breaking at the words.

Could they, though?

'No!' Her eyes were as hard as stone. I couldn't look. I could feel them burning into me. My gaze dropped to the floor. 'You call them and I'll finish you, understand? We'll find her …' She flapped her hand, then flopped her body back, more relaxed now. 'We'll find her, no problem. We sort things ourselves around here. You'll see. She'll be fine. Hopefully she's just with a mate, or having some fun, lucky bloody cow. You have to do this yourself. You can't bring the bloody officials into it.'

I sighed, resigned. Maybe she was right. After all, I had agreed to look after Rubi. And Cassie had messaged to say she was delayed. I didn't have to go bringing more trouble to her door, not yet anyway. And certainly nobody needed hassle, least of all me.

But it would still be good to know where she was.

'What about this Gav?' I asked. 'Even if she's not with him, maybe he might know where she is?'

Jo shrugged. 'I doubt it. He's done with her. If you talk to him about Cassie he'll just tell you where to go.' She burped loudly and took another, longer slug of her drink.

I glanced over at Rubi. She was still stroking the glass on the snake cage, but her head was bowed.

I glanced at my watch; my stomach automatically clenched. I had to be at work soon. What could I do with Rubi?

'Maybe Rubes should stay with me,' Jo said, like she was reading my mind.

Rubi rushed over to me and gripped my arm; I could feel her fingers pinching tightly into my skin. I hated the sensation, longed to tear her off, but resisted. Just felt the sweat build a sheen on my skin instead. I turned to face her. She was shaking her head violently.

Jo swiped her hand across her face. 'Cassie should've asked me anyway. I don't know what she was thinking, asking you! Just look at you, you hardly know her.'

There were things I wanted to say back at her, but for once I managed to keep my tongue lodged firmly in my mouth. This wasn't the right time. As my eyes trailed the room, I could see properly. No wonder it stank in here. I could see the bin with the discarded cans inside. How did I not notice the empty vodka bottle beside the TV? I understood now why she was wobbling. She was properly drunk already; that was why she looked so pasty and unkempt. It really was like Dad all over again. My thoughts moved for a moment to Liam.

Where was he? How was she even caring for him properly?

The only thing that I knew for sure was that Cassie had good reason not to leave Rubi here. She trusted me instead. She gave me the responsibility for her most precious thing. She saw something in me that I hadn't seen for a very long time.

So I did something I never thought I would do. I took Rubi's hand and gripped it tightly in mine. This time it felt good there, even normal.

'It's OK,' I said as firmly as I could. 'Rubi is staying with me.'

And to my surprise Jo put up no resistance. She simply nodded slowly and returned to her can. Her finger trailed the surface, going round and round the tiny opening.

'Yeah,' she gave a bitter half-laugh. 'That's the shitty thing. Maybe she's actually better off with a bloody stranger.'

'Thank you anyway. You've been very helpful,' I said to Jo, not really knowing what else to say, but I felt I had to give her something. I was in her house, after all, and even though she hadn't been exactly hospitable, she had tried to help. She wasn't so bad.

I felt something flash through me, a feeling of sympathy. I felt so sorry for her.

Rubi squeezed my hand and we turned and started to walk out of the room.

'I want to stay with you,' Rubi whispered. 'I like you. And my mum likes you.'

'Does she?'

'Sure.' Rubi grinned. 'Why wouldn't she?'

I could've listed a million reasons, but it didn't feel right to do that now, not while Rubi was looking so pleased with herself.

I didn't see him at first, but I felt Rubi's body suddenly stiffen and then jolt forward, pulling me towards the doorway.

'Liam!' she squealed.

He stood leaning up against the door frame, a hard stare fixed on me. I released Rubi's hand.

'So …' he said. 'I'm guessing you're here to try and find Cassie.'

Rubi ran towards him. She tugged his top, not seeming to care. 'Do you know where my mum is?'

Liam nodded slowly. 'You know – I reckon I just might.'

Chapter Thirteen

We stood in the cramped hallway. Liam had gestured for us to join him there, after casting a sour look in his mum's direction. I guessed he didn't want her involved.

'Well?' I demanded finally, impatience spilling over. 'What do you know?'

Rubi tugged on his arm. 'You know where my mum is? Where? Just tell me.' I could see the sparkle of tears in her eyes. She was fighting to hold it together. I felt a wash of pride sweep over me. She was being so brave.

Liam nodded slowly. 'Yeah, sorry, babe,' he ruffled Rubi's hair. 'I should've said sooner but I didn't think.' He shrugged. 'Besides, I figured she'd be back by now, so I didn't see the point in saying anything.'

'So where is she, then?' I snapped.

'I reckon she's gone back to him, to Gav.'

'But your mum seemed to think ...'

Liam's voice dropped, his gaze drifting a moment to the open door to the living room. 'Mum knows nothing, not now. She barely knows what fucking day it is.' His face tightened. 'But what I know is Gav still has a thing for Cassie; he's mad about her.'

'So she's got back together with him?' I whispered, conscious of Rubi who, as usual, was hanging on our every word.

201

'Aren't you fucking listening?' he said. I flinched, immediately wishing I could block Rubi's supersonic ears. 'Cassie was done with him. Gav can be a bit full on and she wasn't into that. I know he was upset when they broke up.'

I was confused. 'So why do you think she's with him?'

Liam sighed. 'I spoke to Cassie a few days ago. She was really stressed, you know. Proper wound up. She said she couldn't find the money to pay the rent this month. She was scared and said that she might get kicked out. She asked me if I knew anyone – a lender, or someone who could help her out.'

'That makes sense ...' I breathed. 'I found letters at hers. From a loan shark.'

'You were snooping?' His eyes glinted.

'I had to! I needed to find something, anything that could give me a clue as to where Cassie might be.' I felt my defences rising like great, solid walls. 'I'm worried about her, Liam.'

'Sure, I get that,' he said. 'I told her before not to get mixed up with those guys. They're proper mean and you don't want to be going to them when you're really desperate. They can smell it on you. They'd screw her over big time and then want some more on top of that.' He swaggered on the spot, rubbing at his face. 'She should've known better than to go to them, but you can't tell her what to do, can you?'

'So she probably owes them quite a bit?'

'Probably, and I reckon that's why she's gone back to Gav. She needs help, right?'

I nodded numbly. His hard, determined stare was enough to tell me that nothing good came from these people – which was no surprise to me. It was pretty clear that Cassie must've been in a bad situation to even consider contacting such low life.

But when you're desperate you do desperate things. I for one knew about that ...

'She should've gone to the bank,' I muttered.

'You're not for real!' Liam scoffed. 'How is someone like Cassie going to rock up at the bank? They won't help her. She's screwed, man. Totally screwed.'

He sagged, all the bravado suddenly gone. He was so young, too young perhaps to know this much and to be involved with so many people's lives. I wondered how he was coping with it all. Surely it was enough for anyone to deal with. But then again, what would I know? I couldn't even begin to imagine what life was like for him.

Rubi piped up, her eyes wide. 'Is my mum in lots of trouble?'

Liam groaned softly and then bent down, his voice gentle. 'It's nothing to worry about, Rubes, OK? I'm sorry if I worried you. And I'm sorry I keep swearing – my mouth runs away with me sometimes. I'm just saying that your mum might've needed some help, that's all. That might be why she went off last night.'

Rubi nodded very slowly, but her eyes were fixed on Liam. She seemed unsure.

He turned back to me. 'She mentioned that Gav has been calling her up again, asking to see her.' He shrugged. 'I told her that he's doing all right at the moment, he's got a new job on a building site, getting cash in hand. I thought he might be able to help her out.'

'So it was you who told her to go and see Gav?'

Liam had dropped his sneer by this point and almost looked sheepish, his feet scuffing at the floor. 'Well, I said it might be an idea. She wasn't keen, so I didn't think she'd go through with it. That's why I didn't think to mention it before.'

OK. That seemed to make sense. It would also explain why Cassie had been made up when she left the flat. Perhaps she had wanted to charm him.

Liam dropped his voice in an attempt to protect Rubi, who was still listening intently. 'Like I said, Gav still has a thing for Cassie, and she feels bad about that. But – she needs the money badly. So ... I'm guessing she's gone there to, well, get back in his good books.'

'And will he help her?' I asked.

Liam scowled. 'Sure, if he's got it. But he'll expect something in return.'

I was confused. 'Like what?'

Liam sucked his teeth. 'Seriously, lady, are you for real? Do I have to spell it out?'

In the other room, Jo cackled. I hadn't even realised she was still listening.

I felt myself redden and was acutely conscious of Rubi who was looking a little muddled.

'So are my mum and Gav back together?' she asked softly.

Liam snorted. 'Doubt it. I expect your mum will take the cash and leg it. But it might explain why she's taken so long.' He sniffed. 'Maybe she's holding out for more. Or maybe she just feels too guilty, running off quickly? Maybe she's sticking around a bit to be nice.'

'Do you think she's safe there?' I asked. 'Gav won't get angry with her or anything ...?'

I let the words hang.

Liam chuckled. 'Oh God! Gav is sound. He's a bit gobby sometimes, a bit of a loser really, but he'd never harm Cas.'

'Even so, I really would like to speak to Cassie. Do you have a number for him? An address?'

Liam shrugged. 'Yeah, sure. I'll write the number down. But when I tried calling him earlier his phone was turned off.'

'You've already tried him?'

'Yeah. When you first said Cassie had gone away, I wanted to see if she was with him – you know, to check if she was all right ... I tried her too, but no joy. To be fair, her phone is always running out of charge, so I wasn't too worried.'

'Well, definitely write his address down too, just in case.'

Liam held my gaze. 'You're really worried, aren't you?'

'Well ... yes ... to be honest, I am.'

Tentatively I told him about the messages, about my funny feeling and the last call I had made to Cassie where I'd heard a voice in the background.

'But that could be nothing,' Liam said quietly. 'You might have heard Gav speaking. And Cassie could've easily answered the phone by mistake, sat on it or something.' He paused. 'But then again, it could be ...'

'What?'

He stepped back a little, his face creasing into a frown. 'Well, it could be that Cas is in more trouble than we think. Between us we have to work out which one it is.' His voice dropped further. 'And quickly.'

*

At first, we walked back to my flat in silence. I wondered if Rubi was churning over the comments Liam had made, as I was also re-playing the conversation. There was a lot to take in and most of it was quite worrying. Liam had told me he was going to do some digging of his own and assured me he would keep calling Gav. I was relieved that someone else was helping now, at least. I found that I was able to trust Liam. There was something about him – an openness and honesty that I liked. He seemed genuine.

'Why is Jo like that?' Rubi asked suddenly, as we approached my front door.

I hesitated. 'Like what?'

'Drunk,' Rubi replied coolly. 'I know she was. Mum used to say she drinks too much and that's why she gets cross with her. But why does she do it all the time like that?'

Rubi kicked at the floor, her face screwed up in disgust. 'I don't understand why she does it. It makes her horrible and shouty. Liam gets angry with her. She should stop.'

'It's not as easy as that, Rubi,' I said.

'Why isn't it?' She frowned. 'It's really gross.'

'It's not gross.' I bent down and gently put my hand on Rubi's shoulder, made her turn to face me. 'It's not gross, Rubi. It's not nice, but Jo can't help it. She's probably an alcoholic and that's like having a disease.'

'A disease?'

'Yes. It's an illness. It's something you can't help. Very often people drink to cope with the bad things that happen in their life.'

I thought of Dad, how his shaky hand had so many times reached for that can of beer. How his tear-stricken face would turn to me. '*I need it, Duck. I need it to help me through. Please understand.*'

'That's sad.'

'Yes ... yes, it really is.' I rubbed her shoulder. 'It's the saddest thing of all.'

I was glad when we got back home. My safe, familiar white walls soothed me, and I could feel my whole body uncurl and slowly begin to relax. The lovely smell of thick carpets and snug cushions greeted me. Even Rubi seemed a little happier, running over to Boris who was curled up on the sofa. She gently cooed at him, her body turned away from me.

'I'm hungry,' she moaned.

I didn't think I had much food that would interest Rubi. It wasn't as if I kept a wide variety anyway. I hardly needed to, with only myself to worry about. Raiding the fridge, I pulled out the last of the cheese and looked at Rubi hopefully.

'Will you have this in a sandwich?' I sniffed it. 'It's mild, I think.'

'If you grate it and don't put too much inside.' She watched as I buttered the bread, her expression critical. 'And cut off the crusts. I hate crusts. They taste horrible.'

I tutted. 'That's a bit of a waste.'

She smiled and I noticed for the first time the tiny dimples that graced her cheeks as she did so. It was quite endearing. 'I think they taste of dust,' she told me.

'What do? The crusts?'

She nodded. 'Yep.'

'Is dust better than yuck?'

She frowned at me. 'They're both the same.'

'You're wrong,' I told her. 'In actual fact, the crust is the tastiest bit.' And to prove the point, I ate the end of the bread, heavily buttered and sprinkled with the last of the cheese. I had considered toasting it, but there really wasn't much time.

'I have to go to work soon,' I said. 'I really can't be late.'

Her forehead creased into a frown. 'Where will I go?'

I sighed. 'Well, I guess you'll have to come with me, if that's all right? I'm guessing Jimmy won't mind.'

I thought of Jimmy and his cheerful face, and really, I couldn't see him complaining. To be fair, Jimmy complained about very little. It was another reason why he was so easy to be around, but I needed to call him to check. In truth, the last thing I wanted to do was go to work, but I couldn't bear to let him down. Also, a large part of me longed to see him, to talk over my concerns and maybe see if he could help. Jimmy always knew what to do and in the calming surrounds of the quiet bookshop, I might be able to work things out better.

Jimmy answered after the third ring. 'Lucy? Is everything OK?'

'Oh yes, I'm fine,' I insisted. 'I'm still planning on coming in this afternoon, but I have a small problem.'

'Oh ...' I could hear Jimmy's smile through the phone. 'Not another dead animal delaying you, is there? Let me guess, a rat this time?'

'Oh God, no ...' I shivered. 'No, not a dead anything. Actually, she's very much alive. I'm looking after a little girl, Rubi. Is it OK if I bring her into work? She's no bother ...'

'You're looking after a little girl? How did this happen?' Jimmy sounded confused. 'I mean, I didn't think you even liked kids?'

'Well, it's not so much that I don't like them. I'm just not used to them ...' I glanced over at Rubi who was busy entertaining Boris. Slowly I stepped into the hall. 'It was only meant to be for an hour or so, but her mum hasn't come back ...'

'When did she go?'

'Last night.'

'Last night! What the hell?'

'It's complicated. I can explain more when I see you.'

'Shit, Lucy.' He breathed hard. 'You have to go to the police, surely? Something might have happened to her.'

'She's been texting me. She said she was held up.' I closed my eyes for a moment, feeling the tension there. 'Jimmy, it's really complicated. Can I come in? We can talk more there. You know I'm not good on the phone.'

'OK ... sure.' His voice softened. 'Lucy, are you OK? Are you sure you're doing the right thing?'

I thought of what my dad had said earlier and forced my best smile. 'I'm doing what I think is right. That's all I can do for now.'

*

209

Eve Ainsworth

Rubi wasn't so keen to go.

'We'll have to leave Colin, though, won't we?' Her voice was soft, her gaze drifting to the wall, the divide between the two flats. I imagined the small dog back inside, curled up on the sofa and snoring loudly. I prayed he hadn't messed the floor again.

'He'll be fine,' I said, feeling unsure.

'We can't leave him for long. He'll get scared.'

My shift was only four hours. I wasn't an expert on dogs, but I was fairly confident that Colin could be left safely for that amount of time. What other choice did I have? As understanding as he was, I doubted Jimmy would tolerate me turning up to work with a dog and a child in tow. With any luck, Cassie would come back while we were away and sort him out.

'I'll leave another note,' I told her. 'I'll explain where we are. And I'll text your mum again.'

We were becoming experts at leaving notes, as pointless as they were. I was also becoming convinced that Cassie wasn't reading any of my messages, because why hadn't she replied to any?

Rubi was looking at my phone, which was sitting just out of reach on the table. I'd already checked it twice – there was nothing there. No text from Cassie, no voicemail, just a continuing heavy silence. Where was she? Was she OK?

'I wish she would call,' Rubi muttered softly, taking a careful bite of her bread. 'I just want to know ...'

Her voice floated off, but the unsaid words were clear enough.

'I wish she would, too,' I said, but seeing Rubi's face I felt a tug of something. I guess it was a feeling of familiarity.

After all, I, of all people, knew what it was like not to have a mum around. I knew how lonely it could be to look at the door and wish that the one person you loved would walk through it and come back into your life. Being motherless was like being on a boat without a sail. A lot of the time it felt like I was drifting, a part of me missing, constantly tipping and turning in the rushing waves. Rubi's face was like a mirror looking back at me, her wide eyes reflecting my own fears. She wanted her security back. She was feeling as wobbly and fearful as I had for so long. She was another version of me.

'Rubi. Can you be a detective again?'

She nodded.

I dug into my pocket and once again pulled out the photo I had found in Cassie's drawer. I had been reluctant to show it to Rubi before. It was obviously old. However, right now I needed all the information I could get.

'Do you recognise anyone in this photograph?' I asked.

Rubi peered down at it, her fingers trailing over the faces. 'Isn't that ... Isn't that my mum?'

'Yes, it is.'

'She looks different.' Rubi squinted at it again. 'Her hair looks funny.'

'What about the man, Rubi? Do you recognise him?'

She frowned and shook her head quickly. 'No.'

'OK. Have you seen this photo before?'

More shakes of the head. Rubi's finger continued to trace over her mum's face. 'She's really pretty ...' she said sadly, her bottom lip wobbling.

I knew instinctively that I needed to take her mind off her mum for a bit. I swept the photo back into my pocket, out of sight again.

'We need to get a move on,' I said.

'Where?'

'You can come and help me at work, OK? I think you'll be a huge help,' I said, switching on what I hoped was a cheerful voice. 'And then ...'

'And then?' She chewed her sandwich slowly, waiting for me to make some kind of decision.

'Well, then I guess we'll come up with another plan. A proper plan. Just like Columbo would.'

I was about to say something more when my phone vibrated on the table. My heart lifted for a second.

Cassie? Could it be?

But then I saw the familiar 'unknown number'. That stupid insurance company was bothering me again. I certainly didn't have time for them. I cancelled the call, hoping they would get the message and keep my line clear. I needed it open for Cassie.

'Not Mum?' Rubi's face dropped.

'No, not this time.'

'I want her to call.'

'Don't worry, Rubi,' I said. 'We will work this out.'

'Because we're good detectives,' she replied, brightening again.

'That's right, and together we are going to find your mum.'

*

Rubi watched me carefully as I slowly brushed my unruly curls, pinning back the bits sticking up at the side with kirby grips. I tried not to look in the mirror, but of course I couldn't help a peek. I really don't know why I bothered. Nothing had changed. The same dull, sunken eyes stared back at me from behind my glasses. The same long, pallid face. With my hair pulled back, I could clearly see the feathers of grey threading through, even though I was only thirty.

An ageing duckling that would never be a swan.

Time was drifting past at such speed.

'Your hair is so pretty.'

The words were like a jolt, a tiny spark igniting my spine. I stepped back, turning to see Rubi looking up at me, her face serious and pinched, then a shy smile lit up her expression.

'It's so sparkly, like diamonds,' she said softly. 'And it's so curly too, like ringlets. Princesses have curly hair.'

'It does get a bit knotty,' I confessed. 'I'm not sure princesses have knots.'

Rubi ignored me and instead gently touched her own hair.

'We need to go,' I said briskly, trying to change the subject. 'Are your shoes on? We need to go back to yours and get your hair and teeth brushed again.'

She pulled a face. 'If I have to …'

We hurried back to her flat in silence. I noticed that Colin barely moved from his sleeping position in the hallway as we rushed past.

I stood still and watched as Rubi ran the toothbrush robotically back and forth in her mouth. Toothpaste was spilling everywhere and dribbling all down Cassie's lovely clean sink. I never knew one small person could make such a mess. It was quite an achievement.

Next, we found her hairbrush (lodged conveniently under Colin's backside) and I sat her down on the sofa as I tried desperately to work out the tangles. Rubi squirmed and moaned as I did it.

'You have to be gentle,' she scolded. 'My hair is knotty too. Start at the bottom, that's what Mum always does.'

'OK ...' I ran the brush through the ends of the hair and worked my way up. She was right. That was much easier.

'I wish I'd known this when I had long hair,' I said.

'You had long hair?' She seemed surprised. 'How long?'

'Oh – right down to the middle of my back, but it was such a pain. Too curly.' I used my hand to flatten a few loose hairs on the crown of her head. 'I'd look silly now.'

I put the brush down. I could see myself at nineteen staring into the mirror, waves tumbling down my back. It had been like a weight then, so heavy and pulling on me. It had been the feature Mum loved most about me.

'When I moved here, I needed a fresh start,' I said simply. 'So I cut it all off.'

I suppose I thought cutting it all would help in some way, cut some of those ties from the past. Funny how you can be so wrong about something. It was always going to take so much more than a simple hair trim to remove my ties.

'Well. Your hair is still very nice now,' she replied. 'It's pretty.'

'Ha! I'm – I'm far from pretty,' I muttered, more to myself. I laughed uneasily. 'But look at you.' I stood up so I could get a proper look at her. 'With your hair all neat and tidy – well, you look just ...'

I couldn't think of the right word.

'Beautiful?' Rubi offered hopefully.

'Yes. Beautiful,' I agreed. 'Really beautiful.'

'And I think you're beautiful too.'

I knew she wasn't being truthful. She was a young girl – what on earth did she know? But as we left the flat, her tiny hand encased in mine, I felt my head begin to lift.

'So, this is the famous Rubi I've been hearing so much about,' Jimmy said when we arrived at the shop.

I glanced back at him. 'I only just told you about her ...'

Jimmy pulled a face at Rubi, who immediately burst out laughing. 'Well, that was enough for me. I already knew she would be totally fab.'

'Are you sure it's OK – all this ...' I gestured helplessly. 'I know this isn't quite a normal situation.'

Jimmy peered down at Rubi and addressed her directly. 'Rubi, I'm sure you're a big enough girl to know what to do and what not to in this shop. I can trust you to behave in here, can't I?'

Rubi puffed out her chest, eyes gleaming. 'You can!'

'Well then.' He turned back to me, his large, dark eyes sparkling. 'I don't know what you're so worried about, Lucy.'

'I just ...' I shook my head, feeling flustered. 'I don't know. This is all so different.'

His smile curled wider. 'Ah, Lucy, I'm only kidding, but you do worry too much. Rubi will be fine here. It's really no bother at all.'

'How busy has it been?' I asked.

Jimmy's eyes drifted to the door. He shrugged slowly. 'Not great,' he admitted. 'Maybe it'll pick up.'

Jimmy had been managing this place for over fifteen years now and had worked here most of his adult life. We celebrated his fortieth birthday last year in the shop itself. Loads of Jimmy's friends and family came. One friend even made him a giant cake shaped out of a stack of books. I remember how I hung back on the day, unsure of myself and becoming overwhelmed by the number of people who knew and loved Jimmy. He was certainly a popular guy.

But I knew that for all his carefree nature and laid-back manner, he was worried too. Things were changing. It wasn't the same place it had been when he had started here fresh out of school.

A few years ago, this had been a thriving bookshop, chock-a-block with shelves and boxes overflowing with books. But since we'd been taken over by a larger company, the place had lost its independent, quirky feel. The walls were now gleaming white and the floor was so shiny you really could see your face in it. The shelves were neatly stacked with carefully referenced, mainly modern, books. At the front was a table piled high with glossy bestsellers. Jimmy had managed to keep hold of his small antique range by the till. That was his pride and joy.

Although I liked the cleaner, smarter appearance of the shop, I did miss the more unusual books. The self-published wonders, the forgotten joys. It felt as though we were like everyone else now – selling what the masses wanted to read and not catering for the specialist few.

At least Jimmy hadn't changed too much, although the new owner tried to encourage both of us to adopt a sleek professional image. Jimmy reluctantly shaved off his long dreadlocks and always wore smart trousers rather than his favourite vintage jeans. But I still saw his colourful T-shirts peeking out from underneath the jumpers – his rebellion against the Establishment. And he refused to shave his goatee which I thought was a good thing; the dark hair softened his round face.

We settled Rubi in the office at the back of the shop. I held out a battered copy of *The Wind in the Willows* hopefully.

'Would you like to read this? It's one of my favourites.'

She took it from me eagerly. 'Yes, please.'

'That's a great book, Rubi,' Jimmy told her. 'It has all sorts of animals in it.'

'Really? What ones?'

'Well – there's a toad, and a mole and a ... er ...'

'Rat?' I offered.

'Rats can swim really far,' Rubi told him proudly. 'And their teeth never stop growing.'

'Wow, that's interesting,' Jimmy replied keenly.

'Rubi is full of facts,' I told him. 'She really likes animals.'

Jimmy nodded. 'Well, I love hearing animal facts. You can tell me more anytime.'

Rubi's cheeks burned with pleasure. 'Really?'

'Sure. I love learning stuff.'

Rubi settled down happily with the book, her body already looking snug in Jimmy's oversized office chair. As we walked towards the door, I nudged him gently in the side.

'You're so natural at this,' I whispered. 'It's not fair.'

'It's not so hard. She's hardly a wild animal herself!' He paused. 'Anyway, it's easier for me. I grew up in a big family. I've been around kids all my life.'

'I know, but ...' I hesitated. 'I guess it doesn't come naturally to all of us.'

We both watched as Rubi turned the pages, engrossed, and Jimmy smiled brightly. 'See! She'll be just fine.'

We busied ourselves in the shop, concentrating mainly on a new display that needed to be put out.

'So, how long have you known Rubi?' he asked. 'It's not exactly like you, bringing a little person to work like this.'

'I've not known her long, or her mum Cassie. They moved in next door a few months ago.'

'Ah?' His eyebrow was raised. 'And already you're the babysitter.'

I took my place behind the counter, my eyes fixed on the door. 'It wasn't like that. Cassie said she was just popping out and asked me if I could look after Rubi. I was just doing her a favour.'

'Pop out?'

'Yes.' I shrugged. 'But like I told you, she just hasn't come back yet.'

'And when exactly did she go again?'

'Yesterday. Just after six.'

'That's a bloody long time, Lucy.'

'I know. I'm aware of that.'

'And you really don't think you should be involving other people?'

'Not yet.' I shook my head. 'I think maybe I can figure this out somehow. If I can just put the pieces together ...'

'This sounds crazy to me.'

'Maybe.' I shrugged. 'But I want to do the right thing by Rubi. That's all.'

Jimmy rubbed his beard. He seemed to consider this for a moment, his eyes fixed on the open door of the office. He seemed transfixed, as if he expected Rubi to dart out and shout something.

'She's very well behaved, actually,' I said in an attempt to placate him. 'She reminds me a little of Boris.'

'Boris?' His brow creased further. 'Oh. Your cat! Really?' He smiled a little and turned his gaze back to me. 'So, in what way does she remind you of Boris? I'm intrigued.'

I sighed. This was typical of Jimmy. Always probing me for information. Treating me like I was a curious object that he wanted to find out more about. Sometimes I didn't mind humouring him. But today, I felt grumpy and tired and worried about what lay ahead. I was in no mood to entertain him.

'She's quiet,' I said. 'And gentle. That's all.'

Jimmy's eyes widened. He wasn't used to me having a sharp tone. I began tidying the small display of diaries by the till, embarrassed that I had dropped my guard like that in front of him.

Jimmy moved a little closer to me; I could smell his aftershave – fresh and spicy, not like anything my dad would wear. It was nice, if a little strong.

'Are you really OK?' he said finally. 'You seem – well, not yourself ...'

I coughed, either in my fluster or the fact that his scent was clogging the back of my throat. Was it just my imagination or was he wearing more than usual?

'Are you worried about something? Can I help you?'

The door opened and a customer walked in. I didn't recognise her. She was young and pretty, dressed in tight jeans and an even tighter black top. Her blonde hair cascaded over her shoulders in a golden wave and her skin seemed to glow in that way that women on TV managed. What was their secret? How did they do it? She walked confidently over to the counter, clutching a piece of paper. Ignoring me, she thrust the note at Jimmy, flashing him a brittle smile.

'I need to find this book on Dickens,' she said crisply. 'It's for my friend's birthday. He's very particular.'

Jimmy looked down at the scrap of paper and nodded.

'I'll need to check on our system out back to see if we have it. It should only take a few minutes.'

Her eyes narrowed. 'I'm actually in a rush.'

Jimmy shrugged, his soft smile lingering on his face. He never lost it. He was the friendly face of the bookshop.

'I'll be as quick as I can. I'm afraid I have a very old computer. Please wait here,' he said, disappearing into the back.

The woman stood there, examining her nails. Behind me I heard Jimmy talking quietly to Rubi and her replies. Then I heard her light giggle. I realised he must be showing her how to use the ordering system. Rubi seemed so interested, asking lots of questions.

How easily they talked to each other. They had been strangers just moments ago and now all I could hear was soft laughter and easy, breezy conversation.

How different they both were to me. How I wished I could be more like them. Perhaps I could have, if my life hadn't gone the way it had.

Chapter Fourteen

The bookshop was empty again after a strangely busy thirty-minute period. I checked on Rubi, who was happily occupied drawing in the office, her head lying on the table, her pen scribbling furiously on the paper. I also checked my phone, but of course there was nothing there. If I'm honest, I don't think I was expecting anything else. The silence was beginning to chill me. I considered sending another message, but what would be the point? Cassie obviously wasn't prepared or able to answer me yet, and it seemed hopeless to keep on trying.

Jimmy was sorting books in the stockroom and I found myself hovering by the door, my phone still gripped in my hand.

'She hasn't called or messaged me. Should I do something now, do you think?'

He looked up. 'What do you mean?'

'I mean, I'm getting fed up of sitting around waiting for answers.' I frowned at the phone. 'I think I need to be more proactive now. I'm getting worried.'

'Why?'

I explained to Jimmy about the letter I'd found in the flat, the photograph and the odd unanswered phone call when I'd heard voices in the background.

'It doesn't tell you much,' Jimmy said. 'Except she's obviously in debt.'

'And possibly in trouble.' I paused. 'I was thinking, maybe the debt collectors caught up with her ...'

'And are doing what? They just want their money. It's not a film, Lucy. They won't kidnap her for revenge – not unless they were getting money for it.'

'Well, I'm not ruling it out. Her debt is the biggest lead I have.'

Jimmy pushed aside the box he was checking. 'Where else could she be?'

I lowered my voice. 'According to her friends, she could be with her ex-boyfriend, Gav. She's got these money problems and apparently he's been in touch, so they think she might've gone back to him to try and get some cash. But both their phones are turned off, so I can't contact either of them.'

'That seems convenient,' Jimmy mused. 'I wonder why they are both out of reach. A bit odd, surely?'

'It is, isn't it? Also, I've been thinking.' I paused again. 'Cassie moved to the estate in a hurry. She told Rubi to forget about this man, this Gav. Would she really go back to him if she hated him that much?'

'Well yes, perhaps if she needed cash. We all do things when we're desperate, don't we?' Jimmy said carefully.

I nodded slowly. I'd certainly acted in desperation before. Jimmy would never know that, though. He only got to see the quiet me that came to work, that stood behind the counter and busied myself organising the books.

I knew only too well what desperation really was. Those awful feelings I'd had after Mum died – if Cassie was feeling even half as desperate as I'd done in the past, then I could understand her. I knew how it could make you do strange, selfish things. I turned away from Jimmy, not wanting him to see my face. I felt sure he would be able to read the guilt flickering behind my eyes.

'The most likely assumption is she's with this ex. Perhaps they got pissed together and they're suffering today?' Jimmy continued. 'Reminisced over a bottle of wine, took things too far—'

'Oh, I don't know. Maybe.' I shook my head, still unsure. 'It just doesn't sit right with me.'

'Do you think there's a reason to be concerned about Gav?' he asked.

'No, I don't think so. Her friends say he's harmless, but ...'

'But you're still worried?'

'It's just that call, Jimmy. When she picked up but didn't speak. Something about it seemed odd, not right ...'

'Maybe she was drunk? Or picked it up in error?'

'Maybe, that's what I thought at first ...' I took my glasses off, rubbed them slowly against my top. 'But I'm pretty certain she was on the other end. I heard something ... a sigh.'

'A sigh?'

I pushed my glasses back in place and my vision slowly adjusted. 'Well, I think it was a sigh. I can't be sure.'

'It doesn't really tell us anything, then.'

'Not really, but for some reason it makes me uneasy.'

'It *is* concerning that's she's not back yet,' Jimmy agreed. 'I have to admit that makes *me* uneasy. My sister never leaves her kids without the strictest instructions, and even then she's checking in all the time. It's what mums do ...'

It's what mums do ...

And Cassie was a good mum, I was sure of it.

'I know,' I said. 'I don't think she'd be gone this long without contacting me. She must know Rubi would worry.' I dropped my voice to a whisper. 'What if she's hurt? I don't know – been knocked over or something? These things happen, don't they?'

Jimmy paused. 'Well yes, that is possible.' He laid his hands out squarely on the nearby table. 'That's why I really do think you should call the police. Ask for some advice.'

I flinched, thinking of what Jo had said to me earlier and of my own personal worries about involving the authorities. 'And say what? That I'm babysitting for my neighbour and that she's taken too long coming home? That she could be with her ex-boyfriend having a good time and forgotten all about us, or she could be hurt somewhere but I really don't know ...'

'It's not unreasonable, Lucy. She's been gone nearly twenty-four hours. This goes beyond babysitting duties.' He sighed. 'When all's said and done, Rubi is not your responsibility.'

'But she is now,' I said coolly. 'I know it sounds daft, but I do feel responsible. I want to do the right thing by Rubi and I'm not sure calling the police is that. Who knows where she might end up? So I'm going with plan B instead.'

'Which is?'

I checked behind me to make sure no one had entered the shop; luckily it was still empty.

'I think I'll have to find the boyfriend, this Gav. I have his address; The friend of Cassie's I told you about – Liam – gave it to me,' I said, my insides feeling queasy at the thought, but just saying it out loud convinced me. I needed to be brave now. 'I want to know if Cassie is there. Or if not, if he's seen her or spoken to her. He might be able to help. He could know something.'

'Lucy, do you think you've been watching too much *Columbo*?'

I scowled, refusing to answer that. I mean, he had a point, but surely *Columbo* could only help me here.

Jimmy sighed, like he knew he'd gone too far. 'Do you really know that this Gav is OK? Is it safe to go there?'

I had considered that, but I had no real answer. I guessed I just had to trust the opinion of Jo and Liam. After all, they had no reason to lie to me.

'Well,' said Jimmy after a beat. 'Maybe someone should come with you.'

I flapped my hand at him, immediately dismissing the idea. 'No. God, no. Honestly, I'll be fine. I'm better tackling this by myself.'

He frowned at me. 'But how will you even find this place?'

I hadn't really thought about that yet. 'Like I said, I have the address. I thought I'd just grab a cab, or—'

'Or you could get a lift with someone you know. Someone who can help with Rubi.' He sat forward, his face grim. 'Lucy, you are going to a stranger's house on an unfamiliar estate. There could be no CCTV there. This guy could be a maniac for all we know. I can't let you take the risk by yourself.'

I felt myself wobble and tried to keep my voice firm. 'I'll be fine, Jimmy.'

He stepped forward and gently touched my arm. 'Why don't you let me take you? I have the car. I'd feel better knowing you were both safe. Plus, I have nothing better to do this evening.'

'Jimmy, I—'

'Lucy. Please, just let me do this.' His face was serious now, his deep, liquid brown eyes burning into mine. 'For once, let somebody help you.'

I was so relieved when the four hours passed, and we could finally lock the door. Rubi walked out of the office and handed Jimmy back his phone. He had given it to her about an hour ago and she had been transfixed by it.

'I've just got a few games on there.' He shrugged. 'Most of them are pretty addictive.'

'You have some really good ones. I couldn't beat your highest level on Candy Crush,' Rubi said brightly.

'It's mainly for my nephew,' Jimmy said, shoving the phone back into his pocket, but I noticed that his eyes drifted to the floor. 'Well, most of the time, anyway,' he muttered.

'So – shall we go now?' I asked hesitantly.

I honestly wasn't sure about taking Jimmy along, but he did have a car which would make things easier. Plus, I realised that it might be handy to have someone else there to help, especially with Rubi. It would be nice to have a reliable human being beside me. Someone to stop me mucking it up. After all, the best detectives always had a sidekick.

'Why are you looking at me like that?' he asked, as he dug out the shop key.

'Like what?'

'Like I have three eyes or something.'

I smiled to myself. 'I just wondered what you'd look like in an old mac.'

'What?' He looked shocked. 'Lucy, I'm not that sort of guy!'

'No, I didn't mean like that. I was thinking of Columbo.'

'That's her favourite detective,' Rubi piped up. 'She really loves him.'

Jimmy seemed amused; he shook his head as he pulled down the shutter. 'Oh, I know all about the Columbo love; Lucy talks about him all the time.' He turned back to me, smirking. 'I don't mind being compared to the fella, but seriously ...' He gestured at his own face. 'I can't think of anyone I look like less.'

'Sorry,' I said, feeling myself blush. 'I didn't mean it like that. I just feel like we're out on an investigation together.'

He nodded slowly; he seemed to like that suggestion. 'Yes, I suppose we are.'

'An investigation looking for my mum,' Rubi said. 'And we'll find her. We have to.'

'We are going to go and find this Gav,' Jimmy said firmly. 'And hopefully put both your minds at rest.'

Rubi jumped up and down, suddenly excited. 'Gav? Really? We're going to see Gav? Now?'

'Yes.' I tapped her shoulder in an attempt to make her stop. 'We're going to see if your mum is there with him.'

'I hope she is,' Rubi said. 'I like Gav, even though Mum told me to forget him. He was funny and he played loud music a lot.'

'Sounds like my type of man.' Jimmy rattled the keys in his hand. 'Come on, then. My car's parked round the back. Do you still have the address?' I nodded. 'Good. We can shove it into my satnav. It's about time I used the bloody thing.'

Rubi stepped forward and tugged on Jimmy's arm. 'No. We can't go yet.'

He looked down at her, confused. 'Why not? It's best to go before it gets too late.'

'We have to go back to the flat first,' Rubi said. 'We have to pick up Colin. I'm not leaving him on his own.'

I shook my head. I was standing my ground. 'No. Colin can wait. We need to do this first.'

'But you promised me we wouldn't leave him too long.'

'And we won't. Once we're done with Gav, we will go home, I promise. I bet Colin won't even notice.'

Rubi flashed me a look that I suspected was anger. Her bottom lip curled, but she said nothing in return. Her silence said it all.

Chapter Fifteen

Rubi was quiet in the car, staring stubbornly out of the window, her normally placid face now closed to me. Jimmy talked easily, telling light jokes and silly anecdotes about the shop.

'Do you want to play some music?' he offered, pointing at the glove compartment. 'I have some old CDs in there. Take a look.'

I pinged it open. As promised, jammed inside was an array of tightly packed CDs. It was an eclectic mix of reggae, dance and pop.

'You have quite a mixed taste,' I laughed, pulling out one case. 'Hang on, what's this?'

I yanked out a bright album stacked right on the top. It was *Sergeant Pepper*. 'Oh cool.'

'I like all sorts,' he replied casually. 'Hey, Rubi, did you know Lucy has her own song on here?'

Rubi sat up in her seat, suddenly interested. 'Is this the one your dad was talking about? The one about being in the sky?'

I laughed. 'That's the one. Jimmy, did I tell you about that? I'd forgotten.'

'You told me on your very first day.' He screwed up his face, concentrating as we slowed towards the lights. 'I have a very good memory; now every time that song comes on, I think of you.'

I stared down at the case, my feelings rushing inside me. Did he really think of me every time? I wasn't even sure how to feel. No one had ever said anything like that to me before. I wondered if he thought of me in a good or bad way.

'Play it now!' Rubi said. 'I want to hear it.'

I flicked open the case and carefully lifted the disc. It was in perfect condition. I had loads from when I was a teenager, but I had scratched and damaged every single one. Jimmy had obviously taken more care with his. I slipped it inside the CD player, selected the right track and waited for the dreamy intro to start.

'There, that's better,' Jimmy declared. 'This should lighten the mood.'

I sat back, listening as the vocals swept on. Dad used to play this when I was really little, in the happier times when Mum was still alive. He'd sweep me up in his arms and sing along, jigging me up and down with the beat.

'Rubi? Do you like it?' I asked after a moment or two.

Rubi just sniffed. 'It's OK. It sounds old-fashioned.' She turned her attention to the window, clearly losing interest.

Jimmy snorted. 'Old-fashioned! Just shows what you know. This is a classic.'

Above the radio nestled the blinking screen of the satnav; every so often a shrill robotic voice would direct us where to go and which turning to take and Jimmy would follow obligingly, thanking her every time. I laughed.

'Jimmy! She's a robot!'

'I like to be polite,' he replied. 'It's only right.'

'I haven't heard you laugh loud like that before,' Rubi said. She thumped the back of Jimmy's seat. 'She must find you funny.'

Jimmy glanced over at me and grinned. It was infectious, and I did the same back.

'It should take us twenty-two minutes, give or take traffic,' he said, still smiling. 'So not long at all.'

I nodded, feeling more serious now. I just wanted to get this all over with. What if Cassie was there when we got there – would she be angry with me for tracking her down? And if she wasn't there, where would that leave us? Would Gav be able to help us at all? The ominous thought of going to the police still hung over me. I glanced back at Rubi, who was staring blankly out of the window, not complaining at all.

I wasn't sure if I could do that to her. Not yet, anyway.

'Remember we are detectives,' I told Rubi gently. 'We're going to Gav to see if we can find more clues.'

Rubi was squirming in her seat, her face pressed up against the glass. 'That's cool, but I don't think she'll be there.' Her breath was creating a mist on the window.

'Why?' I asked.

Rubi seemed to be slipping further down in her seat. 'Mum made Gav cry before, she said bad things to him. She said she'd never go back because she was bad for him.'

Jimmy flashed me a look. A kind of 'this is interesting' expression with his eyebrows half raised.

'We're just going to talk to Gav,' he said finally, turning right down a side street as directed by his new automated friend. 'He might know something. He might be able to help us find out where your mum is.'

'I just want her back home,' Rubi whispered. Then her voice got louder, more accusing. 'She said she would only be gone a few hours.' She started kicking the back of my seat. 'She's being mean staying away. She told me she'd come right back. Why is she doing that?'

The thumping was shaking my seat.

'Rubi! Stop that!' I snapped finally.

Rubi flung herself back in her seat, but her cheeks were blazing and her arms were drawn tightly across her chest.

'You can't tell me what to do! I want my mum!'

'Rubi—'

'Leave me alone!'

I took a long, shaky breath. I really hadn't meant to upset Rubi. That was the last thing I wanted.

'I'm sorry I shouted, Rubi. We all want your mum back,' I said. 'We want her back and we want everything to go back to normal. I'm trying to help you here, I promise. But you're not helping us by getting angry.'

'You don't care,' she said loudly. 'You don't want to have me. You want to get rid of me.'

'That's not true.' I twisted my face so I could see her. She flicked her angry eyes away from me and towards the floor. I could see she was fighting back the tears again.

'Rubi. I don't want to get rid of you. I want you to be happy. I want to do the right thing for all of us,' I said and then after a few minutes I spoke again, my voice much softer this time. 'Detectives have to be calm and brave. We have to keep a level head so that we can work this out. Can you do that, Rubi? Can you keep calm for me?'

She gave the seat one final sulky kick and then pulled her legs back up. I heard her sigh deeply, then a shaky inhale that suggested she was near to letting the tears flow.

'Can you?' I asked again.

'Yes, suppose ...'

I really didn't know what else I could say to make Rubi feel any better. I just hoped that including her in this 'investigation' was the right thing to do. It was so tiring trying to work it all out.

'Lucy.' Jimmy's voice broke into my thoughts. 'Are you OK?'

I snapped back into reality, my head still swimming a little. Sitting up, I noticed that we were away from the familiar sights of my area and were now driving through the outskirts of North London. This was a grey, hard-looking area where green spaces had given way to car parks and huge, ugly warehouses. Narrow houses lined each street.

'Yes, I'm fine.'

'We're nearly there,' Jimmy said, a bit too brightly.

My head was still muzzy. We sat in silence for a bit as the satnav directed us down a busy main road. I focused on the images outside the window – the houses, the cars, the trees. I took a long, deep breath. I wasn't sure if it was the right time to say what I was about to say, but I was going to anyway. Despite the doubt nagging at me, I wanted Rubi to know that she wasn't alone. I completely understood how she felt. I tried to ignore Jimmy as I spoke. I felt uneasy knowing he was going to learn more about me – more perhaps than I wanted him to – and I hoped desperately that he wouldn't think badly of me. Somehow this felt like the right thing to do.

'I know what it's like to miss your mum,' I said finally, my voice quiet. 'I know what I said to you before, Rubi, that I didn't miss her. But I lied. I miss mine every single day.'

I heard Rubi shift on the seat behind me. 'But she died.'

'She did, yes. But I still miss her.'

'How did she?' Rubi asked. 'Die, I mean?'

I continued to stare out of the window. For the briefest moment, I could see her again. Mum. Walking along the pavement. Her long, confident strides overtaking others. She was tall like me, but she suited her height better, she owned it. I don't remember her slumping. Or trying to disguise it. Her voice was loud and strong, her hand was tight in mine, pulling me along beside her.

'She was sad,' I said. 'Very sad. She didn't want to be here any more.'

And I could have stopped her. I walked into the room that night. I saw her laid out on the bed with the tablet packets scattered around her.

'She looked so small, so lost,' I whispered. 'She didn't even look like Mum any more.'

'Lucy.' Jimmy squeezed my arm again. 'Are you OK? Do you want me to stop the car?'

'No,' I said firmly, lifting up my head. The spell was broken. 'No. I'm sorry. I shouldn't have said all that.' I turned to Rubi again. 'I'm sorry, I didn't mean to scare you.'

'You didn't.' Her eyes were wide and bright. 'But do you think my mum doesn't want to be here any more ...'

'No! God, no!' I tugged on the seatbelt and folded my body through the gap. Reaching across, I took her tiny white hand. It was so warm and delicate, like china. 'That wasn't what I was saying at all. I just meant I know what it's like to feel scared. I know what it's like to miss someone – do you see?'

She nodded quickly.

'Lucy, is that your phone?' Jimmy asked.

I sat up straight and dug inside my bag. The damn thing had slipped right to the bottom. I clawed at it, swiping clumsily at the screen, not even noticing the number.

Oh God, don't say I've missed her. Please don't say I've missed Cassie's call.

'Duckling!' Dad's rough voice immediately invaded my ear. 'What's going on? I thought you were going to me keep updated.'

I managed to persuade Dad that I was OK and that he needed to end the call quickly. My priority, I reminded him, was to keep the line clear. Dad wasn't happy. He told me again that I should be calling the police. He told me that missing people had to be found in a certain number of hours or they were almost certainly dead meat. I didn't tell him what I was about to do. I think that information alone would've made him worry even more.

'Stay safe,' he warned before he hung up. 'And remember to try and do the right thing. Always.'

'I'll try,' I whispered. 'I promise.'

I was quite relieved to end the call. I felt like I was keeping things from him and I could tell he was worried for me. All of these emotions made my head hurt.

Jimmy swung into a small car park outside a low-rise block of red-brick flats. It didn't look so bad actually, but the windows were tiny and mean-looking and a dusting of graffiti decorated the main frontage. It was probably nice once, but the veneer had worn off. Now it was like a lot of this part of North London, run-down and neglected.

Gav lived at number two, which meant he had to be on the ground floor. I was thankful for this. At least I could get away quickly if I needed to.

'Are we all going in?' Jimmy asked.

'I want to go too,' Rubi pleaded. 'I want to see Gav.'

I shook my head. 'No – I think it's better if just one of us goes and someone needs to stay with Rubi.'

'As long as you're sure?' Jimmy frowned a little. 'I really don't mind going with you.'

'Look after Rubi,' I replied firmly, already stepping out of the car to make the point. 'I'll be fine, honestly. What on earth can go wrong?'

Jimmy lightly touched my hand. 'Be careful.' His dark eyes settled on mine. 'I'm just here if you need me. Call, shout, whatever – and I'll be there in seconds, I promise.'

'Thank you.'

His eyes stayed fixed on mine. 'Don't be long, Lucy. I worry about you, OK? Remember that!'

As his hand left mine, I could still feel his heat. My skin was tingling.

*

I walked quickly. I knew it really was best that I went alone. I had to keep Rubi safe, and this was the best way. But part of me longed to have Jimmy beside me.

The flat itself was easy enough to find. Number two was tucked away in the corner of the building. A bright, newly painted red door and a clean doormat welcomed me, along with a few pots with healthy-looking plants. I immediately felt annoyed by my previous assumptions. Why had I expected Gav's place to look different to this? Did I assume it would be tatty and unwelcoming? I could feel the deep bass vibrations of music playing inside. In another flat, further along, a dog yapped loudly.

With growing resignation, I pressed the plastic, well-thumbed doorbell. Then I stood back and waited. The deep thumping sound inside continued. I pressed again.

The door to the flat next to me opened and an older lady peered through the gap. She looked very frail with thinning white hair and an angry expression on her face which she soon lost when she saw me.

'Oh, I thought you were one of them,' she said in a rasping voice, sounding like she needed a good cough. She opened the door wider and began to look me up and down. 'What are you? From the council, are you? On a Saturday?' She tutted. 'About bloody time. That music hasn't stopped. It's giving me a bloody migraine.'

I tried to flash her my brightest smile but was deeply aware of how fake it probably looked. 'Oh no. I'm not from the council. I'm – well, I guess I'm a friend.'

The woman squinted at me, taking in my height, the stupid fixed smile that now seemed to be glued to my face.

'You don't look like *his* type of friend.' She sniffed.

I sighed. 'Well, I'm not. Not directly. But I'm hoping he can help with something.'

The woman snorted. 'Him! You'd be lucky!' She must have noticed my expression change, because her face suddenly softened. 'Well, good luck to you. But you'd have more luck banging on that bloody door of his. His doorbell hasn't worked for months. He's probably asleep, though Christ knows how he does with that racket going on.'

I smiled, thanked her and quickly did as she suggested – three sharp raps on the smooth wood. All the time I noticed that she remained at her door, watching me.

I stepped back, expecting more silence, but just as I was about to admit defeat, the door slowly opened, releasing with it a relentless sound of deep, disturbing so-called music. The man standing behind the door eyed me suspiciously.

'What do you want?' he grumbled.

'Are you Gav?' I asked, fairly loudly over the noise. I tried to sound bright and confident, but it came out a bit squeaky.

'Yeah – and, what? Who are you?'

Gav stepped forward, out of the murky shadows. I could finally see him. Tall, as tall as me anyway, and skinny with an untidy mane of blonde hair. On his chin was a line of rough stubble and his skin looked almost whitish-blue. He pushed a clump of hair away from his eyes and immediately I could see the terrible bruising there, cruel, purple and swollen. One eye was barely open, the other unbruised but still bloodshot, blinking back at me.

'What you want?' he barked. 'If you're here fucking selling stuff, you can piss off now. I'm not interested.'

I hesitated, his words stinging, then I shifted position and straightened my shoulders so that I was level with him. I knew this was something Dad did when he wanted to intimidate people, show them that he wasn't scared.

'I want to know if you've heard from Cassie? It's really important,' I said finally. My voice was surprisingly firm and calm.

Gav blinked at me, his frown deepening. I saw that he was running his tongue across his lip. There was a small cut there, on the corner; it had healed slightly into a hard red scab, but it looked uncomfortable.

'Is she here?' I asked. 'I really need to see her.'

He snorted, then quickly looked around us. His eyes fell on his elderly neighbour who was still standing there, gawping. He glared at her and muttered something incomprehensible under his breath.

'I'm sorry ...' I moved forward, indicating that I couldn't quite understand him. I was beginning to think he was drunk, or worse.

'Doesn't matter ...' he hissed, but his eyes were still fixed on the older woman. He turned his attention back to me. I couldn't look straight at him. I found his one blazing red eye extremely difficult to deal with, it looked so painful.

'Who are you?' he snapped. 'Why do you want her?'

I flinched. 'I'm just a neighbour of Cassie's ... that's all. I need to know ...'

'A neighbour? Like, at her new place? At the Cherry Blossom?'

I nodded. 'Yes, I'm looking after her daughter at the moment.'

His expression immediately changed. His mouth slackened and his entire body seemed to shrink as he slumped slightly against the door.

'You? You have Rubi? Thank fuck – I mean, like, I didn't know. I just didn't know ...' He squeezed his eyes shut. 'Fucking hell ...' He shook his head. 'Can I see her? I'd really like to see her.'

I hesitated. I could tell how upset he clearly was, but my instinct was still to keep Rubi safe. At the moment that meant keeping her with me.

'I have Rubi. She's fine but I can't get her just yet ...' I paused. 'But ... I really need to know where her mum might be.'

Gav remained where he was for a moment and then, slowly, he began to nod.

'You better come in,' he said.

'I can't have that old bitch out there listening to every word,' he explained once the door was closed.

Gav led me into a clean, minimal living room: two leather-effect sofas, a freshly polished table and a huge TV in the corner. The only thing ruining the ambience of the place was the booming music from the surprisingly small-looking stereo, but Gav quickly picked up a remote control and turned it off.

'Sorry,' he said. 'I find it helps me relax – you know, when I'm stressed.'

'It's OK,' I stuttered. 'It was very loud, though.'

The silence was odd now and my ears were still ringing. I smiled again anyway, in thanks.

He looked awkward, his gaze darting from left to right as if he was expecting someone to jump out at any moment. 'Can I get you a drink or something? Tea? Coffee? Water?'

I thought of Rubi and Jimmy sitting waiting in the car. I couldn't leave them for too long.

'No, honestly, but thanks.'

He flapped at the nearest sofa. 'Please then, just sit down – you're making me feel itchy.

'So, Cassie?' he said as I sat down, looking a little sheepish. 'You want to know about her.'

'Yes. Has she been with you?'

He smiled at me sadly. 'No.'

The first word that came to my mind was 'fuck'. It almost leapt from my mouth. I squeezed my hands together instead, cursing my bad luck. Had I got this completely wrong?

'But she was meant to be,' he continued.

I leant forward, my hand gripping the arm of the cool leather sofa. 'Hang on. What did you just say? She was meant to be here?'

Gav sat back. He rubbed his face and sighed. 'Yeah, she was meant to be coming here. I was expecting her.'

'When? I mean, when was she meant to be coming?'

'Yesterday. Yesterday evening. She called me up and everything and I was here waiting for her. I was ...' His voice dropped. 'I was looking forward to it, fucking idiot, I am. She needed money, you see. She told me she was in trouble and I agreed to help. I guess I thought it might be good to see her. I never got over her, you know ...' He rubbed at his face again. 'I don't know what I was thinking. But it doesn't matter now because it never happened, did it?'

'But when she didn't come here, weren't you worried about her?'

His eyes blazed for a second and then he laughed. It was a short, cynical sound. 'You don't get it, do you, sweetheart? She mugged me off. She must've set me up. She showed up with some blokes instead. These fucking big bastards. I'm guessing one of them, the really gobby one, is her new fella. Like, great choice, Cassie!' He shook his head slowly. 'That guy is crazy, man. How do you think I got this?' He pointed to his eye. 'He fucking did me over and then took all the money I had ready for Cassie. I was willing, you know. I was, like, willing to help her out because stupidly I thought we could have another shot of it. But instead, she sent her new man and his heavies to beat the crap out of me.'

'Did you recognise them, then? These men?' I asked.

Gav snorted. 'Her new bloke hissed his name at me – like I should know it or something. Harry Harris. Sounds like a fucking cheesy club singer if you ask me. Told me to stay away.' He half laughed. 'Well, I will now. Don't you worry. I don't need the bloody hassle.'

I noticed that his gaze slid away from me as he spoke, almost like he was keeping something back, but I wasn't sure how much more I could push him.

I hesitated for a moment and then pulled the crumpled photograph out of my pocket.

'Gav, do you recognise this person at all?'

He took the photo from me, studied it. 'It's Cas, isn't it, long ago? The bloke – he looks kind of familiar. I can't be sure, though.' He paused. 'Why?'

'I'm trying to work out where Cassie might be, or even go next. I was told this was an ex-boyfriend?'

He frowned. 'Obviously from long ago. We didn't really talk about stuff like that. I know she was hurt in the past. That's all.' He stared at the photograph a bit longer. 'Do you think he could've been one of the men that beat me up? It all happened so fast, I didn't get much of a look at them ...' He rubbed at his head. 'I can't be sure.'

'I don't know,' I said.

'I don't either.' He handed me back the photo. 'I'm sorry, I don't know where she's gone.'

'I'm sorry they did this to you,' I said. 'It's horrible.'

He sighed. 'Don't be sorry. I'm the fucking mug here. I'm just glad she had the sense not to take Rubi with her.' His voice wobbled. 'He's a nutter, this new fella of hers.'

'But why beat you up? Why do that?'

'Who fucking knows? Like, I had the money for her, didn't I? It wasn't much but it was enough to get her out of trouble. About five hundred quid. They took that. Then they searched the fucking flat. What for I don't know. All the time, that fucking bitch just stood by the front door watching them. I swear she looked happy.'

'But do you really think Cassie set this up?' I asked. 'Why would she do that?'

Gav didn't speak for a moment. I thought that he wasn't going to answer, but then he did. Quietly, almost robotic. 'Yes, I do. Because this whole thing was her idea. She arranged to come and see me, for me to get the money together, she planned the whole thing. And she was there. She was with him at the door. She watched as her man and his friends did me over, looking happy about it, and then she turned and walked away.' His voice broke. 'And the fucking bitch didn't look me in the eye once.'

Chapter Sixteen

As soon as I left Gav's, his music went back on full blast. He didn't bother to say goodbye. He just closed the door quickly behind me, probably relieved to see the back of me.

I paused in the hallway to give myself a chance to collect my thoughts. I needed to stay calm and be methodical like Columbo. I knew that I couldn't get myself in a panic. I had more information now. At least I knew for sure that Cassie wasn't off having a good time, but I wasn't sure this version of events was much better. I took off my glasses and rubbed them on the edge of my coat, before replacing them and considering my options. So, it appeared that Cassie had arranged to meet Gav, whilst at the same time telling a new man, Harry Harris, about the rendezvous. My mind churned these facts over. Was Harry working for the men she owed money to? But why then did they have to beat up poor Gav? Surely it would've been enough for Cassie to have borrowed his money and given it to Harry that way? It was certainly a less messy option. And what were they searching the flat for? Was Gav keeping something from me? He certainly hadn't wanted to say anything more to me and seemed to want me out of the flat as soon as possible.

Even so, I couldn't fail to notice his relief that Rubi wasn't with Cassie. He obviously cared for the little girl, which surely proved that he had some decency. It also showed that he really feared this Harry guy.

Why on earth then would Cassie want to get involved with someone like that?

I remembered what Gav had said about Cassie looking happy and considered this for a moment. Did it mean she had arranged to have him beaten up for his money and wanted him hurt? It didn't fit with the person I had met. The sweet, friendly Cassie I had seen didn't seem callous or evil at all. Could I really have misjudged her character so badly?

Where was Cassie now? Was she still with Harry? Why had she lied if she'd known she was going to be longer than a few hours? I remembered what Dad had said about missing people needing to be found after a certain period of time and felt a shiver. She had been gone nearly twenty-four hours now. This wasn't looking good.

I squeezed my eyes shut. This wasn't about me. I thought of what Dad had also said before about parents leaving their kids home alone so they could go on holiday. I had read similar stories. People always said afterwards, 'Oh, they seemed so nice. I can't believe they were capable of it ...' And Cassie was obviously also desperate for money.

Was this Cassie? Was she capable of all this?

'I saw her, you know.'

I jumped, not expecting to be spoken to. Turning, I saw that the elderly woman was still standing at her door. Had she been there the entire time? She smiled at my shocked expression, obviously enjoying her moment of attention.

'What?' I stuttered. 'I'm sorry?'

'I saw that young girl you're asking about. Cassie, isn't it? Nice girl, she was. She used to live here, of course, with that idiot next door.' The woman smiled, showing gaps in her mouth. 'Can't see what she ever saw in him myself. And she had her lovely little girl with her sometimes – what's her name again? Rosie?'

'Rubi.' My reply was stiff, not liking the fact she'd got her name wrong.

She nodded dismissively. 'Yes, that's it. Rubi. Pretty little girl. Very serious. I always said she had an old soul, that one.'

'What did you see? Did Cassie say anything to you?'

'Well ...' The woman hesitated, her eyes widening. 'You know, I'm not one to gossip.'

That was clearly not true, but I was guessing this might not be the best time to make the point.

'Please. Anything. It might help us.'

'Well ...' The woman leant in closer. 'It was odd. Cassie is usually such a bright, happy girl but she looked different to me, you know? Very pasty. And she didn't even bother to say hello to me, which is most unlike her. Usually, she asks after me. She knows I have health problems and she always used to check up on me when she lived here. She's considerate like that. A good girl.'

'That's odd, Gav said she looked happy,' I said.

'Well, I'm only telling you what I saw. When she was outside his flat, she didn't look herself at all. I don't know what she was like when she was inside.'

I nodded, encouraging her to continue.

'Yes, well anyway. She was with some men. One of them was obviously "with her", if you know what I mean. He was holding her hand and whispering in her ear. Tall bloke, a bit fat and bald as a coot. He said hello, actually, but I didn't like him. Not at all. He was a cocky little so-and-so, acted like he knew me already. One of those types, you know?'

I wasn't sure I did but I smiled encouragingly anyway, not wanting to put her off.

'What about the other men?' I asked. 'What were they like?'

She sniffed. 'Well, one of them I'd never seen before. Great big lump of a bloke. He looked like a nasty piece of work, to be honest. But the other fella – I've seen him before … lots of times.'

'Really? Where?'

She grinned and pointed back towards Gav's front door. 'There! At his. He'd had one of his parties and that guy was there. I saw him going in. He's always hanging around in there, I'm guessing it's one of his mates. He's hard to forget. Lanky like a beanpole and long ginger hair that he wears in a stupid ponytail like a bloody girl. He's always grinning like an idiot too and making smart comments. I can't stand the man.'

This was interesting. 'So, one of Gav's friends was with Cassie?'

'Yes, that's what I told you, wasn't it? It was him that knocked on the door. I saw Gav open it. He seemed surprised to see Ginger Boy but let him in, then the others came in after; Cassie was just behind them. I'm not even sure Gav would've noticed her before that. They ambushed him.'

'You see a lot of things,' I said.

'You have to around here. You have to keep your eye on things. There's so much that goes on, it pays to be clued up. You know what I mean?'

'Yes,' I said softly. 'I do.'

'We used to look out for one another, long ago,' she continued, her voice much sadder now. 'Flats like these, all the neighbours would know each other. We'd take care of one another. We didn't have much, but we had community.' Her eyes drifted towards Gav's flat. 'I might not like him that much, he's a noisy bugger, but I still keep an eye on him. He hasn't been the same since Cassie left and she was such a good girl. Now he has strange, nasty-looking men over and he looks bloody awful. I worry about him. I wouldn't want him to end up on the scrapheap.'

My head dipped. I felt ashamed of thinking badly of her before. She was right, of course. This woman wasn't even that nosy, she was just an elderly lady looking out for others. Surely we needed people like her.

I'd spent so long building a protective barrier around myself, I'd completely ignored the needs of others. OK, I was helping Rubi now, but that was only because I had to. I helped Dad, but that was out of a sense of guilt and duty. It shouldn't have been like that. Could I have done more for the likes of Joy, instead of blindly shutting her away? Look at Jimmy, how he was always there for people without thinking or complaining. It came so naturally to him.

'I don't know what happened after that,' she continued quietly. 'His music went back on loud and that was that. They weren't in there long, though, those nasty men. I peeked out again when they left.'

'When was that?'

'I dunno? Twenty minutes or so. I'd made a tea and watched a bit of *Corrie*. Then I heard the door go. I saw the same lot leaving Gav's flat and that big man was holding Cassie's hand, but he was almost pulling her along. That's all I saw. I assume they drove off. I didn't see Gav until the next day. All those bruises! My God! I told you they were trouble.'

'But did Cassie see you? Did she say anything to you?'

'No – not to me.' She paused. 'But come to think of it, I did hear her say something to the man that was holding her hand.'

'What? What was it?'

Her face screwed up in concentration. 'She said, "You'll never get what you want." Just like that. It was quite cold and nasty.'

Jimmy and Rubi were laughing when I walked back to the car. Rubi was sitting in the front seat and fiddling with the radio. I stood by Jimmy's opened front door, just as Rubi had selected a radio station that obviously wasn't to Jimmy's liking. To be fair it wasn't to mine either; it was awful rap music. Jimmy yelped in mock protest and covered his ears.

'Oh Rubi, how can you like that?' he said, laughing.

Rubi was giggling. 'It's better than all the rubbish you like.'

I stood there staring at them for a moment, a warm, protective feeling swelling inside me. Rubi was safe. I realised that, above everything else, this was the only thing that mattered to me now. I would keep this girl away from harm. A tiny smile settled on my lips. It finally felt as if I had a true purpose. I was important to someone.

But I had been important to Cassie too. This thought kept coming back to me. She had trusted me. She had sought me out for a reason. Maybe it was time that I did the same to her. Did I need to trust her too?

'Lucy!' Rubi said suddenly, obviously noticing me gawping at them like an idiot. I saw her eyes widen, hope and expectation building. 'Did you see Gav? Was he there? Was Mum—'

'I ...'

My words floundered as I realised that I really didn't know what to say next. I didn't want to upset her again, especially as she looked so happy. Jimmy turned to me, his face creased in concern. He shook his head a little, a tiny message between us: 'Wait, tell me in a minute.' Then gently he turned back round to Rubi.

'OK then, smarty pants,' he said brightly. 'What's the worst music you can find on there? I dare you to try and find it.'

Rubi flinched, her eyes still on me. 'Was he there?'

I nodded. 'Yes, he was.'

'And Lucy will tell us both about it in a second, but first I need to talk to her. Is that OK? In the meantime, see what else you can find on there. See if you can find some really horrible music. Burst my ancient eardrums!'

Rubi pouted her lips a little but didn't refuse. Obediently she returned her focus to the car radio and started to fiddle with it. I stepped away and Jimmy came out to join me. We stood a few metres from Rubi, facing the car, not taking our eyes off her.

'Well?' he asked, his eyebrows arched, and he listened without interrupting as I quickly filled him in on the conversation with Gav, trying to remember all the details I had been fed.

'Shit ...' Jimmy muttered. He kicked the ground. 'This just gets more complicated the more we dig into it. What do we do now? If Cassie did set Gav up – well, that puts a different perspective on things, doesn't it? Surely? I'm hardly thinking she's Mum of the Year here.'

'I don't know what to do.' I gestured towards the car. Rubi was sitting back on her seat now, just staring at us, her face deathly serious. She wasn't stupid. She knew something was going on. I shook my head. 'I don't want to let her down. What do I do?'

'I dunno – call the police now, I guess. If Cassie really has buggered off with this bloke, then we need to tell someone, don't we?'

I shuddered a little. 'I don't know, Jimmy. That seems so final.'

I thought of what might happen if I called the police. I imagined Cassie coming home, with a reasonable explanation, to find her daughter gone. What would happen to poor Rubi? How much damage would that cause? My thoughts drifted and I pictured Rubi's beautiful paintings that Cassie had carefully pinned around the arch in her kitchen. I felt something inside me break.

'I'm still not sure I'm ready to give up on Cassie yet,' I said.

'Really?' Jimmy looked frustrated. 'I mean, surely you have enough evidence now to suggest that Cassie is not making very good decisions.'

'I know, but ...'

I hesitated, thinking of what her elderly neighbour had said. 'I think there's more to this, Jimmy. She asked me to trust her. Now I've just heard that she told one of the men that he'll never get what he wants. What does that even mean?'

Jimmy looked confused. 'Get what? Why would she say that?'

'I don't know.' I paused. 'What if Cassie is in some kind of mess she can't get out of, Jimmy? What were they searching for in Gav's flat? They were clearly looking for something. Maybe she's keeping Rubi away from someone who could be dangerous.'

Jimmy shrugged. 'It's possible, I suppose, but surely that's even more reason to involve the police.'

'Maybe. I don't know.' I shook my head, suddenly decisive. 'No, not yet. I must be able to help her some other way.'

'Seriously? What else can you do?' His voice dropped. 'Lucy, I get it. Rubi is a lovely kid, but you need to remember she's not your responsibility. Not any more. You need to tell someone that Cassie has walked out on her or that you suspect Cassie might be in danger.'

'She is my responsibility, though. You don't understand. Cassie left her in my care.'

'For a few hours!' Jimmy threw up his hands. 'How much longer can you keep offering excuses for her?'

'I don't know,' I replied honestly. 'I just have this feeling that she needs my help. I still think she intends to come back for Rubi.'

'How can you know that?'

'I have to keep reminding myself, Cassie was – is – a good mum. I can't imagine any reason why she would run off and leave Rubi like this.' I shrugged. 'OK, we were hardly the best of friends, but I really don't believe that she would intentionally get a man beaten up for money. Or leave Rubi without an explanation. It just doesn't ... well, it doesn't fit with what I know about her. None of this has, really.'

'But you didn't know her that well, Lucy. She's just a neighbour, isn't she? Someone you speak to occasionally. The truth is, she *could* be capable of this. Sadly, sometimes you have to think the worst of people.'

'No, I don't think you do. Not in this case.' My gaze dropped to the ground. 'Cassie is different somehow. She asked me to look after Rubi. She didn't just leave her with a friend she's known longer, who has a drink problem. She didn't leave her on her own in the flat. She didn't leave her with an ex-boyfriend who she no longer loved. She sought me out and asked me specifically to take care of her. She made an informed decision. She also promised she wouldn't be long. And I believed her. And I still do.'

I closed my eyes for a second, trying to gather my thoughts – much as Columbo would gather his evidence. Cassie had asked me to keep Rubi safe. She told me to trust no one else. Then she had texted me to say she was delayed but would be back soon. Next there was the strange phone call – the male voice in the background. This Harry person, perhaps? And what I thought was Cassie sighing. Or was she moaning? I couldn't be sure. I knew Cassie was in debt and possibly in trouble. I'd also been told by those that knew her that she was a good, reliable mother. This wasn't like her. Who could I really trust here? Gav, her angry ex? Jo, an alcoholic friend? Liam ...

'Lucy?' Jimmy insisted.

I opened my eyes. 'I don't know for sure. Not really. But my instinct tells me she needs my help. She trusted me. I'm not letting her down. Not yet. I just need to speak to her. That's all. I just need to know she's OK.' I paused, licked my lips. They were so dry. 'And, if she really has abandoned Rubi, I need to hear that from her mouth first. Then – well, of course I will get some help.' I hesitated. 'I just have to try to speak to her first. One last chance.'

Jimmy was still frowning. 'OK, but what if she's in trouble? Do you want Rubi exposed to that?'

'That's what I want to find out,' I said, my voice firmer now. 'I have to work out what's going on first before I involve other people. What if Cassie is OK? What if she was planning to come back tomorrow and this was all a misunderstanding or there is a decent explanation? If I call the authorities now, they could take her daughter away for good without knowing that. She's a young, single mum, they could judge her. I just can't let that happen. She asked me to help. She trusted me. That means a lot to me, Jimmy.'

But above all, this was about Rubi. I felt obligated to do the right thing by her. I couldn't be the one to destroy her life.

I had to put right my wrongs.

Jimmy slowly nodded. 'OK. I understand. But you need to be careful. Please, Lucy.'

'I will. I'll just try her number a few more times. I'll leave another message.' I swallowed hard. 'And perhaps I could ask Liam for help. He's the lad that gave me Gav's address. I could see if he knows how to contact this ginger-haired person, the one that Gav obviously knows. Gav must be protecting him for some reason, because he didn't mention him to me.'

'That could work ...'

'Well, I've got no other options. And Liam does seem to know a lot of people,' I replied.

Jimmy sighed. 'OK, OK. But this really does feel like clutching at straws. If you get nowhere in the next twenty-four hours, you need to call the police. Yes? This is a young girl we're talking about here. A vulnerable young girl.'

'I'm well aware of that fact, Jimmy.' I paused. 'And she's safe with me, you know.'

I could barely believe the words had left my mouth. She was safe. I would make sure of it. That was my only concern right now.

'Of course she is, Lucy. I never doubted it. That wasn't what I was worried about.'

He smiled wanly and gestured that we should get back into the car. Rubi had a calm expression on her face. Inside, the music was now soothing. A beautiful Bach concerto was playing. I beamed at her.

'Wonderful choice, Rubi.'

She smiled back. 'You asked me to find the worst music ever. This is it.'

Chapter Seventeen

I was quiet at first on the way back. So much had happened in the last twenty-four hours, I could hardly get my head around it all. It almost felt like I was part of some surreal TV show, quite different to the life I had lived only hours before. Rubi hadn't said much, either. I gently explained that her mum hadn't been at Gav's flat and told her that we needed to think of other options. She had simply shrugged and looked away. I wondered if she was beginning to feel defeated and that worried me. I didn't want Rubi to give up on her mum just yet.

'We will find her, Rubi,' I insisted, ignoring Jimmy's nervous glare. 'We are going to go home first, put our heads together and work out what to do next.'

'Is that what your Columbo would do?' she asked carefully.

I smiled. 'Well, yes. I think he would, actually. He certainly wouldn't give up. He always works it out in the end, even the trickiest puzzle.'

I pulled the notebook out of my bag, the one that Rubi had used to write down Cassie's list of contacts.

'Maybe you could draw a map, Rubi, linking all the people that have been in contact with your mum? That's proper detective work.'

Rubi took the pad happily. 'What – like Jo and Gav?'

'Yes, and Liam too. And the ginger-haired man that Gav knows. We want to see how everyone is connected.'

Rubi grinned. 'I can try.' She took the notepad and started to sketch.

Jimmy parked up in the small area behind the flats, sliding in next to a battered old car that looked like it had been dumped there.

'Can Jimmy come up?' Rubi asked. 'I want him to meet Colin!'

'Oh, I'm sure Jimmy has better things to do,' I replied, casting an unsure glance in Jimmy's direction. 'He's helped us so much already. He'll be sick of the sight of us.'

'I really don't mind,' Jimmy said casually. 'Rubi was telling me all about him in the car. I do rather like dogs, and he does sound very cute.'

I shrugged, still uncertain. 'Well, OK then, if you're sure.' I tugged on my coat and then carefully smoothed down my trousers. My stomach was churning, which was stupid as it wasn't like he was coming back to mine or anything. What on earth was wrong with me? 'I'm sure Colin would love to meet you,' I added quickly.

The block was already a hive of activity. As we neared the main building, I saw a group of youths circling in front of the cold concrete lobby. These were the younger ones. Pale kids with spotty skin and hard, fixed glares. These were the ones that usually made the most noise on the estate. They flicked their gazes at us as we passed and then quickly looked away again, uninterested. I used to feel a bit threatened by them in the past, worried that they might try and engage with me. But today was different and I barely acknowledged them. They seemed simply insignificant as I swept past, easing Rubi in front of me. In fact, as I glanced back, I noticed how young they really were. How thin the youngest one looked. How their expressions were bored, rather than angry. How had I not noticed these things before?

Jimmy touched my arm. I flinched, not meaning to, but he kept his hand there anyway, not seeming to mind. Rubi was charging ahead, walking towards the front doors as if she couldn't wait to get back. I realised she was probably hoping that her mum would be there. I hated the doubt that still carved through me, but I quickly pushed it to the back of my mind.

We were nearing the doors now. Rubi was gripping the handles and peering up towards the windows, almost as if she was hoping to catch a glimpse of her mum.

'What do you think is happening?' Jimmy asked quietly. 'What is your gut feeling here?'

I shivered. I didn't mean to, but just the sight of Rubi looking longingly towards her flat was enough to convince me.

'I'm convinced Cassie is in trouble,' I whispered. 'Serious trouble.'

The first thing I noticed was Cassie's door. I found myself just staring at it, wondering why on earth it was hanging off the hinges like that. Surely I hadn't slammed it that hard when I left before? And then I realised what had happened. For a moment it was like I couldn't breathe; something had hold of my throat and I was frozen in place.

'Fuck! It's been kicked in!' Jimmy hissed behind me. He was standing in front of Rubi as if to shield her, but I could see her pale face peeping round, her mouth forming a perfect 'O'. There was nothing I could say to make this look any better.

My brain clicked into gear. Colin! Oh my God! Was he OK?

'What's happened?' Rubi sobbed, clutching the notepad to her chest. 'Who did this?'

Before Jimmy could stop me and before I could stop myself, I ran in.

The flat was a complete mess. I picked my way over scattered cushions, upturned desk drawers and the bin, which had been spilled out on to the sofa and floor, scattering rubbish everywhere.

I imagined Cassie seeing this, looking across her destroyed room. I gasped as I saw the photo of her and Rubi lying smashed on the floor. Ruined.

Carefully I laid the picture beside the TV. At least it could be fixed. That was one thing we could sort out. The sharp glass nicked my finger and I sucked at the skin nervously, tasting the metallic tang of my blood.

Who would do something like this? This was a home. A young child's home.

'The bedroom and bathroom are empty. They've gone,' Jimmy said, coming up behind me. I turned to see Rubi, rooted by the front door. Her pale expression hadn't changed, but I could see her eyes were welling with tears. What would Cassie say when she saw this mess? How had I let this happen?

'A burglary?' I said quietly. 'Maybe I didn't lock the front door properly. Maybe they saw me leave and took a chance.'

Break-ins were relatively common around here. Only a few weeks ago I'd seen cordon-tape around a ground-floor flat and afterwards police had come door-to-door asking questions. But apparently that had been a quick in-and-out job. A laptop and a wallet stolen. Nothing like this.

Jimmy shook his head. 'If you hadn't locked up, why would they kick the door in? It wouldn't be necessary, and it would be too noisy. Anyway, if they were thieves, why did they leave that?' He pointed to the TV, which stood untouched, and a watch of Cassie's which had been thrown down on the sofa, discarded.

I was so angry I felt like I could burst into tears at any moment. 'So why do this?'

Jimmy was moving around the room. Slowly he reached down and lifted one of the desk drawers that had been dumped on the armchair.

'I don't think they were stealing,' he said. 'I think they were looking for something.'

Looking for what? I stared around the room, trying to get a sense of what had happened. And then it hit me.

'Jimmy,' I hissed, desperately not wanting Rubi to hear. 'Colin has gone.'

Chapter Eighteen

In desperation I tried calling Cassie again. My phone had missed calls, but one was from Dad and the other was another unknown number from that stupid call centre. Would they ever get the message? Guilt burned deep inside me as I glanced at Dad's missed call. I hoped he was OK. I usually had time for his chats, but right now he had to wait. Every day for most of my life I had been at his beck and call, but just this one time, I needed to put him into second place. I blinked back the tears. I just hoped he'd understand.

There was only one person I wanted to hear from right now and that was Cassie, no one else. I needed to tell her what was going on. But her phone was on voicemail once again. I didn't even bother leaving a message this time. Instead, I thumped out a short text.

Cassie. We have a problem. A big one. Call me. We need you to come home now.

What else could I say? 'Cassie, your flat has been smashed up' or 'Cassie, someone has been in here and taken Colin.' Although I wanted her to react, to take the message seriously, I didn't want to be alarmist. There was nothing worse than someone who jumped to the wrong conclusions unnecessarily.

Although, to be fair, I didn't know what other conclusions to come to at this point.

Jimmy was still pacing the floor behind me, rubbing his beard and looking particularly distressed. 'We need to call the police, Lucy. This is serious.'

'I know, I just ...' I stared at my phone, willing it to call. 'Cassie needs to know what's going on.'

'I can't believe she's still not answering. Perhaps her phone is dead or switched off,' he said, as I rammed the phone back into my pocket. 'I'm going to knock on your neighbours' doors. See if they heard anything.'

I watched him leave, not bothering to tell him that the old man on the other side of Cassie didn't answer his door for anyone. Joy used to complain about it. Shamefully I didn't even know the other neighbours on the floor. I was dimly aware of an Asian family at the end, of another single mum with three or four kids. How had I lived here for so long and not even bothered to find out who they were?

Rubi stepped towards me. 'Mum put her charger in her bag. I saw her.'

'Really?' I shrugged. 'Well ... maybe she's just not near a power socket.'

I wasn't sure that was true, though. Even I knew there are power sockets practically everywhere nowadays.

'It's more likely she's lost her phone somewhere. Put it down, forgotten where it is, or had it nicked,' I said.

'Why did they mess everything up?' Rubi whispered, looking around the room sadly. 'It's horrible in here now. They've made it horrible.'

Her hand was hanging by her side; without thinking I took it and squeezed it gently. I was pleased when Rubi sank against me a little, her head nestling against me. She gave a tired little sigh but said no more. For the moment, the silence was helpful. It was helping to clear my mind again. I pictured Columbo, standing next to us. He would be calm, of course, and his approach would be thoughtful and considered. Even something like this wouldn't rattle him. He'd still be working on putting the pieces of the jigsaw together.

If someone had come looking for something, what was it? Could this be linked to what had happened at Gav's place? It couldn't have been for valuables, so what else could it be?

What was it Cassie had said to the man as they'd left Gav's flat, the thing about not getting what he wanted? Was he looking for it here instead?

Jimmy swept back into the flat. He looked hot and flustered. 'I didn't find out much. Although Mrs Khatri at the end was very sweet and helpful. She said she heard some banging.'

Mrs Khatri. So that was her name. 'But she didn't see anything?'

'Sadly not. We are calling the police,' Jimmy said firmly. 'Enough of us trying to work out what's going on; we're just going around in circles and this could get messy. We need to formally report this burglary and the fact that Cassie has abandoned Rubi.'

Rubi gasped and buried her head against my stomach. I could feel the vibrations of her body as she sobbed. I shot Jimmy an angry look and watched as he paled.

'I'm sorry,' he dipped his head. 'I'm sorry, Rubi, I wasn't thinking. I spoke too soon. I didn't mean for it to sound as harsh as that. I'm just worried, like you are.' Rubi didn't look up. Jimmy rolled his eyes. 'This all seems to be getting a bit, well, messy, isn't it? You have to admit it, Lucy. I don't mean to be pushy here, but I do think we need to tell the police now. I'm worried, for both of you.'

'I know, Jimmy, but—'

My words were interrupted by a much louder, more confident voice by the door.

'I think I might have something of yours.'

We all turned, alarmed. I didn't immediately notice Liam standing there, a sly grin creeping up his face.

What I did notice was that Colin was clutched in his arms, panting at us quite happily, like he'd never been away.

'Colin!' Rubi ran over to him. 'I thought they took you. I thought bad men had kidnapped you.'

Liam's grin widened and he carefully placed Colin on the floor beside her. She immediately knelt and started rubbing at his fur, making those gentle cooing noises again, like he was a cute baby. The dog seemed fairly unbothered about the sudden attention and simply sat himself down, yawning widely as if we were keeping him up, and then began to lick his backside.

'I found him just now cowering in the stairwell,' Liam announced. 'He must've legged it. Stupid bugger.' He frowned, finally taking in the state of the flat. 'I saw that the door was kicked in and wondered what had happened, but I didn't expect it to be this bad ...'

Jimmy sighed. 'It's pretty bad ...' He stepped forward, held out his hand to Liam. 'I'm Jimmy. I'm a friend of Lucy's.'

My cheeks blazed a little at the term 'friend' and I turned away from Jimmy so that he didn't see. 'Jimmy has been helping us,' I told Liam.

Liam nodded. 'Good to meet you, Jimmy. I'm Liam. I live on the estate too. I know Cas and Rubi pretty well.' His eyes skated over mine. 'And I guess I know Lucy too now. A bit.' He walked further into the room, his arms swinging. 'So, who would've done Cassie over like this?'

'I don't know,' I said. 'I wish I did. I'm just trying to figure it all out in my head. It must be the same men.'

Liam frowned at me. 'What do you mean? The money-lenders?'

'Possibly.' I glanced at Rubi, not wanting to say too much in front of her. 'I went to see Gav and he's had a similar thing happen there. Some men paid him a visit and not a very nice one.'

'Men?' Liam looked worried. 'What were they like?'

'That's what I'm trying to find out, but the thing is Cassie was with them.'

'My mum!' Rubi rounded on me. 'You didn't say she was there.'

'I'm sorry, Rubi. I didn't want to upset you,' I said. 'But she's not with Gav now. We still don't know where she is.'

'You should tell me these things,' Rubi said loudly, her eyes gleaming. 'You shouldn't keep things from me. I might know stuff.'

'I didn't think—'

'Yeah, well you should, because I think I know who's done this ...' she continued, breathing hard.

We all stared at her. This tiny girl with the red face, who suddenly looked like she was ready to fight the world.

'I think it's my dad.'

'Your dad?' I said, now feeling totally confused.

'Yes. I heard you say his name before, to Jimmy. You said Harry.' Her head dropped. 'I shouldn't have been listening, but I told you, my mum always says my ears are really good. You were both talking quite loud, and my window was open ...'

Jimmy frowned. 'I'm sorry, Rubi. You weren't meant to hear us—'

'But you told me before you didn't know who your dad was,' I broke in.

Rubi was picking at the skin around her fingers, not looking at us now. She seemed strangely defiant. 'I don't know him. I've not met him. But I do know his name is Harry,' she said quietly. 'And I know Mum hates him, like really, really hates him. More than anyone.'

'Hates him?' My heart thudded a little harder. 'Are you sure?'

She nodded, her fringe bobbing in and out of her eyes. 'Yes. She told me that before. She told me he was a very bad man and that's why we could never see him. Never.'

I hesitated. 'Rubi, do you think he might be the man in the photograph that I showed you before? The one where your mum looks young. Jo did say he was an old boyfriend of your mum's.'

Rubi shrugged. 'I don't know, I've never seen him – but it might be.'

'Jo said that Cassie would never meet up with the man in the photograph again. That she'd rather cut her own nose off.' I shuddered at the thought. 'Jo couldn't remember his name. She thought it was something twatty.'

Like Harry Harris?

'So why would she meet up with him, if he was such a bad man?' I whispered.

'For the money?' Jimmy offered. 'Was she that desperate?'

'No. That makes no sense,' I said quickly. 'Gav had already told her he could help her. Why would she meet up with someone dangerous when she had a much safer option?'

'Maybe she didn't want to,' Liam said. 'I don't know this guy, but if he's bad, like Rubi says, well, maybe he came after Cassie? Maybe she's not with him out of choice.'

I swallowed, feeling the hard lump inside my throat. My gaze fluttered to Rubi who was looking strangely calm and nodding in agreement.

'I don't think Mum would want to see him again,' she said. 'She said she would never let him find us.'

'Then how did he meet up with her? Was this all just a coincidence?' I spread my arms out wide, indicating the room, Rubi, the entire situation. 'Did Cassie really only just plan to see Gav and then this Harry person just bumps into her by accident? How come she texted and phoned me like everything was fine? She never said there was a problem, only that she was delayed. Wouldn't she tell me if she was worried about something?'

'Everything is clearly not fine,' Jimmy muttered. 'She hasn't come back. Her flat's been turned over. This is all far from fine. We need the police.'

Liam shrugged, seeming to ignore Jimmy. 'Maybe she was stalling. Maybe she had to say those things to keep this Harry geezer happy?'

Could that be true? All this time I had resented her messages, thinking them selfish and flippant – when in fact they could have been hiding a darker truth. Was Cassie in real danger? I'd had fleeting thoughts like this before, but now it was feeling far more likely. My eyes trailed the flat again, taking in the mess and chaos, the utter destruction.

Cassie really was in trouble.

The thought kept re-playing in my mind like a nasty taunt. I paced the room, my gaze trawling the entire room. I was trying desperately to keep myself calm and work through this mess. How wrong I had been to doubt her. Now she needed us more than ever. There had to be some way I could help her – I couldn't let her down.

Then suddenly I spotted it. Something lying discarded by the living-room door. I don't know why, but it caught my eye. It looked like a small, folded piece of brown paper. I walked over and picked it up.

'Didn't Gav tell you that there were other people at his flat? Other men that beat him up?' Jimmy asked me suddenly.

I nodded as I unfolded the paper. 'Yes – some other big guy. And maybe one of Gav's friends. A tall guy, ginger, with a ponytail. He's always at the flat, apparently. I was going to ask you if you knew him, Liam.'

'Charlie?' Liam said, his voice almost a cackle. 'I bet that's Charlie Teasdale. He's a complete wanker. I've got no idea why Gav always chose to hang around with him. He'd sell his mum down the river for a fiver.'

'He didn't say, but his neighbour was convinced that it was one of his mates.'

Liam smacked his hand against the wall, making me jump. 'Well, that's it, isn't it? That little shit has probably been feeding this Harry information. Gav probably told Charlie that Cassie was coming to see him and Charlie fed the info back. Harry must've just been biding his time until Cassie got back into contact with Gav again.'

'But how did he know she would?' Jimmy asked. 'How did he even know about Gav in the first place?'

'I dunno,' Liam said. 'I don't know how he knew about Gav, but I guess if someone has enough contacts, he can get his information somehow, and Gav has always been a blabbermouth when it comes to his girlfriends.'

'I'd like to know how Harry found out about Gav; it's the only thing that doesn't fit,' I said thoughtfully. 'He could easily find out more once he had Gav's details. He probably knew they'd split up recently, especially if Gav has been telling the world about it.'

'Yeah, Gav has never been good at keeping himself to himself,' Liam agreed. 'I'm guessing Harry heard about the split from this Charlie and then heard that Cassie was back in contact and planning to meet up with Gav.'

'I guess it makes sense,' Jimmy agreed. 'But why come here? Why smash the place up? Gav didn't know exactly where Cassie was living, did he? Did she bring him back here? And if so, for what?'

'No,' I said quickly. 'It wasn't Cassie who brought them here, not intentionally anyway.'

I held up the brown envelope. It still had the piece missing where Cassie had ripped it off to write her number for me. How did that seem so long ago? When I flipped it over, you could clearly see Cassie's address stamped neatly on the front.

'She put this in her handbag before she left. She ripped off a piece to write her number on for me and put the rest of the letter in her bag,' I said. 'He must've found it. It would have told him all he needed to know.'

'But what did he need to know? Why did he come here? What was he looking for?' Liam demanded. 'What was he looking for here and at Gav's flat?'

I shook my head. 'It wasn't for *what*. It was for *who*.'

And my eyes rested on Rubi.

Chapter Nineteen

'I think these men intercepted Cassie on the way to Gav's,' I explained. 'It makes the most sense. They knew she was meeting Gav at that time, so maybe they were waiting just outside. The thing is they wouldn't expect her to be on her own.'

Liam raised an eyebrow. 'Go on ...'

'Well, Cassie takes Rubi everywhere with her, doesn't she? Rubi's like her shadow, except yesterday evening Cassie asks me to look after her. She tells me to protect her. She goes alone. I don't know, maybe she just had a bad feeling about it all. But I think Harry was expecting Rubi to be with her.'

'OK. Cassie left Rubi with you for safety,' Jimmy said. 'But why did they still do over Gav's place? What were they looking for?'

I frowned. 'That's the only thing I can't quite work out. There must be something else Harry and his men want, along with Rubi.'

'You need to get Rubi to a safe place. As soon as bloody possible!' Liam snapped.

Rubi screwed up her face into an angry expression. 'No! I'm not leaving. I'm staying here with Lucy.'

'We can go back to my flat,' I offered, thinking suddenly of Boris who had been left for most of the day. I desperately hoped that he was OK. This wasn't fair on him, either. 'It's late now and I'm sure Rubi could use some sleep.'

Liam shook his head. 'No. I don't like the idea of you being so close to Cassie's place. What if this Harry comes back? What if Cassie tells him that you're the one looking after Rubi? He'll know where to go. It's too risky.'

'Where, then?' I bit back, feeling frustrated now. 'If you don't want me to call the police, I don't know where else we can go.'

I didn't exactly have a long list of friends to turn to.

'No, I get that,' he said gently. 'I just want you both to be safe.'

'I want that too,' I said. 'Well, for Rubi anyway.' I couldn't say I was that bothered about myself. Rubi was my priority.

'Maybe Rubi could stay with someone else,' he offered. 'That way you would both be protected.'

Liam was staring softly at me, his eyes wide and hopeful. I was worried he might suggest taking Rubi back to his place and prepared myself for a refusal. I couldn't believe that staying at Jo's would be any safer than mine and I knew that Rubi wouldn't want to stay there.

I also realised I wasn't prepared to let her go. Not now. Not after all this. We'd come such a long way already and as far as I was concerned, she was my responsibility until I could find Cassie. I wasn't prepared to step back now. I made myself stand up straight and looked Liam right in the eye.

'No. I'm sorry. I promised Cassie that I would look after Rubi and that's what I'm going to do. I'm keeping her with me. It's the one thing I said I would do.'

'I want to stay with Lucy,' Rubi added softly. 'I don't want her leaving me too.'

I think my heart split open a little. I turned towards her and gave her a reassuring smile. That wasn't going to happen. I wouldn't let it.

'You can both stay at mine,' Jimmy offered suddenly. 'I have a two-bed place a mile or so away. I mean, the spare room is a bit of a state – it's where I store all my stuff – but if you don't mind a bit of mess . . .'

'Oh, Jimmy. I don't know, I—'

'Sounds ideal, mate!' Liam said.

I glared at Liam and then slowly turned my attention back to Jimmy. I saw he was having difficulty maintaining eye contact with me.

'I'm sorry, Jimmy. I don't mean to sound blunt but I'm not sure it would be appropriate. I mean, you're my boss—'

Jimmy's eyes seemed to blaze. 'Not appropriate? What are you talking about? You've worked with me for five years, Lucy. If I was some axe-wielding maniac, I think you'd have worked it out by now . . .' He stuttered a little. 'I thought perhaps you'd trust me. I've been trying to help you both all afternoon. What do you think of me? I'm trying to be your friend here. I want to help . . .'

I stared back at him, my hands falling uselessly to my side. Part of me wanted to take his hand and tell him just how thankful I was. But the other part of me, the stronger side, was so scared to do the wrong thing, to say something silly or act in a clumsy way. I felt rooted to the spot, paralysed by indecision.

I didn't know the right words to say. It was far easier to see him as my work colleague and nothing more. But the lines were becoming blurred now and it was making my mind buzz with confusion. Was Jimmy really my friend?

'If you're sure?' I said carefully. Jimmy caught my eye and smiled weakly.

'Of course I'm sure. I couldn't be more sure.'

'But what about Colin?' Rubi asked. 'He has to come. He's scared too.'

'Colin is fine to come,' Jimmy said. 'I quite like dogs. I'm sure he won't mind the mess either.'

I looked up again. 'Jimmy, I'm sorry; "appropriate" wasn't the right word. I just don't feel very comfortable in other people's houses. I'm not really used ...'

I let the sentence drift.

Liam walked towards me. He was looking at me differently. His gaze was still quite intense, but it had lost its edge. He tipped his head slightly to one side. 'Lucy, he's making sense, you know. If you and Rubi sleep there tonight you'll be keeping her safe. No one, not even Cassie, would know you were there. There's no way Harry could find her. It's a perfect solution.' He paused. 'And you'll be OK too. That makes me more comfortable.'

'But what do we do in the meantime?' I shifted on the spot. 'If Cassie's in trouble. Maybe I should call the police and tell them. This has gone too far now, hasn't it?'

Liam shrugged. 'And what will you tell them exactly? That Cass left Rubi with you and disappeared? What do you think they'll do next? They'll talk to Gav and find out she was there when he got beaten up.' His voice lowered. 'Do you really think they'll believe she's in trouble, that she needs their help, or do you think they'll come to the helpful conclusion that Cass is a nasty con artist who's dumped her kid on the nearest neighbour and legged it? They never fucking believed my mum when she reported my old man for beating her up. They just assumed they were two pissheads out of control.' He sighed. 'I told you before, it's different for people like us. We're not well-spoken, middle-class types – we're nobodies that no fucker cares about. They will take Rubi away from her mum, away from the people who love and care about her, fuck off and leave a mess behind.'

He stepped back as if exhausted. My eyes found his again and I nodded. A tired smile settled on his lips. I think, finally, I understood him completely and he got that.

'You're right. It's different for us,' I repeated.

My background hadn't caused what had happened to me, but it hadn't helped. As soon as Mum died, and Dad lost his job and got swept into the world of benefit queues and smoky pubs, our destinies changed.

So many bad things had happened to us. Things could've been different.

'I'll sort this all out,' Liam said. 'I'll speak to Gav's mate, that bloody weasel Charlie. I'll find out who this Harry is and where exactly he is, and we can go from there.'

'But ...' My voice faltered. 'Do you really think you can?'

Liam simply grinned. 'Never underestimate anyone, Lucy. Least of all me.'

*

I was temporarily back in my own flat, numbly throwing a few clothes into an old Tesco bag that I found in the kitchen. I didn't want to stay away, not again. I was worried about Boris. I didn't want to leave him in the flat again for so long – just the thought was making me feel unbalanced and nauseous. I left enough food to keep him going and whispered that I would be back the next day, but as he purred between my legs, I felt so guilty.

'I'll be home soon, Boris,' I promised. 'All of this will be over soon. Rubi will be with her mum. Everything will be back to normal.'

My fingers ran quickly through his fur, working back and forth, trying to settle my thoughts.

Next door, I knew they were still talking, making plans, deciding the next best move. Jimmy seemed to like Liam and, more importantly, trust him. If I was honest, I didn't really know who or what to trust any more. All I knew for certain was that we were running out of both time and options. I kept thinking of Cassie – kept picturing her pretty, determined face. Was she OK? Or had she been hurt? Cassie would know how to look after herself. Surely she would be all right?

Around my feet Boris continued to purr, snaking his soft fur against my skin. He was so desperate for attention. I cleaned his litter trays and refilled his bowls, whilst desperately trying to reassure him, and myself.

'I will be back soon. Back to snuggles on the chair and long, comforting TV programmes. Back to silence and solitude. Back to our safe, boring life.'

I sighed. My God, I'd done more this weekend than I'd done in who knows how long. I'd probably need a week of not speaking to people to recover from it.

I hadn't put much in my bag, just a change of clothes, fresh underwear, my roll-on deodorant and a toothbrush. After all, it was just one night. That was all. Hopefully Liam would be able to sort this all out and we would know where Cassie was after that. We could find her and bring her home.

And if not? I paused and squashed the bag between my fists. Well, if not, I would call the police whether Liam liked it or not. I still absolutely hated the idea of involving them and social workers, but this situation couldn't carry on indefinitely, it just couldn't. It might be time to stop playing at being Columbo and call in the real experts.

But what about Rubi? What would they do with her?

I marched past Boris and let myself out on to the balcony. The burst of sharp night air was what I needed. Tentatively I leant up against the railings and peered over. Of course, everything was the same as before – the lit-up flats opposite, the snaking paths below, the overgrown shrubs, the hard, unforgiving concrete; but at the same time so much was different now. I'd never really seen the estate as anything other than a place to live before. I would walk quickly across the grounds and hurry into my flat, not bothering to get to know anyone else who lived here. I'd never noticed Jo or Liam before, and if they hadn't made an effort with me, I would never have known Cassie or Rubi. Not properly, anyway. After all, what effort did I put in with Joy, really? I only ever did the basics; I never let her into my life. If I'd had my way, they would've been just more strangers in this block. Faces that I would never bother to get to know.

It had never worried me before, but now I thought back to what Joy had said. I needed to let people in. For so long I had pushed them away – scared of what they might do to me and, more significantly, scared of what I might do to them.

I wasn't sure if I could do that any more. The little girl with the heavy fringe and piercing stare had changed everything.

She'd made me want to feel wanted.

I was exhausted and the headache that had been threatening to erupt for so long was now drilling behind my eyes. I looked over at the balcony of Cassie's flat, to the tiny, battered chairs that she had put out there and the fairy lights she had pinned around her own railings, making her side so much more inviting and fun. In the corner I could see Rubi's bike, a pair of roller-boots and a pair of discarded wellingtons. Cassie and Rubi's life, still contained in this one scene. I remembered I'd seen Cassie standing a few inches away from me, peering out over her own balcony, cigarette dangling from her hand so that the grey smoke danced in the air in front of her. How long ago had that been – just a few weeks? But it seemed like years now.

'Just look out there,' she'd said when she noticed me. 'And you see life. Everyone else living. Getting on.'

I had been a bit irritated at the time, too busy reading my book to join in her conversation. But I had looked up, nodded, acknowledged her. I don't think she minded my aloofness, though, because she just smiled and carried on.

'It makes you realise you're never alone. Not really,' she'd said, not looking at me. Just staring out into the space.

I put my book down then and thought about that statement.

'I'm always alone,' I told her. I wasn't looking for her pity. It was just a fact. Something I was used to.

Cassie did something then that had surprised me. She laughed. A real, hearty laugh, her cigarette bouncing up and down in the air.

'Alone! You silly bugger. You're not alone! You just choose to be. There's people all around you just waiting for you to get to know.'

And then she'd turned, winked at me and gone back into her flat, leaving me churning over those thoughts – not really understanding what she meant.

I found I was staring now at the space where Cassie once had been, wishing so badly that she was still there, so that I could hear her laugh again. So that I could ask her what she had meant and then I would ask her how she'd worked me out in such a short amount of time. How was that possible?

'Lucy?'

I blinked and shook myself out of my trance. I hadn't noticed Rubi creep in, yet there she was standing next to me. Colin was clasped in her arms. Her pretty, round face was staring up at me. She looked worried and so tired. Darkness smudged under her eyes like bruises.

'Rubi? I'm sorry, I was just—'

Rubi nodded, smiled a little. 'It's OK,' she said.

And then, wordlessly, she sat on the chair next to me and we both gazed out in silence. At the space where Cassie had once stood.

*

Jimmy was quiet as he drove us back to his house. He seemed different now, less cheerful and more thoughtful. He turned on the radio low and focused most of his attention on the road, barely talking to either of us. Behind me, Rubi was curled up in the back seat looking suspiciously as if she might sleep at any moment. We had already filled her with a McDonald's Happy Meal from the drive-through. She had been delighted by the second McDonald's of the weekend. I figured it wouldn't hurt her this once.

Liam had left us earlier, his phone glued to his hand and with a barked promise to us that he would do all he could to track Cassie down.

'He's probably no biggie, this Harry,' he shrugged as he walked away. 'Just some idiot who likes pushing women around, and Gav, who's a pussy anyway. If the right people have a word I'm sure all of this can be sorted out.'

The right people? I shivered at the thought. I had a horrible idea that the 'right' people were probably as far away from that word as you could get. I thought it best not to ask any more.

So now what could we do but wait? Liam had both our numbers. In my hand I clasped my phone, just in case he called with an immediate update. Or even on the off-chance that Cassie made contact. I think a part of me was hoping that her phone had simply run out of charge. Or was broken. I had to believe she would find a way to contact me.

I checked my missed calls again. Just Dad and those unknown numbers. The call centre, of course, but then a cold sensation washed over me. What if it wasn't those annoying buggers? What if Cassie had tried to contact me another way? I groaned at the thought.

'Are you OK?' Jimmy asked.

'I'm not sure ...' I was still staring hopelessly at the missed numbers. 'I just hope I haven't messed up. I'm going to answer every call from now on, no matter what it is.'

'Sounds wise.'

'But if it's those insurance idiots again – I might lose my rag.'

Jimmy chuckled. 'I wouldn't blame you.'

I couldn't believe how tired I felt. It was getting late now, almost nine, and the quiet, soulful music on the radio was lulling me into a trance. I longed to close my eyes and fully relax, but that felt wrong somehow, with so much going on. What would I normally be doing around now? A small smile escaped me. Saturday night. Usually, I would have a long soak in the bath, with the temperature just right. Then I would wrap myself in my soft, soft dressing gown and watch a film. Saturday nights were always film nights, the older the better.

'What are you grinning at?'

Jimmy's voice broke my spell. He glanced over at me, an eyebrow slightly raised. I felt myself redden.

'Oh – it's silly really.'

'What is? Go on, tell me.' He was coaxing me. It was hard not to be encouraged. I carefully shifted in my seat, waking myself up a little.

'I was thinking that Saturday is usually my film night. I always put one on. It's one of my things.'

'One of your "things"?' He grinned. 'Isn't that what makes you so special? What's silly about that?'

I concentrated my gaze out of the window, aware that my cheeks were properly burning up now. Did he really just call me special? He couldn't have meant that, surely? This normal, down-to-earth guy driving the car. What would he think if he knew everything about me? He wouldn't think I was special then.

'You know I have my silly, dull routines,' I said, feeling unusually unguarded. 'I guess it's because I've been on my own for so long now, I like to keep things the same. I guess I usually eat the same food on the same day. I watch *Columbo* every Friday. Saturday is film night. I like to take my long walk on a Sunday.'

'That's not silly. That's just the way you live your life,' he said. 'And to be honest, I quite like *Columbo* too.'

I wasn't looking at him, so I didn't know whether he was smirking at me or not. Was he just humouring me, trying to make me feel nice? I kept staring out of the window, feeling a little light-headed.

'I have things too,' he said casually. 'I like watching box sets on a Friday and having a curry on a Saturday. It's not so unusual to have little routines.'

'Really?'

'Really.' He chuckled. 'You're not weird, Lucy. Not at all. But maybe, you're just a little bit lonely. Like me?'

I turned, my head still fuzzy and light, my mouth strangely dry. 'Maybe. Maybe I am.'

Jimmy glanced at me. His eyes were sparkling, his lips curved into a smile. 'Actually, I think—'

But I was already flapping my hand for him to stop talking. My phone was ringing. I snapped it open quickly, eager to hear Cassie's voice on the other end.

'Lucy!'

'Dad,' I replied, trying to hide the disappointment. 'Are you OK? I'm a bit busy.'

He laughed, his wheezy laugh that came from deep within him. It was particularly loud this time. It sounded like tiny stones were rattling around his chest cavity. 'Busy? Blimey, Duck. What's with all the excitement this weekend? You seem to be very popular all of a sudden.'

I glanced over my shoulder at Rubi; her eyes were closed, her mouth ever so slightly open as she slept. I wasn't sure I could call this whole situation exciting. In fact, that was probably the last word for it.

'Where are you?' he asked, sounding a bit sad now. I heard him resettling himself, banging something around next to him. His cigarette tin, most probably. 'I keep phoning you. Why don't you answer?'

'I couldn't answer, Dad. I'm sorry. It's been a crazy day. I have Rubi still. I need to get her to bed.'

There was a pause. He sniffed. 'You still have that poor girl? Why? What's going on? Why haven't you called the police yet?'

My heart rate was soaring again, I hated this. Dad always knew when I was lying. He always said I was rubbish at it.

'I've just been asked to look after her a little bit longer.'

'But why you?' he probed. 'Listen – are you in some kind of trouble?'

I moved the phone to my other ear, glanced at Jimmy as if I could get him to help me, but his eyes were on the road.

'I'm fine, Dad. Everything is fine.' I tried to be firm.

He snorted. 'Nah – something's up. I can tell. Are they blackmailing you? Bribing you? Is she trying to get you to have her girl while they go out partying? I bet she's not even paying you!' He muttered something under his breath. 'You know you're a soft touch, Lucy, people take advantage ...'

'No, Dad!' I took my glasses off, rubbed at my sore eyes. 'No one is taking advantage of me.'

'Are you sure?'

'Yes ...'

'That girl needs to be with her mother.'

I nodded my head weakly. 'I know. I'm sorting it.'

'You come over tomorrow morning first thing and we can talk then. Bring the girl with you if her mum still isn't back. We need to sort this out.' He coughed. I heard the deep wheeze once again and wondered if he was OK. It sounded particularly nasty.

I breathed out hard, feeling the roll of sickness inside me. I sensed Jimmy shifting in the driver's seat but I couldn't bring myself to look at him. I didn't want to see the questions blazing in his eyes.

I went to reply to Dad, but the line had already gone dead. He had gone. Satisfied that I would do as I was told, as I always did.

'What did he say?' Jimmy asked. 'Your dad's an ex-copper, isn't he? He must have a view on this.'

'He has a view, all right …' I said. 'He's not happy about it. He thinks Cassie is scamming me, but he doesn't know the full facts. He wants me to see him tomorrow.'

'And do you want to see him?'

I shrugged. 'I guess he might be able to help.'

Although right now everything felt so surreal. Was I really going to be turning to my dad for help with this mystery? When did my life suddenly become so chaotic and, well – interesting? I hated to admit it, but my body and mind were buzzing with anticipation. Was a small part of me actually beginning to enjoy this? Surely not …

Jimmy swung the car into a parking space. 'We're here!' he said brightly. He pulled up the handbrake and turned towards me. 'Are you sure you're OK?'

'Yeah, it's just all a bit crazy …' I sighed. 'I just want to do the right thing here. I want to solve this puzzle once and for all.'

Jimmy nodded slowly, like he was thinking that through. 'Look, I'll give you a lift to your dad's in the morning. That'll save you some time. You're right, he probably will help, being ex-forces and that.'

'Jimmy – you don't have to. You've already done enough. I'm sure you have better things to do.'

'It's Sunday tomorrow. The shop is closed. I've got nothing else planned. Besides, I want to help you, I really do,' he said, his voice firmer than I'd ever heard it before. 'And you're going to let me.'

Chapter Twenty

Jimmy's flat was in a modern block on the other side of the city, a part I rarely visited. This was where all the main office blocks and nice residential apartments were. I knew there was a lake nearby and that we were walking distance to the mainline station. I noticed that the grass verges around the blocks had been neatly trimmed and the trees were pruned and in keeping with the modern design. I felt weirdly nervous approaching the building. This was the first time I had been inside anyone else's home who wasn't on my estate, or wasn't my dad.

I looked up at the flats themselves. They were so different to my dull concrete tower. This building was lower, a more human scale, built with a characterful textured buff brick.

'Like it?' Jimmy asked, as we walked towards the main lobby. He glanced at me shyly, like he was keen to hear my opinion.

'It's really nice,' I said.

'It's really posh,' Rubi said, which was actually what I was thinking too. Strange, really, as I never thought of Jimmy as being particularly posh or wealthy. I suppose I always naively assumed that people who could afford these places would be uppity and rude, and Jimmy was neither of these things. In fact, he was one of the most laid-back people I knew.

'I was lucky, I bought it at the bottom of the market with money I inherited from my uncle.' He shrugged. 'I'm not posh at all.'

He led us in through the access-only doorway. There were no lifts, so we had to go through the stairwell to the second floor. It was a cleaner, fresher block than ours, but I couldn't help thinking how soulless it was, too – almost like it had no character to mark it out as its own.

'Here we go.' Jimmy led us towards number thirty-three and thrust his key in the door. It was very bland from outside, just a simple white door with its brass letterbox. No WELCOME mat. No ornaments outside. No hand-made sign like mine, telling people to go away ...

God, why did I do that ...

We walked inside. Rubi was still sleepy and dragging behind us. Jimmy, seeming to notice this, guided her gently towards the first door.

'This is my spare room,' he said softly, opening it up. 'It's a bit of a state, as you can see, but the bed is really comfy, and it's already made up. I don't really have that many people stopping over, but I like having it looking nice.'

The room was small but compact. The bed was rammed up against one wall, a navy cover pulled tight across it. The rest of the room was made up mainly of boxes and a large glass cabinet in the corner. I peered at it, curious. Inside was a collection of figures. Some of them I vaguely recognised.

'The boxes are full of books. Videos. All sorts of collectables. My ex made me hide them away, she couldn't stand the sight of them.' Jimmy shrugged. 'What can I say? I love *Star Wars*.'

'I've never seen it,' I admitted.

Jimmy gasped; his mouth actually dropped wide open in shock. 'You're not serious? Not even one? Not even the very first one? Surely you *must* have seen that one?'

I shook my head. 'No. Unless you count the five minutes I saw once before Dad snapped it off.'

'My mum likes *Star Wars*,' Rubi announced in a small, tired voice. She sat down on the bed and yawned. 'She keeps saying that we're going to watch them all together. One day ...'

'Your mum has good taste,' Jimmy told her. 'And one day you really must watch them all.'

Rubi smiled lazily, her eyes heavy. 'I will.'

'And so should you, Lucy.' He paused, his gaze lingering on the boxes. 'I mean – I could put one on now if you like?'

Rubi shook her head, her eyes immediately snapping open again. 'No, I want to watch them with my mum. She promised me.'

Jimmy sighed. 'Of course. That makes sense. Well, you can borrow them any time.'

'You can watch it with us,' Rubi said to me. 'Would you like that?'

I stuttered a little. 'Oh ... yes ... maybe, Rubi.'

What I couldn't quite tell her was how much I would like that. The words were there, but somehow, I couldn't quite bring myself to say them out loud. In all honesty, I was surprised by my own reaction. This wasn't like me at all, and yet, I knew this was something I really wanted to do. I *wanted* to watch a film with Rubi.

In fact, I knew that I would love to.

*

Rubi's teeth were brushed and she was tucked up so tightly in bed I could barely see her face, just the tip of her nose and her eyes, which were half closed by now. I still wasn't sure what I was really meant to do next. I had no story to read her. What did parents usually say to their children at bedtimes? I had nothing to go on. For as long as I could remember, I had taken myself off to bed, reading or staring at images in my book and then turning out my light when I was ready.

Jimmy stepped into the room. He glanced over at Rubi in bed and me folding the edge of her duvet carefully into place. His eyes settled on mine; there was a softness there that immediately made me feel relaxed and calm.

'Are you girls OK? Is there anything more I can get you?'

'I think we're fine.' I patted the duvet gently. 'Rubi looks ready for sleep already.'

'I'm not sleepy ...' Rubi muttered, but her heavy eyes betrayed her.

Jimmy rested his hand carefully on my shoulder. It felt odd there, but not uncomfortable. A warm feeling tingled down my spine. 'Just shout if you need anything. Anything at all.'

'Thank you.' I smiled weakly and felt a sense of dis-appointment as his hand left my body. I quite liked it there, the weight and presence of it. I felt suddenly empty.

He left the room quietly, creeping out with surprising grace for a man of his size. I watched as he carefully pulled the door closed.

It was just us again, alone. Rubi drew a shaky breath.

'When will Mum call, Lucy?' Her voice was now barely a whisper.

291

I shifted on the bed; I was tired also. It was all I could do not to curl up beside her and drift off to sleep.

'I don't know,' I said. 'But I do know that she loves you and she will want you to sleep right now.'

'We don't even know where she is.' Rubi shuffled further down in the bed. 'I'm scared.'

'What are you scared of?'

'I'm scared she won't come back at all. That I'll never see her again.'

I could've said more to her. I could've told her that I understood and that I was still haunted by the fact that I'd never see my mother's face again. But I knew it was different for me. My mother hadn't been Cassie. Towards the end, she had periods of being quite cold and distant – as if she was slowly switching off from this world. Having a young child hadn't been enough to save her. But I was sure Cassie wasn't like my mum. She loved Rubi. That was one thing I had to believe. I was holding on to it for dear life.

'Your mum won't let that happen,' I said. And I just prayed I was right.

Rubi breathed out softly. For a moment I thought she was finally going off, so I eased myself up and got ready to leave the room.

'I know something ...'

'Rubi. You need to sleep now, really.'

'Jimmy really likes you, you know,' she said quietly.

'Don't be silly ...'

'He does ... I heard him tell Liam. He said, "She might be difficult to get to know, but there's something special about her." He told Liam that you were special. He told Liam he should be nice to you.'

'Why would he say that?' I said, confused.

She giggled gently. 'Because he really likes you, silly.'

I frowned. I couldn't believe he'd feel like that about me. Why would he? This was kind, funny, sociable Jimmy. A man who had been in love before and had his heart broken and didn't have time for that nonsense again. He'd never like someone like me. Not like that.

Why on earth would he?

I found Jimmy in his small living room, making up a duvet cover. He was humming softly under his breath and barely noticed when I walked into the room. I quickly scanned around me. It was nice in here, uncluttered – not at all like the room Rubi was in. The sofa and armchair were expensive-looking black leather. The walls were completely bare apart from a large abstract painting on the far wall. It was a mixture of smudgy, swirly colours and just looking at it for too long made my eyes ache a little, but that could've been the tiredness. I turned hastily away and moved instead towards Jimmy.

He looked up and smiled brightly.

'I've already changed my own bed,' he said matter-of-factly. 'You can sleep in my room tonight and I'll kip on here.'

I shook my head. 'Oh no, Jimmy, don't put yourself out like that! I'll be fine on the chair.'

He smiled at me, still gripping the bedding. 'It's no bother, Lucy. I'd much prefer you were in comfort and, to be honest, I'm used to sleeping here – the number of times I've crashed out here ...'

'Only if you're sure?'

'I'm sure.' He laid out the duvet, smoothing it down. 'It's no problem, honestly.'

I hesitated, watching him work for a moment, but I realised I couldn't keep quiet much longer. The frustration was building inside me.

'Why did you tell Liam to be nice to me?' I said a bit too quickly.

He looked confused. 'I—'

'I'm not some charity case.' I was shaking now, trying so hard to stop myself. 'I don't need people to keep looking out for me because they feel sorry for me.'

Tears stung my eyes; I looked away. I couldn't bear the way he was staring back at me. He looked wounded, like I had just struck him in the face.

'It wasn't like that, Lucy.' His voice was weak.

'Then what was it like?' I rammed my hands up against my eyes. 'It feels like you think I'm some kind of poor soul that needs looking after. Poor lonely old Lucy. I just want ... I just want ...'

'What? What do you want?' He was louder now, more insistent.

I was drifting, unbalanced – no longer angry, just miserable and so, so bloody tired. 'I just want to feel normal,' I said.

I just want the bad feelings to go away ...

Jimmy snorted.

'And what the fuck is normal?' He gestured around the room. 'Is this normal? Eh? A forty-year-old man, lonely, living on his own and collecting *Star Wars* dolls? Some days he's so fucking bored he even talks to himself. Is that normal? Honestly?'

I stared back at him. He didn't know the rest of it.

He still didn't know the real me.

Jimmy stepped forward; he hadn't finished.

'Is it normal for a young mum to be struggling to make ends meet? That this same mum is so desperate that she contacts an ex-boyfriend and gets into God knows what trouble?'

I hugged myself tightly, looked away.

'Is normal a young boy, hanging around in gangs because his mum is too off her face to deal with him?' He nodded. 'Yeah, Liam told me a bit about his situation. It's not nice. That kid has been through a lot. That's why I asked him to look out for you, because deep down he understands. He knows what it's like to feel alone.'

'I like being alone,' I said, my voice wobbly. I was clenching and unclenching my hands. My skin was so hot it felt on fire.

It's easier that way.

'Do you, though? Really?' He shrugged. 'Yeah, sure it's nice to be by yourself sometimes. But it's also nice to have people with you on occasion. If only you let them in ...'

'I'm different to you.'

'No ... you're not so much.'

I bowed my head. Wasn't it true that I had enjoyed Jimmy's company today? And Rubi ... Even the thought of Rubi sleeping in that room made my heart stir a little. I never thought emotions like that could be possible.

Jimmy's voice was much softer now, barely a whisper.

'Is normal this? A sad, desperate man, trying every single day to get his work colleague to notice him because he can't stop thinking about her.'

I shivered, my skin prickling, my legs feeling like they were floating. 'Me?' I whispered.

'Yes, you. You daft bugger.' His cheeks were glowing. I could see beads of sweat on his brow. 'I've been struggling to say anything. After my relationship with Ria went so badly wrong, I didn't want to mess up our friendship too, but ...' He paused. 'I just need you to know how I feel.'

I frowned, unsure.

'I'm sorry ...' I muttered. 'I can't ... You don't know—'

'I don't know what?' His eyes fixed on mine. I could see warmth there again, real, deep warmth that made my insides fizz with confusion. 'Lucy. Just tell me. What is it?'

I shook my head. 'It's me. I'm complicated. There's stuff, so much stuff you don't know about me.'

'So! I don't care. We all have history.' He rubbed his chin, studying me, and then slowly he stepped towards me. 'What won't I understand? Lucy, please – just talk to me.'

'No!' My voice was sharper now. I held out my hands to stop him.

'OK, OK,' he said, his voice barely a breath. 'I get it.'

'I'm sorry, Jimmy,' I stuttered. 'It's just ...'

'It's fine,' he said, his voice still soft but with a hint of resignation. 'I get it. I really do.' He moved away from me and towards the hall. 'You look tired, Lucy. Shall I show you your room? I think we both need some rest now.'

I nodded, not knowing what else to do. Anything I said now would be clumsy and wrong and would probably make things a million times worse. I moved mechanically behind him. I was so churned up inside. I couldn't believe for one moment that Jimmy liked me in that way ... and yet ...

I wasn't sure I could properly explain the reasons why I froze. I hadn't meant to offend him. In fact, I was mortified that I had – but he had caught me totally off guard. I didn't know *how* to react to emotional outbursts like this. It was all just very overwhelming. I felt like my head was about to burst.

He showed me into his bedroom. It was clean, tidy and light. The bed was massive and inviting me to sink into it. I almost groaned in anticipation of the soft mattress and fresh sheets. How was I so tired? Suddenly all my bones seemed to be aching and struggling to keep me upright.

'Jimmy ...'

I wanted to tell him then. I really did. But as he turned to face me, his expression open and ready to listen, I felt the same resistance come back. The overwhelming fear that Jimmy might not really like the true me, that this was just him feeling sorry for me and trying to make me feel better. My throat thickened and the words trickled back within me.

'Thank you,' I said instead.

The words drifted, hanging between us. I wanted him to know how much I meant this. I opened my mouth to say more, but then I saw something in Jimmy's face I hadn't seen before. Something so unfamiliar and foreign on his features that it made me freeze. It was disappointment.

I had let him down. Oh God, I really had. My heart felt suddenly heavy.

My mouth stayed open, but nothing came out. I was struck dumb again. Useless.

'It's OK,' he said.

Then he walked out, closing the door softly behind him.

I slept better than I had expected. Despite all the confusion and dramas of the day, my brain allowed itself to be turned off. Even stranger, I managed to sleep right through until morning. This was pretty much unheard of for me. Usually, I would struggle to get to sleep, or wake up several times in the night and have difficulty drifting back off. It was actually a relief to open my eyes and feel rested.

Almost immediately, I recalled the events from before. Cassie still not returning. Gav being beaten up. Cassie's flat being turned over and then Jimmy's strange confession to me before bedtime. There was just too much to deal with.

I sat up and stretched, my eyes adjusting to the new space around me. I reached for my glasses and welcomed the new sights that greeted me, liking how Jimmy had kept everything minimal and tucked away. On the table beside his bed was a book, some fantasy novel with a silver dragon on the cover. Judging by the state of it, he'd had the book for some time. There was also a glass of water and a small clock radio beside it. I glanced at the time: seven thirty. I wondered wearily whether Rubi was up yet but felt strangely awkward about leaving the room. What if Jimmy was still asleep in the living room? I didn't want to disturb him. I listened hard, hoping to hear some sounds of movement in the flat – but there was nothing at all. They must both still be sleeping.

Sinking back in the bed, I reached for my phone which I'd left on the floor. The light was flashing, indicating that I had a message. Suddenly, I was wide awake.

It was Cassie.

Luci. I'm so sorry, it's been a nightmare. My friend is coming to pick Ruby up for me. Let him take her, it's OK. I don't need you now. Are you at the flat now? Thank you

I read and re-read the message several times, my stomach sinking on each occasion. I didn't have to be Columbo to work this out.

No. This isn't right.

This isn't good at all.

I threw the phone on the bed, took my glasses off and rubbed my eyes, trying desperately to fight back the nausea that was now rising up my throat. The only thing I knew for certain was that I didn't like this message at all.

It was telling me that things were now much, much worse.

Chapter Twenty-One

'How do you know?' Jimmy was re-reading the message, a puzzled look etched on his face. Rubi, thankfully, was still sleeping, but we kept our voices low just in case. I had been caught out too many times before by her sharp hearing.

I moved closer to Jimmy. I must've looked awful, having rushed out of the bedroom and just thrown on the clothes I'd worn yesterday. Still, I was glad to discover that Jimmy was awake. He had been so quiet I had assumed he was still in bed, so I was surprised to find him pottering around in the kitchen.

'Look how she spelt Rubi. With a "y". And she spelt my name with an "i". Who would make that mistake twice?' I said, pointing at the message. 'I'm pretty sure it's a clue. Maybe Cassie was made to send this, but she's telling us something is wrong. It's her way of warning us,' I hissed at him. 'I can understand her misspelling my name, but what mother gets her own kid's name wrong?'

Jimmy wasn't as convinced. 'It's just a misspelling. Everyone does that, especially when they're in a rush.'

I snatched the phone back, frustrated. 'I don't think so. Not twice like that, it's too much of a coincidence.'

'But isn't Harry Rubi's dad?' Jimmy asked. 'Surely he'd know her name? Wouldn't he have noticed?'

'But he hasn't been around for years, has he? I'm guessing he forgot how Cassie spelt it.'

Jimmy shook his head. 'I dunno. I feel like we're clutching at straws, thinking the worst. This could just as easily be Cassie sending out a quick message telling us what to do next. Shouldn't we listen to her?'

'Should we?' I sat myself down on the edge of the sofa. 'This text made me rethink everything. I remembered Cassie's first voicemail message to me, something was bugging me about it, so I replayed it this morning. Listen . . .'

I dialled up voicemail then handed my phone to Jimmy. 'I'm sorry,' I apologised. 'You'll have to skip through my dad's messages, but Cassie's message is there too. I saved it. It's on Friday. Just wait.'

Jimmy stood with the phone pressed up against his ear, moving his head from side to side when my dad's voice came on. Then his expression changed. I could tell he was concentrating. He held the phone away from his face and pressed redial, then listened again. Finally, he gave it back to me, his frown much deeper.

'I'm not sure what this proves,' he said. 'I'm sorry, I can't hear anything strange.'

'Listen again.'

This time I played it out loud, so we could both hear the message. Not that I needed to; I already knew it off by heart, having listened to it several times already this morning.

'Lucy – I'm so sorry . . . Look, something has come up. I'm, I'm being held . . . OK, OK. I'm being held up, yeah? Yeah, do you

understand? Please – please just look after Rubi for a bit longer. I'll be home soon, Lucy, I promise – just keep her with you ...'

'Did you notice the emphasis on "being held" the first time she says it?' I whispered carefully so Rubi couldn't hear. 'How she asks if I understand?'

Jimmy shrugged. 'I just assumed that she meant "held up" but she didn't finish her sentence. She repeats it again, so that makes sense.'

'That's what I thought at first, but her voice doesn't drift off. It's a sentence of its own.' I shook my head, frustrated. 'I'm beginning to think that's her way of telling me she's in trouble. She adds the "held up" after because she has to. Maybe someone is listening in?'

'I'm really not sure,' Jimmy said. He began pacing the room. 'This seems too over the top. Are you sure you've not been watching too many *Columbo* episodes? You're even beginning to sound like him!'

I glared at him. 'So what if I am? Columbo would have worked this all out in minutes! He'd never miss something as obvious as this.' I took a breath, trying to calm myself. 'Jimmy, this is serious. I have a horrible feeling I was missing the clues Cassie was setting out for me. I could've been wasting time, thinking Cassie was messing me around when in fact the whole time she was trying to tell me something bad was happening to her from the start.'

'Maybe.'

'And then there's the call I made to her, when I heard voices in the background. I thought I heard her sigh.' I paused, my skin prickling. 'But maybe she couldn't talk. Or wasn't able to?'

'Lucy, you can't be sure of that.'

'And the missed calls? Look, I've had at least four from unknown numbers. I ignored them because I thought it was that stupid call centre again. But what if I was wrong? What if she was trying to make contact another way?'

Jimmy rubbed his chin. He looked uneasy. 'This isn't for us to work out, Lucy. We're not detectives.'

I flicked through the messages, the few texts she had sent afterwards. 'None of these seem right,' I muttered. I landed on the latest one and my stomach churned. 'Especially not this one.'

'Because of the spelling?' he asked.

'Yes, maybe ...' I pushed a sheet of paper in front of him. 'This is what Rubi was doing for me. She was linking up all the names on the map. See how everything connects – Cassie, Gav, the debt collectors, Harry. All these potentially dodgy people link into Cassie. They could all mean her harm. There's no one here I trust or think she could be safe with. Even Gav has reason to be angry with her.'

'Yes ... yes, I can see that.'

'Not only that,' I said softly; my voice was shaky now. 'But when Cassie left, she made me promise to stay with Rubi and wait for her. In her voicemail she insists I keep her with me. But this text message is completely different – this one is telling me to give Rubi to someone else. A stranger. I'm pretty sure Cassie would never agree to that. It goes against everything else she said before.'

'What are you saying?' Jimmy's voice was barely a breath.

'I'm saying that maybe Cassie didn't send this message at all. Or if she did, she's trying to tell me something. She's warning me.' I paused. 'Maybe Cassie is in even more danger than we first thought. And if she's in danger, so is Rubi.'

'OK, now we call the police, surely?' Jimmy was looking more and more uncomfortable. 'I dunno. This feels all wrong now. It's going too far. I think we should call them and ...'

'And what?' I sighed. 'It's like Liam said, they'll probably just jump to conclusions. They might think that Cassie was neglectful, or I might get into trouble.'

Jimmy screwed up his face, not seeming to like the thought of that.

'I might get into trouble for not reporting it straight away,' I continued. 'I'm pretty sure now I'd be judged for keeping hold of Rubi. Would they really understand?'

Jimmy nodded. 'There is that.'

I thought of the things Liam had said. I had been uncertain about him before, thinking he was too young, too reckless, perhaps, but now I could understand why we wanted to keep Rubi safe and close. After all, it wasn't like Rubi was at risk with us. Not really. Me and Jimmy had moved her away, we were keeping her safe. We were doing all we could to fix this.

We just needed more time. I squeezed my eyes shut, wishing I could solve this.

'We need to talk to Rubi,' I said finally, opening my eyes again, noticing how Jimmy was looking back at me, really looking at me. I couldn't remember the last time anyone had noticed me like that before. Although it was a little unnerving, it was also really nice. It made me feel like I mattered.

'OK,' he said. 'And then?'

'And then we go to my dad like we planned,' I said firmly. 'He'll know what to do.'

Jimmy didn't look convinced. 'Really? We've got time for that now?'

'He used to be a policeman, Jimmy. He was one of the best. He'll know what to do. He'll have an answer to all of this.'

I just hoped that I was right.

Jimmy insisted on making us all breakfast. It was a lovely touch, I had to admit. We sat around his small breakfast bar while he busied himself frying eggs and heating beans. For once, he insisted on cooking unhealthy food. He'd decided that we needed it. All the time, he sang softly under his breath, his hips moving gently with the beat. I sat back watching him, a feeling of contentment washing over me. I wasn't used to someone looking after me this way. I had to admit, it was really nice. Even Rubi seemed relaxed; she was playing on Jimmy's phone again and the tiny frown on her face had melted away for a moment.

'I love the apron,' I said, giggling.

He peered down at the offending article. It had a huge chilli pepper drawn on it and the words HOT STUFF COOKING. 'It was a gift. I'm not going to lie, though – I am hot stuff in the kitchen.'

'We'll see.' I smiled.

He winked at me. 'Maybe you will.'

I felt myself blush and quickly looked away.

'Do you like eggs?' he asked Rubi.

She nodded. 'I like them all gooey and runny.'

'Of course you do, that's the best way to have them.'

After we had eaten and I had insisted on helping Jimmy clear up, we sat Rubi down on Jimmy's comfortable sofa. I watched as she instinctively curled her legs under her body, leaning forward slightly. Her hands were on her lap and she kept moving and twisting her fingers. It made me edgy.

Jimmy sat beside Rubi on the sofa. She seemed tired despite her long sleep, and her long hair lay in unbrushed waves against her shoulders. She looked up through her heavy fringe, her gaze already filled with anxiety.

It was Sunday. Only two days ago my life had been normal. Boring to some maybe, predictable maybe, but I could cope with it. I knew what was happening, I was in control. And now, where was I? Standing in my boss's flat, having just slept in his bed, staring down at a small, scared child who was now in my care. What was it Dad used to say? Life can turn on a sixpence. I'd never really understood it before, but now I did. In a matter of minutes, from the moment that Cassie asked me to keep an eye on her little girl, my life had changed completely.

But what about Rubi? I peered more closely at her now. She was the small child that had been left with a practical stranger, who kept forgetting to brush her hair and didn't have a clue what to feed her. How on earth was Rubi coping with all of this?

I knelt down beside her, keeping my voice soft and tender.

'So, how are you this morning?'

Rubi was now picking at the skin around her fingers. She made a snorting noise. A kind of 's'all right' sound.

'Rubi, so much has gone on these last few days. You're bound to feel a bit confused and upset. That's normal, you know. And you can tell us if you're feeling upset.'

She nodded. Then sniffed a little.

Jimmy leant forward slightly. I was still on my knees; my legs were already beginning to cramp up and I was feeling out of place again, awkward. But I didn't move. I maintained my position.

'Is there anything you want to ask us?' I kept my voice light, like Jimmy; it seemed to work better. Rubi looked up immediately, locked her eyes with mine and I made myself maintain contact.

'I …' She chewed her lower lip. 'I … I don't know what will happen to me …'

'Happen to you?' I probed as gently as I could. 'What do you mean?'

'If my mum doesn't come back … if Dad does really hurt her.'

That word. That simple one-syllable word hung in the air between us. It was so threatening, so real that I could almost reach out and touch it. I rocked back on my heels, unsure what to say next. Rubi had mentioned her dad only once before, but she had said that she didn't see him. Nothing more. I shook my head. I was so silly; I should have probed her further.

Jimmy touched her shoulder softly. 'Oh Rubi, this must be hard for you.'

Rubi flinched. Her head lifted again, her chin jutting out in a determined way. 'We couldn't go back to live at Nanny's before because he might find us. He'd kill Mum,' she said loudly. 'I heard Mum say it. I heard her say it out loud. And I'm scared.' Tears were flowing now, rushing from her eyes in a steady stream. 'I'm really, really scared that's what he'll do to her now.'

I moved forward and pulled Rubi into my arms. It was an odd feeling at first, holding this sobbing, shaking child against my chest. Feeling her heat radiate into me. But then I began to relax and a calmer sensation flowed through me. Her body seemed to mould easily against mine and instinctively I began to rock her; her emotions seemed to blend into my own. Rubi was so brave and so honest. She didn't shut her feelings away like I did.

'It's good to cry,' I said softly. 'You need to let it all out.'

After all, what good did shutting myself away ever do for me? If I could have been honest with my dad and told him the pain and anguish I was in, maybe things would have been better for us. If I could have told the truth about that awful night, maybe my pain would have lessened.

I could see now that locking my hurt away was never the answer. It had nowhere to go. It only grew bigger inside me.

'Will it be OK?' Rubi sobbed into my top.

'I don't know, Rubi. But we will do everything we can to help you.'

'Will I be taken away?'

I peered down at her head. At her glossy black hair. The neat parting that was still there despite my failed attempt at brushing it earlier. She was so small, so helpless, so sweet. Like a vulnerable kitten.

'Not if I can help it,' I said.

And I meant every word.

As we were getting ready to leave for my dad's, Jimmy took a call on his mobile. He raised his eyebrows at me and gestured that he needed to take it in the hall. Rubi and I were left in the living room. Colin was circling the room looking suspiciously like he needed a wee. I prayed Jimmy wouldn't be too long, as my plan was to let Colin run around on the patch of grass outside before we got into the car.

Poor dog, I thought, watching his plodding movements. He'd been moved from place to place, too. Not only that but he was bound to be missing Cassie. I wondered how scared he'd been when Harry and his men had showed up at the flat and turned it over. No wonder he ran. He must have felt like his world was in chaos. And poor Boris! My thoughts shifted to him, alone at mine. I hoped I would be back to him soon. At this rate, he would be sulking for months.

I wandered over to Colin and scratched the rough fur on his back. 'Not long now, boy,' I said. 'We'll be home soon.'

Rubi giggled. I glanced over to her and she was grinning widely. 'Look! You love him too now! I thought you didn't like dogs.'

'I suppose he's growing on me,' I admitted. 'And I do like dogs, sort of, but I've never been around a particularly nice one before.'

'Mum says that all dogs are good. It's the owners that make them bad. Did a dog hurt you?' she asked.

I nodded, still fussing Colin who was now curled up by my feet. 'A long time ago now. I was about eleven or twelve ... my dad had a friend round who had this huge Rottweiler-type dog. Anyway, they weren't taking too much notice of him ...'

In other words, they were both passed out drunk, but Rubi didn't need to know that detail.

'... I walked in. And the dog, not knowing who I was, jumped up at me.' I laughed nervously. 'It's silly really. He only wanted to say hello, but I was so scared because of the sheer size of him, I ran up to my room. I didn't even tell my dad afterwards. But I've always been a bit wary since.'

'That's so sad. Most dogs are good,' Rubi said softly. 'Did you know that pugs are a really ancient breed? The Chinese emperors used to treat them like kings and queens. Some had their own palaces!'

'I didn't know that.'

'So, we have to look after Colin. He's really special.' Rubi paused. 'And he's family.'

I patted her hand gently. 'I can see that now.'

Jimmy came back still holding his phone in his hands. He looked at both of us in turn and smiled.

'That was Liam,' he said softly. I looked back at him, confused, and Jimmy shrugged. 'We swapped numbers back at Cassie's place; we thought it would be useful. He's just told me he's got an address for this Harry down near Brighton.'

Rubi jumped up. 'Brighton! I think that's near Nanny's house.'

Jimmy nodded as he slid his phone back into his pocket. 'I think that's certainly where his main place is. But Liam seems to think Harry has houses all over the South East. This Charlie told him he was renting out a house nearby.'

I breathed out. 'He's been working quickly.'

'Exactly. But that's the thing, Harry has contacts. If he wants something, he can get it. That's kind of the drift I was getting from Liam.'

This didn't sound good. 'What do we do next?'

'I'm not sure. Liam's still digging around, but he managed to find something else out.' Jimmy gently moved me so we were facing away from Rubi. He lowered his voice.

'He told me Harry also has a place in Cyprus. Apparently, he's been boasting about it to anyone who listens. Recently he's been talking of relocating there.'

I shook my head. 'So ...'

'So ... What if that's his intention? What if he wants to take Cassie and Rubi there?'

I stared back at him anxiously. Cyprus?

Surely he couldn't be planning that? I glanced over at Rubi and my entire body stiffened. Was that what he'd been looking for before at the flats? Passports?

'I'm not going there,' Rubi said loudly. 'He can't make me.'

'No, Rubi. He can't,' I said calmly. 'He can't make you do anything.'

He'd have to get past me first.

Chapter Twenty-Two

We parked up on the small, cluttered road outside Dad's house. I took in the familiar sight, the huge shadow of the warehouse and even Dad's bashed-up car on the drive. The street seemed brighter this morning somehow, warm and welcoming. Dad's compact garden still showed splashes of late-summer colour. This had been part of my routine for so long, but I'd been looking at it with a narrow gaze, only seeing the gloom. And yet there was so much good here. There was life. There was growth. There were memories.

'Are you sure you're OK?' Jimmy said, his hands still gripping the steering wheel as if he was prepared to pull away at any moment. 'We can just turn around and go to the nearest police station; it's not too late, you know that.'

Behind us I heard Rubi shuffling on her seat. She didn't say a word, but I could almost feel her worry burning into the back of my head.

'He'll know what to do,' I said. 'The one thing he was good at was being a policeman. He has that kind of rational brain. He can help us.' I reached across and touched Jimmy's arm. 'It'll be fine. You'll see.'

I think my move surprised both of us and immediately I withdrew, embarrassed and a little uncomfortable. I put my hands back on my lap, squeezing the skin tightly. The burning sensation helped to refocus my mind. Quickly, I grabbed my bag and turned to Rubi. She was sitting upright, watching intently. Beside her Colin snoozed. That dog always seemed to be asleep, lucky bugger.

'Come on,' I said as lightly as I could. 'Let's go inside. We need a plan, and even though my dad can be ...' I struggled for the right word '... grumpy at times, he's very clever. He might actually be able to help us. We can show him all the work we've put together.'

'Do you think he'll be pleased?'

'I think he'll think we've been very good detectives,' I said, even though doubt lingered. I knew what Dad would really be thinking. He'd be wanting to know why I hadn't listened to him and gone to the real police. Would he understand my reasoning that I was listening to my gut? Would that be enough for him?

Dad opened the door with his usual charming demeanour, coughing roughly into his sleeve and then wiping the spittle away with the back of his hand. He clung on to the doorway, eyeing us up. I noticed how yellow his skin was looking now. And his eyes too. He looked like a slow-rotting piece of fruit. I moved in closer, but I still couldn't smell the familiar scent of stale beer. Only tobacco and dry sweat. This was a good sign. I felt myself sag with relief.

'Who's this?' He stared up at Jimmy and grinned wickedly. 'Big lad, aren't you?'

Jimmy didn't seem concerned by the comment. He simply held out his hand. 'I've been called worse, to be fair,' he said cheerfully. 'I'm Jimmy. I work with your daughter.'

'It's a Sunday.' Dad was clearly confused. 'My daughter doesn't work on Sundays.'

'The shop is closed today,' Jimmy said. 'I don't work on Sundays either.'

'So I don't understand—'

'Maybe it's better if we go inside,' I interrupted. I gestured towards Rubi, who Dad didn't seem to have noticed. 'There's something really important I want to talk to you about.'

Dad's gaze darted from Rubi to Colin and then back to me. He sighed and I could hear the deep rattle in his chest. 'Aw, so you still have the little one, I see, and that bloody dog ...'

I nodded. 'And we need your help.'

His eyes widened with surprise. He didn't speak for a second or two, his hand brushing the rough stubble on his face. Then his slow smile reappeared, and he opened the door wider to let us in. 'My God, Lucy, you must really be in trouble if you're asking that ...' He turned and shuffled back into the house.

'I can make us a cup of tea,' I said. 'Then I'll explain.'

'I need to sit down first,' Dad grumbled.

I have to admit, I was a bit self-conscious as I led Jimmy through the dark hallway. I wondered what he made of the house, what he must see. Old-fashioned prints of boats and seaside scenes on the wall, faded floral wallpaper and chipped paint. I was used to the smell, but today it suddenly gripped me, my senses on a higher state of alert. I noticed how the tobacco lingered in the air, stinging the back of my nose and making my throat feel hot. Even worse, the boxes were still packed up everywhere – although Dad seemed to have made a half-hearted attempt to move them to one side.

'He's not well,' I whispered.

'You don't have to explain,' Jimmy murmured.

Dad was waiting in the living room, sitting forward on his worn armchair, rolling himself another cigarette. He looked like he belonged in this room, amongst the clutter and dust. In the corner, the TV was on but muted; it looked like some cookery programme, which was ironic as Dad had barely cooked anything in his life. At his feet were a pile of newspapers and a box of battered old paperbacks. I saw Jimmy's eyes light up when he saw them.

I couldn't help glancing over at Mum's picture on the mantelpiece. It was the only one, crammed on the shelf amongst chipped ornaments, stacked-up leaflets and a dying house plant. It was of their wedding day, Dad stiff and formal in a pale blue suit, her wispy and pale in a floaty eighties dress. Their hands were locked, their smiles fixed towards the photographer. The only other photo was of me, aged about four, small, chubby and sitting in the garden, my focus completely riveted on the small cat that had trespassed on to our land. I still remembered his soft ginger coat, the way his body rumbled as I stroked him.

The photos stopped after Mum died. Dad had no longer seen any point in marking our lives, in celebrating or even attempting to be happy with Mum no longer there. It was as if we were in constant mourning, with his only enjoyment coming from a cheap can.

'You look like her.'

Rubi was standing next to me, Jimmy just slightly behind. It was funny, I had almost forgotten that they were there.

Dad snorted, settled back on the chair. 'Lorraine was a beauty. An absolute beauty.' He sighed. 'There's not a day goes by ...'

Jimmy was still staring at the photo. He reached out and touched it.

'She does, Lucy. She really looks like you. Same frame. Same shape face. The hair. The smile.'

I wanted to laugh it off. But instead, I remained rooted on the spot. I could see her so clearly, Mum, in this room, so long ago now that I almost ached trying to hold on to the image. The room had been tidier then, of course, and fresher. Dad had been at work a lot, so his smoke was not a constant feature. I could see her standing by the window, peering out, her slender body moving with ease as she whipped back the net curtain and turned her face towards the street.

She had been watching Dad leave for work. The mood had not been good. I had been sitting opposite the TV, chewing on a sandwich – cheese, I think – and trying to ignore the cloud that had fallen over us once again.

'I wish that just once ...' she had said, her voice breaking. And then she had turned, her face white and her eyes flooded with tears. I had been rooted on my seat, powerless, not sure what to say or do, and I just watched as she slipped out of the room again and locked herself in the downstairs toilet. She thought I couldn't hear her sobs, but it was all I could do to block them out. She was always so upset, so stressed. She hated Dad working the night shift; she liked him being at home with her. All the time.

I had crept out to her. Stood by the closed door. Unsure. Scared, I guess. I had called out. I had asked her to come out. I wanted her back with me.

I was just confused. I didn't like the noises she was making. I wanted it to stop.

Her voice had boomed through the wood, cutting through me, making me freeze on the spot.

'Go away! Go away, you stupid girl. I don't want you.'

Just like that. She didn't want me.

Go away.

A bad feeling had washed over me. It took over, sinking into my bones, weighing me down. I knew something awful was going to happen. I simply had no idea what it would be.

And I was right, for later that night, it all got much worse. So much worse.

I knew for certain what had happened when Dad came home from work the next morning. He made a noise like an animal howling and then smashed up the kitchen. He never told me what she did, as I crept into the room to confront him; he never sat down and explained. Not properly, anyway. He just told me Mum had gone and that it was him and me now. We were quite alone.

She'd left us.

I was only six. A tiny thing. I was too young to deal with things like that.

'You're thinking about her, aren't you?' Dad said. His voice was surprisingly soft. He coughed again, the wheeze in his chest sounding angrier than before. 'You're thinking about your mum.'

Behind me I heard Jimmy whisper to Rubi and Colin, coaxing them out of the room and saying quietly that he was going to put the kettle on, get a drink for Rubi and a seat in the kitchen. I didn't turn, but I waited until I could hear their footsteps receding and the creak of the kitchen door.

I faced him. 'I try not to,' I said finally. 'But it's too hard not to sometimes.' I took a deep breath. 'Do you think things would've been different for us if Mum hadn't done it?'

'What?' He blinked at me. 'Killed herself?' He sighed; his entire body seemed to sag. 'I often wonder that too. It damaged us both so badly, didn't it, Duckling?'

'More than I realised.' I moved closer to him. 'I thought I was OK, you know. That I was coping, but I think for so long I've just been burying it.'

His large eyes scrutinised me. 'When did you realise that?'

I shrugged. 'I'm not sure. I think looking after someone else makes you see things from another angle. Having Rubi with me has made me see how much I've been shutting myself away. How I've been stopping myself from having to confront what happened.'

He nodded. His face was so old now – how had it got so bad? I was here most days and I had refused to see it. I ignored the death rattle inside him. I just did what I always did and locked myself away from the truth. We both did.

'I've made too many mistakes,' he said. 'I need to right some of them while I still can.'

'Why now, though?' I demanded. 'Why the urgency? We never talk, normally. That's not what we do, is it?'

'Duckling, I ...' He shook his head. 'I just couldn't bring myself to talk about it. It was like opening the wound again.'

'Opening it up?' I said, my anger growing. 'It was never properly healed, Dad. That's half the problem. How could I be brave about something that kept hurting me over and over again?'

'I know. I know ...'

'I've been alone for so long. I've had no one. No one to talk to.' My voice was shaking now. 'What am I to you anyway? Just your silly little Duckling. Your big, clumsy joke. I'm simply here to wash your clothes and do your shopping, nothing else. You never once ask if I'm all right. If I need any help ...'

My voice broke. I couldn't say another word; my body was shaking and my eyes were wet with tears. When I finally looked back at him, I saw that he was crying too.

'When she died, I think I did a bit too,' he said finally. His voice was flat, expressionless. It was as if he had announced that he had just this minute taken the bins out or something else equally mundane or trivial. 'I couldn't be the father I should've been to you. I blamed myself for everything. I thought it was my fault. If I hadn't worked those long hours. If I'd listened to her, not neglected her ...'

I sat myself down on the sofa opposite him, aware of how saggy and threadbare it had become. It had always been here, as much a part of the room as we both were. I still placed myself at the end, nearest the left arm. It was where I had always sat as a child. There was a small worn patch where my arm or head had always rested. Some habits were hard to break.

'She told me to go away,' I said finally, my voice cracking. 'That day before she died. She was crying and she told me that she didn't want me.'

He looked up, his eyes wide. 'I never knew that. You never said.'

'I didn't know how to.' All of this was so hard to say – and yet, I knew it was finally time. 'Dad, there's something else you don't know.'

He swallowed; his tongue licked his dry lips. 'Go on ...'

'I ... I went in to her that night. I had a bad dream. So I got up and went to her room. I wanted her to make it better. I wanted my mum.'

'Oh, Duck ...'

I turned my face away. I couldn't look at him. I needed to get this out now. The words had been inside me for so long, it was like a darkness growing bigger and bigger inside me. I had to let some of it out before it imploded.

'She was in her bed; the pill containers were spread over the covers. She was lying there. Her mouth was open and her eyes – her eyes were awful, just glazed and staring up at the ceiling. I called out to her. But she didn't move. She *couldn't* move. I was so scared, Dad. I knew she had done something bad, but I was so scared, I ran and hid in my bed.'

He slumped back. 'You found her like that? Before I did?'

'You were still at work. I didn't know what to do.' I paused. 'I thought if I buried my head under the covers, it would all go away. I thought I might wake up and it would be OK. But it wasn't.'

'Oh, Duckling ...' he said weakly.

'I should've done something,' I muttered. 'I could've stopped her. I should've done something.'

He shook his head slowly but said nothing.

'Was it because of me that she died? Did she hate being a mother that much?'

'It wasn't that,' he said flatly. 'It wasn't your fault.'

'I could've saved her.'

'No, you couldn't. You were six years old. You couldn't help her.' He paused. 'Oh God ... You must've been feeling like this all the time. Oh Duck ... this explains so much ...'

I nodded, tears burning. 'I felt guilty. I thought I should've done more.'

Dad still had the roll-up in his hand; he manoeuvred it between his fingers, back and forth, not lighting it. His focus seemed entirely fixed on that cigarette. Neither of us spoke. I was aware of the sounds around us, the ticking clock, a bluebottle buzzing angrily against the window, the ebb and flow of Rubi and Jimmy's voices from the other room.

'She was very poorly, Duck,' he said finally. Then he reached towards his small side table and picked up his blue butane lighter; his thumb pressed down on the mechanism, once, twice, three times before the flame finally burst through.

He leant forward, groaning a little, and lit his cigarette, taking a huge lungful of the smoke, nicotine, tar.

Another puff. Another sharp cough. His hand wiping more spit away from his lips. I noticed it was shaking slightly.

'She was very, very ill.' He sighed. 'And so incredibly sad. I wish I could've done more to help her, I'll live with that guilt forever, but it was never about you. She loved you.'

His voice broke and he sucked again on the fag, greedily, as though he really needed the poisons inside his body.

I couldn't say anything more. There was nothing left. I slumped in my seat, deflated, beaten.

'I know,' he said finally. 'I know how much it messed you up. I should have been there for you more. If I had, maybe your life would've turned out better. For that I'm so sorry.'

I didn't answer. Instead, I turned away from him.

'Duck. I know you're hurting, but there's still something else I need to talk to you about.'

I heard the tone of his voice, the hint of what he was on the verge of saying, and something froze inside me. I knew what it was. Of course I did. I'd already worked out what he was so desperate to tell me.

But I wasn't ready to hear it yet. I couldn't deal with it now. I had to get out.

'Not yet, Dad,' I said.

I quickly left the room.

In the kitchen, Rubi was drawing with a biro on the back of an old bit of cardboard Jimmy had found. She looked relaxed, quite settled and relatively happy. It made me feel a bit better just looking at her, making sure she was still in one piece.

'Are you OK?' Jimmy asked, staring at me with concern.

'I'm fine. We had a lot to talk about.' I smiled nervously. 'I guess it's taken it out of me a bit. Now, who still needs a drink? I said I'd make it ages ago.'

I made the tea and took Jimmy with me back into the living room and we quietly closed the door. Dad took his tea and began sipping it slowly and eyeing us both up. We told him everything that had happened with Cassie up till now and I showed him the notes that Rubi and I had drawn up. I told him the bad feelings I had deep inside my gut. Strangely, Dad was silent. This wasn't what I'd expected. I'd assumed he would be bombarding us with questions.

'I keep telling Lucy that it's time to go to the police,' Jimmy stated. 'I think we're just wasting time now.'

Dad nodded. 'I would have agreed with you before, but now I'm not so certain ...'

'Really?' I said, surprised.

Jimmy seemed shocked, too. 'Surely it's the most sensible thing to do now. We're out of our depth.'

'And what will the police do exactly?' Dad asked. 'At this point I'm not sure they'll be much help.'

Jimmy's smile was uncertain. 'Well ... investigate. A young woman has gone missing.'

Dad held out his finger. 'There. Stop there. That's the assumption you are making. At the moment we have no actual proof that Cassie is missing —'

'The messages,' I interjected. 'I told you. They don't read right at all. She wouldn't keep spelling Rubi's name wrong, or mine for that matter.'

'She could have been rushing, like Jimmy said.' Dad sipped his tea. 'The phone could've auto-corrected the name. It's a weak argument and not one the police are necessarily going to believe.' He shook his head. 'Before, I was all for going to the police, but that's when I thought this Cassie girl was just mucking my Duckling around. Now I'm not so sure.'

'She wouldn't leave Rubi this long,' I said. 'I don't believe it.'

Dad pursed his lips, seeming to be considering this. 'Look at the facts. A woman leaves you with her child, doesn't tell you where she's going and gives some vague details of when she will be returning. Next, she messages you, asking that you hold on to Rubi for longer. Then she is seen with another man, who is doing over her ex-boyfriend ...' He shook his head again. 'None of this looks good for Cassie. The police will follow the most logical route: Cassie dumps her young child on you while she goes on a crime spree with an old flame.'

'She wouldn't do that,' I said firmly.

'And you know her that well?'

'I know her well enough to know this doesn't fit. Rubi told us she moved them away from this man, this Harry. By the sounds of it, Cassie gave up contact with her own mum to keep away from him. Who would do that unless they were truly scared?'

Dad shrugged. 'It's a good point. But then why did she go back to him?'

Jimmy sat forward. 'Liam – one of the kids on the estate – has been doing some digging. He spoke to Charlie who was friends with Gav, the man who was beaten up.' Jimmy paused, checking with my dad that he understood all of that. Dad flapped his hands in a gesture that said he should continue.

'OK. So Liam, or one of his contacts, hunted down Charlie. Turns out Charlie had been approached months ago by this Harry. Harry had managed to track Cassie as far as Gav – let's just say the man has contacts. A *lot* of contacts. It turns out Gav was probably not the greatest person for Cassie to turn to – OK, he's harmless enough, but he's still the sort of loudmouth that gets himself known very quickly to the wrong type of people. It wouldn't have taken Harry long to discover Gav and Cassie were connected. Anyway, Harry got himself in with Charlie, paid him a lot of money to find out what he could about Cassie now that she was no longer with Gav. Apparently Gav had been boasting only a few days ago that Cassie was coming back to him, that she needed him again. So, as we suspected, the men decided to catch Cassie in the act and ambushed her outside Gav's.'

Dad sighed. 'That's a hell of a lot to digest.'

I thumped the arm of the sofa in frustration. 'Bloody Gav. What an idiot! Why couldn't he have kept his mouth shut?'

Jimmy shrugged. 'As you guessed, Lucy, Harry assumed that Cassie would be bringing Rubi with her on Friday. After all, usually those two go everywhere together.'

'But instead, she asked me to look after her,' I said.

'Maybe she knew she had to keep her most precious thing safe and away from harm,' Dad said.

'The question is, what do we do now?' Jimmy said. 'Take this additional information to the police? Try to contact Cassie again? Liam is going to dig around some contacts in Brighton – although it's unlikely he's there, maybe someone knows where Harry is.'

Dad took another sip of tea. 'I reckon this Harry will be lying low somewhere quite close. If he really wants Rubi, he won't want to be far away. He'll be planning his next move anytime now.'

'Well ...' Jimmy said. 'That's possible, but this still feels like we're playing a daft guessing game.'

I realised that they had both gone quiet. They were looking at me, waiting for me to chip in and say something of use. But I had already been distracted. My phone had just buzzed in my hand.

Cassie had messaged me again.

'We're not guessing,' I said softly. 'Because now I know exactly what they want us to do next.'

Chapter Twenty-Three

Luci. You need to meet my friend Harry with Ruby. Please trust him. We are making a fresh start – just us two. I think I need to get away from the ghosts in the flat! It has to be only you that comes. And you have to bring Ruby. Please confirm this is OK and I'll send the address.

I blinked, reading and re-reading the message. Then another one appeared.

Please Luci. Please do the right thing. I trust only you. x

I didn't know whether to be relieved that Cassie was OK, or frightened that she was somehow still in a situation she didn't want to be. Either way, these messages had caused certainty in me. This had to be her – because why else would she mention the ghosts in her flat? Who else would've known her worries about that except me?

'This is Cassie,' I said. 'She wants us to take Rubi to them.'

Jimmy took the phone from my hands and read the message himself. 'It might not be her,' he muttered. 'You can't be sure.'

'It is. This is her way of telling me it's her. She mentioned the ghosts in her flat, which is something we talked about when I first met her properly. It's so random to mention that without it meaning something. Why else would she say it? I think she's proving to me that it's her – that I should trust her.'

Dad snorted. 'So why not call you? It would've been a lot easier, surely?'

I took the phone back from Jimmy, stared at the words again. 'I don't know. Maybe she just didn't want me asking a load of questions. Texts are quicker and neater, aren't they? And other people can't hear what you're saying ...'

Jimmy nodded, rammed his hands into his pockets. 'It makes sense.'

'OK, so you think it's her and this is a good thing – why?' Dad said crisply.

I looked over at him, confused. He was perched forward now, a cushion rammed up behind his back. It made him look weirdly awkward, like the chair was about to tip him out at any moment.

'It means she's OK,' I said.

I didn't go as far as to say, 'It means she's still alive,' but I kept remembering what Rubi had said before about Harry killing her mum. The threat was like a weight on my chest.

Dad rubbed his knee. He caught me staring. 'Bloody thing aches like a bitch these days. In fact, most of me is falling apart.' He shifted, frowning a little. 'OK, I understand what you're saying. She's well enough to send a text – that's a good sign. Let me see it a minute.'

I got up reluctantly and walked over to him. He snatched the mobile quickly as though I might change my mind. Maybe I was thinking about it. I certainly didn't want him to put a negative spin on things. Especially as I was starting to feel a bit more confident.

I just wanted everything to be all right. I wanted to make everything fixed so that I could have my old, safe life back.

I rocked back on my heels. I mean, I did want that, didn't I? So why then did these thoughts, that usually gave me comfort and relief, suddenly feel so sad and depressing?

Was the life I had before really what I wanted now? Was it *ever* what I truly wanted?

I sighed a little. It had to be the stress making me overthink everything. That was all. I wasn't quite myself at the moment. It wouldn't take long before I was back to my old self.

Peaceful. Calm. Quiet.

And lonely, I now realised.

So achingly, awfully lonely.

'Hasn't she spelt Rubi's name wrong again?' Dad asked, breaking into my thoughts. 'And Lucy's.'

'Yes!' I exclaimed. 'At first, I thought it was Harry, but now I know it's her. I don't know why she would make those mistakes.'

'Unless it's a way of warning you?' Jimmy said. 'You did think that before.'

I sighed. 'It could be, but we are just second guessing. Maybe I'm being dramatic. All I know is that Cassie has sent this message. I don't want to let her down.'

Dad murmured something under his breath, his eyes squinting down at the message, then he handed the phone back to me.

'Well, what do you think?' I asked.

'Yeah – I agree. I think it's her. She sent this message.'

'So do we just do what she asked then?' Jimmy said softly. 'Agree to take Rubi to her. I guess, it's not an unreasonable request. She is her mum. This is what she wants. The name thing could just be a simple mistake. Or it could be the phone changing it.'

'Maybe, but there's something else in this latest message that I don't like,' Dad said suddenly. 'Didn't you both see it? Have another read. Does anything stand out to you?'

I brought the message up again. I squinted at the screen for several minutes, feeling confused, my overloaded brain struggling to see what Dad did.

And then suddenly the words jumped out at me.

It has to be only you that comes.

Please do the right thing. I trust only you.

She only trusted me. This was the same thing she had said when she had left Rubi with me. And what was it she had said? My memory swept back to before.

'Please don't let Rubi go anywhere with anyone else. Just keep her with you, OK? Keep her safe, until I get home.'

'Only me,' I said in a half-whisper. 'She only wants me to go.' But I could feel Dad's gaze bearing down on me. I could understand that he might not be happy with that.

'What do we do?' Jimmy asked. 'This is like some sick game that Cassie is trapped in. How do we help her without putting Rubi and Lucy at risk?'

Dad chuckled. 'Oh, that's easy, son,' he said. 'We play along.'

I stared back at him, confused. 'And how exactly do we do that?'

Jimmy shook his head. 'Cassie was clear that she wants Lucy to go, but I'm not prepared to put her at any risk. No,' he said, more firmly this time, his cheeks reddening. 'I don't want Lucy hurt.'

'Well ... neither do I,' Dad replied smoothly. 'I hope that we can find a way that keeps everyone safe.'

'Well, there isn't, is there?' I shot back. 'Whatever we do is risky. But I'm not prepared to do nothing.'

'The police ...' Jimmy started again weakly.

'No!' Dad held out his hand. 'No. I really don't think we can. Not yet, anyway. We have even less to tell them now, for fuck's sake. Rubi's mum has asked Lucy to bring her kid back – where's the crime in that? They'd laugh us out of the station.'

'But the message ...' Jimmy was losing ground, he looked to me for support. 'We all agreed there was something wrong with it.'

I took my glasses off, rubbed my eyes. I could feel the pressure building inside my head. This was all too much. Then I put my glasses back on and looked at the text again, at Cassie's words. I allowed my mind to refocus, to take in all the information. I realised that both men were staring at me. They were waiting for me to say something, to make a decision.

'Sometimes the easiest option is the best one ...'

Who had said that to me before? I clawed my memory, trying to recall. I could hear her voice, light but determined.

Cassie, of course. She had said it to me so long ago and yet it had never felt so relevant.

'We're not calling the police,' I said firmly. 'Not yet anyway. We are going to her – like she asked. Well, I'm going, anyway.'

'No!' Jimmy started.

'Not alone, anyway,' Dad barked. 'I'm coming with you.'

'But not Rubi?' Jimmy looked confused. 'Surely you don't think it's a good idea to take her?'

I rubbed at my forehead, at the slight pressure point there. 'I don't know. Maybe if she just waits in the car. If this Harry sees her it might be enough. Maybe I'll have a chance to talk to Cassie. Check that everything is OK.'

Jimmy shook his head. 'No. It's too risky.'

He was right, of course. I closed my eyes. What was I thinking? Cassie trusted me. How on earth could I take the risk that Rubi might be harmed? It wasn't an option at all.

'I'll just have to go without her,' I muttered. 'I'll just have to hope—'

'Or you could play the game,' Dad interrupted sharply.

I looked over at him. He was sitting calmly, rolling himself another cigarette.

'What game?' I said. 'What are you on about?'

'They want you to bring Rubi. So, we bring Rubi,' he said, his eyes twinkling in the light. 'Or at least something that looks like her.'

Chapter Twenty-Four

I stood outside my old bedroom again. I could feel the disappointment and sadness most heavily here. Like a memory I had left behind, it was waiting to be rediscovered and overwhelm me. I always thought this room was my sanctuary, my place to get away from the bad memories, from the drunken exploits of my broken father. I used to believe that I was better off in here. But as I pushed open the door and walked inside the empty space, I knew that I wasn't.

This was just another lie I'd told myself.

This room had simply contained me. It trapped all my fears and worries inside like a prison. As I looked around the walls, still decorated in pretty pink floral wallpaper, I could actually taste the pain in the air, still lingering. I remembered the loneliness I'd felt as I lay on my bed night after and night and tried to forget. And when I left home, I did no better, simply closed another door and locked myself away.

Hiding away had never helped me. Instead, it had made things a million times worse.

I found the doll, as Dad had told me, in one of the boxes he'd left for me in the middle of the room. I never knew he had kept it there for all this time. With her long dark hair, she bore a passing resemblance to Rubi.

'I remember when Mum gave this to me. What was I, four?' I said softly to myself, lifting her out. 'It was one of hers from when she was young. She told me to look after it. She said it was special. It was one of the few lovely things I remember her doing for me.'

She was huge, as big as me when I received her, and dressed in old-fashioned clothes. Her face was beautifully painted, yet strangely creepy. I remember I had been quite frightened by her. Mum said she was called Polly.

I peered into the box, wondering what else Dad had kept. My fingers dug inside. What was this? Old school reports. Drawings I had done. I pressed the doll against my body, breathing in her dusty scent. I never knew he'd kept all this. Even in his worst moments, he had put this stuff by. He had cherished it. That sentiment alone meant the world to me.

I tucked Polly under my arm and slowly left the room. I then found myself stuck at the doorway, quite unable to move. I was now facing my parents' bedroom. From here, I could once again picture the run I had made all those years ago, staggering from Mum's bed to my own. I could almost see my tear-soaked face, my thin, goosebumped arms reaching for my bedroom door handle, trying desperately to flee from what I'd just seen.

'It wasn't your fault,' I whispered. 'You were six, Lucy. Six years old. What could you do? You didn't know what it would do to your dad. You couldn't stop it. You couldn't.'

I don't know how long I stood there, staring at the empty space, but my hand was numb by the time I pulled myself away and headed downstairs to join the others.

'Dad ...' I said hesitantly, still feeling unsteady. 'Do you really think this will work?'

'Sure. Why not?'

He placed the Polly doll squarely next to Rubi. The doll was smaller in height but stood together I could suddenly see why he'd had this idea. It was the hair that did it. They both had full-fringed, glossy dark hair.

'Dad, I don't know ...'

Dad nodded smugly. 'It will be fine. Trust me.'

'I don't understand it either,' Jimmy snorted in frustration. 'I mean, I'm assuming that Harry or Cassie or whoever will be a little bit miffed if Lucy rocks up with that thing under her arm.'

'Mum?' Rubi interrupted, her attention drawn away from the doll. 'You're going to my mum?'

Dad ignored her. 'No, that's not what I'm suggesting at all. My idea is much simpler. We drive up with Polly in the back seat. With a few cushions underneath her she'll look taller, and from a distance it might be enough to trick them. I'll park a little away from the meeting point; I'm hoping that will be enough.'

'Enough for what?' My mouth was dry.

'Enough to convince them that Rubi is in the car, waiting,' my dad said gently. 'Maybe I should go out to Cassie, or Harry or whoever. I'll find out if Cassie is all right and if I can I'll bring her back to the car.'

'And what if Harry decides he wants to check? What if he goes instead of Cassie?' Jimmy demanded. 'This plan is full of holes.'

Dad shrugged. 'It's not perfect, I grant you, but it might work and that's enough for now. Me and Lucy can agree a signal. If Harry is coming, I'll let you know, and she can drive off and call the police immediately. That can be our back-up plan.'

'I can't drive,' I muttered. 'Remember?'

Dad's gaze dropped to the floor. 'Shit. I'd forgotten that. Damn, I'm sorry, Duck. I should have taught you. I was never good at this stuff, was I?'

'It's OK ...'

'Well, we might both have to leg it.'

Jimmy was pacing now and looking really wound up. 'This is crazy. I can't see it working.'

'I agree, it won't,' I said firmly. 'It has to be me that goes out to the house.'

Jimmy spun round to face me, his face deathly pale. 'Lucy, you can't mean that! This man is dangerous, possibly Cassie too. Look what they did to Gav.'

I had to hold back a laugh at the thought of Cassie being dangerous; it was too ludicrous.

'She asked for me. So it has to be me,' I said, pressing my lips together.

I had to do this right. Cassie had asked for me specifically.

'OK, well, I should drive, then,' Jimmy said.

'No, Jimmy,' I replied quickly. 'If I can't be with Rubi, I want you to be. My dad doesn't know her as well.'

Dad agreed with me. 'That makes sense. And I can drive—' He coughed dryly into his fist. 'Just about. I can get us away if necessary. I can get us to the police.'

Get us away. The very thought seemed insane, like we were in some crazy film. How had I been caught up in this madness? This sort of stuff was never meant to happen to me.

'And what if Lucy gets hurt?' Jimmy hissed, his eyes blazing. 'Are you seriously prepared to put her at risk like this?'

Dad frowned a little. 'Of course I'm not. But hopefully we can get to talk to Cassie and check out that everything is OK and get her out of there. Lucy shouldn't go into any building or put herself at risk. She just needs to speak to Cassie and find out what the score is, nothing else. We can make sure you and Rubi are nearby, so if everything is fine and dandy, we can reunite them. Everyone will be happy ever after. This idea is just a safety net – just to ensure we have covered all the angles.'

'So why not just take Rubi anyway?' I asked, still confused. 'Wouldn't that be easier?'

Dad lowered his eyes. 'I don't want her there. Just in case, that's all. It pays to be cautious when there's kids involved.'

'I want to see my mum,' Rubi said, louder this time.

Dad reached out and touched her arm. 'And you will, sweetie, hopefully very soon. But first we need to find out where exactly she is. Lucy, you need to send that text. Confirm you're coming. Ask her where and when.' He paused. 'Tell her that you're happy to help her.'

Once again, I pulled out my phone and began tapping away.

I just hoped that Cassie saw it in time.

*

I read out the address she had texted back. Jimmy fed it into his own mobile, mumbling under his breath, obviously unhappy.

47 Shipley Street. Milton Bank
2pm

Instinctively, I looked at my watch. It was already eleven. Where on earth had the morning gone? In the blink of an eye my weekend had almost disappeared.

I thought back to the weekend before, to last Sunday. What had I been doing? I'd got up late, of course, I always did on a Sunday, and then watched American sitcoms whilst eating my muesli. By this time, I would be preparing for my walk. A brisk stroll, twice round the park – stopping on the way back at the small café on the end of Hedge Street. There I would eat chicken and chips and sip stewed tea whilst reading the supplied newspapers. Usually, I would manage to get the same seat by the window – I always felt so irritated if it was taken – and I would sit facing the door so that I could watch people coming and going. They knew me well in there. The owner, Brian, would also welcome me with a smile and call me 'flower' which was both slightly inappropriate and quite charming.

I wondered if he'd be concerned if I didn't show up today. Would he worry? Would he think something bad had happened to me? Or wouldn't he even notice my absence? After all, I was just a shadow in the corner, quietly eating my food and ignoring everyone else. What was there to miss? Who'd look for me if *I* was missing?

I blinked, surprised to find that tears had collected under my lashes.

'Lucy? Are you OK?' Jimmy was looking at me, puzzled. Rubi was kneeling next to him, carefully stroking Polly's hair. Occasionally her fingers would get stuck, and she would have to tug to release them. She caught me looking at her and tipped her chin upwards, her eyes fixed on mine. I smiled sadly back at them. This really wasn't the time to be self-involved. I had to pull myself together.

'I'm fine. Absolutely fine.'

Jimmy nodded. 'I've looked up the address. It's on one of the new estates on the other side of town.'

Dad scowled. 'Bloody state they are, too. Churned up a nice piece of countryside for what? Stacked-up chintz for posh wankers to live in.'

Jimmy chuckled. 'I won't invite you to my place then, Tony. I dread to think what you'd make of that!'

Tony? I looked from one to the other. When did Jimmy find out Dad's name? Had they suddenly become best mates? My world was becoming even weirder.

'So … by my calculations it'll only take twenty minutes or so to get there. Plenty of time to get our plan laid out,' Dad said.

Jimmy shrugged. 'I still think it's lunacy but I'm obviously outnumbered.'

'What do we do now?' I asked. 'Just wait here? Kill time?'

'We could go out. Get some lunch?' Jimmy suggested hopefully. 'I'm starving. Breakfast seems ages ago now.'

Rubi looked up. 'Yes. I'm hungry too.'

I knew just the place.

Jimmy pulled away and started chatting jovially to Dad. It was as if this was a completely normal day, and we were used to each other. I studied him more closely. Although he was smiling brightly as he spoke and laughing at what seemed to be the right points, I noted the soft bags under his eyes, the way his mouth seemed to strain itself into a grin. Perhaps this was more of a performance, designed to put us all at ease.

Rubi sat up against the other side window. Colin was lying on the floor, his squashed-up face resting on my foot. It was rather comforting.

Between Rubi and me was Polly, propped up in the middle like another little girl, her glassy eyes fixed forward. My arm kept brushing the cold plastic of her skin, reminding me she was there. Rubi was happy, though. She kept stroking Polly's hair and pulling gently on her dress.

'It's so cool we're bringing her,' she told me excitedly. 'I wish my friend Esme could see her. She'd be so jealous. She has so many Barbies, like a hundred. But she hasn't got a doll like this.'

'She certainly is very different,' I made myself agree.

'Can I take her into the café with me, please? Can I show her to Mum when we find her?'

'Yes, of course,' I said softly.

She smiled widely. 'Mum will love her. I know it.'

'I'm sure she will.'

Rubi's fingers were now lightly stroking the doll's legs, up and down in a soothing rhythm. 'She said she would get me a big doll. Not this big. But big ... If I was good at school ...'

'And have you been?'

Rubi looked up, blinking. 'Yes. Miss Gibson said I've been working very hard.'

'What year are you in, Rubi?'

She looked bewildered, like this was a fact I should already know. Perhaps I should.

'Year two.'

I nodded slowly. She really was so young; it was easy to forget that because of her quiet, resourceful nature. So, what did that mean? It was September now; was I correct to assume that she was at school? I seemed to have a distant memory of the term starting around this time, which meant she might be going back tomorrow. I flexed my fingers, anxiety building – why hadn't I thought of this? Rubi would need her school things ready for the morning. There would be things to prepare. I couldn't even phone her in sick because I wasn't her parent. I closed my eyes for a brief moment. I didn't even know where she went.

'What school do you go to?'

'St Jude's,' she replied. I knew the school, of course. It was just across from our estate, a small brick building surrounded by rusted chain-link fencing. It was very different from my first school. A smaller Catholic school down the road from Dad's house, it had been set way back off the road and surrounded by greenery. I had quite liked it there; in fact, I had spent most of my break times roaming the fields alone. No one seemed to mind.

'Do I have to go tomorrow?' Rubi asked, interrupting my thoughts. 'I don't want to go if Mum's not here.' Her bottom lip was sticking out.

'We'll sort something,' I replied vaguely. It wasn't exactly a yes, but it wasn't a no either.

I glanced out of the window, almost relieved to see that we were here. The familiar sight of my usual Sunday eating place was reassuring. This was a good place. Just looking at the faded sandwich board outside, the painted white façade and curtained windows made me feel safe.

Jimmy swung the car into a parking space outside the café. I noticed he and Dad were discussing football now. I couldn't help smiling. They were getting on like two old friends.

Rubi peered out across me, getting a better look at where we were.

'Is that it? It's small.' Her snub nose wrinkled.

'It's perfect.'

We got out of the car and there was a moment of mild panic when we realised we still had Colin to contend with.

'Well, he can't go inside,' Dad said matter-of-factly. 'There's a ruddy big sign there banning dogs.'

'He'll have to stay out here,' I decided, walking Colin over to some metal railings near the window of the café. 'At least here I can keep an eye on him.' Colin seemed reluctant to comply; his head immediately dipped and his tail dropped between his legs. He looked like a dog being led to his death.

'What if someone steals him? I'm taking Polly in case they take her,' Rubi whined, clutching hold of the doll, who was half propped on the ground. The doll was far too big for her and she looked almost comical standing there with this huge plastic creation dominating her.

'They won't,' I replied firmly.

At least I hoped they wouldn't …

'They might. What do you know? My mum said pugs are expensive.' Rubi scuffed at the pavement with her foot, Polly jiggling unstably in her arms. 'You don't always tell the truth.'

The accusation hurt. I stepped back a little, still clutching the lead. I looked down and saw that my hands were shaking. I bent down and continued the task of looping the lead tightly around the metal pole.

'Lucy hasn't lied,' I heard Jimmy tell Rubi.

'She has. She keeps saying stuff, telling me things that aren't true,' Rubi said coolly. 'And she keeps telling me my mum is coming home, even though she isn't.'

'I don't lie …' I whispered, the words falling from my lips like dust in the breeze.

Or at least, I don't mean to.

'I was just trying to do the right thing,' I said weakly. 'That's all. That's all I'm ever trying to do.'

I stood up; Colin was now safely secured. My eyes locked with Dad's. He smiled at me gently. Rubi was staring back at me defiantly, her cheeks puffed out, her eyes welling with tears.

'I told you what I believed to be true. What I hoped to be true. How can I lie when I don't actually know myself what is going on?'

Rubi blinked slowly; her bottom lip trembled.

'I don't lie, Rubi. Not to you, not to anyone. Not if I can help it.' I sighed, rubbed the palms of my hands against my trousers. 'There's just some things I chose not to tell you for your own protection. There's a difference.'

'OK,' she whispered. She wobbled and I saw how she was struggling under the weight of that huge doll, her knees buckling. Gently, I eased the doll from her grip and tucked it under my arm. Then, carefully, I reached for her hand; it slotted in so nicely with mine. A perfect fit.

'Let's get some food,' I said as brightly as I could. 'And then we're going to work out how to get you back to Mum.' I reached down and stroked Colin's head. His fur was incredibly soft. 'And we'll sit right by the window so we can keep an eye on this fella. OK?'

'OK.'

Her fingers curled around mine. Soft, warm and intimate.

It was all going to be just fine.

It had to be.

What a sight we must have looked staggering into the café – Dad complaining about his back, Jimmy trying to break the tension by laughing at one of his own jokes and Rubi barely able to stand upright as she clung on to her great, awkward doll which she'd insisted on carrying again. Brian looked up and waved as we made our way to the table in the corner. I saw him raise an eyebrow, obviously surprised that I had company today.

I chuckled to myself as we settled ourselves down. 'The loner is no longer alone,' I murmured, looking around at my small motley crew.

Dad looked back at me, confused, rubbing his ear. 'Eh? What was that, Duck?'

'Never mind, Dad.'

We ordered the food quickly, keen to eat and get our plans underway.

I settled myself on my chair, watching as Rubi placed Polly on the seat next to her. She carefully pulled down her skirt and neatened her hair, fussing over her as if she was a little mum herself. She actually looked like she'd make a good job of it.

'Do you agree with that, then?' Dad said suddenly.

'Er, what?' I looked up, confused.

'With the plan. With what you need to do?' Jimmy said, gesturing with his fork. 'Are you still happy to do this?'

'Er ...' I glanced down at my plate, at my practically untouched chicken and chips. My stomach felt too small and tight, my throat dry. I took a mouthful of the strong sweet tea and was grateful for the liquid warmth. 'I'm fine to do this.'

Jimmy was still looking at me; he pursed his lips together and then slowly shook his head. 'I can't believe we're doing this. It's bloody madness. I suppose it's an interesting way to spend my day off, though ...'

Dad was sitting back, sipping his own tea. He seemed relaxed now, one arm curled round the seat next to him, the seat where Rubi sat, slurping her milkshake, listening to us all with wide, knowing eyes.

'You're overthinking it all,' he said smoothly. 'It'll be fine. All Lucy has to do is knock at the door and tell Cassie we're in the car. If it's Harry and he gives her trouble, she walks away. Quickly.' He took another sip. 'Just stay outside, Lucy. Stay where I can see you. If this bloke is out for causing trouble, he won't want to do it in public. Especially not in such a nice area.' He winked at Jimmy. 'Nobody likes to draw attention to themselves, do they?'

Behind us, Brian cleaned a nearby table. I knew he was trying to listen in to the conversation. I smiled at him to indicate that everything was OK and he drifted off, sponge still clasped in his hand and an uncertain look on his face.

Jimmy placed his phone on the table. He had brought up Street View. On the screen I could see the tiny image of a brand-new housing estate, red-brick semi-detached houses packed tightly together. Jimmy pointed at a row of three taller, town-house types, facing a small patch of green.

'The house is one of these,' he said.

I nodded. It looked nice enough. Like somewhere a nice businessperson would live. Someone respectable. Someone who bleached their toilets and folded their clothes every night before bed.

Not someone who hurt people or beat them up and kept them hostage.

'I wonder why he picked here,' I said.

Jimmy shrugged. 'Not sure. According to Liam, Harry would've only found out where she was this week. My guess is that he's renting the place or borrowing it from a mate.'

'Makes sense, I suppose.'

Jimmy swiped away from the address, moving further down the road, out into the main street. 'There!' he said, zooming in. 'There's a small park just here. Even a little field for the dog. Me and Rubi can wait for you there.'

'I like that idea,' Dad agreed. 'You're safe enough there.'

'I want to see Mum,' Rubi complained, spitting out her straw. There was a small drizzle of chocolate milkshake on her bottom lip. 'I don't want to wait in a park. I want to go with Lucy. It's not fair.'

She looked so determined, her eyes blazing, her lips pouting. I picked up the straw that she had left on the table and gently placed it on the side of my plate. Using my napkin, I cleaned up the trail of milk.

'Colin needs a walk,' I said softly. 'He might not get a chance when we get your mum back, you'll be too busy having fun together. You're the best with him, Rubi. He'll miss you too much if you go with me. You'll still be helping us by doing this.'

Her eyes lowered. 'I just want my mum.'

'I know you do.' I paused. 'And she wants you too.'

And very soon, I was going to get her back. Not for my sake. Not even for Cassie's – but for this little girl who missed her mum so badly, who needed her and who didn't understand why she'd had to go. A little girl who had the chance to get her mum back.

I was doing this all for Rubi.

Chapter Twenty-Five

The house seemed so innocuous from outside. Dad had parked the car a little further down the road, but from here we could easily see the set of three houses. They looked so tidy, so normal, it was difficult to compute my feeling of raging anxiety. The cars parked outside were all premium models. Behind us Polly sat propped up on two cushions that Jimmy had retrieved from his boot. She looked a bit lopsided and weird. She certainly didn't look like Rubi. I just hoped we would get away with it at a distance. I saw Dad cast his gaze over a nearby black Audi, licking his lips slowly.

'There's money around here, that's for sure,' he said quietly.

The car seemed strangely empty with just us two in it. I was trying to remember the last time Dad and I had driven out together. There had been short drives to his darts matches when I was younger. I used to sit in the back of the car, munching crisps while he played his music. Did we even talk much? I didn't think so.

I certainly couldn't recall days at the seaside or trips out to the park. A wave of icy sadness washed over me. Why couldn't anything have been normal for us after she had gone?

Dad turned to me, his face unreadable. 'Are you scared, Duck?' he asked.

Scared was the wrong word. I've never been scared. Not really. I could watch any horror film and be unimpressed. I could go on a roller-coaster ride and leave feeling dissatisfied. Anxiety was a different thing. It was the worry of the unknown, the fear of being caught out, of not being able to cope. It was a horrible, chewed-up feeling at the pit of my stomach that I couldn't seem to stop.

'I'm not scared, not really,' I said truthfully. But I did feel really sick. I kept picturing Rubi in my mind, using her face as my focus. I couldn't let her down.

'You're a good girl,' he said softly. He gave a rasping cough and then floundered, looking for a tissue in his pocket. 'I'm sorry. This is no good ...' He beat his chest with his hands. 'My lungs are truly fucked now.'

'You should stop smoking.'

His eyes twinkled. 'Stop smoking? Seriously? It's too late for me now, Lucy. I'm too old. Too stubborn ...' He coughed again. 'I know my fate.'

'You don't have to think like that,' I said. 'It's defeatist.'

'Is it?' His hand suddenly reached out and squeezed mine. His skin looked so grey next to mine, like old, overworked clay.

'How bad is it?' I asked.

He sat back a little, his eyes wide and sad. 'You knew? You knew that's what I wanted to talk to you about?'

'I guess I worked it out. You stopped drinking for so long. You're packing up your things.' I paused, smiled at him wearily. 'And you look bloody awful.'

'Thanks.'

'Shouldn't you see a doctor again?' I asked him. 'You probably need to get checked over. Get a second opinion?'

349

He smiled sadly. 'Oh, there's no point. Not now.' He raised an eyebrow. 'Don't look like that, Duckling. I wanted to talk to you about it for a while, but I figured you had enough on your plate. I didn't want you to worry about me too. But this week I've been feeling a lot worse. I knew it was time you should know.

'They said I've got a few months,' he continued. 'But who knows?'

'Oh Dad …' I took his hand again, held it in mine. 'Is there nothing they can do?'

His smile was so sad, I felt like it could rip me in two. He didn't need to answer that question. His face told me all I needed to know. Finally, he spoke again.

'You've been through a lot, Duck, and at such a young age. Losing your mum and then me messing up. It's a lot …'

'I'm not young now, though. I'm thirty.'

'That's still young. But you've carried it with you all this time like a lead weight.' He coughed softly. 'I should've talked to you before; I know that now. I should've helped you more.'

'No, Dad. It's my fault. All of this. Not yours.'

'Duck. You can't say that!'

'But Dad,' I whispered, my voice cracking. 'It was my fault that you started drinking, that you lost your job. If I'd stopped Mum … If I'd done something …'

I realised my entire body was shaking. Nausea washed over me like a wave.

'If I had done something that night …'

He shook his head. 'I told you she was ill, Duckling. It wasn't your fault. She had made up her mind. You couldn't stop her.'

'But—'

'Me turning to drink was my weakness, not yours. You have nothing to blame yourself for.' He squeezed my hand again. 'You need to stop it.'

Silence filled the car. I leant my head against the window. I couldn't bring myself to look at him. It felt like every part of me was on fire. Tears licked at my eyes, but I couldn't cry.

He's right. I've been hurting myself for far too long.

Finally, he sighed. I could hear the faint wheeze like a balloon deflating. 'I have advanced emphysema, Duck. It's severe. My lungs are screwed. They reckon my heart is failing too … fucking joke. My heart failed me years ago. The day your mother died …'

His voice broke. Suddenly I was struggling for breath too. 'Dad …'

He removed his hand from mine and raked it through his thinning hair. 'It's true though, Lucy. Everything died for me when she died that day. I could barely go on. I screwed it all up, the job, relationships – you. I was just too weak.'

'You weren't. You were grieving.'

'I just miss her so much,' he said bitterly.

'I know. So do I.'

We sat there for a bit longer, just staring out at the view in front of us. The car clock read one fifty. It was nearly time to go. The streets were deserted, it was deathly silent outside. Inside, my heart was hammering loudly; my blood seemed to be coursing at top speed through my veins.

'I'm sorry I let you down,' he said finally. 'I never put you first, did I? I never tried to understand you.'

I shrugged. 'I guess I'm not the easiest to understand.'

'Are any of us?' He half laughed. 'But you're a good person. That's all that matters really, when it comes down to it, and I'm so bloody proud of you.'

'You are?' I blinked, unsure. 'You think I'm good?'

'I know so.' He paused. 'You said earlier that I call you Duckling as some kind of joke. Because I see you as clumsy or something. But it was never that.'

'What, then? What is it?'

He grinned. 'Don't you see – a duckling is a creature finding its way. It's hopeful, innocent. A duckling is someone with their life ahead of them, waiting for their opportunity to fly.'

I stared back at him. 'You think I still can, Dad?'

'I've been so worried about you being afraid to do things, to put yourself out there, but seeing what you've done for that little girl – well, it makes me so bloody proud.'

'Dad ...' My voice cracked.

His smile was tired now, but his eyes still sparkled. 'Lucy, can't you see? Your life is yours to live now. Please enjoy it. For me.'

I felt sad that this conversation had never happened before. It wasn't just that it was so late in coming, but I felt regret for all the years I had spent waiting for Dad to say something like this to me. All that time, I'd thought I was a disappointment to him. All that time I'd carried the secret deep inside me, too scared of his reaction if he heard the truth. It was all for nothing. Dad had understood. The awful thing was, he always did. It was our lack of communication and openness that had caused so much of our pain.

If we hadn't shut ourselves away, if we hadn't hidden from each other, maybe it would've been different. Maybe we would've healed properly. Instead, we had wasted so much time, and for what? Dad was seriously ill now. I was alone. What had we done to each other?

I couldn't bring myself to look at him. I think it was the combination of tiredness, fear and forgiveness. I was so scared I might completely break down into tears. So instead I focused on the clock.

It was two o'clock.

'It's time,' I said. 'I'm going to find Cassie.'

As I walked, it felt like a thousand eyes were upon me. I tried to move normally even though I felt stiff and uncomfortable. It was as though I was in one of those films where the main character has to deliver money in a hostage situation. I kept imagining someone would jump out of a bush, tell me to put my hands into the air and then they would bundle me into a car.

My mind was working overtime. Again, I kept thinking, what would Columbo do? He would be calm, composed, nonchalant, of course. He would smile politely as he knocked on the door, acting like he didn't have a worry or concern in the world. He would put people at ease. I had to take a leaf out of his book. I had to act more like him.

The skies were grey and heavy overhead, large, pregnant clouds that looked as if they would spill their guts at any moment. The pressure building in my head and the slightly

sweetish scent in the air also suggested that rain was immi-
nent, possibly a storm. My thoughts shifted. Where would
Jimmy and Rubi go if the weather changed? She was only
dressed in a flimsy dress. Why hadn't I thought of this? I
just had to hope that Jimmy would take them into a warm
shop or café to wait it out. With any luck it wouldn't be for
too much longer.

Number forty-seven was the end town house. It looked so
innocent – a tiny square of neatly cut grass, a paved driveway
(without car) and a blank-looking building with white blinds
drawn down against the day and a white shuttered garage
reflecting against the light. I stood for a moment, taking it all
in. There was nothing strange to note. A newish-looking side
gate led round to the garden; two wheelie bins were pressed
up against the garage like silent soldiers. I couldn't hear any
noises from inside.

I walked to the front door, straightening my T-shirt and
pushing my glasses back up against my face. The door was
one of those half-glass designs with a diamond pattern. I
pressed the doorbell firmly and heard a burst of tinny faux
classical music sweep through the house.

I stepped back and looked up at the windows. The house
was still silent. There was no sign of anybody.

Uneasy, I pressed the bell again. I was a little impatient
too. Were they messing me around? I wondered for a second
if I'd got the wrong house, but the numbers were clearly
etched into the silver metal plate beside the door. I had read
the text message enough times to know the number wasn't a
mistake.

Duckling

This time I rapped on the glass, hard, several times. When nothing happened, I bent forward and flipped open the brass letterbox.

'Cassie!' I called. 'It's me, Lucy! Let me in!'

The letterbox sprang back into place. Still silence. Nothing at all.

I walked up to the front window, tried to peer through, but the blinds were tight against the glass so there was nothing to see. My stomach dipped. Was this really it? Another dead end? What the hell were we going to do now?

I went to turn towards the car, to gesture to Dad that it was a no-go. But then I noticed something. The side gate was open slightly.

I was certain that it had been closed when I'd first arrived, but perhaps I was wrong. The gate was a little out of view from the road, blocked by a towering tree in front of the projecting garage. Maybe I had looked too quickly before and missed it.

I walked over hesitantly, calling through the open gap. 'Cassie?'

There was no response. Despite the icy feeling stiffening my limbs, I pressed on. I gently eased the gate further open and peered around it.

Louder now. 'Cassie?'

I didn't see him until much too late. The meaty arm whipped around my neck and pulled me sideways, dragging me through into the garden.

I tried to scream, but the grip was too tight. Instead, I found myself being dragged further backwards.

It had all gone horribly wrong.

Chapter Twenty-Six

He threw me down on the floor. I took some satisfaction in the fact that my sheer height had given him trouble. I sincerely hoped he'd put his back out trying to get me into the house.

My glasses had tumbled on to the floor in front of me. I reached out and shoved them back on; thankfully they hadn't broken. We were in a kitchen – a very nice kitchen by the looks of it. Very clean with a spotless tiled floor and granite worktops. The back door was hanging off by its hinges. It looked as though it had been kicked in.

'Where is she?' he demanded.

I finally looked up at this man who had grabbed me so forcefully. Although my sight was blurry, I still just about recognised the man from Cassie's photo. The cold, wide-eyed stare was the same. This was the elusive Harry. I dimly wondered what Cassie had ever seen in the man. Standing before me was a muscular, squat-looking, balding beast with a bust-up nose, jutting jaw and bad teeth. His eyes were practically bulging out of his head.

I blinked back at him, giving him my best confused look. To be fair, it wasn't hard. 'Where's who?'

'Stop with the fucking games, bitch.' He was breathing heavily, one hand resting on the smooth work surface. 'Where's my daughter? Where's Rubi?'

I didn't have much time to consider my options. I was on the floor and this man was pretty worked up. I wasn't afraid, though. Not of this bully. I wouldn't let myself be. My breathing was calming and my head, for once, was completely clear. This man wanted Rubi and I wasn't about to let that happen. He could do what he wanted to me. I wasn't going to let an angry, sweaty, violent maniac anywhere near her.

'I need to see Cassie,' I said coolly, pulling myself into a seated position. 'I need to see her first. Then I'll tell you where Rubi is.'

'I'm not here to make bargains with you,' he growled. 'I could fucking smash your face in any minute.'

'You could,' I agreed. 'But that's not going to get you Rubi.'

He leant towards me. I could smell garlic and beer on his breath. 'Look at you. Who are you? Keeping a man from his daughter?'

I ignored him. Slowly, I dragged myself up from the floor, flinching a bit from my stiffness. It had hurt where he'd thrown me. I was bound to be bruised all over.

'Where's Cassie?' I asked again. I noticed I was towering over his stubby frame. I wondered if he was used to this, a woman who was bigger than him. Or did he usually just terrorise women who were smaller than him – women like Cassie?

'Cassie's fine,' he said, rooted to the spot. 'You just need to tell me where my girl is. We're all making a fresh start. No one's going to stop us.'

'A fresh start? Where?'

He leant in again. 'None of your fucking business.' He pushed me, but I barely moved. My feet were firmly planted on the floor this time. I was ready for him.

'You really are going abroad, aren't you? That's why you came to the flat. That's why you tore it apart. You weren't just looking for Rubi. Was it Rubi's passport too?'

'I told you, it's none of your fucking business.'

'Oh my God.' The realisation suddenly hit me. 'You never wanted Cassie, did you? This was just about finding Rubi and getting her away from here.'

'Away from that fucking bitch!' he yelled. 'She doesn't deserve her.'

'Liam found out you had a place abroad ...' I mused. 'It all makes sense now. You get Rubi into Cyprus and it'll be harder for Cassie to get her back.'

He shoved me again, with more force this time, and I staggered back, my heel striking the open kitchen door.

'For the last time,' he said fiercely, 'it's none of your fucking business.' His hand snaked around my throat and I felt the pressure building. A burning sensation was working up inside. I wanted to cough, choke, which I tried desperately to fight against. The pressure increased and I kicked out with my legs, but I was hitting the floor. Panic set in as I continued to kick out uselessly, my ears ringing, my head ready to explode. I was going to die like this, on the kitchen floor. I was going to die before I could help Cassie. Before I could stop him getting Rubi. That couldn't happen.

Then, suddenly, he released his grip. I slid to the floor and something slammed into my stomach, making me gasp in an exhausted gust. The pain seemed to radiate across my entire body.

'Tell me!' he said, very slowly now. 'Where is Rubi?'

I didn't see him come in. All I could see was Polly's giant, doll-like head come crashing down on Harry's square one. As Harry turned round in confusion, I saw Dad standing there, broken doll in his hand, his breath a haunting rattle filling up the room.

'Here she fucking is,' he boomed, swinging the doll squarely in Harry's face. 'Here's your fucking girl.'

Harry was more surprised than hurt. I heard him cry out 'what the fuck' before he tumbled, wrong-footed, on to the floor. I pulled myself up, confused, pain stretching in my stomach. He'd hurt me, but I could walk. I bent over and shuffled forward. Dad was surprisingly calm; he looked over at me and mouthed, 'Find Cassie,' and then whacked Harry again with the broken plastic creature. I never thought before that the doll could be such a useful weapon, but I guess the bloody thing was heavy enough.

I stumbled out of the kitchen and into the living room. This was also showroom clean but completely empty. Even so, I checked behind the sofa, all the time softly calling Cassie's name. I was desperately trying to ignore the shouts and cries from the other room. The pain inside me was burning and flaring, but I ignored it. I had to keep moving.

I took the stairs gingerly, wincing with each step, and found myself on the landing. Everything up here smelt dusty and too new, as though no one had lived here for a long time. I checked the first room. The bathroom. Surprisingly small and disappointingly empty.

Downstairs there was a crash. A shout.

What was happening down there?

The next room. I opened the door slowly, expectation mounting, adrenaline pumping, pain still building in my stomach. I stepped inside. It was a single bedroom. A child's room. All pink and pristine. A prettily made-up bed stood beneath the window, and a toy trunk was piled sky-high by the door.

I staggered to the next room, to the closed door. Gently, I eased it open. Everything inside me had seized up. I was struggling to breathe now, but I made myself walk into that room. I had to keep going forward. I knew if I stopped, I would fall.

Cassie was lying on the bed. Her face was bruised and her eyes were closed. Her body was twisted slightly, turned away from me. There were patches of blood on the white duvet, signifying a struggle of some kind.

I wanted to hide. Of course I did. All my familiar feelings of anxiety and panic hit me again, but I made myself stay. I couldn't leave her. Not now. I wasn't going to leave her alone like that, on the bed. She needed me and I was going to go to her.

I wasn't hiding this time.

Instead, I crept towards her.

'Cassie?' I whispered, half in desperation, half in hope.

Her eyelids flickered. She groaned softly.

She was conscious, but only just.

I touched her hand. So small. So pretty. Still warm. It twitched under mine.

'Cassie,' I said. 'I'm here. It's OK now. I found you.'

But I couldn't do it any more. I couldn't stay upright. The pressure in my stomach was too much, my head was too dizzy. I sat down on the floor next to her. I was so tired. My stomach hurt too much. I peered down, confused. And then I saw the blood.

Not hers now, mine. So much blood, and it was coming from me in dark, rippling streams.

I slumped against the bed, her hand still in mine. I clung on to her. Darkness swooping in and out. Stars shining. Lights flashing. A voice came from somewhere, far away. A shout. Was he coming back? Was this the end? Was this how it was always meant to be?

'I'm here,' I whispered to Cassie. 'I'm here … I kept her safe for you … I kept Rubi safe …'

And then I closed my eyes.

Chapter Twenty-Seven

I woke up. Sore, disorientated and thirsty. The first face I saw was his. It seemed to be floating above me, a disjointed picture. Familiar and yet so hard to make out.

I tried to talk but my mouth was too dry, full of dust. I coughed instead and tried to roll on my side, but I couldn't. My body felt restricted, as if I was bound to the bed. I baulked a little. Scared, I guess. My hands flapped uselessly, feeling stiff cotton sheets around me.

A pain was drilling into my stomach. It was muted, like the embers of an old fire, but it was enough to make me cry out.

What's happened ...?

He touched me lightly on the arm. 'Stay still, Lucy. You've been through a lot. You need to rest.'

'Wha ...' I groaned. I blinked my eyes open.

Once.

Twice.

The light was too bright; it burnt my eyes. I could feel them water. Why was it so white in here?

'You're in hospital.' His voice was gentle. I tried to grab hold of it. Stay with it. But I was too tired. My eyelids began to close again.

The floaty feeling was back. It was nice.

I went with it.

*

The next time, he was there again. This time sitting further back, a book in his hands, but he wasn't reading. He was staring right at me.

'Lucy?'

'Jimmy ...' I spoke, but the words were cracked. I ran a tongue across my chapped lips, hating the rough texture. 'What happened?'

I tried to move again. The same pain was there, in the centre of my belly.

'You were stabbed. You lost a lot of blood.' He shifted in his seat. 'They had to operate.'

Confusing, drifting thoughts fogged my brain. I couldn't shift them. I could picture the house – so quiet and calm. Then I saw him, that small, brutal man. His leering face coming towards me. Harry.

'Rubi?' I croaked, my mind whirring.

'She's OK, Lucy. She's with her nan. She's safe.'

I frowned. Her nan? But what about Cassie? I had kept Rubi safe for Cassie.

I remembered Cassie's beautiful, bloody face.

'Cassie? Is she ...?'

I could barely stand to hear the answer. I closed my eyes again for a second, took a shaky breath. There had been so much blood. Too much. When I looked again, Jimmy was smiling at me. He looked so tired and relieved. He took my hand in his and squeezed it tight.

'Oh Lucy, I'm so glad you're awake.'

'But Cassie? Where is she?'

'She's here. She's in a bad way, but she will be OK. We got to you both in time.'

'We?' Still confused, I stared back at him. 'You came? You found us?'

He shook his head. 'No, not that. You know I was uncomfortable about the whole thing ...' He looked down at his hands. 'When you went, I called Liam. Told him what was going on. He didn't like the sound of it either. Despite everything, he agreed with me that it was time to call the police.'

'Liam did?'

'Yeah. He had a feeling something wasn't right. He didn't want you hurt.'

I wasn't sure how I felt.

Tired. Deflated. But strangely calm. My thoughts were no longer rushing around inside me. My mind felt at peace. It was over. Cassie was safe. I had found her. Everything would be all right now. It had to be.

'Dad thought—' I croaked. 'Dad thought it was best to go in.'

I thought of Dad swinging that stupid doll. It seemed laughable now. But what if he hadn't come? He had saved me. He had protected me.

'Dad came,' I whispered. I smiled at the thought. 'He came for me.'

Jimmy looked up again, his eyes glinting. I could see the tears there and I wondered why he was so upset. We were all OK. Rubi was with her nan. Cassie was saved. So why was he crying now?

'Lucy, I'm so sorry,' he said.

*

Hours later, finally alone, I thought of Dad. I thought of our last conversation, and of the things he had said.

It was like he knew we were reaching the end of our journey. He'd opened up to me, finally. He'd been so adamant that we should talk this weekend, that we should finally sort things out, and thank God he'd got his own way.

I shut my eyes. Duckling. His name for me. The name I'd hated for so long and now I clung to it with pride. I never wanted to let it go.

I gripped the bedsheets. Twisted and pulled. The crushing pain deep inside was making it hard to breathe.

I felt like a part of me had been carved away. Destroyed forever.

For so long I'd needed his love, and yet all the time he'd needed mine too. We'd spent so long together, yet we'd never really understood what the other one was going through. If only we had talked earlier, or really tried to listen to each other, instead of hiding, we could have helped ourselves and healed. It was all so sad and so desperately painful.

I gasped, the tears blinding me. The old me would have blamed myself for putting him in danger, but I quickly pushed that thought away. Dad had come out to protect me. I hadn't asked him to, but he did it anyway.

He was brave at the end and I loved him for it.

My dad. Despite everything he would always be my precious dad.

And I would always be his Duckling.

*

Days passed. I got better, stronger. Jimmy visited often and that was nice. I liked having him there. I worried about the shop, but he told me not to, it was sorted. He told me a little bit about his plans to expand the antique and second-hand area of the shop and how he hoped that might improve custom. He was looking forward to having me back to help. He squeezed my hand and told me I needed time to build my strength up.

He also told me how he'd sneaked my keys out of my handbag so that he could pop into my flat to feed Boris.

'I knew you'd worry,' he said. 'I wanted to keep him safe for you.'

I nearly cried all over again.

My wound was healing well. The nurse seemed particularly pleased with my scar. And no one was concerned about my now missing spleen. No one really mentioned the fact that I was missing more than an organ, though. I was an orphan now. Perhaps that was for the best. I wasn't sure I was ready for those conversations yet.

I was spared too much detail about Dad's death. All I knew was that he had continued to wrestle with Harry when I'd left him. Harry had then punched him several times. Dad's weakened heart and lungs couldn't take it and he keeled over. We think that's when Harry legged it. They caught up with him half a mile away, covered in blood and still insisting that he see his daughter.

Thankfully that will never happen.

I knew the person I needed to be now. I was ready to embrace it. The loss of Mum and Dad was balanced with my gains – Jimmy, Cassie and Rubi. They had shown me so much, in such a short space of time. They had made me see that there was a better way to live.

I owed it to all of them to try.

Three days after I woke up, they let me see her. She had been in Critical Care, but now she was in her own room. She looked so small and young lying on the crisp white bed. Her face was still a maze of reddish swellings, one eye blackened, her mouth twisted cruelly out of shape.

He was a monster. The monster who came back for her.

But Cassie was a fighter.

I sat down beside her. I leant right by her ear so she could hear me.

'I'm sorry,' I whispered.

Her eyes opened. A tiny frown. She saw me and something brightened.

'Sorry?' she muttered, each word an effort. 'What for?'

'I didn't believe you. I thought you were being a pain, not coming back to us. I should've worked it out sooner.'

Her frown deepened. 'You did in the end.' She took her time with each word. 'He would've killed me if I hadn't texted you. I hoped you'd notice what I was trying to say. I changed the spellings … I wanted you to work out something was wrong. I tried to call you too. I got hold of his phone and I tried calling on that. I wanted to tell you … that … that I was … that we were in danger.'

'I'm so sorry I missed those calls, Cassie. I thought it was someone else. It was an unknown number.'

'It's ... OK. You ... got there in the end.' She sighed. 'You called me that time, but I couldn't talk. He was next to me ...'

She groaned, shook her head in frustration. But I didn't need her to say any more.

'I didn't bring Rubi. When I knew something was wrong, we didn't want to risk it.'

She smiled, then grimaced at the pain. 'I know ... thank you.'

Her mouth moved slowly, and she carefully told me more.

'He found me outside Gav's. I told him her passport was there to stall for time. I didn't think he'd find my flat.' A breath. A swallow. 'He took my phone. He checked everything. I said he would never see Rubi, that I'd never let that happen, and he just lost it. He just wanted her and ...' She blinked, sighed. 'He wanted to break us apart.'

'I know,' I whispered. 'I know you did everything you could to keep Rubi away from him.'

'Harry ... He found Gav.' She grimaced again. 'It was my fault. I called him once when I was still with Gav.' She closed her eyes. 'Gav had a party. I got drunk. I picked up one of his mates' phones and called Harry ... I just wanted to wind him up. Show him that I was better off without him. That I'd moved on. Stupid thing is, me and Gav split up about a week after that.'

The realisation hit me. 'You used Charlie's phone? So that's how Harry found out about Gav.'

She nodded gingerly. 'He tracked down Charlie and then Gav through him. I didn't know. I'd forgotten I'd done it, I was so pissed. I guess he hoped I'd get in contact with Gav again, and I did.' She pursed her lips together. 'Stupid bitch. If only I'd left him alone, none of this would have happened.'

'This wasn't your fault, Cassie. This is all on Harry.'

We sat in silence for a while. The only noise was coming from the clock on the other side of the room. Then Cassie carefully repositioned herself, took my hand.

'You kept Rubi safe. I knew you would. You saved her. You saved us,' she whispered. 'I'll never forget.'

I shrugged it was nothing, but of course it wasn't.

It was everything.

I was discharged two days later. Jimmy was waiting for me outside, Colin tugging on the lead.

'Will you keep him forever, then?' I asked.

Jimmy smiled. 'Cassie's mum is allergic, so maybe. Rubi wanted one of us to look after him, and Cassie will move back down there, most likely. It seems the most sensible solution. Cassie will need help getting back on her feet.'

'I hope Rubi will be OK.'

'She'll be fine. Her nan has said we can visit anytime.'

I nodded. I would miss her. I would miss both of them.

We walked together, down the narrow path away from the hospital. Jimmy kept close to me, his presence a constant reassurance. I glanced over at him, taking in his large frame, his gentle, expressive features, his beautiful full, smiling mouth. OK, he might not look anything like the great detective, but he was still a Columbo to me. Wonderful, wise and kind. The perfect combination.

'I'll give you a lift home,' he said.

I paused. I was about to tell him that I'd be fine, like I normally would, but then it hit me. Why did I keep doing this? Why did I keep turning down offers of help, shutting people out like they weren't important? Well – no more. I couldn't be this person any longer.

'Actually,' I said brightly, 'that would be lovely. Thank you.'

'Really?' he said, fighting a grin.

'Of course.'

We turned towards the car. It was getting late and our shadows stretched across the car park. I looked taller than ever, but beside Jimmy we matched perfectly. Two long, gangly shadows. I pulled my spine up straight and walked as tall as I could, wondering why I never had before.

'I found this in my pocket,' I said finally.

Jimmy peered over and saw the photo in my hand, the one I'd taken from Dad's house of my mum. She really did look so beautiful in it. Quite different from what I remembered. The woman that my dad loved so much.

'I thought ...' I paused, my fingers clutching the creases. 'I thought maybe I could give it to the funeral home. Dad could have it with him ... You know, so that they're together again. Finally. Like he always wanted.'

'That's a lovely idea, Lucy.'

Jimmy took a step forward; his hand touched my arm lightly.

'You know, I meant what I said before,' he said softly. 'You mean a lot to me. Like a real lot. I know you've had a tough time. But I'd really like to get to know you better.'

I blinked back at him. Disbelief still rattled inside me, but I tried hard to force it away. I had spent too long listening to negative voices in my head. They made me hurt.

Dad was right, I needed to stop hurting.

I needed to start living again. For both of us now. It was time to finally let the wounds heal.

'I like you too,' I said. And then, more shyly, 'Like a real lot.'

He laughed. 'Maybe we could – I don't know, watch some films together? Take things slow?'

'You know I've never seen *Stars Wars*?' I offered. 'You could help to fix that.'

He reached forward and took my hand in his. I didn't resist. I didn't pull back. I simply allowed his warm grip to encase mine.

I shivered. But in a good way. A really, really good way.

'You have a beautiful smile, Lucy,' he said.

This time I didn't argue or resist. This time I didn't refuse to believe. Maybe, I finally could see what he could.

I looked straight at him, at his bright, sparkling eyes, and I beamed back.

'Thank you,' I replied.

After

The knock at Dad's door was insistent and continuous. I took a deep breath before clambering over the boxes towards the door. I flung it open, hoping to see her familiar welcoming grin. I wasn't disappointed. She was wearing bright blue shorts and a pale yellow T-shirt. Her hair was not wild and untamed, but pulled simply back into a ponytail, the fringe now neatly trimmed. She looked restrained but still full of energy. A smudge of what looked like red paint was dotted under her right eye. In her hand she was holding a clutch of paper. This was the first time I'd seen her since I came out of hospital, which seemed like forever ago, even though it had only been a week.

'We're going soon!' she announced. 'Mum's outside in the car with Nan already. But I wanted to see you first.'

'Of course. I would've been cross if you didn't,' I told her.

She peered behind me.

'Lucy!' she tutted. 'You've made it even more messy now.'

'I know. But I have all my dad's things to sort through. There's so much.' I flung up my arms in protest. 'Hopefully I'll be through it all soon. There's only a few bits I want to keep. Jimmy is going to help me later. I'm going to let him take all the books.'

She giggled. 'Jimmy loves you so much.'

'Rubi!'

'What! It's true. Even my mum says so ...'

We stood, suddenly awkward, Rubi swinging her leg back and forth, me gripping the door frame feeling a little unsteady. Finally, her face screwed up into a frown.

'Urgh, what is this music you're playing?'

'Jim Reeves,' I said, glancing over at Dad's old CD player. Finally, I'd had the chance to play it. I'd even dusted her old lampshade and hung it up in my living room. It belonged with me. 'My old neighbour used to love this singer and I promised myself I would listen to it in her honour.'

And realise what an opportunity I'd missed in failing to really get to know Joy. That was something I would always regret now.

'He sounds old.' She rubbed her nose. 'And what is he singing?'

I smiled. 'I like his song the best. He's saying he loves someone for being who they are.'

'That's nice.'

'Yes ... it really is.'

'So ...' I said finally. 'When do you leave?'

'In a minute. Nanny is waiting outside in the car.' Rubi smiled. 'Her and Mum have made up. I think they're friends now.'

'That's good, then.'

'I guess ...'

'And it'll be nice to live with her again for a while. Your mum can ... well, she can get some rest too.'

'But I'll miss you,' she said quietly.

'I'll miss you too.' I paused. 'But you have your phone now, don't you? We can text each other. Whenever we want. And maybe I can pop down and see you sometimes ...'

Rubi's face brightened. 'Yes, you can. I've got this.' She pushed one of the pieces of paper into my hand. I gently uncurled it. It was her new address written in Rubi's neat writing.

'Just in case you ever forget,' she said.

'But I won't,' I told her.

'I have this too – for you.' She handed me the other bit of paper which was folded in half. As I eased it open, I saw the bright colours immediately. The beautiful swirling water, the light ambient sky.

'Oh Rubi – it's wonderful.' I could barely speak.

Rubi leant forward and put her arms around me. I bent down, breathing in the smell of her lavender shampoo, of her crayons, of her sweetness. A lovely, heady mix. I wished I could bottle it and keep it with me forever.

'You found my mum,' she whispered. 'Just like you said you would.'

'We found her together. Both of us. The perfect detect-ives.'

'Just like Columbo?'

'Better.'

I lifted my head, suddenly aware that someone else was watching us. Behind Rubi, I saw Cassie now standing by the front door. Her face was still swollen and bruised. She was staring at both of us. A bright, rich smile lit up her face. She lifted her fingers to her lips and sent the kiss towards me. My fingers fluttered to my own mouth, as if it had just landed there.

Lovely, sweet Cassie.

'Oh,' I said, almost forgetting. 'Rubi. I have something for you too.'

I carefully walked over to the box nearest the door. The box from my old bedroom. I hadn't quite decided what I'd do with it yet, but it would come back to the flat with me until I had. I also had all the books to give to Jimmy. I was hoping it would help his new expanded antique area. On top of my box sat one particular book that I was especially pleased to find. I picked it up.

'I found this in my old book collection,' I said, passing it to Rubi. 'I thought you might want to finish it.'

Rubi looked down at the copy of *The Wind in the Willows* and her face immediately brightened. 'I love it,' she said. 'Thank you.'

My heart was pounding. I squeezed my hands together. 'I'm going to really miss you, Rubi.'

'You'll see us again soon, silly,' Rubi said, her eyes sparkling. 'You have to come and visit. Mum says. We still need to watch *Columbo* together. You promised, remember?'

I nodded. I had.

In my shaky hand, Rubi's picture fluttered, catching the light.

A picture of a duckling, of course. A beautiful duckling. It was high in the sky, the sun shining behind it. Its wonderful wings were outstretched, and its beak was raised towards the clouds. And there, just below, a small girl with dark hair looked up at it and smiled, her hand waving in the duckling's direction. Then further underneath, in her careful, cursive writing, Rubi had written:

Lucy in the sky

I closed my eyes.

At last, I understood.

Not all ducklings turn into swans.

But this duckling had finally learnt how to fly.

Acknowledgements

Writing a book is not a solo journey (although it can feel like it at times) and there are many people I need to thank for helping me to shape *Duckling* into the book that it is now, for assisting its publication and for helping to keep me sane.

First, I would like to thank the wonderful team at PRH: Sonny, Emily and Katie especially have been wonderfully supportive. I'm so excited to start my journey with you all. When I was seven years of age, I received my first rejection letter from PRH and now, some thirty-five (gulp) years later, I'm being published by them. Dreams do come true; sometimes you just have to wait a little.

I also need to thank my lovely agent, Laura Williams, who believed in my book (and in me). Your support during this time is truly appreciated. I definitely owe you a drink or two.

I'm not sure where I would be without my lovely family. Thank you, Tom, as always, for being my first editor – for reading copious drafts and picking up my silly errors. You are also good at picking me up when I'm having a writing wobble, so thank you! *Duckling* would still be hidden away in my drafts file if you hadn't encouraged me to submit it. Thank you also to my children, Ella and Ethan, for putting up with a distracted and sometimes bad-tempered mother. I will reward you by putting your enemies in a book one day, I promise. I also want to thank my lovely mum, my brothers and my gorgeous sisters for their continual support. Cherry and Iain in particular are often the recipients of my plot ideas and I appreciate your patience.

Writing can be a very lonely and isolating craft, but I'm very fortunate to know some amazing authors who I'm proud to call friends. Thank you to the Placers for listening to my anxious rants and being there when needed, and thank you also to the Debut 2022 group – it's been so much fun already. Can I please say a special thank you to fellow authors Rowan Coleman, Jo Nadin, Sarah Harris and Keren David, for helping me throughout my 'ups and downs' and also to my early beta readers – Rhian Ivory, Emma Pass and Sarah Dodd.

I'm lucky to have some wonderful friends and I appreciate their love and encouragement, in particular Amanda, Jodie and the wonderful Rebel Mummies. Thank you for keeping me laughing.

I also appreciate the wonderful bloggers, librarians and readers who have supported my earlier career. It is always remembered.

If I've missed anyone it's only due to my tired, dappy brain and not because I don't appreciate you.

My final thanks goes to my primary school teachers Mr Smith and Mr Anthony. They saw a shy little girl with no self-confidence and gave her the greatest gift of all. They made me see that it didn't matter what background I came from; if I worked hard enough and believed in myself, I could achieve my dream.

Well, I guess they were right.